Christmas Memories

MARILYN PAPPANO
DIANA PALMER

Silhouette Books

Published by Silhouette Books
America's Publisher of Contemporary Romance

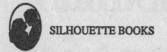 SILHOUETTE BOOKS

CHRISTMAS MEMORIES

Copyright © 1992 by Harlequin Enterprises B.V.

ISBN 0-373-15186-1

The publisher acknowledges the copyright holders of the individual works as follows:

ROOM AT THE INN
Copyright © 1988 by Marilyn Pappano
WOMAN HATER
Copyright © 1987 by Diana Palmer

Printed in U.S.A.

ROOM AT THE INN

"Leah, are you saying that you don't want me living here, in Angel's Peak?"

"No! I think—I think it would be wonderful." Her eyes were practically glowing. "But your job, your friends, are in Philadelphia."

"Nothing is as important to me as you and your family are," he replied.

She was still troubled. "But . . . what if things between us don't work out?"

He left his chair and knelt beside hers. "That's a risk I have to take—just like trusting me is a risk that someday you're going to have to take."

"I'm not sure I'm worth that risk," she said as she hesitantly slid her fingers through his hair.

"*I* am," he disagreed softly.

She smiled through her tears. "You have a lot of faith in yourself, Bryce Cameron."

"No, I have faith in you."

WOMAN HATER

"I don't have to propose marriage to kiss you,"

Winthrop said as he moved closer to Nicole.

"I have a cold—it's contagious!" she exclaimed.

"I have a sore leg, and it's not. But desire is," he whispered against her lips. "Shall I show you how easy it is to catch?"

"It isn't fair," she wailed.

"Probably not. But it's sweet, all the same. Here," he breathed, pressing her hand against his hard, warm chest.
"Touch me." His hand slowly dropped between them to the buttons of her bodice.

"No," she protested.

"Enjoy it," he whispered. His fingers moved to the edge of her breast, tracing it with maddening expertise. . . .

TABLE OF CONTENTS

ROOM AT THE INN

MARILYN PAPPANO

Chapter 1

The rocking chairs evenly spaced on the long porch were dusty from more than a month of disuse, but Leah Cameron didn't mind. With her coat zipped and buttoned up snugly, and her hands hidden inside warm ski gloves, she sat down, rocked back and forth, and watched the snow fall.

It was going to be a busy weekend at Cameron Inn, and she wanted to spend the last peaceful hour outside, alone with the snow and her thoughts. She supposed she ought to be grateful that business was so good—every one of the twelve rooms was booked for the weekend—but it meant she would have little quiet, and very little private time. This weekend there would be even less time for herself than usual when the inn was full; her mother- and father-in-law, who normally helped run the place, had left this morning for Atlanta. Tomorrow would be Peter and Martha's forty-third wedding anniversary, and they were celebrating it in style in the city. She didn't expect them back until Sunday evening, after most of the guests had gone home.

Forty-three years. She gave a soft sigh. That was a long time to stay married. Her own marriage had lasted only twelve years—unhappy years, mercifully ended by Terence's death in an auto accident six years ago.

A car turning off the highway caught and held her attention. The weekend's first arrival. That meant time to smile and be friendly. She took a deep breath to prepare herself.

A man got out of the car, glancing around without noticing her as he pulled on a pair of dark gloves. Maybe he wasn't a guest, she thought as he started toward the house. He had no luggage, and there were no skis strapped to the top of his car. He looked more like a businessman, with his heavy overcoat and neatly creased trousers. A salesman, perhaps, wanting to do business with the inn.

Smiling faintly, she watched him cross the snow-covered yard. Her oldest son, Douglas, had shoveled the sidewalk this morning before school, but it was buried again, marked only by a miniature snowdrift on each side.

As the man drew closer, she grew still, her rocking chair motionless. She had never seen this man before, but she *knew* him. There was something familiar in the way he moved—with such purpose; in the way he held his head up instead of ducking it against the heavy, wet snow; in the color of his hair and the stubborn line of his jaw. When she saw his face, she would know for sure. His eyes would be brown—a dark, warm, chocolaty brown—and she would know who he was.

He climbed the steps and stopped in front of the door to stomp the snow from his feet. For a long moment he just stood there, as unmoving as Leah, unaware of her at the end of the porch.

His eyes were riveted on the brass plaque that hung next to the door. Welcome, it proclaimed, the letters forming a graceful arch over a pineapple, the traditional symbol of hospitality. Then, slowly, as if feeling the intensity of her stare, he turned and moved toward her.

Leah waited until he was standing only a few yards in front of her. Carefully she began to rock again, pretending an easiness that she was far from feeling. "Hello."

He didn't return the greeting right away. Instead he looked at her, as intensely as she had watched him, with eyes that were indeed brown. "Hello."

He sounded stiff, uncomfortable. She suspected that he would have preferred to ignore her greeting, but his manners, as deeply ingrained as her own, had won out. Did he know who she was? She decided that he must. There was probably very little that escaped his attention, and for the past month, they—Peter and Martha, Leah and the house— had received a great deal of that. "I wondered when you would come," she finally said.

How had she known, after talking to him twice on the phone, that he would come? Bryce Cameron wondered skeptically. Had she planned what she would say to him when he came—what strategy she would use to stand in his way?

He looked from her to the other chairs, but found them too dusty. Brushing snow from the railing, he leaned back against it, pushing his hands deep into his coat pockets. "So you were expecting me."

"Yes. Not today, of course, but soon."

Of course. Tilting his head to one side, he asked bluntly, "Why?" He hadn't even known it himself until just this week. After a month's worth of phone calls and letters had accomplished nothing, he had decided only three days ago to fly unannounced to Angel's Peak, to surprise his Uncle Peter and Aunt Martha and the lady with the lovely Southern drawl. And the lady had expected him. "How did you know?"

She lifted her hands, palms up, and shrugged. "You're a Cameron."

That simple answer could cover a multitude of sins, he thought with a grin. Camerons were stubborn; they liked to get their own way. They were fighters who hated to admit defeat. They were also too thickheaded to know when they were whipped, or to realize when they weren't welcome. He suspected that she was referring to the latter. "The black sheep always returns to the fold, doesn't he?"

"Are you?"

"Returning to the fold?" The smile grew cynical and, at the same time, more attractive.

"The black sheep."

He mimicked her shrug. "That's what Peter says, isn't it?"

"Actually, Peter says very little about you or your father. I thought you might tell me."

He pushed himself away from the railing and started toward the door with an easy, comfortable grace that Leah envied. "Sorry, sweetheart," he said over his shoulder. "I didn't come more than six hundred miles to give you my version of the family history."

She watched him take four steps, then five, then six, before she spoke. "I'm afraid you'll have to settle for me."

He turned, looked at her again and smiled, as if amused by the thought of "settling" for her. "Would you like to explain that?"

She told him about Peter's trip to Atlanta as she walked toward him. She held the door open, followed him inside, then closed it with a quiet click. "So," she finished, unzipping her coat, "do you want to have a cup of coffee and talk to me, or do you want to waste a six-hundred-mile trip?"

It took Bryce only a moment to choose his course of action. A few minutes later they were seated in her office, a tray holding a pot of coffee, mugs, cream and sugar on the desk between them. While she fixed his coffee, he glanced around the room. It wasn't much bigger than the closet down the hall where she had hung their coats, with barely enough space for a desk and chair, a set of shelves, a filing cabinet and a straight-backed chair for visitors. But it was charming, with its rose-colored wallpaper and matching curtains, its handwoven rugs and potted plants and photographs.

He looked at *her*, too, all soft and pretty and feminine. She was of average height, but slender, which gave her that delicate, fragile appearance that Southern women wore so well. In her case, he would bet, appearances were deceiving. He knew that she was a widow, raising four children and running the inn; she was probably stronger than he was.

"Have you eaten lunch?" she asked in that soft drawl of hers as she handed him a cup of steaming coffee.

He nodded. Not expecting much of a welcome in Angel's Peak, he had stopped at a fast-food restaurant in Asheville before starting the trip up the mountain.

She sat back comfortably in her chair, her fingers laced loosely around her cup. "I suppose it's time for formal introductions. I'm Leah Cameron."

"You're going to feel very silly if I'm not who you think I am," he warned.

She smiled—not the hesitant, uncomfortable grimace that he expected, but a full-blown, sunlight-bright smile that warmed him all the way to his toes. "I *know* who you are."

Taking in the glow of her smile, he revised his earlier opinion. She wasn't pretty—she was beautiful. Undeniably, achingly beautiful. For a moment he envied his dead cousin for having been able to claim this woman as his wife.

She was waiting—calmly, patiently silent. "All right," he said at last, tearing his gaze from her face. "I'm Bryce Cameron."

She gave a shrug to indicate that she'd known all along, then sobered. "I'm sorry you missed Peter."

"Are you?"

She didn't object to his skepticism. He had tried for weeks to talk to Peter, and she certainly hadn't helped him. He was justified in doubting her. "Yes, I am. I think it's unfortunate that this feud between your father and Peter has gone on for so long. I'm surprised they can even remember what it was about."

His eyes, so dark and warm, narrowed. "Oh, they remember," he said coolly. "Believe me, we all remember." He took a sip of his coffee, then set it on the desk. "What are the chances that you might tell me where Peter and Martha are staying in Atlanta?"

She chided him with her gaze. "Even if I knew, which I don't, I wouldn't tell you. They're celebrating their anniversary. I wouldn't do anything to ruin it for them."

"And you think I would." He said it flatly, knowing her answer before she gave it. Just what had she been told about him? he wondered. Enough to judge him?

"Yes." She had been tactless, but she wouldn't lie to make up for it. "Peter has made it pretty clear that he doesn't want to talk to you. He said a few years ago that he never wanted to see you or your father again."

"That was a few years ago." Six, to be exact. Bryce remembered the occasion well. He imagined Leah did, too. "Maybe he's changed his mind."

"I doubt it." She sat quietly for a moment. There were a hundred questions she wanted to ask him—about his father Frank, about the feud that had split the Cameron family in two, about himself. Especially about himself. Was he married? Did he have any children? What kind of man was he? They were questions whose answers were none of her business, because this man was none of her business.

Her thoughts were wandering, Bryce realized. Selfishly, he wanted to call them back to himself. "How did you know who I was out there?"

She focused on him once again. From the half dozen photographs on the file cabinet behind her, she selected one, handing it across the desk to him. "That's my son, Douglas."

He set down his coffee, took the frame and studied the picture for a long time. Although he didn't know the boy, he knew the face—it was his own about twenty-five years ago. He stared at the picture and envied Leah this big handsome son. He would have liked to have children—in fact, he had insisted on it until the desire had threatened to tear his marriage apart. Then, giving up the dream of being a father, he had held on to the marriage and to Kay. Ten years later, *she* had let go.

At last he handed back the photo. "Gran said we all looked alike—but only the men, fortunately. The Cameron women are prettier."

"I don't think the Cameron men are too shabby," Leah disagreed absently as she set the picture back in its place.

He grinned. "Is that supposed to be a compliment—not too shabby?"

"You don't need my compliments." Smoothly she changed the subject. "Do you have a place to stay tonight? With all this snow, you'll never find a room in town."

"I was planning to finish my business with Peter, drive back to Asheville and fly home tomorrow." He picked up the mug again, just for something to do with his hands. "Are you offering me a room here?"

What could it hurt? she questioned. Peter was about two hundred miles away in Atlanta; by the time he returned, Bryce would be back in Philadelphia, his home since he'd left Angel's Peak so many years ago. "Yes," she replied evenly. "I am."

"Then I'll take it."

"It's not one of the guest rooms," she cautioned. "Those are completely booked for every weekend from now until spring. But I do have an empty room in the family wing. It may not be as quiet as you'd like—I have three other children besides Douglas."

"Matthew, Megan and Laurel. Ages six, eleven and thirteen. Douglas is seventeen." He was pleased with himself for keeping the names and ages straight.

Leah looked dismayed. "You've been checking up on us."

"Not me—Dad. He wanted me to know what I was up against."

"What else did he tell you?"

Bryce shrugged. "Not much. Does that mean I lose the room you just offered?"

The idea of a complete stranger snooping into her life made her distinctly uncomfortable. There were too many things in the past that she wanted to remain there—not deep, dark secrets, just...private things. The place where she had grown up, the circumstances of her marriage to Terence, the details of that marriage. How much did Bryce Cameron know?

But her manners wouldn't allow her to take back her offer. "No," she said slowly. "If you're finished, I'll show it to you."

She led him through a maze of hallways to the family's private quarters. They walked through a small, cluttered living room, with a smaller dining room and kitchen just beyond, and down the hall to an open door. "You can use this room," she said, her voice a bit cooler than before.

Bryce walked into the middle of the room and looked around. This had been his grandmother's bedroom, a place he had been allowed to visit only when he'd been very, very good—which hadn't been very often, he ruefully recalled. Leah had changed nothing. The mismatched furniture was just as Gran had left it—the big brass bed with its incredibly soft feather mattress; the solid pine armoire that was taller than he was at six feet; the hexagonal marble-topped tables that served as nightstands on each side of the bed, holding the antique brass lamps; the oak-framed cheval mirror; and the pine rocker, draped with a wedding ring quilt that had been made by his great-grandmother. Even the old family Bible still stood on one of the marble tables.

Leah stopped just inside the room. "The bathroom is next door. Dinner will be served at six-thirty in the old ballroom. Do you remember where it is?"

He turned to look at her, his smile reaching his eyes now. "I grew up in this house, Leah," he gently chided. "I remember."

She nodded. "There's a phone in the little room under the front stairs, and television in our living room down the hall and in the sitting room. If you need anything, the clerk should be at the front desk, there's always someone in the kitchen, and I'll be around somewhere."

Bryce watched her leave, then closed the door and sat down on the bed, running his hand over the quilted cover. He had planned such a simple trip—talk to Peter, settle the past, return to Philadelphia—but nothing was working out simply. He hadn't considered the possibility that his uncle might be out of town, or that he might feel such a sense of homecoming. He hadn't given any thought at all to meeting his cousin's widow, and he certainly hadn't entertained any idea that he might *like* her—might even be attracted to her.

He removed his suit coat and tie, tossing them across the arm of the rocker, then kicked off his shoes and stretched out on the bed. He was here on business, he reminded himself as he closed his eyes. Strictly business.

He awoke several hours later to the ringing of chimes. For a long moment he remained still, his eyes closed, trying to remember where he was. The bed was softer than his bed at home, and the room smelled of wood and polish and spices, and just the faintest hint of perfume.

The inn. He was in Gran's old room at the estate, in Angel's Peak, North Carolina, and the chimes had to mean dinner, since his stomach was rumbling and the sky outside the lace curtains was dark.

He felt for the lamp, finally finding the key that switched on the light. His shirt was rumpled, but with his jacket on, it wouldn't be too noticeable. Standing in front of the mirror, he knotted his tie and tugged at his jacket. His suitcase was still in the car, so he combed his hair with his fingers before he left the room.

He had gone only a short distance when he met Leah in the main hall. "I was just coming to get you," she said, stopping before she bumped into him. "I couldn't remember if I told you that the chimes meant dinner was being served."

"No, you didn't." For a moment he stood still, letting his gaze sweep over her. She was wearing the same clothes she'd had on that afternoon: jeans and a sweater—casual, easy, comfortable. But she looked good. Very good. The sweater was gray and fitted snugly enough to reveal the soft curves of her breasts and hips without being too tight. Her jeans clung close to long slender legs before disappearing into soft leather boots. Her hair, brown with just a hint of red, curled loosely down to her shoulders. Her mouth was full, her nose small and straight, and her eyes . . .

Her eyes were like the sky—cool, clear and blue. Icy blue.

His expression, faraway and troubled, puzzled her. "Is something wrong?"

Grimly he shook his head. "You're a lovely woman, Leah." And *that* was wrong. She wasn't supposed to be pretty, wasn't supposed to have eyes the color of the sky, wasn't supposed to gift him with rare, fragile, beautiful smiles. And he sure as hell wasn't supposed to like her. Or want her.

Instantly wary, she took a step back. She had no illusions about her appearance. She was passably attractive, but, as Terence had occasionally affirmed, she would never be beautiful. She would never make men stand still in their tracks, or overwhelm them with her loveliness.

That meant Bryce was lying. An odd sense of disappointment shot through her. She had hoped they could be friends—she had precious few relatives, and she would love to welcome a new one into the family—but how could they be friends when he started off by lying to her?

"We'd better go. Colleen, our cook, doesn't like it when we're late," she said. But she made no effort to move; she just watched him with eyes filled with suspicion and doubt.

Bryce grew wary, too. Considering the circumstances, she had been unexpectedly friendly, until he had said she was lovely. His compliment had, for some reason, offended her, but why? Did she expect him to make a pass at her now? If so, she would be disappointed. In spite of the fact that he'd been single—he liked that word better than divorced—for six years, he didn't make passes at women; Kay had taught him that such passes weren't often well received. And he had lacked skill, she'd claimed. Finesse.

The tension between them reminded Leah uncomfortably of Terence; too much of the time spent with her husband had been tense. When the chimes rang again, she gratefully used them as an excuse to turn away. "We'd better go."

He walked silently alongside her, matching his longer stride to hers. When she stopped in the doorway of the ballroom, so did he.

The original dining room had been too small to accommodate the guests, so the ballroom down the hall, which filled half of the first floor, had been converted. The teal-blue walls were stenciled near the top with a floral pattern in deep peach. The same pattern had been enlarged and painted in the center of the high ceiling, where it was shadowed by the lights below. In front of the tall, wide windows, a mahogany table, seating fourteen, gleamed in the light of twin chandeliers. Smaller tables, seating four each, were grouped at each end of the room, covered with dark peach linen cloths and lit with tall, slender tapers in silver and pewter candlesticks. Against the inside wall a fire crackled in the fireplace, filling the air with the sweet scent of pine.

Leah's gaze traveled swiftly around the room, automatically lighting with pleasure at the simple beauty of the room. The large table, along with half the smaller ones, was filled with hungry guests. Her children were waiting at two tables pushed together in the corner, and visitors from town, who made dinner at the inn a Friday night event, filled the others.

As if on cue, the wide doors to the kitchen swung open, and Colleen's staff began serving the dinner. It was roast beef with all the trimmings; Leah knew without looking or even sniffing. The kitchen was Colleen's domain, but planning the menus was Leah's chore.

She wished she could seat Bryce with the guests—there were empty seats at several tables—but that would be rude when there were also empty seats at the family's table. Without looking up at him, she said quietly, "You can sit wherever you like—with the kids and me, or with the guests."

That last phrase sounded hopeful, so he deliberately disappointed her. If she didn't want him around, she would have to say so, though he doubted she could be that ill-mannered. "I'd like to meet my cousins."

She accepted his response with a nod. Greeting the guests as she went, she made her way to the family table, leaving him to follow. There were three empty chairs at the table—two at the closer end and one at the other. She went to the far end, putting the length of the table and one child between them. "We have a guest tonight, kids," she said softly, sliding the chair out. "This is Bryce Cameron. He's your grandfather's nephew."

His brow wrinkled at the odd phrasing. Wouldn't it have been simpler to introduce him as their father's cousin? It started him wondering about her relationship with her husband. During the brief time they had talked, she had never mentioned Terence, not even when she'd explained how she had recognized Bryce. As closely as he and Douglas resembled each other, he and Terence must have looked almost like twins, but she had avoided comparing him to Terence. Because he couldn't compare? he thought with a hint of bitterness. Or because she'd loved her husband too much to bring up his name?

Her soft drawl and the four steady, curious gazes directed his way brought his attention back. She recited the names he already knew, giving each child a gentle smile in turn.

All four children looked alike, with dark brown hair and darker brown eyes. Douglas—who was tall and, judging from the size of his feet, promised to be taller—was at the opposite end of the table. He stood up, circled around and politely shook hands. Laurel and Megan sat on Bryce's right, young and giggling and pretty. On his left, the barrier between Leah and himself, was Matthew. Mimicking his brother, he stood up and gravely extended his hand. "I'm pleased to meet you," he said in a childishly serious voice. "Do I call you Mr. Cameron, Mr. Bryce, or Cousin Bryce?"

When was the last time he'd seen a six-year-old concerned about the proper way to address an unknown relative old enough to be his father? he wondered as he solemnly accepted the small hand. "How about just plain Bryce?"

Matthew shook his head. "We're not allowed to call grown-ups by their first names, are we, Mom?"

She was about to give him permission, as long as Bryce didn't object, when he spoke again. "How about uncle?"

"You can't call him that," eleven-year-old Megan said sarcastically.

"Why not?"

"Because he's *not* your uncle, silly," Laurel replied, sounding bored.

"You can figure it out later." Leah sent a warning look at her daughters as she slid into her seat. "Eat your dinner now, before it gets cold."

The four children monopolized the dinner conversation, relating the events of their day to their mother. Bryce was, for the most part, silent, answering an occasional question from one of the children, observing the way Leah responded to each of them, giving her full attention to each speaker. She was a good mother, he thought with respect. A loving mother. That was the one thing that Kay, in their fourteen years together, had never wanted to be.

As soon as they'd finished eating, the kids left the dining room, leaving Bryce and Leah alone at the table. As he moved with easy confidence into the seat Megan had vacated, Leah wished she had skipped the last cup of coffee so that she could leave, too.

"Your children are very nice. You must be very proud of them."

"Yes, I am." She finished her coffee and set the cup on its saucer.

He glanced out the window at the snow. It was coming down harder, weighing down the shrubs that circled the house. He wanted to talk, to say something that would keep her from leaving the table, but his mind was blank. All he could think of was that he wanted to keep her with him a while longer. "Business must be good."

She shrugged. "We can't complain."

"Is it this crowded during the week?"

"No. We get some guests for a week or two, especially over Thanksgiving and Christmas, but most of our winter business is on weekends."

The silence that settled over them was uncomfortable. He glanced around and saw that more than half the guests were gone. His uneasy gaze also took note of the near-perfect condition of the room. "The house looks good."

"Yes, it does." She scooted her chair back. "If you'll excuse me..."

His mouth thinned into a narrow line. "Why are you so eager to run away from me, Leah?"

Laying her napkin on the table, she stood up and slid the chair back into place. "I have things to do."

And at the top of that list was getting away from him. That was okay, he decided grimly. He could use some time alone.

Leah wanted to flee both the room and the house, but she couldn't just walk away and leave him sitting there alone. She stood stiffly, her hands gripping the back of the chair. "Is there anything you need?" she asked haltingly.

"Nothing that you can give me." He stood up, too, knocking a napkin to the floor, and walked away. All the way across the room he felt her eyes on him, but he didn't slow or turn back. In the hallway he retrieved his coat from the closet and left the house.

He had to brush the snow off the trunk of his rental car before he could open it. The suitcase inside was small and cold against his bare hand. Quickly he slammed the trunk and started back toward the house, bag in hand.

"I would have gotten that for you," came a husky voice from the porch.

Bryce looked up at Douglas. "That's okay."

"It's part of my job. Since you got here this afternoon, I just assumed that you'd already taken your luggage in." The boy watched as Bryce brushed the snow from his hair, then his shoes and trouser legs. "You aren't exactly dressed for this weather, are you?"

Bryce found a smile somewhere inside for his cousin. "No," he agreed ruefully. "I'm not." He noticed that Douglas was bundled up. "Are you going somewhere?"

"Yeah, we have a basketball game tonight. Mark's supposed to pick me up in a few minutes."

"It won't be canceled because of the snow?"

Douglas's grin was engaging. "If they canceled everything every time it snowed, we would have to hibernate all winter. Angel's Peak is the highest mountain in North Carolina, and the town is the highest town. But I suppose you know that, being born here and all."

Bryce put the suitcase down and stuck his hand inside his pocket. "I suppose I must have, but I forgot. I really wasn't expecting this kind of weather."

Douglas leaned back against the wall, seemingly unaware of the cold. "Yeah, the snow's coming early this year. They say we're going to have a hard winter. Of course, a hard winter is great for a town that depends on skiing for its living." He grinned again. "How long are you planning to stay, Mr. Cameron?"

Bryce blinked. "Don't you think there are a few too many of us around here with that last name to be calling me mister? You're almost an adult. Aren't you allowed to call grown-ups by their first names?"

"Only if they say it's all right."

"Well, it's all right with me. As far as how long I'll be here... I don't know. I need to see your grandfather."

"You haven't seen him in a long time, have you?"

Bryce shook his head.

"Why not?"

He liked the boy's straightforward approach. He knew Leah would have liked to ask that, too, but propriety had stopped her from snooping. Still, he had no intention of answering the question. His business with Peter was private.

A car slowed to a stop near the side of the house, and three short honks broke the silence of the night. Douglas pushed himself away from the wall and bounded down the steps. "See you tomorrow, Bryce," he called on his way.

Picking up the suitcase again, Bryce went inside and down the long halls to his room. Unpacking the few clothes he'd brought took only a few minutes; then he sat alone with nothing to do. Most of the guests were in the sitting room—he'd heard their laughter and conversation when he had passed by—but he didn't want to join them. He usually made friends among strangers easily, but tonight the effort seemed too great.

He picked up the heavy family Bible and carried it to the rocker with him. The wooden slats creaked when he sat down and opened the book to the record pages in the middle. Most of the entries, the spidery ones in faded ink, had been made by Gran, the final one dated thirty-nine years ago on the page marked "Deaths": Katherine Johnson Cameron. His mother. Gran's own death had been recorded next, followed by an entry for Terence, only six years ago.

Curious, he turned to the "Births" page and compared dates. Terence had died three months before Matthew's birth. It must have been difficult for Leah, losing her husband in the middle of her pregnancy.

He had told her the truth in the office that afternoon when he'd said that he knew very little about her, other than her name and the names and ages of her children. Now he couldn't resist the urge to find out more, and the family records were a good place to start.

Brief but complete histories of every person who had married into the Cameron family in the last hundred years were listed in the Bible—histories of everyone but Leah. The lines under her name were blank—mother's and father's names, grandparents' names, place of birth, all of them. Her birth date was listed as Christmas Eve; her maiden name was Douglas; she had been seventeen when she married Terence; and less than three months later her son Douglas had been born. That was the extent of the information on her.

Bryce closed the Bible and returned it to the table. He shut off the lights and walked to the lace-curtained window, then stared out at the snow. Leah Cameron meant nothing to him. He was only here to settle his business with Peter, and she wasn't part of that business.

Then he impatiently shook his head. He had never lied to himself before, not even when Kay had left him, and he wasn't going to start now. Leah was a beautiful woman, the kind he should have married—gentle, considerate, kind and loving. It was only natural that he would be attracted to her. There was nothing wrong with that attraction.

As long as he did nothing about it.

Leah stayed busy on Saturday, seeing to the dozens of little details that running the inn required: replacing the fresh flowers in each guest room; helping the staff launder the loads of table and bed linen; making sure the steps and a path to the parking lot were kept clear; overseeing breakfast, lunch and preparations for dinner; checking the firewood supplies, and so on. She saw little of her children and nothing of Bryce.

She told herself that she should be grateful he wasn't around. The man disturbed her more than anyone she'd ever known; at least he was making it easy for her to do her work by avoiding her. No, she corrected herself, it was possible for her to work, not easy. Even though he'd stayed out of her sight all day, he hadn't left her mind. With an awareness far more acute than she would have believed possible, she could *feel* him—a strange, unfamiliar and somehow compelling presence in the house she knew so well.

She told herself it was silly to pay so much attention to him, even if it was only in her thoughts. She had male guests at the inn on a regular basis—men who were more handsome and more charming than Bryce Cameron—and she had never let any of them affect her this way.

But she wasn't *letting* Bryce affect her. It just happened—the way the sun came up each morning and went down each evening. She had no power to control it, and trying just made her tense with frustration.

Taking a break from the piles of mail in front of her, she swiveled her chair around to face the window. The snow had stopped earlier, after depositing more than eighteen inches. The yard and the woods beyond wore a heavy coat of white, presenting a romantic picture from the warmth of her office.

What did she know about Bryce Cameron? Not very much, she admitted with a rueful smile. Peter had done little more than confirm his nephew's existence, something he could hardly deny, since it had been documented in the family Bible. The only child of Frank and Katherine Cameron, Bryce was in his early forties and lived in Philadelphia. He was obviously a businessman of some sort and, judging from the expensive quality of the suit he'd worn yesterday, a successful one. That was all she had learned about him.

A slow smile lighted her face. No, that wasn't all, honesty compelled her to admit. She knew that he was handsome—better looking than Terence, but perhaps not as attractive as Douglas showed the promise of becoming. She knew that he had the warmest, kindest, darkest eyes she'd ever seen. She knew from the captivating smile that came so easily to his lips that he was good-natured and charming. And she knew, from the brief time they'd spent together, that something in him could reach through her defenses and touch her in ways, in places that she'd never before been touched.

The problem was that she didn't want to be touched—not by Bryce or any other man. She had spent more than one third of her life married, relying on a man to meet her physical and emotional needs. Although Terence had met the physical needs—with food and shelter—emotionally, she would have died a slow death, had it not been for the children. She liked her life the way it was now, with no need and no desire for a man—any man.

"And that," she said to herself softly, "most definitely includes Bryce Cameron."

All this worrying was probably for nothing. She felt a strong pull toward the man, but he'd given no indication that he felt the same tug. He was here on business—business that didn't include her—and probably had no interest whatsoever in his cousin's widow. Philadelphia was a big city; if he wanted a relationship, he could easily find plenty of willing women right there at home. He wouldn't bother with one who lived six hundred miles away.

She turned back to the mail on her desk. It was divided into three piles—bills, reservation requests and deposits. The junk mail went directly into the trash, and there were no personal letters. She couldn't remember the last time she'd gotten one of those; her life revolved around her business.

The chimes, faint and distant, interrupted her sometime later. She straightened her desk, stood up and stretched, found a suitable smile and headed for the dining room.

She spent a few minutes talking to the guests, asking the skiers about their hours on the slopes and the nonskiers how they had spent their day. By the time she reached her table in the corner, she was wishing Peter and Martha would return soon. They interacted with the guests so much more naturally than she was able to; after less than two days of playing hostess, she was all out of small talk.

She got her first glimpse of Bryce as she approached the table. He was sitting near the end again—the end where Douglas usually sat. The end where Leah *always* sat. His dark head was bent as he listened intently to something Matthew was saying.

Whatever problem she personally had with Bryce's presence at the inn, she couldn't fault his behavior with the children. So few adults took the time to really listen to kids, and often they were patronizing. Bryce seemed to offer her six-year-old son the same respect that he would give an adult, and she admired that.

She didn't need to look for things to admire about the man, she scolded herself. What she really should do was concentrate on becoming oblivious to his presence.

Strengthening her smile with a deep breath, she slid into the chair on his right and greeted everyone with a soft hello. Matthew paused to return the greeting, then picked up his thought in midsentence.

"...Diplodocus wasn't so bad, because he only ate plants and not other dinosaurs. But Triceratops—he was tough. He had three horns and could even kill Tyrannosaurus, and Tyrannosaurus was the king of the meat eaters," he finished, wide-eyed and breathless.

Bryce's smile was warm. "Maybe you could show me your dinosaur collection after dinner."

"Okay, sure."

Bryce turned his head to include Leah in his smile. "Have you noticed that he can rattle off names just like that—" he snapped his fingers "—that you and I probably couldn't pronounce with a guide?"

"Speak for yourself," she responded. "I've read too many bedtime stories about dinosaurs. I can tell you anything you want to know about Archaeopteryx or Ichthyosaurus or Pteranodon."

His smile deepened, bringing a gleaming light to his dark eyes. "You like being a mother, don't you?"

She raised her hand to indicate the children. "If I didn't, I would be in serious trouble, wouldn't I?" In spite of her light tone, her thoughts were serious. Was there anything she wouldn't do to receive smiles like that on a daily basis? There was such warmth, such genuine goodness in his smiles, and they made her feel good, too.

"I asked Douglas to trade seats with me tonight. Do you mind?"

"No. Why should I mind?" She spread her napkin as Colleen began serving them. "This looks wonderful, as usual," she told the older woman.

"Don't you know by now that everything I make looks *and* tastes wonderful?" Colleen set a plate in front of Bryce, then stood back, hands on her hips, and studied him. "You must be Frank's boy," she said bluntly.

"Yes, I am." He turned his attention from Leah to the other woman. "Do you know my father?"

"I used to, years ago—and your mother, too. They were good people, Frank and Katherine. When did you get back?"

"Yesterday."

Colleen directed a mock glare at Leah. "And you didn't tell me?"

"I didn't know you knew his parents," she said, defending herself, unable to hide the smile that said she knew Colleen wasn't really angry.

The cook picked up two plates from the tray behind her and set them down in front of the girls. "Peter will certainly be surprised to see you when he gets back."

He noticed that she said surprised—not pleased or happy. Just surprised. "I'm sure he will be," he agreed. A quick look at Leah showed that she concurred.

"I was sort of hoping you would leave before Peter and Martha get home," she said hesitantly when Colleen had gone. She was trying to be tactful, but how could she tactfully tell someone that his welcome was about to run out?

"Why are you so anxious to get rid of me? You don't even know why I'm here."

He spoke in a good-natured tone, but Leah sensed that his question was serious, and that he would like a serious answer. "You're right, I don't know," she said after a glance confirmed that the children were involved in their own conversation. "But I *do* know that Peter doesn't want to talk to you. I know that he doesn't want to see you."

He sighed as he picked up his fork. "Do you think I came here because I wanted to? If my reasons weren't important, I wouldn't care if I never saw Peter or Angel's Peak again."

She stared at him, her mouth hanging open. "You don't mean that. He's your family."

"And do you know what family means to the Camerons? Nothing. Not a damn thing. You look out for yourself, and everybody else can go to hell."

She was still staring at him, her expression both troubled and dismayed. He had disappointed her, Bryce thought, regretting his harsh words. Obviously his opinion of Peter as an uncle differed greatly from her opinion of him as a father-in-law and grandfather.

"Look," he said quietly, wearily, "you worship your family, but don't expect me to do the same."

Leah dropped her gaze to her plate. Growing up without a family, she had dreamed and hoped and prayed for one. When she had gotten one through marriage to Terence, she'd made them the most important thing in her life, and now Bryce was telling her that they didn't mean a damn thing. What had happened between him, his father and Peter to make him feel that way?

Bryce laid his fork down again and touched her hand where it rested on the edge of the table. She jerked her eyes upward to meet his. "I'm sorry," he said. Sorry he had offended her. Sorry he had disappointed her. Sorry he had even opened his mouth in the first place. And sorry he couldn't do as she wanted—as *he* wanted: go back to Philadelphia and never see her, or Peter, or Angel's Peak again.

"It's all right," she murmured, but he could tell by her downcast eyes and troubled expression that it wasn't.

She remained quiet through the rest of the meal, grateful when it ended and she could make her escape. A quiet walk in the woods soothed her nerves, but not her worries about Bryce and the effects his presence might have on her family. On *her*. Putting her troubling thoughts aside, she returned to the house in time to read Matthew a story and tuck him into his bed.

"I like our cousin, Mom. He's awful nice." The words were interrupted with a yawn. "Do you think he'll be here very long?"

Disturbed by her son's simple sentiments, she gave a casual response that hid her concern. "I don't know, honey. I don't think so." She smoothed the covers over him, then laid his favorite stuffed dinosaur on the pillow next to him.

Matthew tucked the dinosaur under the blankets and snuggled him close. "He treats me like I'm all growed up. I hope he stays a long time. I hope he lives here with us forever. I love you, Mom. G'night."

Leah turned off the lamp on the bedside table, then watched her son. Within minutes he was deep in sleep, a soft, innocent smile touching his lips.

She loved all her children, but Matthew was her baby. He needed her caring and protection more than the older kids did. And protect him she would, she vowed. Bryce Cameron wasn't going to come here and destroy her family. He wasn't going to break her son's heart. She would make sure of that.

Chapter 2

Bryce lay in bed Sunday morning, staring at the ceiling. He had heard Leah leave her room more than an hour earlier, but he remained where he was, warm and comfortable and troubled.

If he had any sense, he would get dressed, make the reservation for his return flight and leave Angel's Peak once and for all. But each time he decided to do just that, he remembered the sorrow in his father's eyes, his voice, his entire manner. The old man was going to die, and he wanted to make peace with his brother first; he wanted to live out the rest of his life at home. Was that so much to ask?

And was it so much to ask of Bryce that he make the arrangements with Peter? He had come here prepared to cajole, beg, bribe or threaten his uncle—to do whatever it took to get permission to bring his father home again. Now, after only a few hours' exposure to Leah, he was ready to give up and go back home, without even setting eyes on Peter.

Twenty-four hours more. That was all he needed. Peter would be home this evening, Bryce would work out an agreement with him tonight, and he would leave for Philadelphia in the morning. It was another simple plan—one that he was determined to carry out.

Outside the window he heard laughing voices, the slamming of car doors, the revving of engines. The guests were heading out for the day, to the slopes or to do some snowy sight-seeing, he supposed.

There was a knock at the door, sharp and heavy—one that couldn't be ignored. Bryce rolled onto his side and called out an invitation.

Douglas stuck his head in. "Last call for breakfast," he said cheerfully. "The food's on the stove in the kitchen. Everyone else has already eaten. We're all going to church. Want to come?"

Bryce politely declined, and the boy's grin grew wider. "I didn't think so. That's why I brought these—in case you want to go outside." He opened the door wide enough to slip through a pair of waterproof boots. "My feet are probably bigger than yours, but at least you'll stay dry. See you at dinner."

In a few minutes the house was quiet. Bryce got up, showered and shaved, and dressed in his last set of clean clothes. He tugged on Douglas's boots, which were at least a size too big, then went to the kitchen to see what was left over from breakfast.

The silence in the house was eerie. He couldn't remember any place other than his own house in Philadelphia that was so still. Uncomfortable, he drank a cup of coffee and made a sandwich from a biscuit and a slice of ham, then got his coat and gloves from the closet. This was as good a time as any to go outside, as Douglas had suggested.

By the time he'd reached the edge of the yard, he had chosen his destination. Back in the woods, far away from the inn and the two guest houses, was the family cemetery, where his mother had been buried almost forty years ago, and where Gran had been laid to rest fourteen years later. He hadn't been there since he was fifteen, but he easily found the path that led into the woods. There was a road farther back, barely wide enough for a car, but he chose the winding path that circled and snaked through the densely growing trees. It was quiet here, too, but this was a natural quiet, the only noises the tramping of his footsteps and the occasional crackle of a twig.

Suddenly he emerged into a clearing. Surrounded by an iron and stone fence, the cemetery was large and filled with crosses and headstones. The oldest grave was that of old Abraham, the man who had built the house in 1787, then died three years later. The ones Bryce was looking for were side by side near the back. He had to brush the snow away to read the names.

Katherine Johnson Cameron, wife of Francis Patrick Cameron. She had died when Bryce was barely two. His only memories of her came from old photographs in his father's albums. She had been a rather plain woman, fragile and unsubstantial-looking. He didn't know her, but she had been his mother.

Next to her was Anna Dawson Cameron, his grandmother. She was the one he remembered—the one who had raised him, comforted him, punished him and loved him. She had taught him about life, about joy and satisfaction and peace. She had prepared him for the day when all this— the house and the land—would be his. Then she had died; and Peter, not Frank, had inherited the estate, and the family had been torn apart. Was it too late to put it back together? he wondered.

He realized that he was cold and that he was being watched at the same time. But when he first turned, he saw no one, and he put the feeling down to his location. Even on sunny, bright winter Sundays, a cemetery wasn't the most pleasant place to be. Then he heard a crackle and found the slender figure that was trying to slip away, unnoticed, into the woods.

"Always running away," he said softly, shaking his head.

Leah stopped and approached the gate. "I wasn't running away. I didn't know you were here until I saw you, and I thought you might like to be alone."

"Why? It's a cemetery. These people aren't here—they're gone forever."

She pushed her hands into her pockets. "This is the last place I would expect to find a man whose family doesn't mean a damn thing to him."

His face flushed a dark bronze. "You're not going to forgive me for saying that, are you?" Without waiting for an answer, he continued. "My father is the only family I have, and I love him. Peter, Martha—they can go to hell."

"Does that include your cousins?"

"My—" He realized that she meant her children. He hadn't quite gotten used to the idea of having cousins. "I like your kids, but it's not as if we're really family. I didn't even know they existed until a month ago."

Leah gestured to Anna's tombstone. "Your grandmother was proud of being a Cameron—proud of her house and her land, of her sons and her grandsons. It would break her heart to hear you talk this way."

He opened his mouth to argue, to ask where she got off telling him anything about Gran, then shut it again. She was right. If Gran knew what had happened to her family after her death, she would be ashamed to claim any of them.

Walking through the gate, Leah followed his footsteps in the snow to stand beside him. "How is your father?"

The sun glinted off her hair, setting the auburn tints afire. Resisting the urge to touch it, to see if the curls were as soft as they looked, Bryce turned his gaze away. "My father?" he echoed.

"Yes—Frank. How is he?"

"He's all right," he answered cautiously. There was enough truth in the statement to keep it from being a lie, but not enough to be called honest. "Why do you ask?"

She bent to wipe more snow from the front of Katherine's marker. "Your father's an old man—in his seventies now, isn't he? And after spending more than half your life elsewhere, you suddenly come home, determined to see Peter.'' She waited silently, hoping that he would tell her something, anything, about the reasons for his return. It was more than curiosity that prompted her—she wanted trust. She wanted him to trust her enough to confide in her. She wanted honesty.

Bryce looked at her for a long, long time, his dark eyes solemn and unrevealing. He weighed the merits of telling her the truth, knowing that she might take Peter's side and use it against him, versus lying, knowing that she would probably guess it was a lie and look at him with the same disappointment that still haunted him from last night. Or he could say nothing at all. Still holding her gaze, he chose the latter course and kept silent.

She nodded and took a step back, breaking his hold on her.

To stop her from turning away, he asked, ''Why aren't you at church with the kids?''

''Someone has to stay at the inn.''

''But you aren't at the inn.''

She smiled. ''I will be in ten minutes.''

''Can I walk back with you?''

She wanted to say no, but she couldn't. Giving him a tight little smile, she started away, leaving him to follow.

''So what do you do when you're alone at the inn on Sunday mornings?'' he asked, catching up with her.

''Paperwork...check on Colleen's dinner...enjoy the quiet.''

''Too much quiet can drive you nuts.'' He knew that from experience. There were times when he hated to go home to his empty house. It had taught him the meaning of the term ''deathly silence.''

She gave him a chastening look. ''I have four children, two in-laws, between three and thirty guests, and ten to fifteen people on staff. There's no such thing as too much quiet around here.'' When they crossed the driveway Leah turned on impulse and walked to the front of the house. Bryce un-questioningly followed.

She walked at a leisurely pace, scuffing her feet in the snow, enjoying the clean, fresh wintry scent in the air and pretending to ignore the man at her side. She loved winter—the weather was cold and the snow was plentiful. More importantly, it brought the holiday season. Every holiday was celebrated at Cameron Inn, but the winter holidays were special. Thanksgiving, Christmas and New Year, added together with Douglas's, Megan's and Leah's own birthdays, made November and December a joyous season at the inn.

Her birthday. She gave a soft sigh that brought Bryce's chocolate-dark eyes to her. This year she was going to be thirty-six years old, give or take a few months. No one at the home had known when she'd been born—they had taken her word for her age, and the day had been chosen at random. Long ago she had quit questioning it, had quit longing for a real birthday, a day to celebrate that was her own. She was content to call herself a Christmas baby.

"Something wrong?"

She stopped walking to look up at Bryce. With a faint smile she shook her head. She didn't mind growing older—she didn't feel old, anyway, until she realized that, a few days after her birthday, her oldest child would turn eighteen. Could she possibly be the mother of a newly matured adult?

Bryce wanted to bring her attention back to him. He wanted her to look at him, to talk to him in that soft, sensuous drawl he found so enchanting. His gaze settling on the house in front of them, he fixed on a subject. "Whose idea was it to turn Gran's house into an inn?"

Together they studied the house. It was two stories tall and painted a pure, brilliant white. A veranda completely encircled it, its roof was supported by slender round pillars. Sets of black wooden shutters flanked every window, and the wide ornate door was also painted black. Wide stone steps led to the veranda, and at the top sat a basket spilling over with pumpkins left over from Halloween and the multicolored gourds and ears of Indian corn that had been gathered for Thanksgiving.

"It was my idea," she admitted softly. She had spent many long hours fixing up the house that had been her inheritance when Terence died. Seeing what she had accomplished filled her with pride. Old Abraham would be pleased to know that the house he'd built with his own hands had survived two hundred years in such a lovingly cared-for state. He might not like the fact that it was now an inn, Leah acknowledged with a wry grin—she had definitely detected a note of hostility in Bryce's voice—but at least it was cared for.

When Terence died, opening an inn had seemed logical. The huge old house was far too big for Leah and the children, and Peter and Martha had insisted that they were happy living in the guest house. It had been a big gamble, but Leah had seen no other choice. She hadn't worked outside the home during her marriage, so her only marketable skills had been her ability to run a household efficiently and her willingness to work hard. She had wanted a job that would allow her to spend time with the children, and she had needed one that would let her keep the house she loved so much. Opening an inn had been the perfect answer.

She tilted her head back to meet his eyes. "You don't approve, do you?"

He didn't try to deny it; instead he smiled sheepishly. "I have to admit, when I first heard about it, I didn't like the idea. The only thing worse than an inn would be making it a museum."

"The Camerons do whatever it takes to keep what's theirs," she said with forced lightness.

And to take what they wanted, he grimly added. His uncle Peter had taught them that lesson well twenty-six years ago. "What about you, Leah? Are you a Cameron in name only, or would you do whatever it takes, too?"

She gave him a long, cool look. "I suppose that depends on what's at stake."

"The inn? Your children? Your comfortable little life?"

He saw the flash of emotion before she succeeded in hiding it—annoyance, anger, defensiveness. She was fiercely protective of the things that were important to her—the inn, the children, Peter and Martha. Would she love a man as fiercely? he wondered. Had she loved Terence that way? He wanted to know—needed to know—but knew she would freeze up and walk away if he asked.

"I need to get to work," she said quietly, warily. "Excuse me."

He wanted to keep her with him, so, perversely, he let her go. When she left him standing alone in the center of the yard, some of the warmth went with her, making him shiver.

He had a couple of hours to kill before the kids returned from church. Inside, he changed from Douglas's boots into his own shoes, then set off to explore the house, to see what changes Leah and her inn had made.

The living room was at the front of the house, across the broad hallway from the ballroom. It was a large room, with pale yellow walls. Graceful moss-green leaves curving around tiny dark gold flowers were stenciled at the tops of the walls, and the dark yellow was repeated in the fireplace, the window trim and the moldings over the doors. Elegant draperies in white striped with gold hung at each window, framing the winter views outside. Portraits of long-dead Camerons hung on the walls, keeping watch over their home. The furniture was old, some of it faded or scratched, but all of superior quality. The rug in front of the fireplace was old, too, its rich reds, blues and greens faded after more than a hundred years of use.

The next room was the sitting room. Here the color scheme was reversed, with dark gold walls and pale yellow accents. The furniture was sturdier, not so ancient, and most of it was grouped around the single piece that spoke of the twentieth century: the television set.

There were other rooms—the ballroom, the original dining room, the library, the study, another smaller sitting room—and they were all the same: polished and dusted and waxed, lovingly kept in perfect condition. The only concessions to the present were electric light and television.

He chose not to climb the stairs. All the rooms up there were bedrooms, and all were occupied by guests this weekend. He would have to ask Leah to show them to him when the guests were gone.

He sank down into a wing chair in the second sitting room, tilted back his head and closed his eyes. He liked what she had done with the house—or rather, what she *hadn't* done. It was still beautiful—still home. He had almost hoped to find terrible changes, reasons to dislike her, but she had given the house the same respect Abraham had had when he built it, and the same love Gran had shown when she lived in it.

There was a timid knock at the door, one that he ignored in the hope that whoever it was would go away. But the door swung silently open, then shut again; and a soft little voice inquired, "Are you asleep or just resting your eyes?"

He opened them to see. Matthew standing beside his chair. "Just resting them," he replied. "You have to do that when you get old."

"You're not old, not really. Grandpa is, but you're only about as old as my dad. Were you and my dad friends?"

"Sort of—we were cousins."

"Can't you be friends with cousins? 'Cause that's what we are."

Bryce easily lifted the boy over the high arm of the chair into his lap. "Yeah, we can be friends."

Matthew relaxed easily against Bryce's chest. "But you didn't like my dad," he continued.

How could he tell a six-year-old boy who had never known his father that he was right—that Bryce had never liked Terence? "You know how sometimes Laurel and Megan tease you and don't want you hanging around because you're too young?'' he asked, hoping that the girls were like all the girls he'd known when he was a kid.

Matthew rubbed his nose. "Yeah, I know."

"Well, you still love them when they're mean to you, because they're your sisters, but you don't really like them. That's how it is for cousins sometimes. Sometimes your father and I just didn't get along." Like ninety-nine percent of the time, he finished silently.

"You look a lot like my dad. I seen a picture of him at Grandma's house."

The innocent remark raised several questions in Bryce's mind. Why didn't Peter and Martha live in the main house along with Leah and their grandchildren? And why did Matthew have to go to his grandmother's house to see pictures of his father? Why didn't Leah have pictures of her husband in their living quarters, for the kids, if not for herself? That brought him back to his earlier unasked question: had Leah loved Terence deeply? Did she still love him? Or had their love died, the way his and Kay's had?

"His name was Terence, and he died 'fore I was born," Matthew said solemnly. "I don't know much about him—Mom never likes to talk about him." He gave a heavy sigh. "I wish he was still here. I'm the only kid in my whole first-grade class that don't have a dad."

Bryce didn't know what to say. Even though his mother had died when he was small, he didn't really know how the boy felt. He'd had Gran to replace his mother, so he had rarely missed Katherine. "Do you like being in the first grade?"

The boy raised his head and gave Bryce a knowing look. "You're changing the subject. That's what Mom says Douglas does when he does something wrong and doesn't want to get in trouble for it." He rubbed his nose again. "Yeah, school's okay. But I don't like homework, and I don't like going when I could be outside playing in the snow." His stomach growled, and he looked down at it, his eyes lighting. "I knew I was supposed to tell you something. Mom says dinner is ready and for you to come on. She says someone always has to find you when it's time to eat.''

Bryce could practically hear Leah saying it. "Well, come on," he said, getting to his feet, holding Matthew in his arms. "Let's not keep people waiting."

"Oh, they won't wait. Miss Colleen says that if us kids aren't at the table on time, then our food can just get cold, because she isn't gonna keep it warm for us." He wriggled to the floor when they reached the dining-room door and led the way to their table.

"I was beginning to wonder if you'd gotten lost," Leah said as Matthew sat down next to her.

"Mom." He spread his napkin over his lap, then said with a strong dose of self-importance, "I was talking to my cousin."

The girls snickered, but were silenced by a stern look from Douglas. Leah frowned at all three of them before glancing at her youngest son. Matthew still hadn't decided what to call the older man—his sisters had vetoed "Uncle"; he didn't like "Cousin Bryce"; and he didn't want to use the first name alone. It amused his sisters, but Leah was worried about the importance Matthew had placed on the title and, through that, the man. Once Bryce completed his business with Peter, he would return to Philadelphia, and they would probably never see him again. How would Matthew feel then?

She looked at Bryce, who was cutting the roast chicken on his plate. "Peter called about an hour ago."

He met her gaze, surprised, but hiding it behind an expressionless mask. He waited patiently for her to continue.

"He and Martha will be home around five o'clock."

"Did you tell him that I'm here?"

She flushed. "No."

She was hoping he wouldn't be. She was hoping he would be polite enough, well-mannered enough, to leave before then, without causing trouble. He wasn't. "I guess he'll find out soon enough, then."

There was another flare of disappointment in her eyes, which set off a responding flare of anger in his own—anger, not surprise. He wasn't measuring up to the standards she had set. Well, according to Kay, he rarely measured up. His failures with his ex-wife had been many and painful. Why should Leah be any different?

He didn't speak to her during the rest of the meal, although he took part in the children's conversation. Leah was torn between relief and regret. The last thing she needed was Bryce's attention. The last thing she wanted was his anger.

When dinner was over, she sent the kids off to play, then headed for the front desk. Vicky, the clerk, wouldn't be in until four o'clock, so Leah was filling in for her. She began checking through the records, preparing bills for the guests who were scheduled to leave that evening.

"Can I talk to you?"

The sound of Bryce's voice made her stiffen, and the little hairs on her neck stood on end. Slowly she raised her head to see him leaning his elbows on the polished mahogany counter. "What do you want?" she asked cautiously.

Now that she was listening, he wasn't sure what to say. He wanted to talk to her about Matthew, but the boy was really none of his business. If Leah perceived his concern as meddling or criticism, she would be offended or, worse, hurt. But he felt that what he had to say was important—out of line, maybe, but important.

She waited quietly. Four children and occasionally demanding guests had taught her patience.

He chose to overcome reluctance by leaping in—possibly over his head. "It's about Matthew. We were late for dinner because we were talking. About his lack of a father." He watched her closely and saw the dismay pass through her eyes. He had been right: she was offended.

She rose slowly from the high stool. Standing in front of him, she could see directly into his eyes. "If you have any questions about Terence, I would prefer that you ask them of me and not of my children."

He was definitely in over his head—way too deep. Her eyes were angry and bright, as frigid as the sky outside. He broke contact with them and took a step back. "I didn't ask him anything!" he snapped in self-defense. "He mentioned that I looked like the picture of his father that he'd seen at Martha's. Why don't you have any pictures of Terence here? Why don't you ever talk to Matthew about his father?"

"This is none of your business." She spoke in a calm, flat, unemotional voice, then turned away with a dismissive gesture.

But Bryce wasn't going to be dismissed so easily. He circled the counter, blocking her only escape. "Whatever your feelings for Terence, he was Matthew's father. The kid has a right to know about him."

"'The kid' is *my* son, and I will decide—" She stopped suddenly, forgetting what she'd been about to say. He was too close. Her pink sweater came within a breath of touching his green one, and she could feel the heat from his body. She could sense his eyes on her, willing her to look at him, and at last she did.

His eyes were just like Terence's—dark and mesmerizing. His nose was a little too big, his mouth too hard, his jaw too square, but he was more handsome than any man she'd known.

Bryce, too, had forgotten their conversation. He breathed slowly. He couldn't name her fragrance, couldn't even think of words to describe it. It was simply...wonderful.

He drew in a deep breath so his voice would be steady when he spoke. Instead the increased intensity of her scent made his mind go blank. The only word he spoke was her name, and it was merely a whisper.

Leah trembled. She wanted to move away, to run as fast as she could and hide, but she couldn't take a step without touching him, and she knew that would be a mistake. She had to stand there, had to wait until he let her go.

Without thought he lifted his hand. Briefly, hesitantly, gently he laid it on her hair. A coppery mix of brown and red, it was soft and sweetly scented.

Would one kiss cost either of them too much? he wondered, gliding his fingers over her curls before dropping his hand to his side. He was leaving tomorrow; would it be too risky to kiss her, just once, before he left?

Before he'd found the answer to that, he'd already taken action—by tentatively brushing his mouth against hers. He felt her stiffen, might even have heard her gasp over the pounding of his heart. But she didn't push him or run away or demand that he leave her alone, so he did it again.

Her lips were soft, bare of color, and her mouth tasted warm and sweet. He resisted the urge to pull her to him; instinct told him that she wouldn't accept his embrace so easily. He had to satisfy himself with her mouth, with its moist softness and the shy touch of her tongue.

The telephone on the desk beside them jangled, startling them apart. Leah gasped, and Bryce swore silently. He took a step back as she answered the phone with a welcoming, "Cameron Inn." After a moment she extended the receiver to Bryce.

He took it, wrapping his fingers around the warmth left behind by hers. His heart rate, which had been slowing after the kiss, was increasing again. Only two people knew to call him here—his secretary and his father's doctor—and neither would call unless it was an emergency.

"Mr. Cameron, this is Dr. Upton." The cardiologist's voice, for all its feminine softness, was businesslike.

"What's wrong?"

"Your father has had a little setback today. He seems to be all right, but this morning, and again this afternoon, he's had a series of transient ischemic attacks. These attacks are associated with hypertension and atherosclerosis, both of which he has. The first attacks lasted only a few seconds, but the last ones have been between five and ten minutes each.''

Bryce stared at Leah but didn't see her. His voice was quiet and hoarse when he asked, ''Is this serious?''

Leah busied herself sorting the registration cards with fingers that trembled, but she couldn't stop herself listening to his end of the conversation. She wished she could leave, to give him privacy for the call—to give *herself* privacy to deal with what had just happened—but he was still blocking the only way out and showed no interest in moving.

''It can be,'' the doctor answered. ''T.I.A.'s are often the precursors of strokes. Now, I've made arrangements for your father to be examined right away by a neurologist. There don't seem to be any problems at this time. In the periods between attacks he's lucid and understands what's going on, but to be on the safe side, I think you should cut your trip short and return to Philadelphia today, if at all possible. I've talked to Frank about it, and he would like to have you here.''

''All right. I'll be there as soon as I can.'' There were thin, tight lines around his mouth when he hung up the phone. His hand remained on the receiver. ''Do you have the airline numbers handy?''

Wordless, she found them for him. Bryce dialed the first number while speaking to her. ''Well, you were hoping I'd leave before Peter got home. You're getting your wish. Can you get my bill ready?''

He couldn't make it to Asheville to catch the next flight, so he booked a seat on the following one. When he hung up, he looked expectantly at Leah.

''There's no bill,'' she said with a shrug. ''You were our guest.'' She wanted to say more, to offer him some sort of reassurance. The news he'd received had obviously been bad; he suddenly looked tired and ten years older. She wished she could offer him comfort or just a shoulder to lean on, but she couldn't.

He looked at her for a moment. There were things he should say—things he should do—but he had waited too long. After a moment, she looked away. Turning sharply, he went to his room and quickly packed his bag, then went to find Matthew. In his search he found each of the other three children and said goodbye, but Matthew, the most important and the most elusive, wasn't around.

Leah was still at the front desk when he was ready to leave. "We'll continue our conversation at a later time," he warned her.

She looked up with a calmness she didn't feel. "Will we?" Would he be back? Would he care to see her when he came back?

"We will." He studied her for a moment, his gaze on her mouth, full and soft and set in a very faint smile. She was thinking about the kiss. He smiled, too. "I'll be back, Leah, and we'll finish that, too," he promised. He took a few steps toward the door, then turned back. "I couldn't find Matthew. Tell him I'll call—"

"No." Concern for her son overrode her concern for Bryce. "I'll tell him that you had to leave unexpectedly. I'll tell him that you said goodbye, but I won't tell him that you're going to call."

His eyes narrowed suspiciously. "Are you forbidding me to call him?"

"No." Clasping her hands together to hide her uneasiness, she continued softly. "Matthew is a cute kid—he's polite, friendly, bright, and he likes you. He's pleasant company while you're here, but when you get home...? How long will it take you to forget a nice six-year-old kid?"

He was angry—blindingly angry. Only the realization that she was trying to protect her son from disappointment stopped him from unleashing his temper on her. "I like Matthew—better than I like anyone else around here. I'm not going to string him along, then let him down. I don't take my pleasure in life from hurting kids."

Leah took a deep breath. She was shaking—both from her own emotions and from the intensity of Bryce's. "I didn't mean to imply that you did. But he's a little boy—a little boy who never knew his father, who's always wanted a dad, who's finally met you. You not only look like his father, but you like *him* as much as he likes you. Don't you see what that means to him?"

He did. Matthew was looking for a father, and he thought he'd found a good candidate in Bryce. It was something he would worry about later. "I'll call him," he said flatly. "Goodbye, Leah."

He closed the door behind him and walked quickly to his car. He was almost there when Matthew came racing up. His little brown eyes took one look at the suitcase, then met Bryce's gaze. "Where're you going?"

Bryce put the suitcase into the trunk, then lifted Matthew. "I was looking for you inside. I have to go back to Philadelphia. Something's happened, so I have to leave today."

Matthew clasped his hands behind Bryce's neck. His gloves were cold and damp from the snow. "Something bad?"

Bryce thought of his father, so thin and frail in his hospital bed, and nodded gravely. Yes, something bad.

"When will you be back?"

Not "*will* you be back?" Bryce noticed, but *when*. He was beginning to understand the saying, "the faith of a child." It hadn't occurred to Matthew that he might not return, that he might not care enough about the family home or his new cousins to come back again. "I don't know," he said softly, honestly. "First I have to take care of the problems at home."

"Okay." Matthew hugged him, then slid to the ground. "Be careful."

Sometimes the boy was so serious that he reminded Bryce of a three-and-a-half-foot-tall adult. "You, too. I'll see you soon." As soon as he said the words, he knew that Leah wouldn't approve. Well, that was too bad. He *would* see Matthew again soon, and he couldn't care less what Leah thought about that.

Early Sunday evenings were busy at the inn. Most of the guests, who were scheduled to be back at work the next day, waited until the last possible moment to check out, so Leah and Vicky had their hands full.

It was during a brief break that Peter and Martha arrived home. Leah left the desk to hug her mother-in-law. "Did you have a good time in Atlanta?"

"It was wonderful." Martha looked at her husband and actually blushed. "It was just wonderful. Did you have a good weekend? You weren't too busy, were you?"

"We got along fine—but I'm glad you're back." She rose onto her toes to kiss Peter's cheek. "I'm glad you're back, too," she teased.

"Did anything interesting happen while we were gone?" he asked gruffly as he helped Martha remove her coat.

"Just had the same old stuff," Vicky said.

Not quite the same old stuff, Leah silently corrected. She would have to tell her father-in-law about Bryce's visit—but not yet, not when he and Martha hadn't even settled in. Maybe after one of Colleen's delicious dinners, when the kids were tucked into bed and everyone was satisfied and relaxed . . .

But the choice of when to tell them was taken from her by the arrival of Megan and Matthew. Peter swung his grandson into his arms and gave him a bear hug, then demanded, "Did you miss me?"

Matthew was grinning. "Sure did. But guess what, Grandpa? I met my cousin—we all did—and he's really nice, and I liked him, and he told me—"

Leah didn't hear what Bryce had told Matthew, because her troubled blue gaze was locked with Peter's. The old man's smile was fading, and his eyes were dark with that stubborn look that she was beginning to associate with the Cameron men. Martha was looking worriedly from her husband to her daughter-in-law, and Vicky seemed puzzled. Even Megan felt the tension between the adults in the room.

Sensing that he'd lost his grandfather's attention, Matthew laid his hand on Peter's cheek. "Grandpa, are you listening to me?" he asked impatiently. At least his cousin always listened, even when other grown-ups were around.

"What cousin, Leah?"

If she hadn't known Peter so well, the coldness in his voice would have frightened her. Linking her hands together, she came forward, brushing her hand over her son's hair. "Bryce Cameron."

The sound Peter bit off was a curse, swiftly stopped when he recalled that the children were present. "He was here?"

"Yes."

"In this house?"

"Yes. I don't think this is the time or the place to talk about it, Peter."

He looked from her to the children, then nodded. "After dinner?"

She silently agreed.

"Well, where are Laurel and Douglas?" Martha asked, reaching for a bag she'd set down when she greeted Leah. "I believe I have some small gifts here for my grandchildren, if someone could find the missing two." Her cheer sounded false, but the kids didn't notice.

"I'll find them, Grandma," Megan offered.

"And I'll help," Matthew chimed in.

Finally tearing his eyes from Leah, Peter said quietly, "I think I will, too." He took Martha with him when he left.

Alone once more with Vicky, Leah sat down behind the counter. The clerk pretended to be busy for a few moments, then gave up and faced her boss and friend. "This Bryce—who is he?"

Leah knew that Vicky had seen him over the weekend; she was asking for specifics. "Bryce's father Frank is Peter's older brother."

"I didn't know Peter had any family besides you and the kids. Where has this brother been hiding?"

Leah's smile was strained. "Frank and Bryce left Angel's Peak before you were born. They live in Philadelphia." When the younger woman would have asked another question, Leah quickly and transparently changed the subject. "Do we have any more brochures on the inn around here? I think we're running low. Could you check and make a note to order more if we need them? I'm going to see if Colleen needs any help with dinner."

Only a handful of guests remained for dinner that night. As soon as the meal was finished, Leah asked Douglas to put Matthew to bed while she, Peter and Martha went to the small sitting room down the hall for a private talk.

Peter barely gave her a chance to sit down before he demanded, "Tell me about Bryce. What did he want? What did he say?"

Leah clasped her coffee cup in her hands, feeling the warmth seep into her fingers. Outside the narrow windows snow was coming down again, a light, fluffy white powder. An unusually harsh winter had been predicted for the Blue Ridge Mountains, and these early heavy snows seemed to bear out those predictions. She didn't mind. She liked snow.

"Well?"

"He wanted to see you, Peter. I don't know why—just that it's important to him." She remembered their conversation in the cemetery that morning and added, "I think it might be about his father."

Peter's eyes shifted away from hers—almost guiltily, she thought. "What about Frank?"

"I don't know. I think you should see him, Peter. He's your nephew, and Frank is your brother. Except for us—"

she indicated herself and Martha with a nod "—and the kids, they're the only family you've got left in the world."

"You think family is so important, don't you?" He smiled at her with a touch of pity. "Just because someone is family doesn't make them worthwhile. Families aren't perfect, wondrous, magical creatures, Leah. They're human beings—people just like you and me. They've got flaws."

Family *was* important to her. It came from all those years of growing up, of wishing more than anything in the world to be part of a family—anyone's family. "What flaws could Frank and Bryce possibly have to make you act this way? You've spent a third of your lives separated by some old argument. How can you refuse to even talk to Bryce, just to find out what he wants?"

Peter's scowl was fierce. "The last person in this world I want to talk to is Bryce Cameron! You want to know about his flaws? He is a selfish, deceitful, lying son of a—" Once again he bit off the word. Lifting one trembling hand to his face, he rubbed his temples for a moment.

A selfish, deceitful, lying son of a bitch. Leah tried to reconcile those words with the man who had spent the weekend with them. The man who had treated her six-year-old son with more respect than most adults afforded other adults. The man who had kissed her, who had made her feel things she'd never felt, who had made her long for things she'd given up hope of having.

"The man who came here was polite and friendly," she said carefully. "The children liked him." And so had *she*.

Peter's smile was sardonic. "He fooled you, didn't he? You looked at him with those damn naive and innocent eyes, and he knew exactly how to make you believe what he wanted you to believe."

Leah didn't like what he was implying, but she couldn't argue. For a woman who had been married twelve years, she *was* naive. She *was* innocent. Had it been that obvious to Bryce? Was that the reason behind his warm, friendly gestures, his compliments, his faultless behavior with her children—to get all five of them on his side? Had he strung them along to achieve his purposes?

"He's coming back, Peter," she said, ignoring her punctured ego. "He's not going to give up until he gets what he wants."

"What he wants is to destroy me!" His voice thundered in the quiet elegance of the room, making Martha jump.

"You don't know that!" Martha exclaimed, unable to remain silent any longer. "Bryce is not a vindictive man—"

"How do you know? How do you know what kind of man he is?"

Martha sank back in her chair. "No, you're right," she agreed sadly. "Thanks to you, I haven't seen him since he was a boy. I *don't* know what kind of man he's become."

"Well, *I* do! Remember when I called him, when I tried to talk to him? Remember what he told me?" Peter was enraged, his face white, his breathing ragged.

"Yes." Martha's answer whispered in the air. She laid her hand on her husband's arm. "I remember. But that was six years ago—*six years*. How long does it have to go on? Bryce is no more stubborn, no more difficult than you. Why can't you forgive him for being a Cameron and meet with him? See what he wants?"

He shrugged off her hand and surged to his feet. "He can rot in hell for all I care!" he shouted. "Do you understand me? In hell!"

The room was eerily, heavily silent following his departure. Martha's shoulders sagged; Leah was uncomfortably still. At last she spoke. "He's going to come back, Martha." She was more sure of that than anything else in her life. "What do you want me to do?"

Her mother-in-law shook her head. "I don't know." Bowing her head, she gathered herself, then looked up. Now, she seemed stronger, younger, more vital. "Do what you feel is right, Leah."

"Even if that means welcoming him to the inn again?" She knew that was a good possibility, in spite of Peter's reaction. "He makes Peter so angry."

"It's not Bryce," Martha said. "Peter is angry with himself, I think, more than anyone else. What he said—about not being worthwhile just because you're family—I think he was talking about himself. I don't think he feels he deserves to be on good terms with Frank again."

Leah wanted to ask what had happened so many years ago between the two men, but she kept the question to herself. As much as she wanted to know, the details would have to come from Peter himself. She wouldn't pump her mother-in-law for information.

"Well, dear, I guess I'll go home." Martha laid her hand on Leah's shoulder.

"Let me get my coat and I'll walk with you." Leah got her jacket and a knitted scarf and gloves from the closet, then stopped in her room long enough to change her moccasins for knee-high waterproof boots.

"We really did have a lovely time in Atlanta," Martha remarked as they strolled across the back lawn.

"I'm sorry this had to spoil the weekend for you."

"Did it spoil *your* weekend, Leah?"

Giving the older woman a sidelong glance, Leah saw the smile touching her face. What would Martha like to hear? she wondered. That Bryce had been an unwelcome burden? That the family had liked him? That Leah had been attracted to him? "No. For the most part he was pleasant company."

"For the most part?"

"He seemed a little bitter, especially about the family. He said... that the Camerons look out for themselves and everybody else can go to hell." She repeated the sentiment hesitantly, not wanting to upset Martha. The other woman's laugh surprised her.

"Well said, Bryce." Then she tempered her words. "In a sense he's right. The family as he knew it *was* selfish. Peter wanted what was best for himself, Terence and me, and Frank wanted the same for himself and Bryce.''

"That's called love, Martha, not selfishness.''

"A wrong committed in the name of love is still wrong.''
Martha climbed the steps to the porch of the guest house, then turned back to Leah. "Are you going to take a walk?''

"Yes.''

"Be careful.'' She sighed softly. "I can't tell you what to do about Bryce, Leah. Trust your own judgment. Do what you think you should.''

As far as advice went, Leah thought as she wandered into the quiet woods, Martha's was worthless. She wanted her mother-in-law to tell her what to do, what to say, what to feel. She didn't want to trust herself; when it came to men, she wasn't a very good judge of character. She only had to look at the mistake she'd made with Terence to know that.

If only Bryce hadn't touched her, hadn't smiled at her— Lord, if only he hadn't kissed her. When was the last time she had received such tenderness from anyone, let alone a man? When he'd laid his fingers against her hair, he had been so gentle that she had barely felt it. When he had kissed her...

Her cheeks burned with the memory. If a mere kiss could have such an effect on her, she was even more naive and innocent than Peter suspected. But Terence had never shown her gentleness—not before their marriage, and certainly not after. She had always believed that someday he would change, but she had finally accepted that he wasn't a gentle man.

Since his death, she had kept herself neatly divided into compartments. There was the mother, the daughter-in-law, the friend, the innkeeper—and, buried down deep, there was the woman. No one had been allowed to touch that part of her; no one was allowed to make her feel the things a woman felt—the wants, the needs, the desires.

Until now. Bryce Cameron made her wonder. How would it feel to be loved by a man? To be held and touched so gently, to be liked as well as loved, respected as well as desired? How would it feel to be loved by Bryce?

Some tiny bit of romance that had survived Terence was curious, but clearheaded common sense prevailed. She didn't need a man. She didn't need Bryce. She had her children and her in-laws. She loved them, and they loved her. It was enough. She would make it enough.

Chapter 3

Bryce stood next to his father's bed. The old man was asleep and had been since he'd arrived more than half an hour ago. On the opposite side of the bed stood Dr. Upton, one of the best cardiologists in the state. She definitely had to be one of the prettiest, too, Bryce thought with quiet detachment.

"The symptoms of transient ischemic attacks vary a great deal," she was saying. "As do the effects. But the neurologist was with him earlier, and it's his opinion that at this time there's been no permanent damage."

Edging forward, Bryce picked up his father's hand. It was bony, covered with papery-thin skin. "Why?" he asked. "Why him?"

"As I told you, they're associated with both hardening of the arteries and hypertension, and they're more common in men. Your father was at high risk."

"His heart attack had nothing to do with it?"

"No. T.I.A.'s are a disease of the brain, not the heart."

"You said these usually mean the patient's going to have a stroke."

"Well... generally. But that doesn't mean he *will* have one. It just means that he's a strong candidate." Dr. Upton looked at her patient for a moment, then turned her attention to Bryce. "Why don't you go home and get some rest? Chances are good that he'll sleep through the night."

Chances were also good that he could have another attack, or a stroke. Chances were looking really good that he could die. Bryce shook his head. "I'll leave in a little while."

She shrugged. "All right. But don't wear yourself out."

When she left, the room was still. All the lights but the one above the bed were off, casting dark shadows in the corners. Bryce sat down in one of those corners and watched his father, simply watched him.

After Katherine's death, Bryce had been raised by his grandmother. When she died, too, Frank had completed the job, giving his son every bit of love he possessed. Now it was time for Bryce to give it back. Whether his father had a few more weeks, a few more months, or—please, God—a few more years, Bryce was going to see that he was happy. He was going to take Frank back to Angel's Peak. He was going to do whatever it took—*anything*—to see his father living once again in the Cameron family home, in the house that was rightfully his. No one could stop him this time— not Peter, not Martha and the kids, not even Leah.

The memory of Leah, so soft and sweet when he'd kissed her, made him smile, but only briefly. In the six hours since he'd left her and Angel's Peak behind, he had been trying to convince himself that an involvement with Leah Cameron was the last thing he wanted.

He couldn't deny that she was pretty—outright lying was out of the question—but there were thousands of prettier women right here in Philadelphia, starting with Dr. Upton. He wouldn't deny, either, that she had touched him in ways no woman but Kay ever had. But look where it had gotten him with her: he'd had fourteen years of a marriage that had ended in pain and heartache.

There could be no future with Leah for him. As much as he liked children, he wanted his own, not another man's. Her home, her life, her friends, all were in Angel's Peak; his were in Philadelphia. He knew instinctively that she wasn't the type of woman to indulge in meaningless affairs; any relationship she established with a man would be a serious one. There was no way she would settle for the only thing he could give—the only thing he was *willing* to give: occasional weekends, and nothing more.

He had less than a week to make himself believe all his well-meaning excuses. Friday, if Frank was all right, Bryce was going back to Angel's Peak. He would see Leah again, and this time he would see Peter. This time he would fulfill the only request his father had ever made of him.

Leah's steps slowed when she heard a childish giggle from behind the closed door of the telephone room under the front stairs. There were only four guests at the inn this week, and all of them were out for the day. That giggle had to come from Matthew, home with a cold. Just who would he be talking to on the phone when all his friends were in school?

She knocked at the door and waited until he invited her inside. He was curled up in an armchair, the phone braced between his ear and shoulder, looking as if he was thoroughly enjoying himself. Leah took a seat in the other armchair and waited until he said, "Just a minute. My mom's here."

"Who is that?"

Matthew didn't think to cover the receiver. "My cousin."

She stared at him, bemused. So Bryce *had* called. Although she hadn't mentioned the possibility to Matthew, she was both surprised and grateful. It was nice to know that he'd kept his word. Honorable men weren't that easy to find.

Matthew listened for a moment, then held out the phone. "He wants to talk to you."

To say, "I told you so"? Leah wondered. She accepted the receiver and raised it to her face. It smelled of lemons, like Matthew's cough drops. "Go ask Miss Colleen to give you some orange juice, sweetheart," she suggested. When he was gone, she said a cautious hello.

"You were wrong about me, weren't you?" Without giving her a chance to reply, Bryce continued. "I told you I would call him. This is the first chance I've had."

"What do you want? Congratulations? An apology?" She sounded testy. "One phone call is easy. What if he expects more?"

The good humor left over from his conversation with Matthew fled, leaving annoyance in its wake. "You are damn hard to please, lady."

"I'm not asking you to please me. I'm asking you to leave my son alone, not to let him expect more than you're going to give. When do you get bored? When does someone else catch your interest? When will you call him again? When will he ever see you again? There's a lot of responsibility to the kind of relationship you're starting here—"

"Don't preach to me about responsibility or relationships," he interrupted sharply. "I don't get bored with people, Leah, and I'm perfectly capable of showing interest in more than one person at a time. I don't know when I'll call him again, but as for seeing him . . . I'll be there Friday."

She was silent for a long time. What was she thinking? he wondered. Would she welcome him . . . or throw him out the door?

She had known that this time was coming. Since her talk with Martha Sunday evening, she had known that Bryce would return and that she would have to decide how to deal with him. In the three days since then she had done a lot of thinking about him, but she hadn't yet reached a decision.

"Leah?"

Loyalty pulled her in different directions—loyalty to the family, and loyalty to Peter. Family was so important to her, and she hated to see Peter pretend his brother and nephew didn't exist. She wished she could make him appreciate that side of his family, too—could make him at least talk to them. For that reason, she wanted to tell Bryce that he was welcome.

But Peter was also very important to her. It was only his influence that had persuaded Terence to accept his responsibility when she was seventeen, alone and pregnant. Had it not been for Peter and Martha, her twelve-year marriage would have been as bleak and cold as the home where she'd grown up. If he didn't want to see his nephew, what right did she have to interfere?

"Leah, I'm not trying to cause trouble." Unless trouble was what it took to gain Peter's cooperation. "I just want to see my uncle. I want to settle some things. No one's going to get hurt, believe me."

"You don't know how angry he was when he found out that you'd been here."

His chuckle was soft and intimate. "I can imagine. He and Dad were always too much alike for their own good. They're both hotheaded and more stubborn than mules. Leah..."

Why did her name sound so soft and sensuous coming from him? It was only two little syllables that took about a second to say, yet it brought to mind images and emotions that she knew were better left forgotten.

Trust your own judgment. Do what you think you should. Martha's admonition echoed in her mind, and it prompted her to answer his unasked question. "All right."

Now it was Bryce's turn to sit in silence. What was she agreeing to? Just a visit? Or a return to the house? "Then . . . you don't mind if I come."

"No." She closed her eyes and hoped she wasn't making a grave mistake. "You're welcome to stay here, if you'd like."

He could think of nothing he would like better. "Thank you. Then I'll see you Friday."

"Have you made your reservations yet?"

He hesitated. Admitting that he had seemed rather arrogant, but he couldn't lie to her. "Yes, I have. I'll get into Asheville about five."

"I have to pick up some guests at the airport at five-thirty. If you don't mind waiting, you can ride back with us...unless you prefer to rent a car." She squeezed her eyes shut. She was digging herself in deeper and couldn't seem to stop. Why had she offered him a room and a ride? Why couldn't she let him take care of his business with Peter himself, with no help from her?

Because he was family. Not hers—she couldn't think of him as one of her relatives; that persistent romantic in her refused—but her children's, and Peter's.

"I'd like that," he was saying. "I'll be waiting. Could I speak to Matthew again?" Quickly he qualified that. "Just to say goodbye, okay?"

She sighed softly. "Okay. Hold on."

Matthew was waiting outside the door, his eyes bright and shining. This phone call from Bryce had been better than all the cold medicine in the world, Leah reflected as she left her son alone. She just hoped that Bryce knew what he was doing.

Bryce didn't expect Leah to meet him at the airport; when it was time for her guests to arrive, he supposed, she would show up. Until then he could pass the time thinking. Planning. Scheming. In spite of the transient ischemic attacks, Dr. Upton had pronounced Frank ready to leave the hospital in a few days, and this was where Bryce would bring him. To North Carolina. Home. He just had to make Peter see it his way.

Even without expecting Leah, he picked her out of the crowd the moment he saw her. He stood motionless, quiet, watching her approach. In the time it took her to reach him, he'd made a complete inspection—and found everything to his liking. She was wearing a hip-length silver coat with a rose-colored scarf wrapped around her neck. The sweater underneath the open coat was blue, and her jeans, tucked into a pair of dark brown boots, were relatively new and unfaded. Her hair was a bit tamer than it had been last week, the curls more orderly. The memory of how silky they had been against his fingers made him want to touch them again. The memory of her softness, her scent, her warmth, made him want to do a lot of other things—things he couldn't allow himself to think about. Not here.

Leah tried to ignore the increased tempo of her heart. It was just because she had hurried inside, out of the bitter cold, she insisted. Nothing else.

"Hi."

She echoed his soft greeting, then said, "The others will be here in about half an hour. Would you like to get some coffee while we wait?"

Bryce nodded. He would like anything that meant time alone with her, time to look at her, to talk and to have her undivided attention.

She shrugged out of her coat, then led the way to the coffee shop, taking a seat at the first empty table she came to. She ordered two cups of coffee from the waitress, then folded her hands together on the tabletop, suddenly tongue-tied. What could she say to this man, this stranger who had entered her life such a short time ago and taken such a strong hold that she couldn't wrench herself away? She had decided only five days ago, on a snowy, late-night walk, that she didn't want or need a man in her life, not Bryce Cameron or anyone else. She wasn't going to be charmed by him, she had thought, or kissed by him, or touched—physically or spiritually—by him. And now here she was, sitting across from him, her good intentions shot to hell. She was unable to remember *why* she didn't want a man; all she could think of was why she wanted *this* man, the kiss he'd given her, the longing he had awakened in her.

Bryce broke the silence after the waitress poured their coffee. "Aren't you glad to see me?" he asked, but Leah didn't answer. She was too well-bred to tell the truth and too polite to lie, he thought. "You know, you *did* tell me that I would be welcome," he good-naturedly reminded her.

She inclined her head. "Yes, to stay at the inn."

But not to get too close to the innkeeper. He didn't mind her distance. He would deal with that later. "How is Matthew's cold?"

"Fine."

"And how are you?"

She smiled faintly. "I'm fine, too."

If it had been left up to her, that would have been the extent of their conversation, but Bryce wasn't inclined to sit in silence. That made it too easy to look at her, to appreciate her loveliness, to think about her softness, to hunger for her tenderness. "Do you always play chauffeur to your guests?"

"No, only to the special ones." She flushed slightly as she realized what her reply implied—that Bryce was special.

It made him smile. She didn't give easily . . . but when she did, she would give everything. Everything that he'd told himself he didn't want and couldn't have.

"Providing transportation isn't a regular service of the inn," she went on awkwardly. "But these three people were our very first guests, and they've come back ever since on a regular basis, every few months. They deserve a little special treatment."

He let the ensuing silence lengthen while they drank their coffee. Finally, twining his fingers together around the warm cup, he raised his eyes to hers. "I'll give you two topics of conversation to choose from: Matthew, or Peter. Which would you like to discuss?"

Talk of Peter might very well lead to an argument, which she didn't want. But talk of Matthew would *definitely* lead in that direction. She chose her father-in-law.

"Does he know that I'm here?"

She shook her head. She still hadn't resolved her guilt over keeping Bryce's visit secret from Peter, but, as Martha had told her, she had to do what *she* thought was right.

"Why didn't you tell him?"

She traced a neatly rounded fingernail over the pattern in the tabletop. "He was very angry when he found out that you were here last weekend. I thought it would be best not to tell him that I had invited you back."

He laid his hand over hers, stilling its motion. "Wait a minute. *You* didn't invite me—I invited myself. Keep that straight, all right?" After a pause he asked, "What did he say?"

His hand was big and warm, lightly clasping hers. Leah concentrated on that warmth, that slight connection, so she wouldn't have to look at him. "He said you can rot in hell for all he cares."

Bryce absently rubbed his thumb over the back of her hand. The skin there was soft, fragile—like the woman. With an effort he forced his mind back to the conversation. So Peter wanted him to rot in hell. Was that the reason for the distance Leah had placed between them? Had Peter told her about his past attempts to be reconciled with Frank, when Bryce had stood in the way, adamantly refusing to allow brother to speak to brother? If he had, Leah, so loving and loyal to her family, probably would have condemned him and his actions to hell herself.

But she had agreed to let him return. She had offered to pick him up at the airport, and she was letting him touch her. He thought it more likely that his uncle had simply given Leah his opinion of Bryce's character, rather than any specific details about the past; otherwise she wouldn't be here with him.

"What else did he say?" His eyes were grim, his mouth a thin, taut line.

"That you're a selfish, deceitful, lying son of a bitch." And that you used my children and me. That you knew I was naive enough to fall for whatever line you wanted to feed me. But she couldn't say the last aloud. If it wasn't true, his actions would bear it out. If it was, she would be ashamed to see it in his eyes.

"Do you believe it?"

She allowed herself to look at him. The expression in his eyes was somber, almost bleak, as if her answer truly mattered to him. She searched her mind for the answer but found it in her heart. "No."

Maybe she was being foolish. She had warned herself only last weekend that she wasn't a very good judge of character—especially male character. But her reply was honest. She didn't want to believe that Bryce was the kind of man who could callously use her and the kids, especially Matthew, for his own purposes. She didn't want to believe that she could be attracted to a man like that.

He smiled then, that full, bright, warm smile that made her forget her troubles. Raising her hand to his lips, he pressed a soft kiss on it. "Thank you." Then he quickly released her hand before he could think about keeping it forever and stood up. "It's almost five-thirty," he said in an almost-normal voice as he pulled some money from his pocket to pay for the coffee. "We'd better meet your guests."

As soon as she found her passengers, Leah introduced them to Bryce, then suggested that they get their luggage so they wouldn't miss Colleen's dinner.

The guests, a husband and wife and their teenage son from Charleston, insisted that Bryce sit in the front seat of the station wagon with Leah. Familiar with every member of the Cameron family, they questioned Bryce with friendly curiosity most of the way to Angel's Peak, making private conversation impossible. Very much aware of him at her side, Leah was grateful for the respite. Once at the inn, though, she was left alone with him again, while Vicky checked in the guests.

"You'll have the same room," she said as she walked along the broad hallway, Bryce at her side. "Dinner will be served in about five minutes, so don't be late."

He went into the room, setting his suitcase down next to the bed. One lamp was already on, the covers had been turned down, and a dish of spicy-scented potpourri was sitting on the marble table. The room was almost as welcoming as the woman behind him.

Bryce returned to the doorway and leaned against the frame. Leah had continued past his room to the sole door on the opposite side of the hall. "Is that your room?" He hadn't asked last weekend—not because he hadn't wanted to know, but precisely because he had. Now he couldn't stop the question.

She looked over her shoulder. "Yes."

He caught a glimpse of the bed right inside the door. She would be sleeping less than twenty feet from him. He liked that idea. "Who else has rooms around here?"

Leah felt the color warming her cheeks. "The children's rooms are upstairs."

His smile became a grin. "So it's just you and me on this floor."

She nodded.

Interesting. He crossed his arms over his chest and watched her enter the room and close the door. He remained there for a moment, alone in the hall. If he could keep his mind on business, this trip could end quickly, and he could return to Philadelphia, to his father. But as he turned back into his room, he caught a faint whiff of Leah's fragrance, and he knew he didn't want any of those things— didn't want to keep his mind on business, didn't want to end the trip quickly or to return to Philadelphia. He wanted to stay here a while in Gran's old room, and he wanted to watch Leah—to look at her, listen to her, smell her scent. He wanted to see her smile, maybe even hear her laugh. He wanted to touch her, to hold her and kiss her.

He wanted to make her his.

Damn it, he wanted too much. He'd always been satisfied with what he had; even as a child, he had never fallen into the trap of wishing for things he couldn't have. And Leah fitted both categories: she was too much, and he couldn't have her. He told himself that sternly—how many times had he repeated the warning in the last week?—but he was beginning to resign himself to the fact that he was still going to want. He was still going to wish.

Leah was on her way to the dining room a few minutes after the chimes sounded when Douglas stopped her in the hallway. "How do I look?" he asked, running his fingers through his hair.

She took a step back to study him. He wore a crewneck sweater in a creamy beige with neatly pressed jeans. She looked wistfully at him for a long moment. He was almost eighteen—all grown-up. For so many years he had been her little boy, but now she could see the man in him. When had he gotten so big, so old?

"Mom?"

She smiled almost sadly. "You look fine, honey. Where are you going?"

"Tonight's the dance at school. I told you about it, remember?"

Her thoughts had been so full of Bryce that she had forgotten. Now she nodded ruefully. "Yes, I remember. Are you taking Tiffany?"

Blushing faintly, he nodded, and Leah smiled. Tiffany Wells was the dream girl in this year's senior class—very pretty, head cheerleader, homecoming queen, class president, talented actress, honor student, and a nice girl, as well. All the girls were jealous, and all the boys were in love with her. *And my son's dating her,* Leah thought with vicarious satisfaction. How things had changed from her own high school days in Angel's Peak, when no one had even known that she existed.

"You won't wait up, will you?"

She raised her hands palm outward. "If I'm up, it won't be because of you, I promise." More likely because the guest across the hall from her wouldn't leave her thoughts long enough for something as unimportant as sleep. Rising onto her toes, she kissed his cheek. "Be careful, please."

He returned the kiss quickly, then shrugged into his coat. "See you tomorrow."

When the door closed behind him, she continued her trip to the dining room. As usual on Friday nights, it was full.

"Does Douglas have a date?"

She looked over her shoulder to see Bryce standing there. "Yes," she murmured in answer.

"Doesn't that worry you? How old is he—seventeen?"

Her eyes narrowed and chilled by ten degrees. He knew—somehow he knew the circumstances of Douglas's birth. And those of her marriage? Had he found out from his father's sources, or his own? "Douglas is a good kid, and his girlfriend is very nice," she replied stiffly.

Belatedly he remembered the dates he'd found in the family Bible last weekend—dates that had shown that Leah, seventeen at the time of her marriage, had given birth to Douglas less than three months later. He had spoken carelessly, but he hadn't meant to offend or criticize her. Lifting his hand to rest it lightly on her shoulder against the silkiness of her hair, he said softly, "Even nice girls sometimes get trapped."

Trapped. Leah moved away from his touch, suddenly, sharply. How many times had she heard that word from Terence—that she had trapped him in a marriage he didn't want, with a woman he couldn't love and children he didn't need?

"We'd better sit down," she said stiffly, gesturing to the corner table where the younger three children sat. "They're waiting."

"Douglas has a date tonight," Megan said as soon as her mother sat down. "With Tiffany Wells."

"I know, hon, I just saw him." Leah spread the dark peach linen napkin over her lap, then glanced at Bryce as he took the seat next to her.

Laurel and Megan gave him the warm greeting reserved for family members, while Matthew left his seat, solemnly shook Bryce's hand, then suddenly reached up for a hug. The scene tugged at Leah's heart. Earlier she had refused Bryce the opportunity to discuss his friendship with Matthew, hoping to avoid the confrontation, but now she knew that she couldn't put it off much longer. Matthew was a friendly boy, but he rarely offered physical contact to anyone outside the family; now here he was, giving Bryce his heart. She had to assure herself that the man knew what to do with it.

"Where are Peter and Martha?" Bryce asked. "I assumed they had their meals here, with you."

"Grandma and Grandpa went to eat in town," Laurel informed him. "There's a new restaurant, and Grandma asked Grandpa to take her there."

"A French restaurant," Megan added with a scowl. "I bet their food isn't as good as Miss Colleen's."

"No, honey, I'm sure it isn't." Leah smiled at her younger daughter, then turned her head to include the other two. The warmth stopped just short of Bryce. Resentment of the three children flared to life inside him, then died just as quickly. She would smile at him—*for* him—soon. He promised himself that.

When dinner was over, Bryce went with Matthew to the boy's second-floor room, and Laurel and Megan went to the sitting room to watch television. After making sure that everything was in order for the night, Leah followed a routine she had started many years ago: she gathered her coat, scarf and gloves from the closet and went outside for a quiet, moonlight walk.

The idea of walking for pleasure was one Terence had never quite grasped. Walking was something you did when you had no other choice. So Leah's nightly walk had been a solitary one, even then. At times it was the only peaceful hour she found.

The woods surrounding the inn and the guest houses were quiet, the snow knee-deep in places. She made her own trail to the cemetery, still and peaceful in the glow of the moon. The tombstones were odd-shaped humps of stone covered with snow. Only two inscriptions were visible, those that Bryce had cleared last weekend, marking the graves of Katherine and Anna Cameron.

"You actually hang around graveyards in the middle of the night?"

She hid both the brief spark of fear and the following stronger spark of pleasure that his voice had brought. By the time she turned to face him, her face was calmly, serenely blank. "It's not even eight-thirty."

Bryce checked his wristwatch in the bright moonlight. "It's eight forty-nine. Why are you here?"

"Why did you follow me?"

"To see where you were going."

"Why?"

He answered simply, honestly. "I wanted to be with you." It was that easy to explain. One moment he'd been in Matthew's room discussing dinosaurs and had seen Leah through the window; the next, after changing into the boots he'd brought with him, he'd been following her tracks in the snow. "Do you often come out here alone at night?"

She tilted her head to one side, and the end of her scarf swung free. Bryce resisted the urge to tuck it back into place. "There's nothing to be afraid of in a cemetery. Dead people can't hurt you. It's the ones who are still alive who do that."

Amen to that, he silently whispered. He moved closer to her, until only two feet of snow separated them.

His next question came out of the blue, softly, gently, and totally unexpected by either of them, but once it was asked, he realized that he wanted to know. He needed to know. "Did Terence hurt you?"

Leah stared at him for a long time, sensations racing through her—shock, surprise, fear, pain. She rewound her scarf, giving him a gleaming glimpse of her hair before the dusky rose fabric covered it again. "I'm going back to the house."

He laid his hand over her wrist. "Wait." He wanted an answer. He wanted to hear her say no, her husband hadn't hurt her. He wanted to hear that she had loved Terence, and that he had loved her. He wanted to hear that their marriage had been long and happy, because he had to believe that, sometime in her life, Leah had been happy.

Her eyes, as cool as his were warm, dropped to his hand. He wore gloves, and the thickness of her coat sleeve and her own glove protected her from his touch, but she felt it anyway. She wished that he would remove his glove and her scarf and touch her hair. She wished that he would touch *her*, in those ways that made her feel.

Dangerous wishes. Dangerous man. Pulling her wrist free, she took a step back, then another, until she'd reached one of several small paths that cut across the cemetery. "I'm going back to the house," she repeated numbly.

Bryce walked alongside her, not bothering to talk. He knew she wouldn't answer him, and he didn't like the sound of his own voice enough to break the night's stillness.

When they reached the house, Leah started up the back steps. Bryce took her arm once more. The tension that held her captive was strong enough for him to feel it through her sleeve. He released her and linked his hands together behind his back. "You don't have to run away from me, Leah."

"I'm not running away."

"Are you afraid of all men . . . or just me?"

She stood two steps above him, looking evenly into his eyes. "Are you so sure of yourself with all women . . . or just me?"

He leaned back against the railing and stared up at the sky. What would she think if he told her that the confident air was just that—an air? What would she think if he told her about Kay and the words she had used to describe him? Selfish. Boring. Unsatisfying.

Sometimes he forgot Kay's insults, like when he'd kissed Leah at the desk last Sunday. Other times he didn't care. Tonight he did. Would Leah find him an unsatisfying lover? Would he ever have a chance to find out?

He climbed one step, bent his head, brushed a kiss across her lips and murmured, "Good night, Leah."

After the door closed behind him, she pulled one glove off and touched her fingers to her mouth. Just a kiss—that was all it had been. A brief, insignificant little kiss. It wasn't enough to satisfy, yet it was more than she could handle.

"Please," she whispered, her fingers still covering her lips. "Let him go home soon...before it's too late."

With a shiver she went inside the house to her office, hanging her coat on the back of the chair. She heard the laughter from the sitting room down the hall before she closed the door, but wasn't tempted to join in. The family and the staff took turns playing host to the guests. Usually Leah enjoyed their company, but tonight she was grateful that it was someone else's turn—anyone else but herself. Tonight she preferred working alone to gaiety and cheer.

She turned her attention to the schedule for the holiday season's parties. The first would be next Saturday, the weekend before Thanksgiving; she and Martha had completed the arrangements for it several weeks earlier. It would be followed by nine more celebrations, including holidays and birthdays, in the next seven weeks. She would be exhausted by the end of the year, but pleasantly, comfortably so.

When the knock came at the door, she knew without asking that it was Laurel; only her older daughter could manage to sound so timid. "Come in."

"We're ready for bed, Mom," Laurel said, tugging her robe around her. "Do you want to read to Matthew, or should I?"

Leah pushed her papers into a file and rose from the desk. "Why don't you read to Matthew *and* me?"

"Okay." Laurel slipped her arm around her mother's waist as they left the office. "Grandma says you work too much."

She chuckled softly. "Someone's got to do it, honey."

"When I'm a little older, I can help with your paperwork. That'll be more fun than doing dishes or making beds." She made a face as she spoke to indicate her dislike of housework.

"When you're a little older, honey, you'll have too many other things on your mind to worry about paperwork."

"You mean like boys." Laurel gave a shake of her head, sending her long brown hair swinging. "Not me. I'm not ever going to like any boys."

"She's only saying that 'cause Travis is going steady with Darla Wells." Megan was sitting on the back stairs, her feet hidden in fuzzy pink slippers with huge rabbit ears flopping to each side. When they passed, she jumped to her feet and followed.

Laurel's only response to her younger sister's teasing was to stick out her tongue. When they reached the private living room, Matthew was waiting on the sofa. He handed his book to Laurel, then climbed into Leah's lap to hear the story.

It was a cozy little family scene, Bryce thought from his position in the dark kitchen, with Laurel in the center, Megan on one side, and Leah and Matthew on the other. All that was missing was a father.

How many times, early in his marriage, had he envisioned just such a scene—Kay and himself and their children? It had taken four years of Kay's unyielding insistence that she didn't want children to chase such thoughts from his mind. He had loved his wife and had accepted her decision. Now he was forty-one, almost too old to have children, and Kay was gone. If he had known, back when she was refusing to have a baby, that eventually their love would die and their marriage end, maybe he would have gotten a divorce then and found a woman who wanted kids—a woman like Leah.

But Leah had already been taken.

He cut off that train of thought and stepped farther back into the shadows. He should have made his presence known when Matthew skipped into the room a moment ago. Now he couldn't leave without being seen by the family in the living room. He felt ridiculously guilty, as if he were spying on them—and wasn't he?

Laurel read in a low, quiet voice that sounded so much like her mother's. Lamps at each end of the sofa cast bright circles of light over its occupants, but the rest of the room was deep in shadow. It was warm, snug and peaceful.

When the story was over, each of the children gave Leah a hug and a kiss, then trooped down the hall. The second floor of their wing could be reached only by the back stairs near the kitchen. Bryce listened until the scuffling sounds of their feet were gone, then waited for Leah to leave the living room so he could go to his own room.

She reached across to turn off one lamp, then stood up. But instead of leaving, she turned toward the kitchen. When she flipped on the light switch and saw Bryce standing there, she stopped short, folded her arms across her chest and waited.

His expression was a cross between embarrassment and guilt. "Only a mother could look so disapproving."

She moved past him to take a glass from the cabinet. After filling it from a pitcher of water in the refrigerator, she gestured toward his glass. He held it out for a refill and murmured his thanks.

"Do you do that every night?"

"Usually." She took a long, cold drink.

"That's nice."

"Yes," she agreed quietly. "It *is* nice. It's one of the few private times we have as a family."

She was too polite to say it more bluntly, but he received her message, anyway: he had intruded on their privacy. He changed positions uncomfortably. "I didn't mean to eavesdrop. You were all there before I had a chance to leave."

"You could have passed through at any time."

"Correct me if I'm wrong, but I got the impression after our walk that you'd really rather not see any more of me tonight."

It wasn't "our" walk, she silently protested—it was *hers*. She didn't want to think in terms of "our" with Bryce. She didn't want to share anything with him. It was too pleasant, too warm, too lovely a thought, and it would be too painful. After pouring the remaining water into the sink, she set her glass on the counter and turned to leave. At the bar that separated the kitchen and dining room, she looked back. "You're right," she said quietly. "I'd rather not see you again." She walked away.

Bryce set his glass next to hers. If she had said the words as an insult, he wouldn't have minded. But she hadn't spoken in anger; she had simply told the truth: she would be happier if she never had to see him again.

He was amazed at how much the truth could hurt.

Leah awoke early Saturday morning. For a few minutes she took the luxury of doing nothing, simply lying in bed and listening to the stillness. It was barely six-thirty; the younger children would sleep until at least eight, and Douglas, who had sneaked up the stairs shortly before one-thirty, would probably sleep even later. She doubted that many of the guests were up yet, and those who were, were considerate enough to be quiet.

With a sigh, she rolled from the bed, her feet making contact first with a braided, heart-shaped rug, then the cold wooden planking. Tugging on her robe, she hurried down the hall to the bathroom, closing the door quietly behind her. She adjusted the water temperature in the shower, tugged a brush through her hair, then shed the robe and stepped into the tub, drawing the plastic curtain shut.

Minutes later she stepped out again, drying herself quickly with a pale green bath sheet that reached to her knees. She towel-dried her hair while the steam cleared from the mirror. For a moment she studied her reflection.

Last weekend Bryce had called her lovely. Now she looked at herself and saw what he had seen and wondered again at his lie. She wasn't lovely, wasn't pretty, not even attractive. Her hair lay in wet curls more suitable to Laurel or Megan than to an almost thirty-six-year-old woman and was touched at the temples with a few silvery-gray strands. Her nose was crooked, her mouth was too thin, and her eyes were such an odd shade of blue.

Turning on the hair dryer, she began running her fingers through her hair while the warm air moved over it. Every woman deserved one man who thought she was beautiful, she mused. For a time she had thought Terence was that one man for her. It hadn't taken long for him to shatter her illusions. He hadn't thought she was beautiful. In the last years of their marriage, except for his occasional visits to her bed, he hadn't thought of her at all.

Working quickly and efficiently, she used the blow dryer to relax her curls, then changed them into soft waves with a curling iron. She spritzed the waves with hair spray, letting that dry while she dusted her body with her favorite powder, sprayed her wrists and throat with perfume and switched the towel for her robe.

After styling her hair so that it curled gently away from her face, she tidied the bathroom and returned to her room to dress. The steel-gray crewneck sweater that she tugged over her head barely disturbed her hair; she brushed it back into place with her fingers. She added her favorite pair of snug-fitting, button-fly jeans and a pair of white leather high-top tennis shoes, then left the room.

* * *

She looked more like a kid than a mother and business-woman, Bryce thought, waiting for her in the hallway. It was only when he reached those ice-blue eyes that he could see her age. There was something somber in their depths that came from years of learning and growing. Some of her lessons, he realized, hadn't been easy.

He pushed himself away from the wall. Before he'd taken two steps toward her, he could smell her fragrance—faint, sweet, enticing, sexy—and it tied his stomach in knots. It was too early in the morning to be feeling this way, he protested silently. After the encounter in the kitchen last night, he hadn't slept well; then he had awakened to the sound of the shower next door and known that it was Leah. Now he had to look at her, to smell her sweetness, to hear her voice. Did she know she was causing him this torment? He didn't think so—not yet, at least. He was going to have to tell her, though, because they were going to have to do something about it—together. And soon.

Leah closed her bedroom door, then waited for Bryce to speak. He looked so comfortable, so at ease with himself and his world, as if nothing ever bothered him. Seeing her had no effect whatsoever on him, while seeing *him* sent her whole system haywire. He was so handsome in khaki slacks and a navy-blue sweater that she couldn't even think of the proper words to say in greeting.

"I want to see Peter this morning."

She tried to ignore the faint disappointment that suddenly curled in her stomach. Hadn't she expected as much? Peter was his reason for being here—certainly not her.

"I'll call him and see if—"

He interrupted. "I just want to go over there, to his house. Let me talk to him." He realized that he was asking for her permission, even though he didn't need it. Since he knew she wouldn't give him her approval, he at least wanted her permission.

She nodded once. "All right. They live in the guest house across the driveway."

He nodded, too. He was familiar with the house; his aunt and uncle had lived there long ago, too, when his grandmother had lived in the main house. Stepping forward, he laid his hand on her shoulder. "Leah..." The tip of his finger slid underneath the knit ribbing and rubbed slowly back and forth. Her skin was soft, powdery and warm. Was she that soft all over? he wondered, adding another finger and letting them glide farther until the sweater covered them to the joint.

"Don't do that." She sounded husky but very certain.

He drew back his hand. "Where will you be when I finish with Peter?"

"Around the house."

Once again he nodded; then he turned and walked away. Wearing a heavy leather jacket, he left by the back door.

It was cold outside. Every breath he took seemed to freeze a little more of his insides. It had to be that, he insisted to himself. It couldn't be nervousness at finally seeing his uncle again.

The two guest cottages stood behind the main house, separated by the driveway. He passed the one he and his father had shared and carefully climbed the snow- and ice-covered steps to the second one.

Martha answered his knock with a warm smile that slowly faded when she recognized him. Bryce was preparing himself for a less than welcoming greeting when she took a step forward, wrapped her arms around him and hugged him close. "Welcome home, Bryce," she whispered.

Chapter 4

Martha led him through the living room to the eat-in kitchen, where Peter was seated at the table, the remains of his breakfast in front of him. He was pouring cream into his coffee when he saw his nephew, and the thick white liquid dribbled onto the lace tablecloth. Forcefully setting down the pitcher, he stood up and faced Bryce. "What the hell are you doing here?"

Pretending that he hadn't given the reason at least a half dozen times already, Bryce patiently repeated it. "I need to talk to you."

"If it's about your father, I don't want to hear it."

"You know it's about my father, and you *are* going to hear it." He paused for a moment while he looked at his uncle. Tall, thin, gray-haired, he was proof that the family resemblance never faded away; Peter looked as much like Frank now as he had thirty years ago—just a little bit younger and a whole lot healthier.

Realizing that his uncle was staring back at him, and that Martha was staring, too, Bryce said what he'd come to say, quietly, forcefully. "I'm bringing my father back to Angel's Peak. He's coming home."

Peter was angry, and as stubborn as an old mule. "I won't have him here! Not in this house!" he declared once Bryce's meaning sank in.

"No," the younger man mildly agreed. "In that house." He gestured through the bay window to the inn. "He's going to stay at the inn. He's going to die in the house he was born in." He paused. "In the house that should have been his."

Martha was in the process of pouring a cup of coffee for Bryce. Her hand shook, splashing the dark liquid. "Is Frank sick?" she asked, her eyes wide with concern.

"He's been in the hospital in Philadelphia for more than a month now. He's had two serious heart attacks in the last year and a half." Bryce spoke dispassionately, but his aunt could see his emotion.

"Is he dying?"

"He could live another twenty years, or he could die next month. He wants to come home. He's been away too long." His voice hardened when he looked at his uncle. "And I promised him that I would arrange it."

"I don't want him here," Peter said with a scowl.

"He's your brother, Peter," Martha chided. "Apart from us, he's the only relative you have left in this world."

"I *don't* want him here!"

Bryce gripped the back of the chair in front of him. "Damn it, Uncle Peter, I don't care what you want. He's an old man, and he's sick and he's scared. I'm bringing him back."

"Hmm. He's just looking for a way to get us out of here. He swore he'd never forgive or forget what happened then."

Bryce rolled his eyes upward and sighed. "He's an old man," he repeated. "He doesn't have the strength to try to get the house back. He doesn't care about it anymore."

Peter walked to the window to stare at the inn. "Do you expect me to believe that? That this place means nothing to you or your father anymore?"

"Of course it means something. It was our home for a long time."

"You plan to take it back, don't you? That's why you've been using Leah and the kids—getting close to them so you can turn them against me."

Bryce reached the end of his patience with a jolt. "My friendship with Leah and her children has absolutely nothing to do with you. Don't ever, ever suggest that to her." There was both a warning and a threat in his voice. If Peter did anything to hurt Leah ...

Taking a calming breath, he dragged his fingers through his hair and sighed. "Look, my life is in Philadelphia. I don't want to live in Angel's Peak again. I'm here for Dad, no other reason. He wants to see his home, and you. He wants to set the past aside and enjoy what's left of the future, and he thinks he can't do that without you. He needs you, Peter."

His uncle's laugh was ugly. "He needs me?" he echoed. "Remember when *I* needed *him*? Remember when my son died, and I needed to talk to Frank, to see him? Remember what you told me?"

Bryce lowered his head, a flush of shame burning his face. His response to Peter's request six years ago had been cruel and brutal. It didn't matter that Bryce had been going through the worst period of his life, arranging his divorce from Kay; that for weeks he'd been unable to deal with anything except on the most basic level, without emotion, without feeling; that he had been bitter and angry and willing to strike out at anyone to lessen the pain that was eating away at him. Nothing changed the fact that he had been cruel, and wrong.

Finally he looked up, his eyes troubled. "I'm sorry about that. I'm sorry about Terence. You can hate me for that for the rest of your life . . . but don't punish Dad for it. Please, Peter . . ."

Peter looked ready to say no until Martha added her own, soft, "Please?"

He sank into his chair, bowed his head in his hands and closed his eyes. He wanted to say no, but he knew it would be wrong. He would be punishing his brother for something that Bryce had done. There had already been so much punishment, so much anger and hatred and sorrow. How could he be responsible for any more? "I'll see him," he said grudgingly. Before Bryce or Martha could show too much joy, though, he quickly added, "But I'm not promising anything. And I can't give him a place to stay. There's no room for him here."

Simply getting Peter to agree to being in the same state with Frank was a major victory in Bryce's view. Even so, he decided to press for more. "Why not?"

"Winter is a busy season—the inn is full."

"What about the other guest house, where we used to live?"

"Leah uses that for a workshop."

"What kind of workshop?"

It was Martha who answered. "She makes things—ornaments, decorations, crafts. She mostly uses them at the inn, but there's a shop in Asheville that sells whatever she can send them."

Bryce made a gesture of annoyance. "Leah can use the damn basement for a workshop. I'm asking for two rooms, and I'll pay your rates, Peter. You won't be out any money."

Martha looked up curiously. "Two rooms?"

"I plan to stay for a while, to get him settled in, to be with him."

"How long is a while?"

Bryce shrugged. "A month, maybe six weeks. That's about all the time I can spare from my job."

She nodded thoughtfully. "Until after Christmas. That will be a nice visit." Then she looked at her husband. "Tell him the real reason you can't give Frank a room, Peter. He's family. He has a right to know."

Bryce looked from his uncle to his aunt, then back again. "A right to know what?"

Peter's shoulders sagged as he stared down at his hands. "I don't own the estate anymore."

Shock was written on Bryce's face. In two hundred years the house and land had never passed out of Cameron hands. He had never expected it to happen, certainly not in his lifetime. "After what you did to get ownership of this place, you sold it?" he asked, his voice sharp with disbelief.

"No, I didn't sell it," Peter snapped defensively; then he suddenly looked very old. "I gave it to Terence. When he died, it passed to his widow."

"To Leah." Bryce was dismayed by the news. She wasn't even a Cameron, yet she owned his family home—cool, calm, lovely Leah. "Why the hell did you give it to Terence? Why couldn't you have waited until you died, like everyone else, to pass it on?"

"He was a young, stubborn man, and Leah—"

Peter broke off when Martha laid her hand on his arm. "Your reasons concern several people," she gently reminded him. "Terence is dead, but the others are still living, and you have no right to discuss this with a stranger without their permission."

Bryce turned his frown on his aunt. Not five minutes ago, she had reminded her husband that Bryce was family; now she was calling him a stranger. "What it boils down to is that I have to get *her* permission before I can bring Dad here. Right?"

Both Peter and Martha nodded.

Bryce stared grimly at the tabletop. What had happened to his simple plans to come here and settle this business once and for all? Why was everything in his life suddenly getting complicated with Leah?

He would ask this favor of her, and she would grant it, because she was gracious and generous, and because she understood the powerful ties of family that were drawing Frank back. And to the long list of attributes that connected him to her—attraction, affection, wanting, longing, needing—and now Bryce felt indebted, far beyond the simple price of the rooms.

And what payment would she extract in return for this favor? In his mind he could hear her soft drawl, enticing in spite of her words: "I'd rather not see you again." Would she welcome his father on the condition that Bryce fulfill that one little wish for her?

"I'll talk to her." He cleared his throat. "Thank you, Uncle Peter, Aunt Martha."

Following breakfast, Leah took refuge in the attic. Checking their Christmas decorations was a tedious task that no one but herself enjoyed, so doing it practically guaranteed privacy.

The cartons were stacked in the center of the room, next to a hand-hewn table made more than a hundred and fifty years ago by an earlier Cameron. Leah carefully pulled the clear packing tape from the top of the first box and began removing its contents.

There were ceramic scent pots painted with merry Christmas scenes, ready to be filled with potpourri, and candle holders in wood, glass, silver and pewter. Music boxes in the shapes of reindeer, angels, Santas and snowmen, and bows made of red velvet and green calico. Miniature sleighs for centerpieces and tiny woven baskets to be filled with a few pieces of candy and hung on the trees. Tablecloths and napkins in bright red and green for formal dinners, and place mats in cheery Christmas prints for casual use. Miniature wreaths no bigger than a silver dollar and others as much as three feet in diameter, with every size in between, fashioned out of a variety of materials from pine cones and braided strips of fabric to wheat and Spanish moss. Ornaments in every shape and variety, from expensive delicate china to finger-painted bells made from cardboard egg cartons, and lights—literally thousands of lights. Tiny multi-colored bulbs for the trees, fat round white bulbs to outline the house. Last year, Leah remembered, they had used more than five thousand lights at Christmas. She gave a little sigh. Untangling and checking all those strings of lights was part of her job.

She was unwrapping the broken pieces of what had once been a round green ball when the door opened. Looking over her shoulder, she recognized the dark brown hair immediately. She wished he would disappear before he climbed the final three steps into the room, and yet at the same time she was pleased that he had sought her company.

"Are you busy?"

She continued to sort through the box in front of her. Rather than give the obvious answer to his question, she ignored it and asked one of her own. "How did your meeting with Peter go?"

He crossed to the table, leaned against it and watched her. "It was okay."

"Did you finish your business with him?" She was dying to know what had been so important, and she suspected that Bryce knew it. But if he wouldn't offer an explanation, she certainly wouldn't ask for one, she promised herself as she moved around the table.

"What's wrong, Leah?"

Startled blue eyes met his. "I—I don't understand...."

"Every time I get near you, you try to put distance between us, either physically or emotionally. What's wrong? What have I done?"

She unwrapped a ceramic boy angel, his head bowed to reveal his halo. When filled with sand the angel sat on the mantel, a stocking looped over his upturned foot. There were seven altogether, one for each of them: three boys and four girls, their robes painted in soft Christmas colors—pale pinks and muted golds and mossy greens. Usually Leah admired the workmanship each time she looked at one of the angels, but this morning her hands were shaking too badly. With hardly a glance, she set it on the table.

He asked the question so sincerely; how was she supposed to answer? How could she tell him, "It's not you, it's *me*"? She gave him only half the answer. "It's not you," she murmured.

"Are you afraid of me?"

Afraid of what she felt when he was around, she acknowledged silently. Afraid of what she felt when he *wasn't* around. Afraid because she was helpless against those emotions. But afraid of *him*? "No, I'm not."

He took note of the heightened color in her cheeks and of her trembling hands, and decided that it was a good time to change the subject. "We never did finish our talk about Matthew," he reminded her.

"M—Matthew?"

He picked up a music box, gave the knob on the bottom a twist and set it down again. Santa turned in a slow circle to the tune of "Santa Claus Is Watching You." After a few notes he reached for a heavy glass angel standing next to it. "Matthew," he repeated. "You think I'm a bad influence on him. I think you're cheating him by not telling him about his father."

Leah took the angel from his hands and carefully set it down again. "How much experience have you had with children?"

He gave her a grin. "Almost none. That's why they like me. I don't know how to treat kids, so I treat them like people." While the first music box still played, he set another turning, this one a reindeer twirling to "Rudolph the Red-Nosed Reindeer."

When he reached for a third music box, Leah frowned at him. "Would you stop that?"

He walked to a dusty old rocker in the corner and sat down, folding his hands over his stomach. "Do you want to start the argument, or should I?"

Leah opened yet another box, looked inside and set it aside. "I don't think you're a bad influence," she said slowly, "but you *are* influencing him. I don't think you understand just how much."

"I do understand. Matthew is lonely, and he feels a little cheated, because he's the only kid in his entire first-grade class who doesn't have a father. He's looking for someone to fill in, and he's decided that I'll do nicely." He watched her, gauging the effect of his summary on her. She acknowledged its correctness with a simple nod.

He understood her concern, and that made it difficult to argue, especially when he couldn't explain his feelings to her. He had felt an immediate bond with Matthew—the ties of family, the attraction between a boy who wanted a father and a man who wanted a son. He would never do anything to hurt Matthew, but Leah couldn't know that.

"That's great while you're here, but what about when you leave? Your business with Peter is finished, and you'll be returning to Philadelphia soon. What happens to my son then?"

Nothing, he wanted to say. He wasn't the sort of man who took commitments lightly. He wouldn't get involved with Matthew, then forget all about him when he left Angel's Peak. "You don't think long-distance relationships can work? You know—letters, phone calls, visits?" Even as he asked it, he knew what her answer would be. It sounded implausible to him, too.

"Not when a six-year-old boy is involved." As the strains of music from the Santa slowed and distorted, Leah laid a gentle hand on it to stop it.

What about when a thirty-five-year-old woman is involved? he wanted to ask. Did age improve the odds? "Okay. So why don't you give him a father?"

She stared at him with a hint of derision for his suggestion. "That's a very simple solution for a very complex problem," she said, bringing a low stool from the corner and brushing it off before sitting down.

"Even a one-horse town like Angel's Peak has to have at least a few single men to choose from." He rocked the chair with the toe of his booted foot until he realized he was sending showers of dust into the air. "Terence has been dead for six years. That's long enough to grieve. That's more than long enough to be single and celibate. Why don't you get married again?"

Leah's surprise changed to bewilderment. How on earth had she gotten onto the subject of marriage with him? "It isn't that easy," she protested. "Why aren't you married?"

"How do you know I'm not?"

Her mouth opened, but no words came out. She had assumed, because he had touched her and kissed her, that he was single. She should have known better than that. Not all men felt bound by their marriage vows; she had sometimes suspected that Terence was one of those who didn't. Her face grew warm. She had indulged in all sorts of fantasies about this man without even bothering to find out if he was married.

"I'm not," he said, feeling a warm rush inside because it mattered to her. "But I was—for fourteen years. We've been divorced for six years."

"I'm sorry," Leah murmured, but only because it seemed appropriate. She wasn't sorry—she was relieved. She didn't want to care at all about him, but she couldn't deny the relief.

"So was I." Bryce leaned his head back to study the dusty ceiling beams. He had been very sorry. The end of his marriage had been the most painful time of his life—even worse than Gran's death. It had come as a total surprise to him when Kay had told him about her affair with Derek Wilson, but he had been willing to forgive her, to continue loving her and mend their shattered relationship. But Kay hadn't felt she'd done anything that required his forgiveness, and she certainly hadn't wanted his love. All she had asked for was a divorce, so she could marry Derek. Maybe if he had paid more attention he would have seen what was happening, but his job had demanded so much of his time, and Kay had never complained.

Until the end. He had been stubborn about the divorce, insisting that they could work out their problems; they simply couldn't throw away fourteen years of marriage. *Then* Kay had complained—about the time he'd devoted to his job. About the energy and emotion he'd given it, leaving little or nothing for her. About the dissatisfaction and the emptiness in her life that he couldn't fill anymore. About *his* emptiness, his selfishness, his inability to give or care or feel or satisfy. By the time she'd finished with him, his heart and his ego had been in shreds, and he had given her the divorce—sadly, painfully, but willingly.

Leah watched the expressions that crossed his face as he remembered—sorrow, pain, despair—and wanted to offer him comfort. Painful memories were something she understood very well; she had more than a few of her own. But fear held her back—fear of being rejected, and fear of being accepted. She couldn't let him get too close.

He lowered his head again to look at her. "So... we were talking about finding you a husband." What he had approached in a lighthearted manner had suddenly become a serious subject. He didn't want to think in terms of other men with Leah. He hadn't yet accepted his own attraction to her; how could he tease her about attracting another man?

"No," she corrected firmly. "We were talking about your friendship with Matthew." She reached into the big box in front of her and withdrew a handful of cotton batting. As soon as she began unwrapping it, she could feel the broken pieces inside. For a house filled with people and at least four kids for the holidays, they had very little breakage at Christmas, but she would give anything to know how in the world the few items that did break managed to do so in the packing cartons.

"Do you feel threatened by it?"

She glanced at him as she carefully emptied the contents of the batting into the wastebasket. This ball had been glittery gold. "Why should I?"

"Because you've had Matthew all to yourself. He was born after Terence died, so you never even had to share him with his father. Are you afraid that he'll love you less if he finds a substitute father to love?" Simply saying it gave him a warm feeling. The love of parents and friends was nice; the love of a woman was wonderful; but the love of a child was special. Children loved unconditionally, accepting your flaws in ways that few adults could.

"No," Leah said honestly, her blue eyes making contact with his. "I'm afraid that he'll love you too much. I don't want to see him hurt. He's such a little boy, and he has so much faith. If you disappoint him..."

"I won't."

"How can you be so sure of that?"

"Because I know myself."

Exasperation was woven through her sigh. How had Matthew chosen such a stubborn, single-minded man for a father figure? She had no doubt that Bryce could be a good father—but to his own children, not hers. He had already displayed a degree of patience that Terence had never possessed, and he'd been kind and affectionate and respectful with the children. But they were *her* children, and she would be the one who had to comfort Matthew when the novelty wore off for Bryce.

Her voice sharp with frustration, she said, "He may as well accept the idea that he'll never have a father."

His voice came quietly in the stillness. "Do you hate men so much?"

Her hands were trembling too much for her to be handling the fragile glass ornaments. She pushed the box away, turned her back on him and folded her hands together. "No, of course not."

"Then how can you say you'll never marry again?"

"I didn't."

"You said Matthew will never have a father."

Her knuckles turned white when she squeezed her hands tighter. Risking a glance over her shoulder, she asked, "Do you know many men who want to raise someone else's kids? Four of them?"

The answer, if he chose to give it, was no. Hell, as much as he wanted children himself, he wouldn't choose to take on such a burden—but who could choose when it came to love? If a man fell in love with a woman who had four children, he accepted the children, too, and did his best for them.

"If *you* want to get married again, it's simple: you find a woman you can love, one who loves you. If *I* want to get married, I have to find a man I can love, one who not only loves me but all four of my children, one who they can love in return. What are the odds of six people falling in love with each other?"

"Any man who loves you has to love the kids. You're a package deal."

The frustration flared again. He saw things so simply, in such idealistic terms, while Leah knew from experience that life was complex, full of problems, and that idealism had little or nothing to do with reality.

"I annoy you, don't I?" he asked, sounding both curious and amused.

"You don't understand. You simplify things. You make them sound so much easier than they really are."

"Maybe you make them more difficult than they really are. You had problems in the past, and you expect problems in the future. Life doesn't have to be so hard, Leah."

She shook her head in dismay. "I live my life the only way I know how."

"Carefully. Cautiously. Without taking chances. Without risks." The floorboards creaked when Bryce left the rocker. He took a few steps, then crouched directly behind her. The tall, narrow windows were covered with dust, and the sunlight that came through them was weak, but there was enough to play up the coppery tints in her hair. He touched it with just his fingertips, drawing them lightly over it.

Last week the curls had been wild, tangling together. Yesterday she had combed them into something approaching order. Today they were gone altogether, transformed into soft, feminine waves. His fingertips gently skimmed over them until they brushed her ear.

Leah couldn't control her shiver. She didn't try to move away or tell him to stop, because she didn't want him to. She wanted him to go on touching her this way—gently, lightly, barely there—forever.

Slowly he turned her to face him. Now his fingers moved over her throat and curved upward to her chin. His index finger hesitantly touched her mouth, drew back, then moved to it again. Her lips were soft and smooth, drawing him to test them with his own. He skimmed the very tips of his fingers from one corner of her mouth to the other; then, with great care, he parted her lips with one finger, feeling the moist warmth enclose it.

"Take a risk, Leah," he encouraged, his voice barely above a whisper. "Take a chance with me."

She recognized the first faint stirrings of arousal that swirled in the pit of her stomach. Lord, how long had it been since she'd felt that need? When his mouth touched hers, the need exploded, robbing her of her ability to breathe, to think, to protest. All she felt was desire—hot, liquid, unfamiliar in its intensity.

Bryce laid his hands on her shoulders. He felt the tension in her muscles, but it wasn't because she didn't want his kiss. Maybe it was because she wanted it too much? Her mouth opened to his, welcoming the tentative, easy explorations of his tongue. She tasted dark ... sweet ... innocent.

He changed positions, shifting his weight to his knees. The taste, the feel, the scent of her were weakening him, sending shivers of delight through his body and creating a sudden, erotically uncomfortable swelling of need. One kiss wasn't supposed to be this good, this . . . devastating to his senses.

He slid one hand from her shoulder, over her sweater, until his palm was molded to her breast. Her nipple was hard, easy to find beneath the bulky fabric. But he had barely touched it before she pushed his hand—then him— away.

Her face was flushed, she was breathing hard, and her eyes, for the brief moment that they met his, were uneasy. Hugging her arms protectively across her chest, she dropped her gaze and saw the desire that he made no effort to hide. Her blush deepened. "I—I—" She rose from the stool, shrinking back to avoid contact with him, then circled the table for safety.

Bryce rose slowly, his gaze intent on her face. "What's wrong?"

"N-nothing. Just . . . don't do that again, okay?"

"Do what again? Kiss you? Touch your breast? Arouse you? Make you feel something?"

She didn't know how to answer. Her sensible side wanted to scream, "Yes, all those things!" She didn't want him to do any of them again. The romantic side, though, simply wanted. She sought safety in giving no answer at all.

Bryce watched her ignore him. She was a frustrating woman, he decided—probably as frustrating to him as he was to her. She needed time. Time to get to know him, to learn to trust him, to let herself want him. He could give her that.

Letting her arms fall to her sides, Leah busied herself with rearranging the table. When everything had been neatly shuffled into a new position, she said abruptly, "I'm going downstairs now. Please turn off the light and close the door when you leave."

Bryce was only a few steps behind her. "Will you have lunch with me?" he asked when they reached the second-floor landing.

"You're welcome to sit at the family table—"

He shook his head impatiently. "In town. You don't have to stay here, do you?"

He wasn't the first man to ask for her company in the years since Terence had died, but he *was* the first she'd ever wanted to say yes to—yes to lunch, and a whole lot more. After a moment's hesitation, that was what she said. She might be making a mistake spending more time with him than was absolutely necessary, but she had made a lifetime of mistakes, and she had survived every one of them. Even Terence. "All right. Let me tell Vicky."

Bryce recognized the clerk's swiftly hidden expression at the news that Leah was having lunch in town with him as surprise. So Leah didn't spend much time with men, other than customers. He found that very interesting—and very encouraging. Though he knew that it would probably embarrass her, he chose to comment on it when she returned with their coats. "I take it you don't go out often," he said as they descended the broad front steps.

She didn't look at him. "There's no reason to. Everything I need is right here."

"Everything?" There was her family, of course, and her job, but what about her social life? Didn't she ever need friends, laughter and fun? Didn't she ever need a man?

"This *is* my life," Leah replied, her words a not too subtle warning. "I don't want anything else." Pushing her gloved hand into her pocket, she pulled out a set of keys and offered them to Bryce. He accepted them silently, just as he accepted her warning.

Their drive into town was quiet. He pulled into the parking lot of the first restaurant they came to and followed Leah inside.

"How long have you lived in Angel's Peak?"

She looked up from the menu. "Since I was five."

"Where did you live before that?"

She dropped her eyes evasively. "I don't know." All the important facts about her early life were missing—things like her mother's and father's names, her exact age, her real birth date. When she had been abandoned by her parents thirty years ago, she had been clutching a piece of paper with the name Leah on it. She had supplied the last name and the age herself, but no one had been able to judge the reliability of a hysterical little girl. No one had been able to prove if she was right.

"You've never lived in a city, have you?"

She shook her head. "I've never even seen a city larger than Asheville. I like Angel's Peak. I can't imagine living anywhere else."

After they ordered their meal, Bryce settled back comfortably in his seat. "I can't imagine living anywhere but Philadelphia. I never wanted to see Angel's Peak again."

"Why did you come back?"

He studied her for a moment. Her eyes were cool again, and her emotions were under strict control. Yet he hesitated. He didn't want to tell her about Frank and Peter. He didn't want to spoil this time together by asking for favors. "We'll discuss that later. Right now I want to talk about you."

She sat back, too, folding her hands together in her lap. She was studying him so calmly that Bryce was certain she was going to refuse his request. But after a moment she tilted her head to one side. "Why?"

He searched through a list of possible answers and discarded each one: because I like you; because you interest me; because I want to make love to you. That last one had slipped in unexpectedly, making him remember the kiss in the attic, the feel of her breast, the heaviness in his body, and it made him flush just slightly.

None of those answers were acceptable, but he had one that was. "Because we're family, Leah." She valued her family above all else, and he was going to persuade her to include him in that family one way or another. If she would accept him only as her children's cousin, he would settle for that. For the time being.

She sighed softly. "What do you want to know?"

Bryce restrained himself from saying, "Everything," and offered a nonthreatening question instead. "How long have you been running the inn?"

"Since it opened three years ago."

"Do you enjoy it?"

"Yes. I like meeting people from other places, people who appreciate old houses as much as I do. And I like the responsibility—it's the first job I've ever had."

"The first *paying* job," Bryce corrected. "Being a wife and mother of four is a job, even if it doesn't pay a salary."

She smiled then, shyly. "Yes," she agreed in a soft voice. "It is."

He watched until her smile faded, then closed his eyes. The desire to kiss her again and again was becoming a need, and she wasn't even aware of it. She didn't know that her smile could spread such heat through him that he burned for her. He smiled just a little mockingly. And Kay had called him unfeeling. She would be surprised at just how much he could feel.

Leah was watching him, waiting for his next question. He reached for his coffee cup as he asked it. "Do you like dealing with people?"

She wondered why that surprised him so much. "Of course. I like people."

"You seem so..."

"Snobbish?" she supplied. "Snooty? Stuck-up?"

Those were words that had been applied to her, Bryce suspected, and she hadn't liked them one bit. He chose his own carefully. "No, not any of those. Aloof, maybe. Cautious." As if letting anyone get close to her would be a mistake that she might not survive.

"Cautious." Even the tone of her voice was careful as she repeated the word. "That sounds better. I guess I am cautious. I have to be."

"Why?"

She studied him for a moment. His manner was relaxed, his curiosity friendly, his interest appealing. At this moment, *he* was the best reason in the world for caution on her part. Did he have any idea how strongly he attracted her? Would it matter to him if he did know? "Don't you know any easy questions?" she asked in her smile-softened drawl.

"All questions are easy. Only the answers are hard." He gave the waitress time to serve them before continuing. "So you like people. Is that why you have four kids?"

"I wanted a large family."

"Are you an only child?"

"I don't know." She sprinkled cheese on her fettuccine before meeting his gaze. "I grew up in the home on the north side of town."

He looked down quickly. He remembered the home. The kids who lived there were outcasts in school and in town, sticking together because they had no one else. They lived a tightly controlled, regimented life, with little fun and less affection. Most of them were orphans, but there were always a few whose parents couldn't—or wouldn't—take care of them. Which was Leah? he wondered.

She moved restlessly, her appetite gone. She had made it a rule to rarely offer information about her childhood—reactions like Bryce's had taught her better. Knowing changed the way people looked at her, as if they were trying to figure out what kind of horrible child she'd been, that her parents hadn't wanted her. She waited for him to change the subject awkwardly, as people always did, and wished she had said nothing.

"Are your parents dead, or did they abandon you?"

He spoke in a matter-of-fact tone, as if they were discussing the weather outside. Leah's first reaction was surprise, followed by gratitude that he was still being friendly. "They left me there. I don't know who they were, and I've never seen them since."

What kind of people could walk away from the child that Leah had been—from their own daughter? he wondered. Deep inside he ached for her—for the girl, and for the woman—but he kept it hidden. She would see his sympathy as pity, and she wouldn't appreciate it. "So you lived at the home until you met Terence."

Mention of her husband brought a wariness to her eyes. "Yes. Do you ski?"

He frowned at her graceless change of subject. "If you don't want to talk about Terence, Leah, you only have to say so," he chided.

She gave an accepting nod. "Now it's your turn to answer some questions."

"In spite of your attempts to discourage me, you're interested in me after all, aren't you?" Moving his dinner plate away, he reached for his coffee. "What do you want to know?"

"Did you talk to Peter this morning?"

"Yes."

She waited expectantly.

"We took care of part of my business."

"And the rest?"

He wouldn't get a better chance to tell his father's story and to ask his favor, but, stubbornly, he refused the opportunity. Once he asked her, he would have no reason to stay any longer; he would have to return to Philadelphia to make arrangements for his father's move and his own leave of absence. Even though he would be back soon, he wanted to put off leaving a little longer, wanted to enjoy her company a little longer. "I'll take care of the rest later. Do you want dessert?"

She considered it, then shook her head. "I should get back to the inn."

"You have a perfectly competent staff. I'm sure they can get along for a few hours without you."

She led the way across the dining room, Bryce close behind. "I'm sure they can get along for a few years without me, but I can't get along without them."

He paid the bill, then held her coat while she slipped it on. Facing her, he lifted her hair from beneath the collar, then traced a finger over the rose-colored scarf. "I like this color. It makes you look...soft."

Leah solemnly returned his gaze. How easy it would be to grow used to him, she thought with regret—to his simple outlook and pretty words and easy smiles and gentle touches. How easily she could make him a part of her life. But his presence here was only temporary, while her life was here forever. Forever and ever. Soon he would be gone, and if she let him get much closer, he would take a vital part of her with him.

"I'm not soft," she said in response to his remark. "I'm very strong."

His smile was faint. "You can be both, you know." Taking her arm, he led her outside, where he stopped on the cleared sidewalk, looking at the park across the street. "Let's take a walk in the park."

She looked at the park, too. There were small children in brightly colored jackets playing there, and creations of snow—men, angels, forts, unidentifiable creatures. She was tempted, but there were so many things she needed to do at home. Regretfully she shook her head.

"How about going for a drive?"

Another shake. "I need to get back to the inn," she said a second time, more forcefully.

Bryce's irritation succeeded in overcoming his smile. He dropped her arm and turned toward the car. Of course she needed to get back. At the inn she could busy herself with any number of tasks; she could lock herself in her room or her office; she could surround herself with her employees and her family and her friendly guests. At the inn she could keep him at a distance.

Which was exactly where he belonged. He didn't bother to enumerate the reasons why he should stay away from Leah, although he knew them by heart now. It would just be so much easier if he didn't *want* to be with her, if he didn't find so much pleasure in looking at her, listening to her, touching her and kissing her. Especially in kissing her.

He shoved his hands into his pockets and walked silently at her side, with more than enough distance between them to satisfy her. They reached the station wagon, drove home and entered the house, all without saying a word.

Puzzled by his coldness, Leah hung her coat in the closet beneath the front stairs, then wordlessly extended her hand for his heavier jacket. He gave it to her, then turned away.

"Bryce?"

He paused.

Her hands were cold; she rubbed them together until she realized that they were also trembling. "I take a walk every night after dinner." It was as close to an invitation as she could come.

His smile returned, not dazzling, but gentle. Without a word, he nodded and walked away.

They couldn't squeeze in one more person at the family table that night at dinner, so the two tables were separated to make room for Bryce. After supervising the rearrangement, Leah sat down at one table with Peter and Martha. There was an empty chair on her left, which she fully expected Bryce to claim. She was disappointed when he chose to sit with Megan and the boys instead, leaving the chair next to Leah for Laurel. Leah stared at the back of his head for a moment, then looked away—into Martha's sharp, curious eyes. Blushing, she shifted so that she could no longer see Bryce and turned her attention to her meal.

Was he angry because she had refused his invitations that afternoon? Or had he simply tired of her company? Terence had often gotten tired of her. He had never been cruel; he had simply been incapable of feigning a love—even an affection—that he didn't feel. Was Bryce more like Terence than she'd expected?

She'd made the best offer she could when she had told him about her evening walk. She didn't expect to see him, though, as she left the dining room to get her coat, scarf and gloves. By the time they had gotten back to the house that afternoon, he'd seemed to have lost all interest in spending time with her. But that wouldn't change her routine. She would take her walk alone, and she would enjoy it. She wouldn't let him steal that simple pleasure from her.

She held on to the rail as she descended the porch steps in back, making a mental note to ask Douglas to clean them again; then, breathing in the cold, frosty air, she set off across the yard.

Bryce saw her the moment she stepped outside. Leaning motionless against the tree trunk, he watched her as she moved down the steps, cautious but confident. She knew where the slick spots were. He wished, for her sake and his, that that confidence might be extended into the rest of her life.

As she neared him, he moved out of the dark shadow of the tree and stopped in front of her. "What took you so long?"

Suddenly the prospect of a long, snowy walk seemed much more cheerful. Leah was resentful that he could make such a difference, but resentment wouldn't stop her from enjoying his presence. "I didn't think you were coming."

"You think I'd pass up the only invitation you've given me?" He shook his head. "Not likely." He fell in step alongside her, letting her lead the way across the driveway and into the woods. The walk, like the drive back from town, was silent, but this time there was no annoyance, no irritation—just a simple, warm satisfaction at being with her.

Leah's soft voice broke the stillness. "You never did answer me today when I asked if you like to ski."

"You didn't really want to know, did you?" he asked with a grin, reminding her that the question had been a ploy to shift the subject away from Terence.

"Yes. I do want to know." She wanted to know everything about him—this man who so strongly affected her.

Gratified by the answer, he shrugged. "I learned how when I was a kid, of course. Everyone who lives in or on

Angel's Peak learns how. But I was never very good at it, or very fond of it. What about you?''

"Skiing is a luxury, and luxuries had no place at the home." She answered plainly, without a hint of self-pity or bitterness.

Bryce stopped and touched her shoulder, urging her to look at him. The moonlight shone on her face, touching the wisps of hair that had escaped her scarf. "Was love a luxury, too, Leah?"

He spoke so gently and touched her so tenderly. Did he know that she craved a tender touch—that she was beginning to crave *his* touch? She wanted to run away; she was afraid of revealing her need to him, but she couldn't back away from the hand that was resting lightly on her shoulder. And she couldn't pull her eyes from his.

Bending slightly, he touched his lips to hers. With no more contact between them than his hand and his mouth, he could feel the pleasure that stole through her. Slowly but deliberately, he deepened the kiss, moistening her lips with his tongue. He slid one arm around her, raised his free hand to cup her cheek and closed the distance between them with one gentle tug.

Leah was lost. Warmth spread through her with his kiss, flowing with the heated blood through her veins. With a silent cry of despair at her helplessness, she raised her hands to his shoulders, then wrapped her arms around his neck.

His groan was a soft vibration in her mouth. When his tongue parted her teeth to seek hers, to explore the vulnerable softness of her mouth, he tasted of coffee, rich and hot.

He tugged off one glove, and it fell to the ground, a dark shadow on the moonlit snow. The other glove followed, and he slid his hands into her hair, pushing back her scarf and gliding his fingers through the strands of cold silk.

Holding her, kissing her—God, it felt good! He wished it could go on forever and at the same time wished for more. He wanted to undress her, to caress her, to bring her pleasure beyond belief. He wanted to make love to her. He had needed her for what seemed like ages, and tonight, with hungry kisses and gentle caresses, he knew that he could have her.

But where? The house was filled with people, including her children, and the empty guest house was too close to—

His mind commanded him to end the kiss as common sense took a grip on desire. Sure, he could seduce her—between his desire and her innocence, he had no doubt of that. But this was *Leah*, not some woman he could take to bed and forget tomorrow morning, and Leah wasn't ready to accept him as a lover. If he seduced her now, she would hate him when it was over, and he would lose her. That was a risk he couldn't take.

Abruptly he ended the kiss and pressed her face against the cool leather of his jacket. Although there was warmth in the shelter of his arms, she was shivering; he could feel it through the thickness of their coats. But that was all right, he thought with a rueful sigh—he was shaky, too, inside and out.

Eyes closed, face against his chest, Leah listened to the pounding of a heartbeat, not sure if it was Bryce's or her own, or just the rushing of the blood in her ears. She was unsteady, depending on him for support. Never, not in thirty-five years of living, had she experienced anything like his kisses.

At last he put her away from him. With hands that trembled the tiniest bit, he raised the scarf to cover her hair again, letting his fingers linger there for a moment. When he drew his hand back, he asked, "You're not afraid of me, are you, Leah?" He knew the answer; he just wanted to make sure that she did, too.

She had to try several times to get her voice to work. "I don't think you would hurt me."

"I won't—not ever." He continued to study her face, seeking answers, truths. He wanted to know it all. "Terence hurt you, didn't he?"

Suddenly she swung away, walking briskly through the snow. Bryce ducked to grab his gloves before following her. "Leah, you can't keep running from me!"

She didn't look at him or slow her steps to make it easy for him to catch up. Tucking her chin into the turned-up collar of her coat, she hunched her shoulders against the cold and walked even faster.

They had reached the clearing of the cemetery when Bryce grabbed her hand. "Leah!" When she didn't struggle or speak, he softened both his voice and his touch. "He hurt you, didn't he?"

"Does it matter?"

"Yes."

"Why?" she challenged him, meeting his gaze at last. The softness was in his eyes, too.

Bryce raised his shoulders in a helpless shrug. "Because *you* matter."

She repeated the single word, but this time the challenge was gone. "Why?"

"I don't know, but you do." He pulled back his hand, fighting the desire to take her into his arms again, to kiss her again. "Every time I touch you, every time I try to get close to you, Leah, you pull away. Is it because you still love Terence? Or because he hurt you? Did he teach you to distrust all men?"

"You said today that I don't have to talk to you about him."

He acknowledged that with a nod. "But you've got to talk sometime. Leah, I've got to know."

She walked over to the fence and wrapped one hand around a wrought iron spike. "What difference does it make? It's all in the past—you can't change any of it." Her voice sounded cool and distant and unnaturally calm.

He couldn't change the past, but he could heal the lingering wounds. Once again he followed, stopping behind her. He rested his hands lightly on her shoulders and spoke softly, his mouth only inches from her ear. "What did he do to you, Leah?"

She turned slowly, dislodging his hands, but made no effort to move away from him. Instead she raised her hands to his chest, gripping handfuls of his jacket, and pulled him toward her. "Kiss me again," she commanded. "The way you just did."

Sheer willpower held him back. Gently he unclasped her fingers from his coat, then held her hands together between his. "No, Leah. I won't let you use me that way. Tell me about Terence."

She leaned back against the fence. "Terence was my husband. We were married for twelve years, and we had four children, but he died, and I lived. End of story."

She made it sound so simple. He could make a similar statement about his marriage to Kay. It would be accurate, but it would say nothing about the love and the happiness, or the pain—the incredible pain. How much was Leah leaving out?

Sensing that her simplified answer annoyed him, she uttered a soft sigh. It would be easier to give him an honest response if she knew why he was so intent on getting it. Did it truly make a difference to him, or was he just curious?

"Terence didn't do anything to me. Nothing. He didn't love me ... didn't want me ... didn't need me. Marrying me was the price he paid to get ownership of the estate."

"What do you mean?" he asked, although he'd already picked up enough information to make a fairly good guess.

"I was seventeen, pregnant and alone. Peter and Martha used the estate as a bargaining chip to convince Terence to accept responsibility and marry me."

Bryce tried to imagine how she must have felt, frightened and alone, but he couldn't. He had always had the loving support of his father, had always been able to take care of himself. "Did you want to marry him? Even knowing that he was doing it only so he could have the house?"

She heard the disbelief he tried to hide and smiled faintly. "Yes, I wanted to marry him. I loved him, and I thought that he loved me. And I was carrying his child. I thought that eventually everything would work out all right."

"Did it?"

She shrugged. "He was the best husband and the best father that he could be. He gave me a home and a family, but he couldn't give himself."

Bryce reached for her to offer comfort, but she didn't want it. Moving swiftly, she avoided his hands and slipped away.

"Finish your business here, Bryce," she requested, speaking once more in her soft, angelic drawl, "and go home. Go back to Philadelphia where you belong."

"My business here is with you," he called after her. And that was where he belonged, too—with her. He smiled faintly. If he told her that, she would accuse him of simplifying things again, of making them seem easy when they weren't.

Slowly she turned. "I thought it was Peter you had to see."

"I thought so, too, but it turns out my business concerns you as much as him. More, even." He would have preferred to have this discussion in the morning, in the businesslike atmosphere of her office, but he wanted to stretch out this private time with her. "It's about my father."

"Frank?"

"Yes. He's in the hospital in Philadelphia. He had a heart attack."

"Is he all right?"

He shrugged. "As all right as a seventy-three-year-old man with a history of heart disease can be. He's old, Leah, and he wants to come home. He wants to reconcile with Peter, to see Martha again, to meet you and your children— besides me, you're the only family he's got. He wants to live the rest of his life here, in the Cameron house."

He was playing on her emotions, she knew. He was aware of how important family was to her, and to the kids. He had to know that he was making a request she could never turn down. "All right."

He couldn't believe it was that easy. "All right?"

"Your father is welcome to live here." With a slightly mischievous smile, she added, "You're even welcome to visit him while he's here . . . occasionally."

Should he tell her that his first "visit" would start the day he brought Frank to the estate and last at least six weeks? The answer, of course, was yes, but he said nothing. If he gave her advance warning, she would tell him that there was no room at the inn for *him*—that there was no room in her *life* for him. No, it would be better to surprise her, put her in a situation where she simply had no choice but to accept his presence. She was going to *have* to accept him.

"I realize that this is how you support your family, and I'll pay whatever it costs—"

She raised her hand to stop him. "I don't want your money. This is your father's home."

"But—" He broke off. He'd gotten what he wanted; he wouldn't push her to accept more. They would take up the matter of payment when he and Frank returned. Walking across the snow-covered ground to her, he bent and gently kissed her. "Thank you."

When he offered his hand, she hesitantly took it. His fingers closed firmly around hers, holding on to her, but giving her the freedom to pull away if she chose to. She liked the feeling that he wanted her close but wouldn't use force to hold her there. As with practically everything else about him, she liked it very much.

Chapter 5

Bryce looked out the airplane window at the snow-covered mountains below him. Slowly he smiled. He couldn't pick out Angel's Peak, but it was there. Soon *he* would be there, too. With Leah.

"How much longer until we land?"

He turned to his father. "A few more minutes. How are you feeling?"

"If you ask me that one more time, you'll find out," the old man grumbled. "Will anyone be meeting us?"

"No." Leah had offered to pick them up, but Bryce preferred to rent a car and drive up the mountain. He wanted his father's return to Angel's Peak to be a private one. He also wanted to get settled at the inn before he told Leah how long he was planning to stay. It would be harder for her to throw him out then.

"What are you grinning about?" Frank's faded brown eyes narrowed on his son's face. "For someone who put up such a fuss about coming back here only a month ago, you sure have changed your tune. I suppose this has something to do with Terence's wife.''

"Terence's widow," Bryce corrected. "Her name is Leah, Dad, and she's the one who's letting you stay at the house, so be nice."

Frank made a grimace of disgust. "Letting me stay in our own house. That house has never belonged to anyone but a Cameron, until her."

Bryce reined in his impatience with his father. That had been his first reaction to hearing that Leah owned the house, too. "What about Gran?"

"Well, that's different. She was a—"

"She was a Dawson."

"But . . . well, it was different, anyway. We always knew that she would keep the house in the family."

"Leah has four children who are as much Camerons as you are. She'll keep the house in the family, too." Bryce tensed slightly as the plane began descending. Five days had passed since he'd left the inn to prepare for Frank's move. He had said goodbye to the entire family after dinner before Douglas had driven him to Asheville. He hadn't been given a chance to say a private farewell to Leah, and he suspected she had planned it that way. He didn't know whom she distrusted more—him or herself. All he knew was that he had missed her.

"She must be pretty."

He glanced at Frank. "Yes, she is," he quietly agreed.

The rental car was waiting for them by the time Bryce had collected their luggage, and they set out for their final destination. Frank sat quietly in the seat beside Bryce, looking out the side window.

"It's beautiful."

Frank's first words came as Bryce turned into the long driveway that approached the house. Silently Bryce echoed them. He parked in the lot, then helped his father out of the small car.

Leah was waiting on the porch when they reached the steps, Martha at her side. There was no sign of Peter. She stole a glance at Bryce before stepping forward to greet his father. "Mr. Cameron, I'm Leah." Rising onto her toes, she kissed him, first on one cheek, then the other. "Welcome home."

He took a good look at her before responding. "My son was right. You *are* pretty."

But he spoke in such an unfriendly tone that Leah was sure it wasn't meant as a compliment. She looked at Bryce, who merely shrugged.

"Come on inside, Frank, and leave the girl alone," Martha said, ushering him into the house. "You must be tired after that trip. You'll be staying in Anna's old room. Bryce will bring in your luggage...." Her words faded as the door swung shut behind her.

Leah, wearing a mint-green sweater, shivered and crossed her arms over her chest. "I take it your father doesn't like the idea of anyone but a Cameron owning the house."

Bryce shrugged again. "He's tired, Leah. It's been a long trip, and he's excited about coming home. He's just worn out." He considered moving closer to take her into his arms, then decided that, for a few minutes, he wanted the pure pleasure of looking at her. "Did you miss me?"

A rosy blush tinted her cheeks. "You've been gone less than a week," she reminded him.

"I missed you. I thought about you a lot while I was gone. Didn't you think of me at all?"

Unwillingly, she smiled. "Maybe once." One long, continuous thought, never leaving her mind since his departure Sunday.

"I'll take what I can get." He had looked long enough, he decided. It was time for a proper greeting. Moving across the porch, he wrapped his arms around her and brushed his lips against hers. "I'll take anything you can give me, Leah." Then he kissed her. His mouth was both hard and soft, gentle but demanding, taking yet giving, and instantly the need that had become manageable while he was gone sprang out of control. When he raised his mouth from hers to take a deep breath, he felt as unsteady as she looked. "What are we going to do, Leah?" he murmured, rubbing a finger back and forth over her jaw.

"About what?"

"This. You and me."

Instantly she looked wary. "We're not going to do anything."

He smiled gently. "Oh, yes, we are. Don't fool yourself, honey. When two people kiss, it isn't usually like that. This is special."

She leaned back against his supporting arm to protest. "It was just a kiss."

"Just a kiss?" He grinned at her transparent effort to deny what was happening between them. "Well, I've kissed a lot of women in my life, Leah, and you're the only one whose 'just a kiss' knocked the world out from under me. Do all men affect you this way?"

Reluctantly, she shook her head.

"Then I'll ask you again: what are we going to do?"

She gave the same response, just worded differently. "Nothing. *You're* only here for a few days. *I* live here. My life is here, my kids are here. We can't do anything, Bryce."

He kissed her forehead, then released her, opened the door and waited for her to go inside. "You're being negative about this, Leah. Try looking on the positive side for once, will you?"

She gave him a frown as she turned down the hall toward the family quarters. As far as she could see, there *was* no positive side to their situation. She was falling fast for a man who lived six hundred miles away, whom she would rarely see—a man who couldn't possibly be seriously interested in a widow with four children.

But Bryce *had* found the positive aspects in the five days he'd been gone. All along he had concentrated on the reasons why a relationship between him and Leah couldn't possibly work out. Lying awake late one night, unable to get her out of his mind, it had occurred to him that maybe there were ways around the obstacles. Every problem had a solution; it was simply a matter of finding the solutions to *their* problems.

So Leah was shy, innocent, unsure. He had his own share of insecurities; they could learn to trust together. So she had four children. He had always wanted children, but they didn't have to be his own flesh and blood. He had been surprised to find that he could love another man's children, but it was true. And Leah's kids were good kids—intelligent, well mannered, polite and likable. So her life was in Angel's Peak, and his was in Philadelphia. He wasn't irrevocably bound to the city; with his MBA and twenty years' management experience, he could find a job almost anywhere. Leah could certainly provide him with the proper incentive to relocate, even to a little place like Angel's Peak.

The key was compromise. If he wanted her badly enough, he would compromise for the rest of his life if it meant spending it with her. Now he had to convince *her* of that.

Leah was on her way to her room when she saw that the door to Frank's room was open and he was standing at the window. Tapping on the door, she stepped inside. "Mr. Cameron?"

Slowly, he turned. "My name is Frank."

She smiled faintly. "Frank. I hope you'll be comfortable here. If there's anything you need . . ."

He turned away again to stare out. "I never thought I'd be a guest in my own family home. Do you know how many years this house has been in our family?"

"Since it was built," she said evenly. "And it's still in the family, Frank. When I die, it will go to my children—and they're Camerons, too."

He made a derisive noise. "Why did you have to turn it into a hotel where anybody can stay for a price? Couldn't you get a regular job?"

Leah's smile broadened. "When Bryce called to say you were being released from the hospital, I assumed it was because you were much better. I'm betting now that it was because the nurses couldn't stand you any longer."

He faced her again, leaning one bony shoulder against the wall. "Bryce tells me you have four children—two boys who look like us and two pretty little girls who look like you."

She gave him a chiding look. She knew for a fact that it was Frank who'd told Bryce about the kids first. "He was being kind. The girls look like you, too."

"How old are they?"

"Six, eleven, thirteen and seventeen."

"You were mighty young when you got pregnant with that first one."

"Yes, I was." She admitted it openly, making no excuses, offering no apologies.

"I always wanted grandchildren, but Kay—that's Bryce's ex-wife—wouldn't hear of it. After she was gone, I'd hoped that he would marry again and have a baby or two." His eyes, narrowed and alert, fastened on her. "But he hasn't shown much interest in women until lately. How old are you?"

"Thirty-five."

"They used to say a woman shouldn't get pregnant after she turned thirty, but nowadays they claim it's her health more than her age that matters. You look pretty healthy to me."

Leah choked back a gasp, covering it with a cough. "I—I...uh...need to get back to work. If you need anything, there will be someone at the desk or in the kitchen." She backed out of the room and hurried down the hall. She wasn't fast enough, though, to escape the hearty, satisfied laugh that was coming from Frank's room.

Once his brother had arrived at the estate, Peter turned stubborn and refused to come to the house to see him. He even skipped dinner that evening, although Frank hardly

seemed to notice. He sat at the middle of a long table, surrounded by the children, rarely taking time to even notice
Bryce, Leah and Martha sitting together at one end.

Whatever Frank's objections were to her, Leah was relieved that he showed no animosity to her children. For a
man who'd had little contact with kids, he got along mar-
velously with them, from Douglas down to Matthew, and
they seemed to be good for him. Even in the few hours since
his arrival he looked better—rested and more energetic. Being home with the family was going to be good medicine for
him, she predicted.

She was rising from her chair when Bryce leaned over.
"Meet me out back in half an hour," he whispered.

Aware that Martha had heard his invitation, Leah hesitated before nodding. Half an hour would give her time to
change from the dress she'd worn to dinner in Frank's honor
into jeans and boots. She slid her chair under the table, then
stopped behind Douglas. "Frank, we're having a party tomorrow night for the guests and a few friends from town.
We'd be pleased if you would come."

He looked from her to Martha. "Will Peter be there?"

The older woman shrugged. "Possibly. You know your
brother, Frank."

"Stubborn as a mule," he accused.

"Just like you," she shot back. "You know, it's not impossible for you to walk a few feet across the road to our
house to see him."

"I'm the invalid here. I need my rest."

Rolling his eyes, Bryce helped his father to his feet. "Then
how about going to bed, where all invalids should be?"

Frank pulled his arm free. "All right, I'm going. You
don't have to drag me." He addressed Martha with a steely
stare. "You tell that husband of yours that I'll expect to see
him soon."

"Stubborn old coot," she said, just loudly enough for
him to hear as he walked away. She was smiling when she

turned to Leah. "Why don't I put Matthew to bed tonight? I can read his story as well as you can."

"But Mom always does it, Grandma," Matthew interrupted.

"Yes, but tonight Mom's going to take a long, quiet, private walk in the snow. Won't you let me do it just this once?"

He considered it seriously, then nodded. "All right. Just this once."

Leah gave him a kiss before going to change clothes. When she was done, she left the house and sat down on a bench on the back porch to wait for Bryce.

He joined her a few minutes later. Silently they followed the path they had taken on their last walk. After a few minutes, though, he gave a sigh and said, "I should have warned you about Dad. He isn't intentionally rude.... Well, yeah, he is. It's just . . . he doesn't mean anything by it. That's the way he is with everyone."

"It's all right."

He gave her a sidelong look. "I'm not apologizing for him, Leah," he warned. "I'm just explaining that you shouldn't take anything he says seriously. He's just gruff and cantankerous by nature."

"I don't need an apology or an explanation. I like your father."

"I think he likes you, too—even if he doesn't approve of you having the house, or of what you've done with it."

She smiled then, bright and happy and teasing, and he thought she was absolutely gorgeous. "He may not think much of me as a homeowner and innkeeper, but he seems to think I'd be all right as the mother of his grandchildren."

He had been reaching out to touch her, to capture that smile, when her meaning penetrated the fog that was clouding his mind. It struck him around his midsection—in the region of his heart, he thought numbly. Leah as the mother of his children—it was a powerfully erotic idea.

"Would you have another baby?" he asked huskily.

"I went through most of one pregnancy and part of another by myself," she reminded him. "I couldn't do it again."

"We're talking about me. You know I wouldn't leave you alone."

He was still speaking in that husky, emotional voice that held Leah mesmerized. She shook her head to break the spell and answered him honestly. "No, Bryce, I don't know that. I really don't know very much about you." Except that he was handsome and charming. That thinking of him made her heart beat faster, that looking at him turned her bones to jelly, that simply being with him somehow made everything brighter and better than it had ever been before. Except that if any man could ever make her want and need, if any man could ever teach her to love and to trust, it was him.

She smiled crookedly. Those were the important things, weren't they?

When he moved toward her, she met him halfway, lacing her fingers through his hair as their mouths touched. They kissed hungrily, urgently. When he maneuvered his hands between their bodies to unzip her coat, she made no objection. A moment later she heard his gloves hit the snow with a soft thud; then she felt his hands, still warm, slide beneath her sweater, over her skin to her breasts. He didn't fumble with the thin, soft bra she wore, just stroked and caressed her breasts.

Except for that very brief incident in the attic, no man had touched her so intimately for longer than she could remember. Her husband had never been overly concerned with her enjoyment, had never cared if he gave her pleasure when they were together. She couldn't remember ever feeling so good, so tingly and alive, so needy.

His fingers found her nipples, hard and aching, and gently tormented them until she freed her mouth from his to drag in deep, gasping breaths of frigid air. He turned his kisses to her ear, moistly outlining it with his tongue.

"Touch me, Leah," he whispered. "Feel what you do to me... how you make me need.... Give me your hand."

Slowly she offered her hand, and he removed his from her sweater to accept it. He pressed her palm to his chest, inside the warmth of his jacket, then patiently, slowly but deliberately, slid it over the waistband of his jeans, across his flat abdomen, to the painfully hard evidence of his arousal.

The contact lasted only seconds, then Leah jerked back her hand as if burned and pulled out of his arms, turning her back on him.

"Leah?" There was no anger in his voice, only bewilderment.

"I can't. I can't do this."

Her head was down, her voice muffled, but he heard the quiver of tears. His concern instantly overrode his desire. "You can't... what, Leah?"

"I don't want to do this... don't want you touching me. I—I don't want to touch you." The halting words were lies, every one of them, but they were better than the truth. She didn't want to tell him that she was afraid, that she knew nothing about touching, about giving pleasure and making love. She didn't want to tell him that sex with Terence had been unpleasant, sometimes painfully so, that she didn't want to go through it again.

He knew she was afraid—hadn't he known all along that she needed sweet, gentle coaxing?—but her words still hurt. He needed her touch the way his body needed oxygen to live, but her response had been one of disgust. "Leah, I'm sorry. I shouldn't have done that. I'm not going to hurt you. I won't make you do anything you don't want to do. Don't you know that?"

She took a deep breath, a cleansing, calming breath, then turned to look at him. There was shame in her eyes—shame and fear. "I'm sorry."

He pulled her to him with gentle hands and held her against the hard strength of his body. He stroked her hair, the way he might stroke a tearful child, and murmured to her in soft, soothing tones. "It's all right, Leah. Just don't run away from me. Let me hold you. Let me help you." *Let me love you.*

He would give anything, he thought with a grim sigh, to know all the details of Leah's marriage. The little that she had told him had helped, but there was still so much he needed to know. What had those twelve years with Terence been like? What had she needed and wanted? What had she gotten?

She had needed love in all its forms—affection, physical intimacy, respect, gentleness, consideration, tolerance. Bryce knew that much. Had Terence given her any of those things? Sadly, he suspected that the answer was no. His cousin had taken, and had given little in return beyond the children.

In control again, Leah pushed lightly against his chest, and he immediately released her. "I need to go back and find a room for you tonight."

The cool, untouchable tone of her voice no longer annoyed him, now that he knew the depths of the passion inside her. He retrieved his gloves, then walked alongside her. "For quite a few nights, Leah. I want to stay."

She twisted her head to look at him. "To get your father settled."

Her hopefulness brought him a wry smile. "No. I want to stay until New Year's."

That was—she counted quickly—seven weeks! Her hopes sank to her toes at the same time that her heart sent up shivers of joy. But self-preservation conquered pleasure. "You can't do that. There isn't any room. We're all booked."

He gestured to the house ahead of them as they strolled across the yard. "Look at that house, Leah—look how big it is. Are you telling me there isn't one single room somewhere in there that I could use as a bedroom for the next few weeks?"

"You can't just move in," she protested. "Why? Why do you want to stay?"

"I was with Dad when he had his last heart attack, and it scared the hell out of me. You're not the only one with strong feelings about family, Leah. I'm not going to leave him here and come back for occasional visits. I want to spend some time with him—and with you. We *need* time, Leah, time for you to get to know me, to learn to trust me."

Shaken by the intensity in his eyes and his voice as he spoke, she could only manage a soft hoarseness when she responded. "And time for you to get to know me?"

He smiled confidently. "I need to learn more about your past, but . . . I already know *you*, Leah." He knew that she was going to let him stay. He knew that soon she was going to give him her trust. He knew that he was going to make love with her, and he had a strong suspicion that they were going to spend the rest of their lives together. It would just take time.

She felt helpless—not against him, but against herself. She knew already that she was going to agree to let him stay—not because he wanted it, but because she did. Because, now she had gotten over her initial shock, she liked the idea of having him nearby, of being able to see him every day, of continuing to share her walks with him every night. She knew it wasn't wise—there was a good chance that she would pay for this foolishness in heartache—but it didn't change her mind. The last time she had acted foolishly had been with Terence, but she had survived that. If Bryce turned out to be another mistake, she would survive him, too.

"Well?"

She realized that they had stopped walking and were standing at the back steps. With a slight shrug, she started to climb them. "The only space I have is a storage room on the other side of the downstairs bathroom." And down the hall from her own room.

"That's fine."

"It's very small," she warned. "Years ago my bedroom was the nursery, and this room was used by the servant who took care of the babies."

"That's fine."

"We'll have to clean it tomorrow. For tonight you can sleep in Douglas's room, and he can put his sleeping bag in Matthew's."

"I'll take the sleeping bag." Still more than a little aroused, he knew he wasn't going to sleep well, whether in a soft bed or on a hardwood floor. He closed the door behind them, then brushed a quick kiss across her forehead. "Good night, Leah." Quickly he climbed the stairs that led to the boys' rooms and disappeared.

Leah watched until he was gone, then slowly turned down the hall to her own room. Was she making a mistake in letting him stay? Probably, she admitted. Terence had sorely strained her faith in men. Was the pleasure she found in Bryce's company worth the risk?

She closed the door behind her and began undressing in the dark. As she tugged her sweater over her head, the fabric rubbed against her breasts, reminding her of the feel of his hands there, the taste of his kisses, of the strength in his body and the gentleness in his manner. Was he worth the risk?

Absolutely.

They spent the next afternoon cleaning. Leah, Laurel and Megan scrubbed the windows, floors and even the walls of the small room, while Bryce, Douglas and Matthew carried the room's contents to the empty guest house. On their return trips they brought back a bedstead with a mattress and springs, a single chest and a small table that could serve as nightstand. One of the advantages of running an inn, Leah thought as she and Laurel fitted clean cotton sheets over the bed, was that they always had plenty of furniture. There were other pieces in the guest house and the attic that she could offer, but the room was so small that it was already filled.

"Thanks, guys," she said to the four children lined up in the hall. "Now you need to get cleaned up for the party tonight. Douglas, make sure that Matthew washes his hair—with shampoo this time."

Bryce was leaning against the wall, his head tilted to one side. "What does he normally use to wash his hair?"

"Nothing, if he can get away with it. To Matthew, if it's wet, it's washed." She smoothed a wrinkle from the crocheted cotton coverlet that hung over the bed. "The party starts around six-thirty."

"What should I wear?"

He would look good in anything, she thought, sneaking a speculative glance at him. A suit, a tux, jeans, or nothing at all. That thought made her feel warm all over. She gave a little cough to clear the hoarseness from her throat. "Did you bring a suit?"

"The well-dressed executive never goes anywhere without at least one."

"What do you do?" she asked, realizing that he'd never mentioned his job, and that she had never asked.

"I'm in management with a company that does aerospace research."

She found his response depressing. The job sounded important and exciting and as far removed as possible from anything Angel's Peak—or even Asheville—could offer. "Do you enjoy it?"

"It's a job." And it was responsible for the first serious interest she'd shown in him when she wasn't in his arms.

"How can you take so much time off?"

"The head of the company is a good friend, and I haven't had a vacation in six years."

Since his divorce. Leah was getting more depressed by the minute. Giving the coverlet one last pat, she turned to leave the room.

"Leah? Thanks . . . for everything."

* * *

The guests from town began arriving a few minutes before six-thirty, and soon the living, dining and sitting rooms were full, but Bryce had no trouble finding Leah when he joined the party. He exchanged a few words with a couple from Georgia before taking a place near the door where he could watch her.

"Want a drink?"

He pulled his gaze from Leah to look at her son. "No, thanks."

Douglas mimicked his position, leaning one shoulder against the wall. "There are a lot of people here."

"Your mother must have a lot of friends." He recognized a few of the guests, and the family, of course, but everyone else was a stranger to him.

He felt uncomfortable as he watched Leah circulate through the room, speaking to this guest, listening to that one, smiling briefly at them all. Everyone, male and female alike, lighted up when her attention was directed at them, and he knew the same change came over himself whenever she was near. Still, he resented the little bit of herself that she was giving the others; he wanted all of her.

"You like my mom, don't you?"

Once again he forced his gaze back to Douglas. "She's a beautiful woman."

"And you like her."

"Yes," he admitted honestly. "Very much." He waited, curious about—and a little fearful of—the boy's response to that.

Douglas didn't keep him in suspense long. "Good. We talked it over—the kids and me—and we like you. Just be careful with her, okay?"

"Okay." Bryce watched Douglas leave for the dining room and the food across the hall. When he turned back, he was grinning. He had just been given the stamp of approval by the four most important people in Leah's life—her children. With them on his side, how could he lose?

Leah approached him silently. "You look pleased with yourself."

He looked her over admiringly. Tonight she was dressed to match her cool, elegant voice in a sweater and skirt of cool, wintry white. The simple lines of the V-necked cardigan were softened by a wide lace collar that fell in narrow points over her breasts, and the slim skirt fitted closely, without clinging to her slender hips. His fingers itched to undo the row of round white buttons that fastened the sweater, but through sheer will he kept them at his sides. "No, I look pleased with you," he disputed her statement. "You're lovely, Leah."

The first time he had told her that, she had known that he was lying. She knew she still wasn't lovely—she was just plain Leah—and he was still lying, but hearing him say it made her *feel* lovely, and that was almost as good. "Is your father going to join us?"

"I saw him just a moment ago in the dining room with Matthew and Megan."

"Matthew thinks he's gotten another grandfather."

"The next best thing to a father." He said the words without thought, naturally, simply. The only way Frank could really be Matthew's grandfather was if Bryce became the boy's father, and that, he had already decided, wasn't a bad idea at all.

"And sometimes better." Leah changed the subject. "Have you met anyone?"

"No."

"Would you like me to introduce you to some of the townspeople?"

"No." He didn't try to be polite. "I came here tonight to look at you."

Her blush was automatic. "Why do you say things like that?"

"Because I mean them. Let's go someplace private."

"I can't."

"I'll be on my best behavior, I promise. I won't try to molest you, or anything."

Their gazes met and held, icy blue and warm brown; then Leah quietly, solemnly, said, "I know you wouldn't. But I'm the hostess tonight, and I can't leave."

Bryce accepted her refusal with a wry smile that said he couldn't be blamed for trying; then, with one hand, he gestured to her guests. "How do you do it, Leah? You give them your smiles, your attention, your hospitality, your time, but they don't really touch you, do they? Do you ever let anybody close enough to care?"

You. You've gotten that close. Too close.

When she turned to walk away from him, he was afraid that he had offended her. Then she stopped and beckoned him to follow.

Most of the guests were filtering into the dining room, where the long mahogany table was filled with treats from Colleen's kitchen. Leah led Bryce in the opposite direction, to a small, private corner of the sitting room. "When I was eight, my best friend was named Barbara. When I was nine, it was Katie, and when I was ten, it was Valerie. When I was eleven, I quit having friends, best or otherwise."

"What happened to Barbara, Katie and Valerie?"

"They were adopted, and I wasn't. When I was younger, none of the prospective parents wanted me, and when I was older, I didn't want them. At least I pretended not to want them. I learned not to count on people, not even best friends who promised to be your friend forever and ever."

And not him. Bryce didn't know if she was aware of her message, but he heard it clearly. She was afraid to trust him, afraid that—like her parents, like Barbara, Katie and Valerie—he would abandon her and leave her alone, forever and ever.

He laid his hand over hers, squeezing her cold fingers together. "Leah, no one can promise forever. Circumstances change. People change."

What was he trying to tell her? That he would offer no promises of a future, of a life together? That now he wanted her, but maybe next week, or next month, he wouldn't? "Some people need promises."

He had been talking about her parents and her friends, but now he realized that she was talking about *them*. He lifted her hand to his mouth, placing a moist kiss in her palm. "I can give you this much: I'll never do anything that might hurt you, and I will try like hell to never disappoint you, or disillusion you, or make you unhappy."

She nodded once. Demanding vows and assurances without offering any of her own was hardly evidence of the trust that Bryce hoped she would learn, but she had to do things her way; it was the only way she knew. Maybe one day she *could* repay him with her trust.

From the hallway a strident voice interrupted their quiet moment. "It's about time you came out of hiding, you old goat. I wondered when you'd find the courage to see me."

Leah and Bryce exchanged glances, then rose together and went in search of the voice's owner. In the broad hallway they found Frank facing his brother for the first time in twenty-six years. They had an audience of grandchildren and party guests to witness their dark scowls and less than affectionate greetings.

"Are you calling me a coward?" Peter demanded, and Bryce started to go to his father's side to stop the affirmative reply Frank was sure to make.

Leah laid her hand on his arm. "Let them argue. Have you eaten yet?"

"They're going to ruin your party."

"No, they're not. Come on. Colleen outdoes herself on her party food." Smiling serenely, she led him by the hand into the dining room, greeting Martha on the way.

His aunt, too, seemed unperturbed by the angry exchange that was taking place in the hallway. "I told you they would argue," she said as she picked up a china plate that had been in the family for a hundred years. "Oh, doesn't all this food look wonderful?"

Leah handed a plate to Bryce, then took one for herself. "She may fuss about it, but Colleen loves cooking for parties. It gives her a chance to make the sugary desserts that we all love."

Bryce was puzzled by the women's lack of concern over Frank and Peter. A great deal of preparation had gone into this party: the house was immaculate and decorated with fresh and silk flower arrangements; the children were scrubbed and dressed in their Sunday best; and the elaborate buffet had taken hours to prepare and was being eaten from antique china at tables covered with antique linens. Meanwhile, two old men were in the hallway, calling each other names, and the hostesses couldn't have cared less.

As she slid gracefully into a seat at an empty table, Leah smiled at Bryce, seeing his confusion. "There's nothing wrong with arguing. It's a means of letting off steam, of easing the pressure. Frank and Peter haven't seen each other in years, and they parted under less than amicable circumstances. After all this time, they're not going to suddenly be best friends again. Give them a chance."

"How did you get to be so wise at such a young age?" he teased.

"Personal experience."

His smile faded. Yes, she probably knew all about unfriendly circumstances, about letting off steam and easing pressure. That unflappable control that he had often wished to see her lose was her way of dealing with pressure. He wondered if she ever got mad and yelled the way his father so often did. It was hard to imagine an outraged Leah, but any show of intense emotion—be it anger, joy or passion—would make her beauty come to life.

Passion. The gleaming silver fork trembled in his unsteady hand. He had been given a brief glimpse of her passion, and it had been almost more than he could bear. It would take time, he knew, before she gave herself entirely to him—time he could use to prepare himself for it. Loving Leah wasn't going to be easy—but it *was* going to be magnificent.

The party lasted several hours after the entertainment initially provided by Frank and Peter. Following a heated and loud argument in the hall, Peter had retreated to the sitting room, accompanied by Douglas and Laurel. Megan and Matthew had followed Frank into the dining room, and the two men had remained separated the rest of the evening.

After saying good-night to the last guest, Leah took a seat on the sofa, kicked off her high heels, stretched out her legs till her feet reached the coffee table and tilted her head back. She liked parties—a good thing, since she had to have so many—but she loved being alone in the quiet house when they ended.

"You look tired."

At least, she had once loved being alone. She could very easily grow used to Bryce's company when everyone else was gone or in bed. She smiled without opening her eyes when she felt the cushions give as he sat down next to her.

"Actually I lied. You look tired *and* beautiful."

She opened one eye. "Do you always give compliments so freely?"

"Only when they're deserved." He was sitting sideways so he could study her. Tonight was only the second time he'd seen her in a skirt. As nice as she looked in slim-fitting jeans, he realized what he'd been missing when his gaze reached her legs. Encased in sheer, creamy-tinted stockings, they were long, slender and shapely. They were the perfect length to make their bodies a perfect fit together.

He lifted one hand to touch her hair. It was full and bouncy and unbelievably soft.

"Not tonight, Bryce," she whispered, raising her head to look at him.

"Not tonight what?"

"Don't touch me. Don't kiss me."

"Why not?"

"Because...tonight I feel very...vulnerable. Don't make me want you, because I couldn't say no, and it would be wrong."

The surge of emotion that rushed through him made his smile sweet and very tender. She was the most complex woman he'd ever known—the mother of four children, yet still more innocent than most teenagers; cool and reserved outside, but filled with warmth and passion inside; wounded by love, by a man, but—he hoped—willing to try again with both. She had grown up deprived of the love and caring that most people took for granted, yet she hadn't lost her own great capacity for love. He wanted to take that love, every bit of it, and give back ten times more.

"All evening I've been fantasizing about kissing you...about undoing every button on this sweater so I could see you...." He knew from its smooth, unbroken lines that she was naked beneath it, that only eight buttons separated him from seeing, touching and kissing her breasts—eight buttons, a lifetime of fear and his hopes for their future.

Taking a deep breath, he leaned over her. "One kiss," he promised when he saw the faint alarm in her eyes. "Just one kiss, then I'll go."

Like everything else about him, the kiss was gentle. She could taste the heat, the hunger, the need—all tightly controlled. She wanted more—wanted it all—but when he raised his head, she let him go.

"Good night, Leah."

"Good night, Bryce," she whispered as he left her alone in the quiet, lonely room.

Business at the inn was slower over the next few weeks. A warm spell melted much of the snow, sending the skiers to slopes farther north for their holidays. Thanksgiving was a rather small affair, with only a handful of guests seated around the family table.

Knowing that the snow would come again, Leah was relieved by the slack period. She divided her time between her office, the workshop and the attic. She was inordinately pleased when, more often than not, Bryce joined her in the latter two places. He watched her work on the exquisite Christmas ornaments that she made by the dozen, and helped her by packing the ones for sale in tissue paper and boxes, and stacking the ones for the inn separately. He worked alongside her in the attic, patiently untangling string after string of lights, checking and replacing bulbs from the supply she kept and making suggestions for storage that would avoid the mess next year.

And they talked. He asked her dozens of questions, probing into every area of her life, curious about everything that had ever happened to her, everything she had ever wanted. No man had ever paid so much attention to her, not even Terence, not even in the beginning when, like many young men, he'd been more interested in Leah's body than her mind or her heart. It made her feel . . . special.

It also scared her. Wanting to feel special had led her to make a commitment to Terence—a commitment she hadn't been ready for and one he hadn't wanted. It had led to a long, unhappy period in her life, yet here she was, close to doing it again. She tried telling herself that things were different this time—she was thirty-five now, a mother and a successful businesswoman, not a frightened, lonely seventeen-year-old. And the commitment this time would be to Bryce, who, even on a bad day, was at least twice the man Terence had been. But the fear was still there.

Every time he kissed her, she panicked. She wanted so much more, and knew that he was offering it, but she was afraid to accept. Afraid of disappointing him, of being inadequate. Afraid of making a mistake that would cost her her heart. But she enjoyed him—his kisses, his company, his smiles. It was almost sinful to find so much pleasure in one person.

Bryce's voice interrupted her dreamy smile. "This is beautiful. Did you make it?"

She crossed the living room of the cottage that served as her workroom to join him as he lifted a small house from its protective box. When he set it on the low coffee table that stood in front of the fireplace, he knelt to admire the detailing on it.

"Peter cut out the pieces, Douglas put them together, and I painted and decorated it." Kneeling beside him, she reached out to carefully remove a piece of cotton.

The house stood eighteen inches high and was a perfect replica of the inn, from the snow on the roof down to the brass plaque beside the door. It was decorated for Christmas, with tiny green wreaths and tinier red bows on each window, and miniature white bulbs strung along the top of the veranda and the railing.

He reached out to give her a hug, pulling her off balance, and they both fell to the floor. "You're a talented lady," he said, wrapping his arms around her and lifting her on top of him.

"I'm good with my hands," she replied innocently.

"Anytime you want to show me just how good, I'm yours for the taking."

She raised herself with both hands on his chest to keep from getting too close, but that was a mistake, since the position merely pressed the lower half of her body more snugly against the lower half of his.

Bryce knew the instant she became aware of his arousal, because her face turned the color of the Christmas red around them. When she tried to move, he slid his hands to her bottom, holding her firmly against him. "This is something you need to get used to, honey," he said softly. "There's nothing shameful about it. Every time I get near you or look at you—practically every time I think about you—I get hard because I want you."

Leah dropped her head to his chest, where she could hear the erratic beat of his heart. How could she tell him that she knew nothing about desire, about rousing it or satisfying it? That she knew even less about men and the mysteries of their bodies? It was her naïveté that flooded her face with heat—but she knew her innocence wasn't responsible for the heat that flooded her body.

Carefully she moved away from him, scrambled to her feet and dusted off her clothes. Bryce got up, too.

She busied her hands with some of the more delicate decorations for several minutes before starting to speak. Her eyes were cast down, her voice low and strangely remote. "Sex with Terence was infrequent and sometimes painful and...unfulfilling. I knew nothing when I met him, and I had learned very little when he died."

Bryce was torn between anger for his cousin, sympathy for Leah and joy for himself. She was learning to trust him, learning to give him parts of herself that she'd kept hidden deep inside.

Sensing that she wouldn't welcome any words from him, he instead carefully considered hers. Infrequent, painful and unfulfilling. He had already suspected that the Terence he'd known as a boy hadn't deserved a woman as gentle and loving as Leah. He had apparently been a selfish and ungiving lov—partner, Bryce substituted. He wouldn't apply the word lover to Terence.

She set down the crocheted ornament she was holding and walked to the window. "If you want someone to sleep with, Bryce, you'd be better off finding someone in town. Someone who knows what she's doing. Someone who's... normal."

"Leah, Leah." Bryce put his arms around her from behind and pressed a kiss to her hair. "I quit looking for someone to 'sleep with' when I was twenty. I don't want someone else, Leah, I want *you*. Honey, there's nothing abnormal about being afraid. I haven't lived the kind of life you have, but do you think I'm not scared?" He paused, but she gave no reply. "I'm scared as hell that you'll be disappointed in me. I'm scared that I'm not good enough, handsome enough, smart enough, skilled enough, to make you forget the past."

She slowly turned in his arms. "Really?"

"Does that surprise you?"

"Yes. You seem so confident all the time."

He grinned. "Believe it or not, so do you, a lot of the time." Then he sobered. "I'm not going to seduce you, Leah. When we make love—*if* we make love—it will be your choice. It will be because you want me, because you need me... because you trust me." He kissed her once, gently, then released her and began gathering the strings of big white light bulbs he'd brought with him from the attic. "Douglas, Matthew and I are going to start putting these up after school today, all right?"

That was usually a job she shared with the boys, but she was more than willing to give it up to Bryce. With every day, she thought dryly, there were more and more things she was willing to turn over to him—her home, her job, her kids, her heart. If only he would accept them for forever.

"Leah, where's the ladder?"

She surfaced from her thoughts. "In the storage shed out back. Want me to carry the lights while you get it?"

He chuckled. "I've spent the better part of a week getting your tangles out of these lights. You're not touching them again. I think I can handle it alone."

She watched him leave, the long heavy strings looped over his shoulder, before she returned to her worktable. The top was scattered with an afternoon's work—delicate hearts and wreaths shaped from wire, covered with ecru or white lace and colored glass beads in Christmas red, green and gold, and lavender, pink and light blue—ice blue, Bryce had called it. "The color of the winter sky... the color of your eyes." She smiled shyly, fingering one of the pretty blue beads.

With a sigh she took a book from the tall cabinet behind her. Written by North Carolina's best-known quilter, the book had provided Leah with the patterns for her newest project. Small pieces of wood, only two inches square, were stacked at one end of the table, next to small bottles of red, green, gold and white paint. She had already transferred the patterns to the thin wooden squares; today, with no distractions—particularly handsome, sexy, dark-haired, chocolate-eyed distractions—she was ready to try her hand at painting them.

Her first attempt was a disaster. The patterns, meant to create twelve-inch squares, were reduced to little more than a square inch on the tiny plaque, leaving an unfinished border on each side. Tossing the first one into the wastebasket, she reached for another piece of wood and chose a much smaller brush.

With practice, patience and a steady hand, the results gradually grew better. When she finished the last one, her jaw ached from clenching her teeth together and her right hand was tired from the tight control she'd needed, but the squares were almost perfect. When the paint was dry, she would insert colorful ribbons through the tiny holes she had drilled in each piece and tie neat little bows for hangers, and one more project would be finished.

She cleaned her brushes, resealed the bottles of paint and grabbed her coat from the old sofa. The children were home from school now, which meant that Bryce and the boys would be at work with the lights. If she hurried, she could watch them complete her least favorite job.

She entered the house from the back, intending to pass straight through to the front door, but the sight of Frank in the sitting room, with the television set tuned to his favorite soap opera, detoured her. He wouldn't openly admit to watching the soaps, but it was a habit he'd picked up in the hospital.

"Can I get you anything, Frank?" she asked, stepping inside the room.

"You could change channels for me, so I don't have to watch this drivel."

"Why, Frank, then you'd just have to get up and turn it back when I leave." She perched on the arm of the sofa and gazed at the screen for a minute before turning to the old man. He looked like Bryce would look in another thirty years or so, she decided. He was thin and stooped, but she attributed that to his illness. He had already gained about five pounds on the diet Colleen fixed for him and was looking stronger every day. "You know, if you really don't like these shows, you could do something else."

"Like what?"

"Like get some exercise. The doctor told you to start walking, didn't she?"

He pointed out the window with a bony hand. "That's snow out there, girl. An old man like me can't go wandering around in the snow. I've got a bad heart, you know."

"Your disposition is none too good, either. I take a walk every day. You can go with me. I'll make sure nothing happens to you."

"Hmm. You take a walk every *night*—so you can be alone with Bryce. Where *is* my son, anyway? About the only time I see him is with you. He follows you around like a bull in—"

"Frank," she interrupted gently, "Bryce is outside with the boys, hanging the Christmas lights. Have you seen Peter lately?"

He grimaced at the mention of his brother. "Him? Now why would I want to waste my time with him when there are so many more interesting things to do? I could sit and watch myself grow older, or watch the snow melt, or..."

Leah tuned him out with a fond smile. She had finally reached the conclusion that Frank's greatest pleasure in being here at the estate was bickering with his brother. They groused and griped, but nothing made their day like a good, rousing argument.

"You know, you're a pretty girl—a little bit too prim and proper for my tastes, but pretty all the same. When are you going to quit making Bryce dance around for you and give him what he wants?"

"When are you going to quit minding other people's business?" she countered.

He laughed at that. "I was afraid when I first came here that you were going to be too timid to speak up. If you could have seen the look on your face when we first met—the way you turned to Bryce, as if he could protect you."

"But I don't need protection, do I? You're a harmless old man, Frank Cameron." She stood up, bent down to kiss his forehead, then left the room.

Chapter 6

When Leah stepped onto the porch, she nearly bumped into Douglas, who was perched above her head on the ladder. She swerved to avoid hitting him, calling up a greeting as she did so.

"Hey, Mom," Matthew called. "I'm helping hang the lights." He was up high, too, sitting on Bryce's shoulders, strands of wire and fat white bulbs wrapped around his neck and cascading over his arms. He was feeding the wire to Douglas, who, armed with a staple gun, was attaching it to the porch ceiling. "Don't it look neat?"

"Real neat," she agreed, sliding past them to reach the decorations Bryce had gathered earlier. There were wreaths with big red velvet bows to hang on each of the front windows—both upstairs and down—stacks of fresh pine boughs to form looping garlands along the porch railing and the wreath for the front door.

She leaned her shoulder against a post and watched them until they moved her out of their way once, then again. At last Bryce said, "As long as you're out here, you could help, you know."

"What do you want me to do?"

What a loaded question—and he couldn't even comment on it with both Douglas and Matthew so close. Lifting one hand from Matthew's leg, he pointed to the neat loops of tiny white lights. "You could start putting those in the bushes."

With a salute she picked up the first string and went to work. She had completed the shrubs on one side of the steps when one of their few guests returned. The woman stopped on the sidewalk next to Leah. "The house is going to look so beautiful, all decorated for Christmas," she said with a warm smile. "It's almost enough to make me skip Christmas at home and come here."

Leah murmured a polite response, but her gaze was on Bryce, watching him laugh and talk with the kids.

"Your husband seems to have a wonderful relationship with your sons. So many men these days just don't take the time to enjoy their children—they're busy with jobs and a million other things. Too often we put our children last, and that's such a shame."

Leah colored deeply. She opened her mouth to correct the woman's mistake, then closed it again. It would be easier to let her believe that Bryce was Leah's husband than to explain. Besides, she had to admit, there was a part of her that liked the assumption. She had decided long ago that Bryce would be a good father; now she was beginning to believe that he would be an even better husband. She was falling deeper and harder and faster than she'd dreamed possible. Falling in love.

The guest went inside, and Leah went back to work, putting her thoughts on hold. She concentrated on looping the wires over and through the fragile branches without breaking or damaging them, and on keeping thoughts of love and marriage and Bryce out of her mind.

"When you finish, Mom, come on up and supervise the hanging of the wreaths," Douglas suggested.

She slipped the last cord into the last bush, then hurried up the steps. Even in her boots her feet were numb from being buried in the snow for so long.

They hung a fragrant circle of pine on each of the downstairs windows, straightening the bright red bows; then Bryce and Douglas placed the last one on the door. The wreath was almost as wide as the door, about four feet across, and was simply decorated with two red tin doves. Narrow lengths of red ribbon extended from their beaks to a red tin heart that hung in the center.

"Are we finished?" Bryce asked, joining Leah at the top of the stairs.

Leah was staring at the wreath, seeing the heart and thinking about the serious condition of her own. "No," she replied softly, thoughtfully. "We've just begun."

He looked down at her, gauging the faraway look in her eyes. She wasn't thinking about decorations right now any more than he was. Although he had pretended not to, he had heard the woman's comment about him and the boys. What was more important, he *hadn't* heard Leah correct the mistake.

"Oh, Mom," Douglas groaned. "It's cold out here. Can't the upstairs wreaths and the garlands wait until tomorrow?"

Startled, she looked up, but met Bryce's eyes instead of her son's. "Yes, of course they can. Go on in and get started on your homework."

Both boys hesitated at the door. Leah looked from Bryce to them, then followed their glances upward, way up above her head. There they had hung not just a sprig, but an entire branch of mistletoe, with its thick green leaves and waxy white berries. She laughed softly. "Whose idea was that?"

"I confess." Bryce casually laid his arm around her shoulders. He was mentally holding his breath, awaiting her reaction. Leah disliked any demonstration of affection from him in front of the kids or the guests, an irritant that he'd willingly tolerated until now. But how could their relationship develop any further without some concessions on her part? It wasn't as if it were a secret; everyone, from the kids to Peter, Martha and Frank, as well as a large number of the guests, knew that they were involved.

Laughing again, she reached up to brush a pine needle from his hair. "Why doesn't that surprise me? Well, who am I to argue with tradition?" Locking gazes with him, she laid her hands on his shoulders for balance, rose onto her toes and brushed her lips slowly, teasingly, over his.

Matthew giggled, then clamped his hand over his mouth when Douglas shushed him. Without looking away, Bryce suggested softly, "Why don't you guys give your mother and me a little privacy? I want to show her a new tradition."

"What is it?" Matthew asked.

Douglas opened the door. "He's going to kiss her—a *real* kiss. Come on, you don't want to watch."

"What's your new tradition?" Leah asked, tilting back her head to smile at him.

He caught his breath. "I suppose making love under the mistletoe is out?"

She raised one brow. "On the front porch? In twenty-degree weather? I'm afraid so. Do you have another suggestion?"

Clasping his hands behind her back, he pulled her closer at the same time that he lowered his head. "I suppose we could try a real kiss, like Douglas said." But he sampled her lips, cold and soft and giving, only briefly before pulling back. "Leah . . . how long do we have to wait?"

She knew immediately what he meant. They were both adults. He wanted to make love to her, and she . . . Lord, how she wanted it, too. So why didn't she just say, "Come to my room tonight"?

Because she couldn't. It had to be more than just sex for her, and Bryce had said nothing about more. She knew that he liked her—he was so patient, so concerned, so sweet, so caring—but did he love her the way she loved him? *Could* he love her? Or was he merely enjoying her company while he was here? Would he forget her when he returned to Philadelphia?

A few weeks ago she had been asking the same frustrating questions about Bryce and Matthew. Now she was concerned about herself. How could she stand it if they became lovers, and then he went home at the beginning of January and she never saw him again?

"There's more going on in that mind of yours at one time than in anyone's I've ever known," Bryce said softly. He had been watching her—had almost seen her struggle as she sought an answer that would satisfy him without compromising herself. She was a complicated woman. "Have you ever done anything on impulse, Leah, without thinking about it, without considering the consequences?"

"Yes. Do you want to know what the consequences were?"

He had made a bad choice of question. Instead of showing her that not every situation required detailed analysis, he had given her the perfect opportunity to demonstrate why she shouldn't accept him as a lover yet. "I think I already know," he said grimly. "You found yourself pregnant, without a husband, without a family, without any means of support."

"I was a senior in high school. When I first found out I was pregnant, I was happy. I was naive, I guess. I thought that surely Terence would be thrilled, too, and he would marry me, and we'd be the perfect American family, with Terence going off to work every day, and me staying home to take care of the house and the baby. When he told me that he not only didn't want the baby but didn't want me either..."

He cradled her closer to his chest. When he spoke, his jaw rubbed against her silky hair. "But you're not seventeen, Leah, and I'm not Terence."

"No," she whispered in agreement. His simple argument meant everything—and nothing. She was thirty-five years old now, fully capable of risking an affair with a man who might or might not love her. But she was still so much like that seventeen-year-old girl. She still had the same needs, the same desires. The same doubts and the same fears.

Bryce raised her chin, kissed her hard and let her go. "Whenever you're ready..."

He had to know that if he tried to seduce her, he would succeed. That tinged Leah's smile with gratitude. "You'll be the first to know.... Thank you, Bryce."

Leah saw little of Bryce over the next few days. He wasn't exactly avoiding her—they still shared their meals and their evening walks—but he spent more time away from her, giving her time, she supposed, to think about their relationship. She found that she missed him a lot, even though he was living in the same house. If it was this bad now, how would she manage when he returned to Philadelphia?

When he came to her office Friday afternoon, she was pleased to see him, in spite of the work she had piled in front of her. She brushed a strand of hair from her eyes, making a mental note that she needed a trim before the round of Christmas parties began in earnest. "Hi," she greeted him with a warm, almost shy smile. "I haven't seen much of you lately."

He didn't comment on the fact that they'd had lunch together less than two hours ago. It had been an interesting meal, with Frank at one end of the table and Peter at the other, trading insults so fast and so loudly that Bryce hadn't had a chance to say more than a few words to Leah. "What are you doing?" Circling the desk, he looked over her shoulder at the monthly accounts. "Why are you working on these now? Why not wait until the end of the month when you have all your figures together?"

"Because it'll take me until then to get *these* figures straightened out. I hate paperwork." She bent her head forward to stretch her neck. While it was exposed, Bryce bent to kiss it.

"You need somebody to handle this stuff for you so you can spend all your time doing the important things, like running the inn." Somebody like himself, who enjoyed keeping track of accounts, figures, payroll, correspondence and all the minor details of a business.

"I know, but every time I think of the salary I'd have to pay someone to do it, I decide I can tolerate it a little while longer."

He walked around the desk again, then sat down in the straight-backed chair. "I'm here, and I'm free. Why don't you let me handle it for you?"

Leah wanted to accept his offer immediately, but how could she? They were already into December, and he was planning to return to Philadelphia at the beginning of the year. She had already come to rely so much on him; if she gave him this job, it would be even harder when he left.

Whom was she trying to kid? she asked herself as she leaned back in her comfortable leather chair. Even if he never lifted a finger to help her out, it would be impossible to accept his departure. She had warned herself against getting involved with a man who lived so far away, then had gone and done it anyway. She had fallen in love with Bryce Cameron.

"Where do you go when you wander off like that?" he asked, calling her attention back to him. "Sometimes it's as if we're not even in the same universe."

She attempted to smile. "I was just thinking about something."

"Want to talk about it?"

"No thanks."

"Do you care if I talk about what's on my mind?"

"Of course not. Go ahead."

He stretched his legs out, crossed his ankles and folded his hands over his stomach. In faded jeans and a dark purple sweater, he looked incredibly handsome. "I'm thinking about selling my house."

She stared at him. "I didn't know you had one," she said stupidly.

"I had to have someplace to live in Philadelphia when I was there," he joked. "When Kay left me, I got to keep the house—Derek already had one that was much nicer, according to her. Anyway, I'm thinking about putting it on the market."

"But... where will you live?"

He lifted his arms in a wide embrace. "Here. Not necessarily *right* here, but Angel's Peak."

She swallowed hard. "But..."

"But?" He gently encouraged her to ask whatever she wanted.

"What about your job?"

"I would quit. Six hundred miles is a bit too far to commute, don't you think?" He was acting casual and unconcerned, but his insides were churning. In the last few weeks he had made incredible progress with Leah, but she was still hesitant about committing herself to their relationship. Finally his father had suggested the reason: the fact that Bryce was scheduled to return to Philadelphia at the beginning of the year could be holding her back. So he had found a solution to the problem: he would quit his job, sell his house and move back to Angel's Peak, North Carolina.

He hadn't made the decision lightly. Philadelphia had been his home for most of his life, and he knew the city the way Leah knew tiny Angel's Peak. He had worked for the same company for twenty years; he made a good salary, held a position of authority and knew the personal lives of all his co-workers. He owned a beautiful home there, and his friends were there.

He had asked himself repeatedly over the last few days if he was certain he wanted to make such a permanent move. Angel's Peak offered little to compete with a city like Philadelphia. The services in town were geared toward skiers—

ski shops, motels and restaurants—but little else was available. Shopping for anything more complicated than groceries required a trip down the mountain to Asheville. If he got a job, it would have to be in Asheville, too, leaving him with a two-hour commute each day in less than ideal weather. For entertainment Angel's Peak offered a movie theater with one screen and a good high school basketball team, but nothing as sophisticated as a symphony orchestra or theater. There was one bank, one doctor and one dentist. Was he really considering giving up everything familiar in Philadelphia and spending the rest of his life here?

Yes. Because Angel's Peak had something that Philadelphia could never have: Leah.

"Can you afford to do that?" The questions coming out of her mouth were totally stupid, Leah realized, but she couldn't seem to make her brain work. She was too dazed by the possibility of Bryce remaining in Angel's Peak—with her—forever.

He chuckled. "I have some money from investments and the pension plan at work, but eventually I would probably have to get a job."

"But there aren't any aerospace companies around here."

"Honey, I'm in management," he reminded her gently. "I can work in almost any kind of business. It doesn't have to be aerospace."

"But..."

"Leah, are you saying that you don't want me living here?"

"No! I think—I think it would be wonderful." Her eyes were practically glowing. "You actually want to live here...with us?"

"With you."

"For how long?"

"Oh, not too long. Just the next fifty years or so."

A sobering thought struck her, and the light disappeared from her eyes. Nervously she picked up a pencil, replaced it, then reached for a pen and put it back, too. "Bryce, you aren't doing this just because of me, are you?"

"Sort of." He sat up straighter. "When I first met you, Leah, I told myself all the reasons why I couldn't get involved with you—probably the same reasons you told yourself. One of those reasons was the distance between us. My life, my job, my friends—they're all in Philadelphia. But you couldn't live there. You couldn't give up this house, or Peter and Martha, and uproot your kids and move so far away. But it's a simple matter for me to sell my house and quit my job."

Simple! There he went again, making things seem so easy. He was talking about a change that would scare her senseless and calling it simple. "But your friends..."

"All of them together aren't as important to me as you and your family are."

She still looked faintly troubled. "But...what if things between us don't work out?"

He left his chair and knelt beside hers. "That's a risk I have to take—just like trusting me is a risk that someday you're going to have to take."

Hesitantly she slid her fingers through his hair. It was still hard for her to return the little touches and caresses that came so naturally to him. "I'm not sure I'm worth that risk."

"I am."

Tears were building inside her, and she tried to stop them with a little humor. "You have a lot of faith in yourself, Bryce Cameron."

"No," he disagreed softly. "I have faith in you."

He left her then with a kiss and a hug, before she could argue, before she could think of more worries. She sat motionless for a long, long time, no longer dazed but considering the possibility of Bryce living in Angel's Peak. The excitement built inside her. They could see each other every day, not for the next few weeks, but for the rest of their lives.

She would have unlimited time with him, to get to know him, to learn to trust him, to love him.

Maybe he did love her, after all, even though he'd never said it. She hadn't told him that she loved him, either, but she did. Besides, merely having an affair wouldn't require this kind of major upheaval in his life; only something more permanent would. Like marriage.

That was what she wanted, she admitted—the happy, love-filled, enduring, forever and ever kind of marriage that only Bryce could give her. She wanted to be his wife. Remembering his response the night she'd told him that she had received Frank's approval to bear his grandchildren, she smiled bittersweetly. She even wanted to be the mother of his children.

Ignoring the files in front of her, she left her desk and got her coat and gloves from the closet. If she was going to think about something as important as marriage, she needed to be alone, where no one could disturb her. She needed to take a walk.

As a kid growing up in the home, marriage had been her goal in life; in spite of women's lib, she had wanted nothing more than to be a wife and mother. But marriage to Terence had shown her that there was a great deal of difference between her dreams and reality. After his death, she had decided that she would never again marry and give that sort of control over her life—over her happiness—to someone else.

But Bryce wasn't like Terence. Bryce cared for her, and he was fond of her children. Terence had married her to gain ownership of the estate, but Bryce would gain nothing from the marriage but a wife and a family. He would treat her with the same respect and affection and gentleness that she received now.

She laughed derisively. What grand dreams she had! Here she was thinking about marriage when their relationship had gone no further than kisses and occasional stolen caresses. They hadn't even made love yet. She didn't know when she would be ready for that, but she was already making marriage plans.

Her wandering path had brought her to the family plot, but she wasn't alone there. She stopped short when she saw Frank's familiar figure, heavily bundled against the cold. He was standing in front of Katherine's grave, his head bowed. Even from a distance she could see the emotion that lined his face, and, feeling guilty at intruding, she began backing away. She had taken only a few steps when he heard her and turned.

"Don't go, Leah."

Hesitantly, she walked through the gate and to his side. "I didn't mean to disturb you."

"It's all right." He gestured to the marker. "This is my Katherine. She's been dead a long time."

Thirty-nine years; Leah knew without checking the dates inscribed on the stone. Practically a lifetime, yet Frank had never married again.

"I miss her. All those years in Philadelphia I pretended not to, because I couldn't come back here and visit her. But, Lord, I wish she was still here with me." He wiped one hand across his eyes, then looked at Leah. "Do you believe in life after death?"

"Heaven?" She nodded. "I guess I do."

"Heaven." He nodded, too, solemnly. "That's what it'll be like, seeing her again. She was younger than me by eight years...a bit shy...and not very pretty to other people. But I thought she was beautiful."

Leah smiled a little. She had seen pictures of Katherine. The other woman had been plain, colorless and unassuming—a lot like Leah herself. It said something about Frank's love that he'd found her beautiful.

And what did it say about Bryce that he found *her* lovely? a sneaky little voice inside her asked.

"When she died . . . if it hadn't been for Bryce, I would have given up. But he was just a baby, and my mother was too old to raise him alone. He needed me."

"And you never married again."

"I never found a woman who could compare with Katherine." With a gloved hand, he brushed a thin layer of snow from the top of the stone. "Sometimes love is like that. You meet someone, and you know right away that she's the only woman you'll ever love or want, even if you lose her. You know that you'll never stop loving her, right up until the day you die. And if someone loves you that way, Leah, and you love him back, you can have a happiness that most people only dream about." He raised imploring brown eyes to her face. "Don't be a fool, Leah. Don't throw it away."

She shivered uncomfortably. "I don't know what you mean...."

He waved his hand impatiently. "You do know."

"Bryce has never said—"

"Sometimes the words don't come easily, but there are ways to show love without saying them."

Such as giving up his job and the city that had been his home for twenty-six years? Such as moving six hundred miles to be close? "He was married for fourteen years. How do you know that his love for Kay wasn't the kind you described—the kind that doesn't stop, that goes on forever?"

"Because if it was, he could never look at you the way he does." He laid his hand on her arm. "My son is a good man, Leah. For growing up without a mother and only a crotchety old man for a father, he's a damn good man. You couldn't ask for a better husband or father for your kids." He gave a sigh of exasperation. "What are you so afraid of, girl? Why does being loved scare you so?"

She tried to respond teasingly. "Why do you spend so much time nosing around in things that don't concern you?" But there was no light in her eyes, and her voice sounded heavy.

With a forlorn sigh, she looped her arm through his. "Come on, Frank. Walk back to the house with me."

He wasn't ready to leave yet, but if Bryce found out that he'd walked alone through the snow to the cemetery there would be hell to pay. With one last look at Katherine's grave, he let Leah lead him through the gate and into the woods.

The weekend brought more parties—one for Megan's birthday on Friday night and the annual tree-decorating celebration Saturday. Small evergreens, only two to three feet tall, were placed in each of the twelve guest rooms, the dining room, the sitting room and the family's private living room. A larger one, more than fourteen feet tall, stood in the place of honor in the living room, having been wrestled into place by Bryce and Douglas. All the guests took part in the decorating, shared the lavish buffet prepared by Colleen and her staff, and joined in singing carols when the big tree was finished. It was a thoroughly enjoyable way to spend an evening, Bryce decided when it was over. Having to go to bed by himself afterward, would be the only part of it that he would change. Sleeping alone in a bed for two, while Leah was just a few steps down the hall, was growing more difficult and less restful with each night.

He heard her soft sigh behind him, but didn't turn. It was after midnight, and the guests had all wandered off to bed. The children were tucked in, the house was quiet, and the lights, except those shining on the tree before him, were out.

Leah slipped her arms around him from behind. It was the first private moment they'd had together all evening. "The tree is beautiful, isn't it?"

"Hmm."

"I love Christmas. There was never much money for gifts at the home, but . . . there was always such peace. A feeling that for a while, at least, nothing could go wrong." Then she smiled, pressing her cheek against the soft knit of his gray-striped sweater. "It doesn't make much sense, really—my parents left me there on Christmas Eve—but I still feel . . . safe."

Bryce laid his hands over hers, clasped lightly at his waist. He could imagine her as a frightened, bewildered child, wondering where her parents were and when they were coming back, and his heart ached for her. And Christmas was supposed to be a season of love. He was surprised that she was able to celebrate the holiday at all. "Do you still wonder about them—who they were, where they are...why they left you?"

"Occasionally."

"Have you ever tried to find the answers?"

"The state tried for a while, but there was so little to go on. They didn't even know if Douglas was my real name."

"And you've never tried on your own?"

"No." She hugged him a little tighter. "They didn't want me. They must have had their reasons, and maybe they were good ones, but it doesn't change the fact that *they didn't want me.* I'm not going to show up in their lives now."

"But don't you want to know?" He turned, staying within her embrace, and wrapped his arms around her.

"No. I have everything I need right here—my children, Peter and Martha, the inn...."

He spoke hoarsely. "What about me, Leah?"

With a tremulous smile, she brushed her fingers through his hair. "Yes, I need you, too." Rising onto her toes, she pressed her lips to his, briefly at first, hesitantly, then surely and hungrily. "Stay with me tonight, Bryce," she invited, sliding her hands down to cup his face. "Please."

Clasping her hands between his, he pulled them away, then took a step back. "Are you sure, Leah?"

She nodded.

"Why?"

If he didn't seem anxious to take advantage of her invitation, she wasn't offended. He had waited a long time, willingly, patiently. She didn't blame him for wanting a few answers first. "Because you're a good, gentle man. Because you have faith in me. Because you've cared enough to let me make the decision myself." *And because I love you.* She looked at their hands, locked together, then at his face. She wanted to be with him, to be a part of him. She wanted to share her body, her life, her heart and her soul with him. Forever.

"Are you going to regret it tomorrow?" He couldn't bear it if he saw regret for their lovemaking in her icy-blue eyes.

"I will never regret anything about you, Bryce."

He raised her hands to his mouth for a kiss, then gestured for her to lead the way. He followed her to her room, where she paused, considering the proximity of Frank's room. Taking her hand once more, Bryce led her farther down the hall to his own room.

Laurel had donated a pair of pewter candlesticks from her bedroom to set atop the tall chest of drawers. Releasing Leah's hand at the door, Bryce picked up the box of matches that lay between the candles, struck a flame and held it to each wick.

Leah closed the door behind her. The candlelight gave a soft, warm glow to the small room, providing enough light to see by, but leaving enough darkness to shelter in. She took a few steps into the room, stopping near the foot of the bed, and waited. She had never taken part in a seduction before, and she didn't know what to do. Even her hands seemed to dangle uselessly.

Bryce moved slowly. From the corner of his eye he could see Leah's shadow falling across the crocheted spread, but he didn't look at her. She was nervous...but so was he. Kay's insults echoed in his brain, making his fingers tremble as he removed his watch and laid it on the nightstand. He had sworn to never disappoint Leah, but what if he did? What if she, like Kay, found him unsatisfying?

Slowly he turned to look at her. He loved her. That had to make a difference, didn't it? He didn't know when his love for Kay had died, but toward the end, their lovemaking had stemmed from habit, not passion. Not need. Not love. But what he felt for Leah was all those things—passion, need, love—and so much more. They would give him the skill, the patience, the gentleness, all that he needed to love her.

He bent to take off his shoes and socks. He kicked them under the bed, tugged his sweater over his head, dropped it onto the rug, then finally went to her. "Do you know how much I need you?" He followed her gaze to the bed and shook his head. "Not just like this—in my bed—but in my *life*. I want to spend the rest of my life with you, Leah. Every day and every night."

She raised one trembling hand to touch his lips. "Show me what to do. Teach me how to make love with you...how to touch you...how to please you."

He kissed her palm, then laid it on his bare chest. "Everything about you pleases me, Leah. The way you look at me, the way you smile. The way you walk, the way you talk, even the way you avoid looking at me when others are around."

She gave a soft, nervous laugh. "You're easily pleased."

His shoulders rose and fell in a shrug. "What can I say?"

She dropped her gaze to her hand, pressed flat beneath his against his chest. She could feel his heartbeat, strong and steady. Hers was racing at about a million beats a minute. "Can I...touch you?"

Moved by her timid request, he nodded silently, not trusting his voice to work, and lifted his hand from hers.

His chest was broad and smooth, soft warm skin stretched taut over hard muscles. She glided her hand across, then down to the barrier of his trousers. Bringing her other hand to him, she slid them back up to his shoulders.

The male body was something of a mystery to her. She had rarely touched Terence—cool and withdrawn, he hadn't invited that kind of casual intimacy—and in the twelve years of marriage, she could count on her fingers the number of times that she had seen him without clothing. Now Bryce was standing before her, welcoming her touch and, if the sudden change in his breathing was anything to judge by, enjoying it.

Her hands resting once more at the waistband of his slacks, she raised her eyes to him. Asking permission? Bryce thought, catching his breath. He couldn't stop her now if his life depended on it. He nodded in response.

She easily unbuckled his belt and pulled it free, dropping it to the floor. The button slid open; then, with agonizing slowness, she pulled the zipper to its end and touched a finger to the exposed skin above his briefs.

Bryce closed his eyes, assuring himself that she wasn't deliberately punishing him. She was unsure, innocent, inexperienced. She didn't realize the effect her questing, learning fingertips were having on him. His heart was pounding now, echoing like thunder in his ears, and his blood was heated and rushing to every part of his body, including the hardness that was swelling just below her hand.

Leah touched her tongue to her upper lip, pulled her hands back, folded them together and looked up at Bryce. He opened his eyes in time to see the anxiety in hers. "I—I don't know..."

Her misery was reflected in her flushed face, and her fingers were twisted so tightly that the nails were white. He remembered the night he had kissed her outside, when he had pressed her hand to him and she had pulled away as if shocked. His own fears forgotten, he lifted his hands to her warm cheeks and brushed his lips over hers. "Let me show you, honey," he whispered. "Let me love you."

He kissed her until her breathing was ragged and her entire body was as flushed and warm as her face. Her legs had grown weak, and she clung to him when his hands slid beneath her sweater to her breasts. He removed the jade-green sweater, then her bra, and laid her back on the crocheted coverlet. The mattress gave way under his weight when he joined her there.

Her breasts were small, firm, and aching for his touch. He stroked them tenderly before lowering his head for a kiss. Her hands tangled in his hair when his teeth nipped at her, then gently held her dusky rose nipple while his tongue simultaneously soothed and aroused.

Her cries were soft and helpless, erotically wrapping around him, intensifying his need and his restraint at the same time. He reminded himself that she was counting on him to be gentle, to teach her, to love her. She had never known the love of a man, had never known the pleasure and the ecstasy of making love—only the pain of unfulfilling sex. His needs had to wait; hers came first. Hers were more important.

Her eyes were shut, her breath coming in soft gasps. He was teaching her a new meaning for the word "want." His mouth and hands were unleashing a lifetime of wants until she thought that desire would swallow her up. The intensity of the emotions surging inside her brought her to tears, made her cry out softly, to plead for...more. She wasn't quite sure what she wanted, what she needed, other than to feel Bryce inside her. She only knew she wanted *more*, but she didn't fret over not knowing what she wanted more of. Bryce knew. He would take care of her.

He slid her slacks down her long legs, then removed her panties with one carefully controlled move. She was beautiful—incredibly, heart-achingly beautiful. Just looking at her made his heart swell with love.

She opened her eyes the tiniest bit and watched him remove the rest of his clothes. He was handsome and strong, she thought—her gaze drifting lower—and just a little bit frightening. Then he lay down with her again, and her fear faded away. He wouldn't hurt her. He was too gentle, too caring. Too loving.

"Look at me."

She obeyed his command. He was leaning over her, supported by his upper arms. His hips were fitted intimately against the cradle of hers, his arousal warm and hard against her.

"Trust me, Leah."

She smiled, her ice-blue eyes a little teary. "I do."

Coming from her, he decided, that was almost as good as a declaration of love. His eyes intensely serious, he slowly lowered his body to cover hers, gently probing and finding his place within her.

She had never known such tenderness. He took control of her body, her feelings, her mind, and moved her gently and steadily upward, making her need, making her feel, and finally letting her shatter in an explosion of... She searched her lazy, foggy mind for the right word. Of love. Yes, definitely love.

Bryce's breathing was heavy in her ear, and his heart was pounding so loudly that he was sure she must hear it. He knew he should move off her, but he couldn't; when he had filled her, he had given everything—his seed, his strength, his energy, his love. He wanted to lie with her, inside her, just a little bit longer.

He nuzzled her neck, gently nibbling the sensitive skin there. He realized that he had used nothing to protect her against pregnancy, but he couldn't find it in himself to worry about it. If she got pregnant—God, what a gift! He had given up hope of ever having children of his own—had accepted that he would have to be satisfied with playing stepfather to Leah's kids—but the possibility of creating a child from their love was stunning.

He finally moved to lie beside her, his arms cradling her close. "Are you all right?"

Eyes closed, she raised her hand to his face. His skin was damp, his breathing still irregular. She slid her fingers from his forehead to his nose, then his mouth, where he parted his teeth to capture one fingertip. All right? she echoed silently. She had never felt so good, so special, so loved in her entire life.

The sight of a single tear on her cheek distressed him, and he hugged her tight. "Don't cry, Leah, please. Did I hurt you, honey? Talk to me."

"No, you didn't hurt me," she reassured him, finally looking at him. She was both laughing and crying when she kissed him fiercely. "I never knew.... In all my life, I never knew what making love was like."

He stroked his hand soothingly up and down her arm. He had never known, either—not with Kay or any of the few other women in his past—and for the first time in six years he was at peace, past hurts healed. When Kay had told him that his lovemaking was unsatisfying, he had accepted full blame for it, but now he knew he'd been wrong. No one was to blame. Somewhere in the fourteen years of their marriage their love had deserted them, and without it they had simply been going through the motions.

It had balanced out in the end. Kay had turned to Derek, and Bryce had found Leah. With a sudden swell of emotion, he held her even closer. Now that he had found her, there was no way on this earth that he was going to let her go.

Leah rolled over, expecting to snuggle closer to Bryce's warmth, but the bed was empty. She opened her eyes to a room gray with the first light of dawn, sat up, stretched her arms above her head, then propped both pillows behind her.

When she became aware of Bryce standing at the window, wearing jeans and nothing else, she smiled, her morning suddenly brighter and happier. It was frightening how the mere sight of him could make her life seem so much richer, so much more vital. But this morning there was no room for fear or anything else—just love.

He returned to the bed and sat down facing her. When she started to speak, he shook his head and touched his fingers to her mouth.

She watched, wide-eyed, as he stood up again. Moving quickly, gracefully, he removed his jeans. He was blatantly aroused, heavy with need. He stood beside the bed, awaiting invitation or rejection, welcome or rebuff. Leah didn't say a word—simply lifted the covers for him.

He settled between her thighs, his arousal searing her belly. Ducking his head, he placed a gentle kiss on her breast; then, very slowly, he found his way inside her, luxuriating in the snug, heated feel of her. "This..." He shuddered, closing his eyes until the need racing through his body had ebbed. Then he looked at her and finished the thought. " . . . is heaven."

He didn't know if he spoke aloud—he thought he did, but with every nerve quivering, with every heartbeat echoing, he couldn't be sure. It didn't matter; she understood.

His eyes were dark and alive with emotions—tenderness, desire, need, caring—and in that moment, Leah knew that Frank was right, that *she* was right: Bryce loved her. Maybe he had trouble saying it—a lot of men did—but there *were* other ways to show love than by saying the words, and he had shown her, in the most tender, most lovely way possible.

She smiled so sweetly that his heart melted, and reached up to cup her hands against his beard-roughened cheeks. "Yes," she agreed before bringing his mouth to hers. "Absolute heaven."

Her gentle kiss quickly grew fierce, then hungry, then desperate. She had never known this kind of passion, passion that flamed to life so quickly and so violently, that threatened to destroy her with its intensity. Unlike the tender, sweet loving of last night, this time it was quick and explosive—no lazy, controlled explorations, no gentle kisses, no gradual, nerve-racking buildup—and it left them shattered, clinging to each other, gasping for breath, whispering sweet, soft, meaningless sounds.

Heaven, she thought once more. Absolute heaven.

Bryce watched Leah dress from his position at the head of the bed, the pillows soft behind his back. He was wearing his jeans again, and though he held a shirt in his hands he made no move to put it on yet. He wanted her to stay a little longer, to prolong the intimacy just a little longer, but she had insisted on getting up, dressed and out of his room now, before someone found her. And so he watched her, enjoying the sight. She zipped her light green slacks, pulled on her sweater, lifted her hair free and pushed the sleeves to her elbows. "How do I look?"

Grinning, he left the bed to grasp her at the waist and pulled her close. "Like you've spent the night making wild, passionate love."

She laughed softly, then admitted a little awkwardly, "I feel . . . wicked."

"Why should you feel wicked?" he teased. "Because we made love all night in a house with thirty other people, including my father and your children?" Then gentleness softened his voice. "Don't, Leah. Don't feel ashamed or sorry or guilty, or any of those other things. What we did last night was good and right and—"

"Perfect," she supplied.

He kissed her forehead and repeated the word. "Perfect."

She pulled herself out of his arms and walked to the door. There she hesitated, then turned back. "Bryce...the kids..."

"What about them?"

She shrugged. "I tell them that making love is something very special, that they shouldn't do it just because they want to, or they're curious, or they get carried away."

He pulled his shirt over his head and tugged it down, then straightened the collar. "Did you want to make love to me, Leah?"

"Of course I did."

"Were you curious?"

"Well . . . yes."

"Did I carry you away?"

"You swept me right off my feet," she said with a faint smile.

"Are you a kid?"

"Of course not, but—"

He laid his fingers over her mouth once more. "Making love *is* very special, but you're right: kids shouldn't do it just because they want to, or are curious, or get carried away. But we're not kids, Leah, and we don't live by the same rules. What goes on between you and me is none of your kids' business. We can make our own decisions, Leah, because we have the age, the maturity and the experience to make good ones. You're not maintaining a double standard, or failing to practice what you preach."

She kissed his fingers before removing them from her mouth. "I just don't want them to be disappointed in me."

"Don't you know how much they love you? Do you think they're going to be disappointed in you because you're human, because you care for someone besides them?" His voice grew softer with his smile. "Don't you know how much I..." He started to say "love," but he wasn't sure she was ready to hear that. He wasn't even sure he was ready to say it. Abruptly he changed it. " ...care for you?"

"Yes," she said softly. "I think I do." For once his knack for simplification didn't annoy her. Her children *did* love her, and that wasn't going to change when they found out that she loved Bryce, too. "Your father was right—you're a good man, Bryce Cameron." Leaning forward, she kissed his cheek, then was gone.

Chapter 7

When Bryce saw Leah again in the dining room after breakfast, she had changed from the green sweater and slacks that made her so lovely into a cheery red and white print shirt and jeans. She still looked lovely, he decided. But not as lovely as she had looked in his bed, wearing nothing at all.

They were alone in the house except for Frank, who was in the sitting room watching television. Martha had taken the children to church, and the guests had all gone skiing. He leaned against the door frame and watched Leah spread starched linens of rich red and bright green over the tables. "Can I help?" he offered at last, drawing her attention to him.

She looked at him and smiled. It was as dazzling as the morning sunlight that was streaming through the windows. "Yes, you can." When he started toward her, she raised her hand to stop him. "But not in here. Why don't you go sit with your father? I think he's feeling a little lonely."

"All right." Reluctantly, he left her and went to the sitting room. As soon as he saw his father in front of the television set, a warm sweater around his shoulders and a lap quilt covering his legs, the reluctance changed to guilt. He had taken time off work so he could spend it with Frank, but it seemed the only times he saw his father were when Leah was busy. A fine son he was turning out to be.

He built a fire in the fireplace and closed the doors so the warmth wouldn't escape, then sat down on the sofa.

"Good morning," Frank greeted him. He used the remote control to lower the volume, then turned toward his son. "I was beginning to think I'd have to start tagging along after Leah to see anything of you."

"I'm sorry, Dad. I . . ." He cleared his throat. "I know I haven't been paying much attention to anything else. . . ."

Frank waved off his concern. "I plan to be around here a long, long time. Go ahead and take care of her. After you're married, you'll have plenty of time for the rest of the world."

"Married?" Bryce repeated. Was it that obvious that he wanted to marry Leah? After his marriage to Kay had failed so miserably, he had thought he would never marry again, would never run the risk of failing that way again. Yet whenever he'd let himself think about marrying Leah, he'd never once thought about failure.

"Of course you'll marry her. You can't keep sneaking around behind the kids' backs—you're far too old for that. And Leah deserves more. *You* deserve more."

"I don't know, Dad," he said slowly. "I've been divorced a long time. Getting married is a big change."

"You've been *alone* a long time," Frank disagreed. "Just because it didn't work out with Kay is no reason to refuse to take a chance with Leah."

"You're a fine one to talk," Bryce pointed out, his voice full of love. "You've been alone almost forty years, and you've never given any thought to marrying again, have you?"

Frank's eyes grew misty. "Your mother was the one love of my life. From the moment I first laid eyes on her, I knew she was the only woman for me. If I couldn't have her . . . I didn't want anyone." He stared into the distance, seeing faded memories that Bryce could only guess at, and smiling gently.

Then he looked at his son again, and the smile faded. "Kay wasn't the right woman for you—never was and never could have been. I know you loved her," he added quickly when Bryce started to protest, "but you were too different. You both wanted different things from life. Kay wanted a successful husband, standing in the community, prestige and money, and you wanted . . ."

"Children," Bryce said quietly. "Someone who would give as much as she took. Someone who could share." He had never said those things out loud. Until last night he had never blamed Kay for her part in their troubles; he had taken all the blame himself.

Frank nodded. "Someone who loved *you* more than the things you could give her. Well, Leah's just about the most loving, giving woman I've ever met. Even though she is a bit prim, I couldn't ask for a better daughter-in-law."

A bit prim? Bryce thought of last night, and again this morning, in his bed—of her passion, her heat, those soft little cries she'd made when he had filled her with himself. He was torn in two—amused by the description of her as prim, and hungry to love her like that again.

"Let's go for a walk, son," Frank suddenly suggested.

"All right. Anyplace in particular?"

"Walk over to your uncle's house with me."

"Didn't Peter go to church this morning with Martha and the kids?"

"God would strike him down, the old thief, if he set one foot inside His church," Frank grumbled.

Peter was just as grumbly and cross when he found them standing on his porch, but it was clear that it was to hide his pleasure at his brother's visit. He invited Frank inside, but fixed a cold stare on Bryce. "Are you planning to come in, too?"

Bryce had told his uncle he could hate him until the day he died for refusing to let Peter talk to Frank when Terence had died. It seemed as if Peter was going to do just that. But that was all right. He had better things to do with his morning. Like loving Leah. "No," he said calmly. "I'm going back to the house. To see Leah."

He added the last part with just a hint of malice, well aware that it annoyed Peter no end to see his daughter-in-law with the nephew he despised.

"If she had any sense, she'd throw you right out," Peter mumbled as he closed the door on Bryce.

He returned to the inn and found Leah still in the dining room. The tables wore their Christmas cloths and held Christmassy centerpieces—music boxes, or poinsettias, or pine boughs encircling red and green candles. She was putting the finishing touch on the mantel decoration, a small village of ceramic houses, complete with miniature animals and people and tiny decorated trees.

He scooped her off her feet and kissed her, swallowing her cry of surprise in his mouth. He continued kissing her as he made his way carefully out of the room and through the halls to her bedroom. Delicately balancing her, he got the door open, carried her inside, shut the door with his foot and fell to the bed with her, covering her body with his.

She freed her mouth, laughing helplessly. "Bryce! What are you doing?"

"Make love to me," he demanded. "Now." He was kissing her again, her jaw, her throat, her ear.

"You must be crazy."

He shifted to press his hips against hers, so she could feel his hardness. "If wanting you is crazy, I must be insane," he whispered.

"But Frank . . ."

"Is at Peter's house. I just took him over there."

"My work . . ."

"Can be done later. I'll help you." He nuzzled the softness of her breast, wishing he could remove the shirt that stopped him from tasting her sweetness.

It was becoming more difficult to think of excuses when he touched her that way. Her nipple was budding from the heat of his mouth, swelling and aching for the warmth to enclose it. "The kids..." she whispered.

"Won't be back for at least an hour." She wanted him—he could hear it in the breathiness of her voice, could see it in the hazy blue ice in her eyes, could feel it in the moist heat from her body that cradled him—but she was reluctant. Dragging in a deep breath, he rolled off her onto his back, covered his eyes with one arm and said with mock resignation, "Go on, Leah, honey. Run while you can."

He felt the mattress move as she stood up, then waited for the sound of the door. He would just have to stay in here a while, he decided. He certainly couldn't walk around the house in this condition. As a matter of fact, he wasn't certain he could walk, period.

There was a quiet click—the unmistakable sound of the lock on the door. Uncovering his eyes, Bryce found Leah standing beside the bed, unbuttoning her blouse with slow, confident moves. She pulled it from her jeans, slid it off her shoulders and draped it over the closet doorknob. With one easy tug behind her back, the clasp of her bra came open, and it landed on the doorknob, too, dangling by one thin, peach-colored strap.

He stared, his eyes widened, his mouth dry, his throat too constricted to speak. She was beautiful... exquisite... gorgeous... stunning... lovely.

Leaning against the closet door, she removed her high-top sneakers but left her red socks on; then she unfastened the belt at her waist, but left it threaded through the denim loops. The fabric was old and worn, and the button easily popped loose. Keeping her eyes locked on Bryce's face, she slid down the zipper, then guided the jeans over her hips and to the floor, taking a pair of peach-tinted panties with them.

Stunned and weak, Bryce simply stared at her. She was thirty-five years old, the mother of four, and had the most perfectly formed body he'd ever seen. She was shy and innocent and hesitant, yet she had just made the job of undressing one of the most erotic acts he could imagine.

She moved onto the bed, climbing over him, rubbing against him, drawing an unwilling groan from him. "I've never undressed a man before," she said softly, with just a hint of a blush, as her fingers toyed with his collar. "I—I've never seduced a man before, either. What—" She cleared her throat, her embarrassment deepening. "What do you want me to do?"

He swallowed hard. Her breast was only inches from his hand—or his mouth. He wanted to feel it, to taste it, but he forced himself to lie still and do nothing. "What do you want to do?"

She cleared her throat again. "I—I want to touch you...to look at you.... But we haven't got much time, and most of all I want you inside me...like last night and this morning."

He rose from the bed and quickly removed his clothes, dropping them carelessly to the floor, then joined her once more, sinking into the softness of the mattress, against the softness of her. "Touch me, Leah," he invited, wrapping one strong arm around her shoulders and hugging her to him. "We have time, honey. Touch me."

She raised her hand, and it trembled. With fear or desire? he wondered; then he saw her eyes and knew the answer. She looked solemn, but not afraid. She knew she had nothing to fear with him, that she could stroke him, caress him, kiss him, and he wouldn't criticize or complain. He would find only pleasure in her touch.

The skin that stretched across his chest was soft, the bone and muscle beneath it hard. She touched his nipple and watched it harden, the same way hers responded to his touch. Leaning forward, she bathed it with her tongue, and he bit off a tiny little groan. When she slid her hand across his stomach, he sucked in his breath, and the muscles there flexed convulsively.

She took an innocent delight in his responses, marveling that she could give him such pleasure with no more than the touch of her hand. Then she moved her hand lower, taking the swollen length of his manhood in her palm, and all thought fled from her mind. He was taut, steely hard, yet sheathed in softness. He was heated and pulsing with the need that she had created, that she was increasing as she gently stroked him, up, down, then up again. She closed her palm around the tip, then rubbed her thumb in circles, feeling his moistness. Curious, she raised her thumb to her mouth, to taste him, and Bryce squeezed his eyes shut with a groan.

"Leah, I don't think I can wait...." His voice was unrecognizable, heavy with wanting.

"Now," she whispered, reaching for his shoulders. "Come into me now."

He lifted himself over her, his muscles tense with restraint. Last night had been easy and gentle, this morning violently hungry. This time... He groaned again when he felt her hand enclose him, guiding his way through the silken curls that nestled between her thighs, until the moist heat of her body replaced her hand. Today it would be... She moved tantalizingly beneath him, and he drove into her, filling her with his manhood, and an instant later filling her again, this time with the evidence of his release.

Brief, he completed the thought a moment later. This time it had been brief.

When the shudders racking his body finally subsided, he opened his eyes. Leah was looking at him, just a little bit awed. "I like to watch you," she said, raising one hand to his cheek. "You look so...intense."

He withdrew from her, then slowly began sliding back inside. "I do, huh? Let me see how *you* look when you—"

She chose that moment to arch against him, making him gasp as she took all of him, every inch. He remained motionless, supporting himself above her on one arm while his other hand on her hip urged her to move again, the same way. This time the gasp was hers as she repeated the action, sliding against the hard length of him, up, down, up again. Shivers rocketed through her, growing in strength until she was pleading, wordless cries rippling through her until they were followed by the most exquisite, most mindless pleasure she had ever known. Bryce was with her, accepting once more his own need and reveling once more in his own satisfaction.

He held her, their bodies still joined, his hands soothing her shivers. "Leah," he murmured thickly, pressing a kiss to her forehead. "Lovely, lovely Leah."

She lifted her head long enough to kiss his mouth. "Thank you," she whispered.

"For what?"

Her eyes met his. "For giving me more joy in the last few weeks than anyone has given me in the last thirty-five years. For showing me what it's like to feel...to want and need...and to receive. For being a patient, kind, gentle man and a patient, kind, gentle lover."

He would have told her then that he loved her, but his throat was tight, the lump there blocking his voice. Instead he gathered her even closer, shut his eyes and buried his face in the fragrant silk of her hair. In a heavy voice he said at last, "We need to talk, Leah."

He sounded so ominous that her body stiffened with dread. "About what?" she asked cautiously.

"Last night. This morning. And now. I—I wasn't exactly...prepared for this."

She looked at him without a hint of understanding. "Are you disappointed?"

There were times, Bryce thought, when the innocence he found so captivating could present something of a problem. "No, not at all. That's not what I'm talking about, Leah. I mean...birth control. Contraceptives."

She blushed. "Oh."

That tiny response answered the question he had been about to ask: she hadn't been prepared, either. But he hadn't really expected her to be. He had known that she'd been celibate since Terence's death. Smiling reassuringly, he hugged her closer. "I'll take care of it, okay?"

She smiled, too, with gratitude and relief. "Okay."

Bryce stroked her back, running his hand lazily up and down her spine. "Leah, if you get pregnant...you know I'll be here, don't you?"

The last of the tension eased from her body, allowing her to mold herself against him. "Yes," she said huskily. "I know."

The most delicious laziness stole over her while they lay there in silence. She wanted to stay like this forever, just the two of them, naked and together. But she knew they didn't have forever. Not today, at least. "What time is it?"

He raised his wrist enough to see his watch. "Noon." With an exaggerated sigh he said, "I know, the kids will be home in about fifteen minutes." He rubbed her breast, gently pinching her nipple, then slowly released her. "Run away with me, Leah, to someplace where there aren't any distractions."

She slid from the bed and quickly retrieved a robe from the closet. Shy again, Bryce thought, a surge of protective love rushing through him. Then he saw the wary look in her eyes. Sitting naked on the edge of the bed, he caught her hands. "What's wrong?"

"My kids aren't distractions," she said uneasily. "They're . . . my life."

He stood up and put his arms around her. "Being a distraction isn't always negative. *You're* the loveliest distraction I've ever seen. I just meant that we don't get a whole lot of privacy here, you know? I want to have you to myself. I want to make love to you forever." He heard the front door slam and a familiar voice yell, "Mom?" and quickly released her.

He had just enough time to drag his clothes on. Snatching up his shoes, he gave Leah a kiss and quickly left her room. As the door closed behind him, Matthew came racing around the corner at the end of the hall. "Hey," the boy greeted him.

"Looking for your mom?"

"Nope. I was gonna ask her where you are. What are you doing?"

"I'm going to find a place I can sit down and put my shoes on."

"Why don't you come up to my room? You can sit there, and I have to change anyway." He tugged at the tie around his neck. "Mom says we have to dress nice for church, but I have to change as soon as I get home so I don't get dinner on my clothes."

Bryce followed him upstairs, taking a seat on the bed while Matthew disappeared into the closet. "How long are you going to stay here?" the boy called over his shoulder, tossing a long-sleeved sweatshirt onto the floor. A pair of sweatpants and bright orange sneakers followed.

"As long as I can," Bryce replied, tugging his own shoes on while he studied the orange ones lying near his feet. Kay would have had a fit before she would have allowed a pair of shoes that color inside her house.

Matthew reappeared and stripped to his underwear with the unconcern of a child. Dropping to the floor, he put on a pair of black padded soccer socks, his sweatpants and the shoes, meticulously tying the laces into bows that consisted of four loops and two knots each. Then he lay back, folded his arms under his head and stared up at Bryce. "You keep awful busy."

"I know. I've been spending some time with your mother."

"I haven't seen you much."

Bryce stood up and gathered the clothing Matthew had dropped to the floor. First his father, now Matthew, he thought with dismay. Who would be the next one to prick his conscience? "Well, after lunch, why don't you and I do something together—just the two of us?" he suggested as he hung the child-sized suit on child-sized hangers in the closet.

"Can't. Today's the Christmas parade in town, and we always go to the Christmas parade. You'll come, too, won't you? And Uncle Frank?" Jumping up again, Matthew pulled his sweatshirt over his head while waiting for an answer. "Do you think Mom forgot? We always go, but she's been kind of busy lately, too—with you, I guess."

"I'm sure she didn't forget. If Dad feels like going, we can all go together, okay?"

When Matthew mentioned the parade over dinner, Leah pressed a kiss to his forehead. "Of course I didn't forget. We always go to the parade, don't we?"

"Yes," Martha agreed. "*Everyone* goes." She directed a stern look at her husband, then Frank.

"It's too cold to be standing out watching a Christmas parade," Frank grumbled. "Especially with *him* along." He jerked his head in Peter's direction, but when he saw the disappointment in Matthew's eyes, he relented. "But I suppose I could do it this one time."

The boy was clearly pleased. "What about you, Grandpa? You'll come, too, won't you?"

When Peter grudgingly said yes, Matthew leaped from his chair with a whoop. "Oh, boy, this is gonna be neat!" he exclaimed. "Just like a real family!"

A real family, Leah reflected as they drove in two cars to downtown Angel's Peak. Indeed, they were. But, as soon as they found parking spaces, the family split up, Douglas going off with his friends, Laurel and Megan with theirs. Martha offered to stay near the cars with the two older men, while Leah, Bryce and Matthew strolled along the crowded sidewalk.

When they passed a drugstore, Bryce grinned teasingly at Leah. "Wait here, will you? I need to get something."

"Can I come with you?" Matthew asked, unaware of his mother's blush.

"Not this time. You stay with your mother." He disappeared inside the store, returning less than five minutes later.

"What did you buy?" Matthew asked, reaching for Bryce's hand.

Bryce made sure the package was tucked deep inside his coat pocket before reaching for Leah with his free hand. "You're a nosy child, Matthew, just like your Uncle Frank. It looks like the entire town has turned out."

"They always do," Leah replied. "In a town as small as Angel's Peak, you do what you can for excitement—but you know that, don't you? I keep forgetting that you used to live here. Have you seen anyone you know?"

"The people I knew were kids the last time I saw them. I doubt if I would recognize any of them." Hearing the siren of Angel's Peak's one and only police car, the signal that the parade was about to begin, he slowed his steps. "We'd better head back."

Once they rejoined the others, they took up their places at the curb, Matthew sitting high on Bryce's shoulders. Bryce laid his arm over Leah's shoulders, pulled her close and nuzzled her ear, enjoying her soft fragrance. "Now that *that* little problem is taken care of, will you spend the night with me tonight?" he whispered.

Startled by the question, she turned a delicate pink, then looked around quickly to be sure no one else could hear. "I don't know," she whispered back. "Maybe part of it?"

His smile was resigned. "If that's the best you can offer..."

She knew he wasn't really annoyed, but she tried to explain, anyway. "Sometimes people come looking for me in the middle of the night—one of the kids or a guest or Martha. If I weren't there, they would worry."

"What if *I* come looking for you in the middle of the night? Will you let me stay?"

She looked up at him for a long, long moment. *Forever and ever.* "And if someone found you there?"

"Would that be so bad? Leah, these people—our family, your guests—they're not blind. They know what's going on. Do you think they'd be shocked to find us together?"

Leah couldn't believe they were having this conversation in hushed whispers with Matthew perched above them, Peter, Martha and Frank beside them, and a parade passing by in front of them. "We'll talk later, okay? During our walk tonight?"

Deliberately he bent to kiss her. "All right. Later."

"Later" came much more quickly than Leah would have liked. As soon as Matthew was tucked into his bed—by both Leah and Bryce, something new that the little boy liked very much—they got their coats and set off into the woods.

"Are you ashamed of our relationship?" Bryce demanded, breaking the silence around them.

"No, of course not."

"Then why do you want to pretend it's not happening?"

"I'm not pretending that, but just this morning, Bryce, you told me that what goes on between you and me is no one else's business, and now you're suggesting that we share a room, and the hell with whoever finds out." She said it in one long rush, then caught her breath and looked up at him, only to see him smiling.

"I've never heard you swear before," he teased. "Okay, Leah, we'll do it your way. Whenever you're in the mood to use my body, just let me know—"

She gave him a shove. "Would you stop it? Sometimes you make me want to scream!"

Catching her arms, he held her to him. "I thought you came pretty close to it this morning," he said in a confidential whisper.

She made a halfhearted effort to pull away from him, then burst into laughter. Gently she brushed his hair from his forehead, tickling him with the fuzzy knit of her glove. "Oh, Bryce, you're good for me, you know that?"

Her sudden softening had a devastating effect on his body. He tried to ignore it by continuing with his teasing. "*I* know it, but I wasn't sure if you did. Are you sure you don't want to run away with me?''

Dreamily she considered the idea. ''No responsibilities. No job, no guests, no paperwork, no children...'' Clarity returned to her eyes. ''Not that I mind the children—I love them very much—it's just that I've been with them twenty-four hours a day, seven days a week, ever since they were born. But they're not a burden, real—''

Bryce stopped her with a gentle touch. ''I understand, Leah. You're the best mother a kid could possibly have—don't ever think otherwise. But everyone deserves a break now and then.''

''Where would we go?'' she asked, dislodging his hand, thinking longingly of a day or two in Asheville or Atlanta, or maybe even Charleston.

''Philadelphia.''

She stared at him. ''Philadelphia?''

''You sound disappointed.''

''Well...it's not exactly my idea of a romantic geta-way.'' But then, neither were Asheville or Atlanta. Charleston, maybe—the pictures she had seen of it were romantic enough.

''Philadelphia can be very romantic, if you see it with the right person.'' He paused briefly before continuing. ''I need to go back. I have to put the house on the market, pack up my stuff, turn in my resignation—that sort of thing. It shouldn't take more than three or four days.'' There was another short hesitation. ''I'd like you to go with me, Leah.''

She walked away, brushed snow from a fallen tree trunk and sat down. ''You're really going to do it, then.'' Give up his job, his house, his life.

Bryce crouched down in front of her, where he could see her face. ''Yes,'' he agreed. ''Of course, if it bothers you this much, maybe I shouldn't.'' Quickly he raised his hands in front of him. ''Just teasing.... *Does* it bother you so much, Leah, that I want to live here?''

He was willing to give up so much for her, and what had she given him? Nothing but difficulty. "No," she replied softly. "I think it's wonderful. I think you're wonderful. And I can't imagine what in the world you see in me."

Bryce rested his hands on her thighs, balancing himself, and answered very gently. "I see a beautiful woman who is more giving, more sharing and more loving than anyone I've ever known. A woman I would like to spend the rest of my life with."

It wasn't "I love you," Leah considered, but it was enough. With a soft sigh, she opened her arms to him—her arms, her heart and her soul.

Over the next few days Bryce repeatedly broached the question of a trip to Philadelphia, but Leah repeatedly brushed it off. She couldn't spare the time away, she insisted. She had too much to do—planning the annual caroling party for the coming weekend and the open houses for Christmas week. She hadn't done her shopping yet, and Megan and Matthew needed costumes for the pageant at school. The monthly records for the inn were in a mess that had to be straightened soon, the inn was heavily booked for both weekdays and weekends until after New Year, and who would look after the children and Frank while she was gone?

"You're afraid to go, aren't you?" Bryce accused after yet another futile discussion in the workshop one morning. "Afraid of what the kids will think—afraid of what Peter and Martha will think. For God's sake, Leah, you're an adult! You don't need their permission to do something for yourself."

"No," she responded tiredly, "but I need their respect."

"And you think going to Philadelphia with me for four days—and, heaven forbid, four nights—will cost you their respect?" He tugged at his hair in frustration. "Leah, you've spent the better part of every night since Saturday in my room. Sharing a bed with me here is no different from sharing a bed with me six hundred miles from here, except there I'll be able to wake up with you.''

He added that last part with a sullen frown, looking for all the world like Matthew in a pout. It made Leah smile, but the smile faded quickly. She put down her paintbrush and folded her hands together tightly. ''Is that what this trip is about, Bryce? Having sex whenever you want? Spending an entire night together instead of only part of one? Not having the distractions of the kids or my job?''

She looked disappointed, and he had sworn long ago that he would never disappoint her. He couldn't help himself this time, though. ''Yes, that's part of it,'' he admitted defensively. ''Is it so wrong that I want some time alone with you, not just a few hours here or there, but completely alone?''

She felt honored that he wanted to be with her, and she said so softly. Then she admitted, ''You're right, I *am* afraid. If I walk into that house and tell our families that I'm going to Philadelphia for a few days with you, they'll know that I'll be sharing your bed. They'll *know*. The kids will be upset. And as much as Peter and Martha love me, they're still Terence's parents, and Peter still doesn't like you. I don't want to do anything to hurt them.''

''But it's okay to hurt me.'' He knew he sounded like a spoiled child, but he *was* hurt. She had just admitted that she didn't want her in-laws and her children to know that they were lovers. He understood her reasons for wanting to keep him a secret part of her life, but it still hurt.

''Bryce—'' She reached across the table to take his hands, but he pulled back.

''No, that's okay.'' It was an obvious lie—there was nothing okay about the situation—but he pretended anyway and gave her a taut smile. ''I was planning to wait until next Monday, to see if I could change your mind. But since you don't want to go, I think I'll see if I can get reservations for this afternoon.''

She had never seen him angry, but there was no mistaking the emotion in his face as he shrugged into his coat, and, for the first time in ages, she became angry, too. "That's not fair! You won't even try to understand my position."

"What position? You haven't taken one, Leah. All you're doing is hiding behind the excuse of the kids. They protect you from everything, don't they? And now you're using them to protect yourself from me."

"I wasn't aware that I needed protection from you," she said coldly, "but maybe I was wrong. If I've used the kids as an excuse, it's only because you refuse to accept my answer. *I don't want to go to Philadelphia with you.* Is that clear enough?"

He stared at her for a long time before answering with a single, ice-cold word. "Absolutely." When he walked out, the door slammed behind him.

Leah stood motionless for a moment, then very calmly picked up the paintbrush and turned back to the ceramic stocking-holder angel she'd been working on. The angel was a gift for Bryce, so that the stocking Laurel and Megan were making for him could hang with the rest of the family's. But she was too upset to work, and, her hand trembling, she put the brush down again and rested her fingers on the cool, haloed brown head.

She had lied to him. She *did* want to go away with him—to Philadelphia or anyplace else. It just wasn't that easy. She couldn't leave her kids or the inn during the holiday season simply because she wanted time alone with Bryce. She couldn't so easily admit to her family that her relationship with him was intimate. She couldn't shirk her responsibilities.

But didn't she deserve a holiday? Since Douglas had been born almost eighteen years ago, she had never spent a night away from the kids, except when each of the last three was born. She had never taken a vacation just for herself, not even a weekend trip to Asheville. In three years she had never taken a day off from the inn, not as long as there was a single guest in residence. Wasn't it time now?

Working hastily, she put away her paints, cleaned her brushes and set the workshop in order; then she left for the inn, pulling her coat on as she walked. She went first to Bryce's room, but he wasn't there. With forced calm she searched the house for him, stopping at last at the front desk. "Vicky, have you seen Bryce?"

Sensing trouble, the clerk met Leah's gaze slowly. "He...he left."

"Left?"

Vicky shrugged. "He got the airline numbers from the book, made a couple of calls from the phone room and left just a few minutes ago. With a suitcase." Reading the surprise and hurt in her boss's eyes, she hesitantly asked, "Didn't you know he was going?"

"Yeah. I just didn't think..." She sighed heavily. She just hadn't thought, period. "I—I'll be in my office, okay?"

"Leah? Is anything wrong?" Vicky asked sympathetically.

"No. No, everything's fine." But her smile wasn't fine; neither was the sheen of tears in her eyes, nor the way she bit her lip.

In her office she closed the door on the rest of the inn and immersed herself in the receipts, lists, schedules and inventories that littered her desk. For a while she managed to forget that Bryce wasn't down the hall with his father, or making one of a dozen minor repairs around the house, or waiting for Matthew to come home from school. She forgot that he'd been angry the last time she saw him—angry and hurt. She even managed for a while to forget that he'd left the inn without saying goodbye to her.

He would be back in a few days. He would take care of his business and come home, where he belonged. He would probably even call tonight, and he would tell her that he missed her, and she could tell him that she was sorry.

She told herself all those things through the afternoon and evening, right up to the time she fell asleep. The next day she found it harder to believe them, and by Friday she was starting to worry. Even the children, who had been satisfied with her vague excuse about "business," were beginning to show concern. Just how long would his business take? they asked. And why hadn't he said good-bye? Why hadn't he called? Had he changed his mind about returning to Angel's Peak? Had he decided that he liked the city better after all? She couldn't answer their questions, or ease her own fears.

"You know the nice thing about airplanes, Leah?"

She was supposed to be working but had spent the last half hour staring out the window at the snow. Now she turned slowly to face Frank. "What's that?"

"They fly on schedules. The plane that took Bryce back to Philadelphia—it'll be making that same flight this afternoon, and tomorrow afternoon, and the next day.... Why don't you make sure you're on it next time?"

"I can't do that, Frank."

He settled into the straight-backed chair, crossing his legs and folding his arms stubbornly over his chest. "Why not?"

"I've got too many things to do."

"Like what?"

"Well, there's the party tomorrow night."

"You think we can't go out and sing a few Christmas carols without you?"

"But the buffet afterward—"

His brown eyes were sharp and chiding. "Miss Colleen does the cooking in this house, not you."

She acknowledged that with a sigh. "I have responsibilities, Frank. There's the inn."

"Good Lord, girl, you've got a staff that's efficient as hell. They can get along just fine without you. We can *all* get along just fine without you... except Bryce."

She clutched at that thought, wanting to believe it with all her heart. But if he needed her, why hadn't he called? Why hadn't he given her just one more chance? "What am I supposed to do with the kids, or have you forgotten about them?'' she asked, using her final reason.

Now he looked insulted. "Have *you* forgotten about *me*? I'm perfectly capable of keeping an eye on four kids, and, if I need any help, there's Martha and Peter right across the yard." He hesitated, then looked at her with a kindness she had often seen in Bryce's eyes. "What's the real problem, Leah? Those are just excuses—you know it, and I know it. Why don't you just get on that plane and go to Philadelphia?"

He was right. She'd been through the excuses too many times with Bryce not to recognize them for what they were. They really didn't matter. Only the truth mattered. "He was angry with me when he left, and he . . . he hasn't called. He didn't even say goodbye." She rushed on, not wanting to give Frank time to respond. "He has friends there, Frank, and a job and a house—it's his home, more than Angel's Peak ever was. Now that he's there, what if he's decided that he doesn't want to come back here? What if he's decided that he doesn't really want me?" Her voice grew weak and sad. "I don't have any experience with this kind of thing. If I went six hundred miles without an invitation, and he wasn't glad to see me . . ." She shrugged, unable to continue.

"You had an invitation," he reminded her. "Numerous ones. Leah, we're not talking about some stranger here— this is Bryce. If you love him enough to commit yourself to him, then you've got to love him enough to trust him. You've got to know he wouldn't do anything to hurt you. And you've got to know that if you showed up on his doorstep, he would welcome you."

She wanted to believe that, but she was still afraid. "I've never been on a plane before."

"It's fun. You'll enjoy it.'

"I've never been in a city before, either. Philadelphia is a whole lot bigger than Asheville."

"You'll enjoy that, too. It'll make you appreciate Angel's Peak when you get back." He was gruffer now, more his usual self. "You call the airline and get yourself a reservation on the first flight out tomorrow. That will give you this evening with the kids."

Leah was reaching for the phone when he started toward the door. Pausing, she smiled her first smile in two days and said, "Thank you, Frank."

"You just have a good time."

A good time? Leah felt as if she didn't know the meaning of the words when she climbed into the cab Saturday afternoon. She wanted more than anything to run back inside the terminal and catch the next flight back to Asheville. She had been foolish to come here, to let Frank convince her that Bryce would be glad to see her just because that was what she wanted so badly to believe.

Well, she would find out soon enough. If he didn't want her there, he would say so, and she would go back home and fall apart. But if he did want her... That would make all her jitters worthwhile.

"This is the address," the cabdriver said, glancing over his shoulder at her.

She stared at the house. It was beautiful, of brick, two-storied, with stately white columns that reached to the roof.

"Want me to wait?"

She started to say no, then realized that Bryce might not be home. If he wasn't, she would have to go somewhere; it was too cold to wait outside for him. "Yes, please." She got out and walked up the broad pathway to the door.

The bell echoed through the house, its tones faint through the heavy door. Leah twined her fingers together and waited, and after a moment the door opened.

Bryce's chocolate-dark eyes widened slightly in surprise; then he smiled. "Hello."

Her own smile was weaker. "Hi."

He leaned one shoulder against the door frame, looking unconcerned and relaxed and incredibly handsome. "What are you doing here?"

Leah dragged in a shaky breath. "I'm not sure. Most likely making a fool of myself."

His smile deepened, but was still cool and a little bit guarded. "Somehow I can't imagine the very cool and proper Leah Cameron ever making a fool of herself."

"It happens to the best of us." Why didn't he do something—invite her in, take her in his arms, or tell her to go to hell? she wondered fretfully. She untwisted her hands and shoved them into her coat pockets, then shifted her weight from one foot to the other.

"Why are you here, Leah?" He folded his arms over his chest, unmindful of the cold. He wanted to greet her the way a man should greet his lover, with an embrace and a long, hungry kiss, but he remained where he was, waiting for her answer. In his heart he knew why she had come, but he wanted to hear her say it. He wanted to hear the words out loud, so he could treasure them.

He was asking a lot of her, but she knew she owed him a lot. If he would just give some sign that he was glad to see her, it would be so much easier, but he was simply watching and waiting, patient as always. She took a deep breath, wet her lips with the tip of her tongue and plunged in. "I'm here because I've missed you. I—I lied to you that day in the workshop. I *did* want to come here with you, but...you were right—I was afraid. I've spent half my life alone, and I've lived the other half for my family. Everything I did, I did for them. They were the most important part of my life." She dropped her gaze, away from the solemnity in his, then looked at him again. "This is new to me, Bryce. I've never had a lover, never had anyone to care about, anyone to give to. I don't want to hurt you. I don't want to lose you. You've given me so much, and I've given you nothing in return, but . . . I'm trying."

If he had waited one instant longer to respond, her heart would have shattered into a million pieces, but he didn't wait. He stepped forward, his arms open, welcoming her into his embrace. Into his heart. Into his love.

They shared a kiss that left her weak and him hard. He wanted to make love to her right there on the floor, to remove her clothes and suckle her breasts, to stroke her until she cried, to fill her body with his again and again. He wanted to hide away inside her, to make up for the loneliness of the last three days, to chase away the bleakness that had come from living without her. His need was sharp, hard, unrelenting, but he forced it back. Raising his head, he smiled lazily and said, "You've given me everything, Leah." Including a hunger that couldn't be filled. "Would you be disappointed if I said that I really need to make love to you now?"

It sounded like a wonderful idea to her. She had been wanting and needing him for most of her life. "I would be disappointed if you didn't. My bags are in the taxi. Let me pay him—"

"I'll do it." But for a moment he made no move to release her. For just a moment he needed to hold her. Then, quickly, he let her go and went out to the cab.

Leah looked around curiously while she unzipped her jacket. To the left were wide doors leading into a very formal living room, and to the right was a broad, curving staircase. The entry where she stood was sparsely furnished with only a Queen Anne table, an oriental vase and a painting, but the overall impression was one of elegance.

A rush of cold air brought her attention back to the door as Bryce came in. He set her suitcase and shoulder bag on the floor, took her coat and hung it up, then wrapped his arms around her again. "How long can you stay?"

"How long are *you* staying?"

"I was planning to go home Wednesday. Is that all right?"

She wondered if he realized that he had called Angel's Peak home, or if he knew the rush of happiness that gave her. Rising onto her toes, she pressed a hard, excited kiss to his mouth. "That's perfect," she murmured. "Absolutely perfect."

She expected him to take her straight to bed, but instead he gave her a tour of the house, delaying the inevitable. Prolonging the anticipation. When they went upstairs he carried her bags, showing her the two guest rooms before they reached the master bedroom. In the doorway he paused, his eyes questioning.

The choice was hers, Leah realized. Did she want the respectability of a guest room or the comfort, the security, the sensual pleasure, of sharing Bryce's room? It was no contest. Taking her shoulder bag from him, she carried it to the center of the room, set it on the floor and turned in a slow circle.

There was an air of elegance in this room, too. It was large, dominated by a queen-size, four-poster bed of rich, gleaming cherry. There were matching pieces—a dresser, chest, nightstands—and a heavily upholstered sofa, chair and chaise. The rose print cushions were coordinated with the bed linens and the soft rose wallpaper. It was a woman's room—not frilly enough to make a man uncomfortable, but definitely decorated by a woman. By Kay.

Bryce watched her from the doorway, judging her response to the room. When she completed her slow, assessing circle, she faced him, her expression serious. "You have a lovely house."

Why didn't that feel like a compliment? he wondered. "Thank you."

"It's very elegant. Very rich." She slipped her shoes off, and her stockinged feet sank into the thick silver carpet.

He responded with a simple nod.

Grasping the hem of her sweater, she pulled it over her head and let it fall across the chaise. "Kay decorated it, didn't she?"

"Yes." He watched as she tugged her shirt from her slacks and unfastened each button. His throat was dry, his chest tight.

The plaid blouse joined the sweater, a vivid splash of turquoise against the subdued rose. "She's been gone six years, hasn't she? And you haven't changed a thing." She dropped her bra and undid the button on her slacks. Finally she stopped and looked at him. His chest rose rapidly under his gray-striped sweater, and beneath the soft charcoal fabric of his trousers, she could see the evidence of his arousal.

Raising her eyes to his face again, she asked solemnly, "Am I the only one taking part in this?"

The suitcase that Bryce still held hit the floor with a thud. He closed the door behind him and walked across the room to her. He replaced her hands with his own, pulling the zipper to its end, sliding her slacks and panties to the floor, then hastily discarding his own clothes.

Secure in the circle of his arms, she gently cradled his hardness, caressing the heated length. "Did you miss me?" she asked, nipping at his lower lip.

"Only once," he insisted, backing toward the chaise and pulling her with him.

"When was that?"

"It started the moment I left you—" he sat down, his legs stretched out, and lifted her on top of him "—and lasted until I opened the door and saw you there." He helped her settle across his hips, then reached down to cup his hand over the satiny curls between her thighs. With one finger he stroked through the curls, touching the budded, aching part of her, sliding gently inside her. She was ready for him, moist and heated, but he didn't take her, not yet.

He kissed her mouth and her throat, traveling a familiar path to her breast. Holding her nipple between his teeth, he suckled it, torturing her with his tongue while, much lower, he tortured her with his hand, stroking gently over her heat.

Desire simmered through her veins, growing more intense, more desperate, until she cried out, helplessly pleading, unable to bear his torment any longer. Shuddering with the force of her release, she sank against him, struggling to breathe, to relax, to regain control of herself.

But Bryce didn't give her that chance. Using his greater strength, he lifted her onto him, arching into her, surrounding his aroused flesh with her warmth. He guided her with the gentle pressure of his hands, aroused her with the soft taste of his kisses, encouraged her with the erotic whisper of his words, and this time, when the end came, it claimed them together.

Chapter 8

"It didn't matter."

Leah opened her eyes slowly. The sun that had been so bright in the sky when she'd arrived at Bryce's house was gone now, and twilight was settling over the room. "What didn't matter?" she asked after a delicately hidden yawn.

"The house. I never changed anything after Kay left because it didn't matter." He yawned, too, then settled Leah more comfortably at his side. "It wasn't a home. It was just a place to sleep at night." He looked around in the dim light, then hid his face in her hair. "It's pretty awful, isn't it?"

"No, it's beautiful."

"Just like in a magazine. The kind of place that you can't believe anyone actually lives in."

Leah stifled a giggle, because that was precisely what she had thought. The house was elegant and beautiful, but unreal. A setting for his elegant ex-wife. "Do you see her often?"

"Kay? Once in a while. We have some of the same friends." He glanced at the luminous numbers on the clock beside the bed and groaned. "Damn, I forgot—"

Leah was unceremoniously dumped from his arms as he left the bed. Rising onto one arm, she warily watched him. "Am I in the way here?"

He grinned at her from the open closet, where he was going through the pockets of a classically tailored gray suit. "Don't be ridiculous. I turned in my resignation at work Thursday, and my boss wanted to give a little party for me. I knew it was tonight, but seeing you erased it from my mind." He found the scrap of paper in the trousers. "Eight o'clock. There's still time."

It was six-thirty, Leah noticed. The caroling party at home would be starting about now, and she was missing it. Instead she was going to spend the evening alone in Bryce's house while he went to a party of his own.

"Did you bring a pretty dress?"

Her eyes jerked to his face. "What?"

He repeated the question. "Marv's wife Tara likes to show off her new clothes, so their parties are always pretty dressy."

She was still staring at him, her expression blank. "You want me to go with you?"

"Of course I do. Come on, Leah, you don't think I'd leave you here and go alone, do you?"

"But they're your friends. I won't know anybody. I won't fit in."

He walked to the bed and leaned over her. "You'll know me. And you fit perfectly with me." His lips brushed hers in a gentle kiss. "If you don't want to go, honey, we don't have to."

She didn't—the idea of meeting his friends made her nervous—but she couldn't let him skip a party in his honor. "The only dressy outfit I brought is that white sweater and skirt." She stretched sinuously, her arms high above her head, then left the bed. Her suitcase with her robe was across the room, but the sweater Bryce had worn was at the foot of the bed. Modestly she reached for it, pulling it over her head. It was warm, too big, and smelled of him. She lifted her suitcase to the dresser, opened it and pulled out the clothes. "Will this be okay?"

Bryce's smile was slow, sexy and lascivious. "I've had fantasies about you and that sweater since the first night I saw you in it. Maybe tonight I can fulfill some of them." Then he sobered. "That will be fine, honey. How quickly can you get ready?"

The party was being held at his boss's house, he told her as they drove across town. He had gone to work for Marvin Jordan right out of college, and over the years they had become close friends. Tara Jordan was about Leah's age and very nice, but he felt compelled to warn her that some of the other women who would be there were friends of Kay's and might not be very welcoming.

As he drove along a narrow lane that led to a house about twice the size of the inn, Leah gave him a tight smile. "Thank you. My confidence needed that."

He squeezed her hand, then laid it on his thigh. "Don't be nervous. Just act naturally, and you'll charm everyone there."

They were met at the door by several servants. One took their coats; another escorted them to the living room, where a third offered them drinks. They paused in the doorway, Bryce looking for their hosts while Leah simply looked. "Tell me that Mr. and Mrs. Jordan don't live here alone," she said, awed by the sheer size of the room.

"Marv and Tara," he corrected. "Yeah, they do."

"How many rooms are in this house?"

"Thirty or forty. I'm not sure." He glanced down at her and smiled. "Don't let it intimidate you, honey. They're normal people, just like you and me."

She scanned the room again, this time paying more attention to the guests, particularly the women. Her own simple outfit, while nowhere near as expensive as most of the women's dresses obviously were, wasn't out of place, but she felt naked without jewelry. She couldn't see a single woman without some sort of stone on her fingers, her ears or around her neck. "Are all these people your friends?"

He clasped her hand tightly. "Not really. You'll meet my friends, starting with Marv and Tara. They must be around here somewhere."

The party had spilled over into several other rooms, so it took them some time to find their hosts. Leah followed Bryce through the crowd, trying to ignore the speculative glances that were being sent her way, yet growing increasingly uncomfortable with them.

They found Marvin Jordan in the den, where a small group of men were gathered around a big-screen television set. He was tall and rail-thin, his brown hair giving way to gray. He greeted Bryce, then turned his warm gaze to Leah. "Basketball," he muttered, gesturing toward the screen. "I considered telling them that the TV was broken, but then they would have skipped the party—no offense to you, Bryce. So... you're the first date Bryce has brought to one of our parties in a long time. Are you new to Philadelphia?"

"I'm just visiting," Leah replied.

He smiled broadly. "Ahh, that explains it." But before he could comment further, they were joined by a slim, pretty redhead.

"So the guest of honor has finally arrived." Tara Jordan brushed a kiss across Bryce's cheek, then slipped her arm through her husband's. "How is your father? I heard that he'd been released from the hospital. Is he all right?"

"He's doing really well. He's back home in Angel's Peak and says he feels better than he has in years."

"Angel's Peak." There was a hint of derision in Tara's voice. "I couldn't believe it when Marv told me that you're leaving Philadelphia to live in some tiny little hillbilly town in North Carolina. What could you possibly find in Angel's Peak that you can't get here?''

Leah stiffened slightly at the other woman's characterization of her hometown. If this woman was what Bryce considered nice, then she herself was definitely out of place here, she thought uneasily. She wished she had stayed home.

"Honey, before you embarrass me any further, maybe we ought to let Bryce introduce his date," Marv said with a grin. "You haven't given her a chance to say a word, and she speaks with such a lovely *Southern* accent."

Tara looked at Leah, and her face turned as red as her hair. "You're from Angel's Peak," she guessed. "I'm sorry. I didn't mean... Marv and Bryce will both tell you that I'm completely tactless, but I don't mean any harm with the things I say."

"She's right," Marv teased, enjoying her discomfort. "She *is* tactless, isn't she, Bryce?"

"Completely," he agreed.

The other woman was blushing even more as she extended her hand. "I'm Tara Jordan."

"Leah Cameron."

She wasn't prepared for the shock on the other couple's faces. Tara released her hand and grasped Bryce's, demanding, "Did you get married behind our backs, without an invitation for your dearest friends? Bryce, how could—"

"We're not married," he interrupted, then added so softly that only Leah could hear, "yet."

"So you just happened to find a woman with the same last name?" Marv asked dryly.

"Leah was married to my cousin," he explained. "We met when I was visiting my aunt and uncle."

Leah could see the questions in the other woman's eyes. The first chance Tara Jordan got, she would ask every one of them. Was she prepared to answer?

It didn't take Tara long to find an excuse to get her away from the men. On hearing that Leah owned a two hundred-year-old house, the redhead insisted on giving her a tour. "So...you're divorced," she commented as they climbed a long, broad staircase to the second floor.

"No," Leah said softly. "My husband was killed in an accident a few years ago."

"Oh, I'm sorry. Do you have any children?"

"Four."

Tara raised one eyebrow in surprise. "A ready-made family," she commented. "Bryce likes children, but I guess you probably know that. How long have you known him?"

"About a month. Your home is lovely."

"Thank you. It's too big for just the two of us, but then, it would be too big for twenty of us. They did things in grand style back in the old days, didn't they?" Tara led her through a series of bedrooms, each lavishly decorated with antiques. "Bryce seems quite fond of you."

Leah stopped to admire a collection of candlesticks. Without looking at the other woman, she cautiously echoed her words, "I'm quite fond of him."

"Let's be honest, Leah—you don't mind if I call you that?"

She shook her head.

"Bryce has been friends with Marv for twenty years, and I've known him almost fifteen. I saw what Kay did to him— the hell she put him through. You're the first woman he's gotten serious about since she left him, and I don't want to see him hurt again."

Tara's concern for Bryce was so obvious that Leah forgave her meddling. She looked at the other woman, her eyes cool and steady and sincere. "I don't want to see him hurt, either."

"He's giving up a lot for you."

"I didn't ask him to do it. It was his decision. He didn't even mention it to me until he had already made it."

"His friends are here."

"His family is in Angel's Peak."

"His father could come back here. He would, if Bryce asked him to."

Leah began walking again. Tara had no choice but to follow. "But Bryce wouldn't ask him. He knows that Frank is happy in Angel's Peak." She sighed softly. "Why do you feel it's so important for him to stay here?"

"If you disappoint him—" Tara let her words trail off.

Leah understood. It would be better for him to be in a familiar place with familiar faces. "Do you think I will?"

She studied Leah for a long time, then replied, "No. I think you're in love with him, aren't you?"

She smiled but didn't answer the question. The first time she acknowledged her love out loud, it wasn't going to be to anyone other than Bryce himself.

"When you meet Kay—"

Forgetting her manners, Leah interrupted her. "I have no intention of meeting Kay."

Tara laughed, a husky, throaty sound. "Oh, but you will. A lot of those women downstairs are friends of her. Before this night is over, at least one of them will have told her that Bryce came back from a month in North Carolina with a beautiful woman with a Southern accent. She'll find some excuse to show up at his house, believe me."

"Are *you* a friend of hers?"

She laughed again. "Are you kidding? I couldn't tolerate her even when she was married to Bryce. Kay comes from old money, and it shows. She's very elegant, very refined and cultured—and snooty. I, on the other hand, come from your average, run-of-the-mill, middle-class family. I married money, and that makes me less acceptable in her eyes. Anyway, when you meet her, don't let her intimidate you."

Leah looked troubled by the warning. "Why should she care if Bryce is seeing someone else? She left him a long time ago—she doesn't still care for him, does she?"

"No, she doesn't *care*. It's just her ego. As long as Bryce remained single and uninvolved, she could believe that he wasn't over her, that she was the great love of his life, that losing her was more than he could handle. It's petty and selfish, but some people are like that. They don't want something for themselves, but they don't want anyone else to have it, either.''

''I hope you're wrong.'' Leah didn't want to meet Bryce's ex-wife, to come face to face with the woman he had once loved.

''About Kay wanting to check you out?'' Tara shook her head. ''I *know* her. Just be prepared, and don't let her get to you. Come on, we'd better head back downstairs, or Bryce will come looking for you.''

Indeed, he was waiting for them at the bottom of the stairs. With a teasing remark for Tara, he reclaimed Leah and guided her into the living room, seeking out the people he considered friends for introductions.

Most of the people she met were nice, Leah reflected with some surprise. So they had money and were sophisticated and highly successful. Like Bryce, like Marv and Tara, they were basically nice people, extending the warmth and affection they offered Bryce to her, too. Of course, there were others who weren't so nice, who watched her with a mixture of curiosity and suspicion, who pumped her for information when Bryce wasn't nearby. Kay's friends, she guessed. When the evening was over, she was both relieved and sorry—relieved because she was tired, and now she could be alone once more with Bryce—and sorry because she would probably never see these people again.

''Was that so bad?'' he asked as they walked through the cold, starry night to his car.

''No, I had a nice time.''

''You sound surprised,'' he said with a chuckle.

''I am. Maybe I'm something of a snob, but I didn't expect people who live like this to be nice, especially to an outsider. Of course, they weren't being nice to *me*, but to your date.''

He opened the door and waited until she'd settled herself in the front seat before closing the door again. Life would certainly be easier for both of them if she had more confidence, he thought as he circled the car. She could find so much more pleasure in living if she didn't have so much self-doubt, and he could give her more pleasure if it didn't require so much energy to convince her that he was sincere. But he had no right to complain. He had fallen in love with her, knowing that she was shy, innocent and insecure.

At home he led her through the house to the kitchen. It was the one room that she really liked, Leah decided as she watched him build a fire. Filling the entire rear half of the house, the room was divided into three separate but shared areas—the kitchen, dining room and family room. It had lots of warm brick, plenty of windows, good lighting and the big brick fireplace that filled an entire wall.

"Tonight was the caroling party," he remarked as he slipped out of his suit coat and dropping it onto a chair.

Leah nodded.

"This is the first time you've missed it, isn't it?" He tossed his tie on top of the jacket.

She nodded again. Slipping off her heels, she propped her feet on the low table and leaned back. The sofa was over-size, cushiony and as comfortable as her bed at home.

"Why didn't you wait until tomorrow to come? That way you still could have gone to the party."

Leah waited until he was settled next to her, his arm a comforting weight around her shoulders. "There are always plenty of parties. I wanted to be with you."

He liked the way she said it—simply, honestly, sincerely. "I'm very glad you came." He pressed a kiss to her forehead, then raised one hand to the V-neck of her sweater. "Does the family know that you're here with me?"

"Yes."

"And do they mind?"

She dropped her gaze to watch his fingers, long and narrow, as they toyed with the first button of her sweater.

"No," she replied, her voice breathy. "Matthew was a little upset because he couldn't come, too, and Peter wasn't too thrilled, but..."

He slid the button free, and she lost her train of thought. His hand was a shadow against the winter white of her sweater, a soft, tantalizing, arousing, teasing shadow. There were eight buttons on her sweater, and now he had another one undone. He folded back the fabric, revealing the soft curves of her bare breasts.

"Remember the night you wore this outfit?" he asked hoarsely. "At the party before Thanksgiving?"

All Leah could do was nod. Her throat was dry, her heart pounding erratically.

"You said, 'Don't make me want you, because I couldn't say no.'"

She nodded again.

"Do you want me tonight, Leah?" A third button came undone at the gentle tugging of his fingers, followed swiftly by the fourth.

"Yes," she whispered.

"I want you, too. Sometimes I want you so badly that it scares me. No matter how much you give me, I still want more." The next button slipped loose. "I'll need you until the day I die."

The last three buttons gave way, and he pushed the two sides apart, revealing a broad strip of flesh. For a moment he simply looked at her; then he lowered her onto the sofa. He took one taut, swollen nipple into his mouth, bathing it with his tongue, and felt his own body swell in response until he thought he would explode with unrelenting need. Together they removed their clothes, and Leah opened herself to him. Feeling her warm, moist welcome, he squeezed his eyes tightly shut and breathed her name in an agonized groan. "Oh, Leah..."

Leah lay back on the sofa, propped her shoeless feet on the coffee table and listened intently, but beyond the cleaning sounds Bryce was making across the room, she heard nothing. "There's no noise here—have you noticed?"

He thought of all the nights he had come home to the empty house and grinned wryly. "Yeah, I've noticed." It made him appreciate the bustle of the inn, the warm friendly voices, the sounds of the kids running in and out, or listening to the stereo, or even arguing. "How are the kids?"

She glanced at the phone. The first thing she had done as soon as they finished dinner was call home. Although she was having a wonderful time, after three days she was beginning to miss her family. "They're fine. Are you sure I can't help you clean up? I feel so lazy lying here while you work."

"You cooked. I can clean."

She finished her wine, set the glass on the table and uttered a satisfied sigh. Bryce was pampering her, spoiling her rotten, and she was loving every minute of it. For the first time in her life there was nothing for her to do. No children to get ready for school in the morning or bed at night, no mail or phone calls to answer, no reservations to handle, no million and one problems to solve. He had promised her a good time, and he was keeping that promise. He had taken her to his favorite restaurants, gone shopping with her, given her tours of his adopted home city, but most of all, best of all, he had made love to her. He had shown her things she'd never even dreamed about, made her feel things she'd never known existed. His lovemaking was sometimes lazy, sometimes fierce, sometimes easy and sometimes savage, but it was always tender and always absolute heaven.

When the doorbell rang, she started slightly. The inn didn't have a doorbell, since the door was always unlocked and guests were invited to walk right in. It was an intrusion she didn't want to grow accustomed to. "Want me to get that?"

His hands immersed in soapy water, he nodded. She walked down the hall, her socks slipping on the waxed floor, and reached the door just as the bell rang again.

The woman standing on the porch smiled coolly when she saw Leah. "Hello," she said in a perfectly modulated voice. "I'm Kay Cameron Wilson. And you must be Leah."

There was a brief moment of surprise, but it faded quickly. Tara Jordan had insisted that Kay would come, and somewhere in the back of her mind Leah must have expected it. She leaned against the doorjamb and answered almost pleasantly, "Yes, I guess I must."

The other woman studied Leah openly, curiously, causing her to shift uncomfortably before she returned the assessing gaze. She didn't like what she saw. Kay Wilson was a beautiful woman, her blond hair sleek and stylish, her makeup flawless, her voice cultured; in short, she had an aura of wealth and elegance. She wore a full-length fur coat, with diamonds and emeralds sparkling in her ears, at her throat and on her fingers. "Kay comes from old money, and it shows," Tara had said. Lord, did it ever! Leah thought with a hint of envy.

Her appraisal complete, Kay smiled. There was no mistaking the condescension in it. "Is Bryce here?"

"Yes, he is." Leah made no effort to step back and offered no invitation to enter. "Did you want to see him...or me?"

"He warned you about me, didn't he?" Kay asked with a smugly satisfied smile.

Leah's answering smile was polite but cool. "No. He's never mentioned you at all." It wasn't exactly the truth, but was close enough to count.

Some of Kay's satisfaction faded. "You're from North Carolina."

"Yes."

"And he's moving to North Carolina."

Leah nodded. "Why are you here?"

Her bluntness drew the other woman's approval. "Curiosity. It took him a long time to replace me, and I wanted to see who he had chosen."

"After so many years, does it matter?"

"Yes, in a way, it does."

Leah took a step back. "You may as well come in. It's too cold to stand in the door." She waited until Kay passed her, then shut the door firmly.

"Who was it, Leah?" Bryce called just before he appeared at the end of the hall. He was far more surprised by his ex-wife's visit than Leah had been. "What are you doing here?"

She smiled at Leah again. "I even have an excuse." Then, to Bryce, "I heard you're putting the house on the market. There are a couple of pieces of furniture I'd like to take off your hands—for a fair price, of course."

He looked from her to Leah. With her dismal lack of self-confidence, he expected her to be dismayed and upset, comparing herself to Kay and coming up short. But she was leaning against the wall, her long legs crossed at the ankle, her hands pushed into the pockets of her trousers, looking vaguely interested but unaffected. Turning back to Kay, he said, "You'll have to talk to the real estate agent about that. He's going to dispose of everything for me."

"Who's handling it for you?"

He got his briefcase from the shelf in the closet behind Kay, removed a business card and handed it to her. "Is that all you want?"

"More than enough." She smiled once more, then left, leaving the door standing open behind her.

Bryce closed the door, twisting the lock until it clicked. Then he looked at Leah, waiting for her to respond in some way to Kay's unexpected visit.

She moved away from the wall and walked back to the kitchen. "Did you finish the dishes?"

He ignored the question. "Don't you want to say anything?"

Sitting down on the sofa, she turned sideways to face the fire. "She's a beautiful woman."

He sat down behind her, automatically putting his arms around her. "Yes, she is." After a brief pause, he added, "So are you."

An afterthought, she guessed, as if it had taken him a moment to realize that he shouldn't compliment his ex-wife without offering a similar compliment to his current lover. What had he thought, seeing Kay and herself side by side? Beautiful, elegant Kay in her designer dress and fur coat and diamonds, and Leah in her jade-green sweater, navy trousers and socks. Next to Kay, Leah looked and felt like the original country bumpkin. Had Bryce noticed that? she fretted, then answered herself with another question. How could he have overlooked it?

"I'm sorry, Leah. I don't know why she was here."

"She came to see me."

He tilted his head to one side to look at her. The firelight touched her face with a golden glow, brought out the coppery shades in her hair, warmed the ice blue of her eyes. A moment ago he had called both her and Kay beautiful. It was a cool, unemotional word that suited his ex-wife perfectly, but it didn't begin to do justice to Leah.

She knew he was watching her, and she allowed herself a small smile. "Tara told me she would come, that she would want to see who you were involved with. And she did. She admitted it."

"Does that bother you?"

"She was curious. So was I. I'd wondered about the woman you loved for so many years, about the kind of woman who attracted you."

"Are you satisfied, now that you've met her?" he asked cautiously.

She smiled again, but this time there was a hint of sadness in it. "No. We're as different as day and night. Fire and ice. Ordinary and extraordinary."

He pulled her back against his chest, and she let him. "You got the first two right, but the last one's backward. You're the day, the sunlight, and Kay's the night. You're the fire, and she's the ice. But *you're* extraordinary, Leah, not her. You give love and happiness and comfort.''

''But you gave *her* your love. For fourteen years.''

He sighed softly. ''Do you want to know about Kay and me?''

Did she? One part of her did, but another part was afraid—afraid of what he would say, afraid that she would hear love and longing in his voice as he spoke. At last she shook her head to indicate no, but her mouth formed the word yes.

Bryce settled her more comfortably against him. In the last six years he had rarely discussed the details of his marriage or his divorce—because they were too painful, he had thought. But he discovered now, as he began, that there wasn't any pain; there were only dull-edged memories that no longer held joy or hurt, happiness or sorrow. ''We got married when I graduated from college. I was going to work and be the provider, and she was going to be the perfect wife. So I worked, and I bought her this house and her fancy clothes and expensive cars and jewels, but it was never enough. She always wanted more. I worked harder, usually twelve to fourteen hours a day, and I made lots of money, and Kay made a beautiful home for us and got us invited to all the right parties, to join the right clubs. We had everything a young couple could want . . . except a family, so one day I suggested to Kay that she cut back on her social activities so we could have a baby.'' He laughed softly. ''You would have thought I'd asked her to cut off her arm. She had no intention of having a baby, she told me. Not ever. It might have ruined her figure, and it definitely would have interfered with her life-style.'' His hand slid over the soft curve of Leah's breast to her flat stomach. Four babies certainly hadn't hurt her figure.

''So . . . I worked even longer hours, and the rare times I was home, Kay wasn't. She had to attend this social function or that one, and, more often than not, she attended them without me, because I was working, or because I was too tired from working. Then, one day shortly after our fourteenth anniversary, she told me that she'd met a man at one of those parties. He was handsome, charming, wealthy and ten years younger than me. She had been having an affair with him for the last year."

He remembered the ugliness of the scene, but was still untouched by the bitter pain. "I was going to be noble and generous. I was going to forgive her for the affair. After all, she was my wife, and I loved her. I had been neglecting her for my work. I was going to forgive her, shape up and be a better husband. But you know what? She didn't want my forgiveness, and she didn't want me for a husband, either. Derek had offered to marry her once she'd gotten rid of me. The confession about her affair had been a prelude to telling me she wanted a divorce."

Leah raised her hand to his, sliding it into his bigger palm. She couldn't judge by the emotionless tone of his voice if the memories were painful for him, but she offered him support all the same.

"I fought her on the divorce. We had promised to stay together forever, and I just couldn't let it end that way. *Then* she got nasty."

In that low, blank voice he related the insults, every one of them, sparing himself nothing. Selfish, unsatisfying, boring. The list went on. Then he took a deep breath, smelling Leah's fragrance. It was sweet... innocent. "Finally I let her go. I couldn't fight anymore. There was nothing left to fight for."

Leah broke the heavy silence that fell when he finished. Twisting in his arms, she faced him, her expression sympathetic but filled with dismay. "And you *believed* her?"

He lifted his shoulders in a shrug. "In the last years of our marriage, sex with Kay was...just sex. It wasn't exciting or particularly satisfying. She blamed me, and I accepted the blame."

She shifted positions again, carefully maneuvering until she was straddling his thighs. "You don't still believe . . . ?" she asked, wrapping her arms around his neck.

Bryce laughed—an honest, healthy sound—and the somber mood was broken. "Good Lord, no. One night with you erased all my doubts. Kay and I were judging sex as lovemaking and were disappointed because it didn't measure up. But you can't make love to someone you don't love. It just doesn't work that way. It wasn't her fault, or mine. Between her social life and her refusal to start a family, and the hours I spent at my job, the love just got lost, and we couldn't get it back again."

You can't make love to someone you don't love. The simple sentence set Leah's heart soaring. What they did together in bed absolutely had to qualify as making love— nothing less could be so good. He *had* to love her. Even if he couldn't say it—and after hearing the story of his marriage and meeting Kay for herself, she could understand why he might find it difficult—he had to love her to make love to her.

She leaned back, thrusting their bodies into intimate contact. "Take me to bed, Bryce."

"You're a greedy little thing, aren't you?" he asked with a willing grin.

"Mmm. I want to make love to you. I want to show you . . ." She moved against him, finishing the thought silently. . . . *how much I love you.*

He lifted her to one side, then stood up and pulled her along behind him. "You can show me anything you want, honey," he promised. "Anything at all."

Leah rolled over, fitting herself snugly into the curves of Bryce's body. She was almost asleep when she remembered the question she had forgotten to ask. "Did I show you?"

"Show me what?"

Her voice was fainter, more distant. "How much I love you . . ."

Suddenly wide awake, Bryce carefully rolled over to face her, but she was asleep. The moonlight touched her face, illuminating the peaceful, innocent smile she wore. He touched her cheek gently with one finger, then brushed his mouth over hers. "I love you, too," he whispered. "Oh, Leah, I *do* love you."

He lay on his back, holding her close. Tomorrow would be their last day in Philadelphia. Wednesday morning they had to return to Angel's Peak. He wanted to make it a special day for Leah, and he could think of one way to make it *very* special: he could ask her to marry him. He wanted to take her home with a ring on her finger and the wedding date set.

What was the proper way to propose marriage these days? he wondered idly. Kay was the only other woman he had ever asked to marry him, and that had been so long ago that he couldn't even remember when or how he'd done it.

But it didn't really matter how he asked, as long as he *did* ask. As long as she said yes. As long as she agreed to spend the rest of her life, forever and ever, as his wife.

Tuesday morning they finished packing the items that Bryce wanted to take to Angel's Peak with him. Leah was surprised at how much he was leaving behind. The boxes stacked in the hallway, ready to be shipped, were filled with clothes, books and a few personal items. Everything else was to be left behind.

"Don't you want to take any of this?" she asked, opening her arms wide to include the furnishings around them. "Isn't there a single piece of furniture in this house that means something to you?"

Bryce looked around, then grinned. "I've got some fond memories of the bed and the chaise upstairs, but I don't need to take them with me, not when I'm taking *you*. Kay can have all of this if she wants it."

Leah sat down, a popular mystery novel in her hands. "You don't resent her at all, do you? Even after what she did to you." There was a curious mix of puzzlement, disbelief and pride in her voice.

He took the book from her and added it to the box that stood between them. "I resented what she did—her refusal to have children, the affair with Derek, the things she said— but not *her*. She was a part of my life for a very long time, Leah. She helped make me what I am today. I can't resent her for that."

"I try to feel that way about Terence, but it's hard. Sometimes I look at you, and I wonder why he couldn't have been more like you—more patient, more giving."

Bryce leaned back against the sofa and watched her while she looked through the stack of books he'd decided to keep. So far, she hadn't made any reference to last night's declaration of love. Did she even remember saying it? He wanted to ask her, to ask if she had meant it, but he forced himself to show some of that patience she had just credited to him. She would say it again, in her own time.

He forced his wandering mind back to the conversation. "Did Terence mistreat you?" He sounded normal and curious on the surface, but there was a thread of steel behind the words.

She heard it and hastened to reassure him. "He wasn't abusive, not at all. He never hurt the kids or me, at least not in that way. He was just very reserved, very untouchable. He couldn't give any part of himself to anyone else. He was…"

"Cold. Selfish."

Leah started to protest, then nodded. "At times. Most of the time. I finally accepted that he would never love me, but I couldn't accept that he didn't seem to love the kids, either. I was always so surprised that he didn't love his own children." She gave a little laugh. "That's silly, isn't it? Of all the people in the world, *I* should have been prepared for that. After all, my own father…" She slipped a few more books into the box, then held the flaps together while Bryce taped them.

"Honey, you don't know why your father and mother left you at the home," he said quietly. "Maybe they couldn't take care of you. Maybe they thought you would be better off with someone who *could* care for you, could feed and clothe you."

She shrugged, reaching for an empty box as Bryce moved the full one aside. "Their reasons don't really matter now, do they?"

Only, he suspected, because she didn't allow them to. She preferred to forget the parents who had abandoned her and to concentrate on the family who loved her.

Leah returned to the original subject. "If Terence had been different, if my parents had been different, then *I* would be different, too. And I'm glad I'm not. I like myself the way I am now. I wouldn't mind being prettier, or more sophisticated, or more confident, but I *like* me."

He pushed the box out of the way and tugged on her hand until she was lying on top of him, her breasts against his chest, her hips pressed intimately to his. "I like you, too," he said with a broad grin. "I like you a whole lot.... Marry me, Leah."

So much for the romantic proposal he had intended. The words had just popped out, without thought. But he wouldn't call them back for anything in the world.

The startled expression on her face was comical. She stared at him for a long time, then moved back until she was kneeling between his legs. "Are you serious?"

"Absolutely." Reaching out, he laced his fingers through hers, but didn't try to force her closer. "I want to spend the rest of my life with you, Leah. I want to know that, whatever happens, you'll be there. You'll be mine. I want to live with you and the children. I want to help you take care of them, to raise them and love them. I want you to be my wife, Leah. Forever."

There was more he should say, more he needed to say. *I love you.* But he couldn't quite form the words. Except for the brief, secret whisper last night, Kay was the only woman he had ever said those words to, and it had brought him so much heartache. Leah was nothing like his ex-wife, but that last protective barrier was firmly in place. It would take time, security and a lot of love to remove it.

She was quiet, giving serious consideration to his proposal. The sentiments he had expressed were lovely and touched the deepest part of her, but one thing was lacking. In his entire beautiful little speech, he had used the word love only once, and then in reference to her children. Did he love *her*?

She wished she had the courage to ask, but she couldn't face the risk of hearing him say no. She simply had to believe. He had shown her love in everything he did, in every part of their lives. She was insecure, but surely she could recognize love when she saw it, when she felt it, couldn't she?

She wanted to marry him with all her heart, with every ounce of feeling she possessed. He would be a good husband and father, one who would share himself with his family. He would make her life complete. There would be no more longing, no more loneliness, no more aching need to know a man's love.

Bryce didn't push her for an answer but simply waited. She was considering the idea of marriage from every angle, looking for any problems. He couldn't do that himself. The complexities of the issue meant nothing to him. All he knew was that he loved her, loved her family, and wanted to marry her. He counted on the strength of their shared love to solve any problems that cropped up.

"It wouldn't bother you to raise Terence's children?" she asked tentatively.

He shook his head.

"Would you want children of your own?"

"I don't know. It would be nice, but...you're almost thirty-six, and you've gone through that four times. I wouldn't ask you to do it again just for me. Your kids are great. I'm happy with them."

"Would you work at the inn, or would you want an outside job?"

"I could do all that paperwork you despise, but if I get in your way, I could get a job in Asheville."

"You know, Angel's Peak is a big change from Philadelphia. It's been all right for you so far, but you've only been there a few weeks. What about in a few months, or a few years? Will you still be happy there?"

He pressed a kiss to the back of her left hand. "I like Angel's Peak, Leah, and everyone I care about lives there—my father, Matthew, the other kids, and you. Especially you. I'll be happy wherever you are."

She still had difficulty accepting that. Traditionally, when conflicts arose between a man and a woman, the woman was expected to give in, to make the sacrifices, to please her man. Yet Bryce was willingly reversing the situation, sacrificing everything to be with her.

"Do you need time to think about it?" He had hoped that they could spend the afternoon picking out their rings and celebrating, but he couldn't pressure her to give an answer now. Marriage was a big step for her. She was cautious by nature, and he knew she would want to be certain that her answer was the right one.

"No." She smiled shyly. "I think in some ways I've been thinking about it ever since I met you. I love you, Bryce." Her smile grew brighter when she saw his surprise. "You thought I'd forgotten about saying that, didn't you? I wasn't *that* sleepy." Then she wet her lips nervously. "I love you, and I would like very much to be your wife."

He tried to speak the simple vow again, but fear held the words in his throat. Soon, he silently promised. He would tell her soon, but for now he would have to be satisfied with showing her. He pulled her to him and sealed her acceptance with a long, tender kiss.

Leaving the packing unfinished, he took her shopping. He bought her an engagement ring, a beautiful brilliant-cut diamond, that to Leah, unused to rings of any kind, seemed to weigh down her hand. They also chose simple matching gold bands for the wedding.

"Can we tell the family when we get home tomorrow?" Bryce asked as they dressed for dinner that evening.

Leah looked down at her left hand. Light reflected and sparkled from the multi-faceted gem. "Do you really think we could keep it from them?"

"You could take the ring off," he quietly offered. "You don't have to wear it yet."

She smiled slowly. "I wasn't talking about the ring. I've never been so excited or so happy in my life. I couldn't hide it from them, and I wouldn't want to try. We'll tell them as soon as we get there, all right?"

They rented a car in Asheville and drove to Angel's Peak, savoring their last hour of privacy. As soon as they arrived at the inn, Leah called the family together in the small private living room.

Their announcement met with little surprise but a great deal of happiness. Leah received kisses and hugs from the children, and they welcomed Bryce into the family. Martha embraced both of them, murmuring in Leah's ear, "Be happy with him, honey."

Frank hugged his son, kissed his future daughter-in-law and proudly said, "I told you so."

Matthew was the happiest of all. "Now I don't have to find something else to call you," he told Bryce, who held the boy in his arms. "As soon as you and Mom are married, I can call you Dad."

Bryce held him tighter. "I'd like that," he said in a husky voice. "I'd like that a lot."

Only Peter offered no congratulations. He stood in a corner, scowling darkly, and said nothing until Matthew called Bryce "Dad." His expression thunderous, he left the room, pushing past them without a word of excuse.

There was a moment's silence; then Martha spoke. "I'm sorry, Leah—"

She raised one hand. "It's all right, Martha. I'll talk to him." After gently touching Bryce's arm, she left to find her father-in-law.

He was in the small sitting room. Appropriate, Leah thought, since their first argument about Bryce had taken place in this room. He was standing at the tall, narrow window, looking out but seeing nothing. Closing the door quietly behind her, she went to stand near him.

He glanced at her, but said nothing. After a moment he looked out again. "Remember when you first came here?"

She nodded. "I was seventeen, pregnant, newly married and scared half out of my mind."

"You were a paradox—so timid and shy and afraid, yet determined to be a good mother to your unborn baby and a good wife to your new husband." He smiled at her, but it was sad. "You were, too. You were a better wife than Terence had a right to expect."

She said nothing.

"Terence was my son. My only child. I know he had flaws, but I loved him, Leah. He wasn't a very good husband, but he *was* the father of your children."

"Matthew never knew Terence," she said softly. "Douglas and the girls never knew him, either, because he never let them get close. He fathered them, but he wasn't their father. He never loved them, never made them feel wanted, never gave them anything—respect, time, affection, attention." She dabbed at the corners of her eyes. "Matthew needs a father, and Bryce wants a son. He's good to Matthew, Peter—doesn't that mean anything to you? He's good to all of us—good *for* us."

"He's using you." He made the accusation flatly, his voice empty of emotion but full of certainty.

"No."

He turned to look at her again. "Don't you find it odd that he stayed single for six years after his divorce, and now, in less than a month, he's fallen madly in love with you and can't wait to be married?"

The tears spilled over, rolling down her cheeks. "Do you find it so hard to believe that he could love me? Am I so worthless that no man could possibly want me?"

He pulled her into his arms. "Of course not. But Leah, I *know* him. I know what he's like. I know he can't be trusted. I love you, Leah, and I don't want to see you hurt, but I just can't see anything *but* hurt coming from him. He's a selfish man. He uses people when it's convenient and discards them when he's finished."

"I don't believe you." She pulled away from him and got a tissue from a corner table. "I know you blame him for part of your problems with Frank, but you're wrong about him. I love him, Peter, and he loves me. Can't you be happy for me?"

Looking at her with disappointment and dismay, he touched her hair lightly. "You really do love him, don't you?" His voice was heavy with acceptance. "Let's go back."

With his arm around her shoulders, they rejoined the family. Peter stopped in front of Bryce and, after a moment, extended his hand. When his nephew took it, he said, "I hope you two live a long and happy and loving life together. Take care of her."

Bryce knew how much Peter's blessing meant to Leah. Knowing that his uncle didn't approve of him, he was doubly grateful to receive it. "I will. Thank you, Peter."

They all sat together at dinner, where wine was served to toast Leah and Bryce's engagement. The guests and staff joined in, turning the meal into a gay celebration that lasted past the children's bedtimes.

When the impromptu party finally ended, the guests of honor sat alone in the living room, snuggled together on the sofa. The room was dark, with only the glow from the fireplace and the many-hued bulbs on the Christmas tree to light it.

"Considering the circumstances, I'd say the news of our impending marriage was well received," Bryce said, placing a kiss on top of Leah's head. "I know Peter wasn't happy, but...the kids took it well. Matthew's happy...and I am...."

"Me, too." She laid her head on his chest, where she could feel the steady beat of his heart. "Peter will come around. I think he's just concerned about you taking Terence's place in the kids' lives." It was a tactful lie, one that Bryce didn't believe for a moment.

"Maybe that's part of it, but the other reason is that he hates me." He raised her hand so he could see her ring. It pleased him to see it on her finger, a tangible symbol of their love. When it was joined by the slender gold wedding band, his life would be perfect.

"Why?" she asked softly. Long ago she had promised herself that if Bryce wouldn't offer an explanation about the past, she wouldn't ask. Now she needed to know, needed to break that promise. "Why does he dislike you so much?"

He gazed at the tree, admiring its beauty, pretending that the question she had asked didn't fill him with dread, but he couldn't stop the stiffness that spread through him. He had hoped that she would never have to know the details of the family feud and his own role in it, but he couldn't ignore her.

For a moment he looked at her, his eyes probing and a little sad. Would knowing change the way she felt about him, the way she looked at him, her blue eyes all soft and dewy with love?

"Bryce?"

He sighed deeply and turned back to the tree. "After my father and I left Angel's Peak, we didn't have any contact with Peter and Martha for twenty years—no letters, no phone calls, no secondhand gossip. It was as if they had never been a part of our lives. Then one evening, out of the blue, Peter called me. I don't know how he found out where I lived, and at the time I didn't care." At the time he hadn't cared about much of anything, he added silently. His life had been a living hell, and his uncle's problems had been the least of his concerns. "I was still holding a grudge about what had happened, but I was also curious about what he wanted after so many years, so I talked to him."

Leah shifted against him, and he lifted his arm away until she was comfortably settled; then he hugged her close again. He needed that contact with her while he talked. "He wanted to talk to Dad, but he didn't know how to find him. I refused to tell him. He was pretty upset, grieving. He told me that Terence had been killed in an accident. It had made him realize that nobody lived forever, and that when you were dead, that was it. There wouldn't be any second chances. So he wanted to talk to Dad, to settle things before it was too late. He needed him."

"But you didn't think your father needed Peter," Leah said softly.

He shook his head. "You don't know how it hurt my dad to have to leave here. The pain that Peter caused him... I couldn't forgive him, Leah. It had been twenty years, and I couldn't forget what he had done to my dad. I told him that I didn't give a damn about Terence's death, that he had probably deserved whatever had happened. I was pretty cold. He had lost his only son, and all he wanted was to talk to his only brother, and I wouldn't let him. I never even told Dad that he had called until last month."

They sat in silence. A log in the fireplace crackled and fell, sending a shower of sparks into the air. The tension dancing through him was also crackling, awaiting a response from Leah.

"That was around the time when Kay left you, wasn't it?"

She had made the connection that he'd deliberately left out. He hadn't wanted to make any excuses for his behavior. In his eyes there were none. "Yes."

"You were dealing with your own grief then, Bryce. Don't punish yourself for it now."

He looked down at her, holding her head with his hands in her hair. "Losing a wife to divorce doesn't quite compare to losing a son to death."

"In a sense it does. You and Peter had both lost someone you loved very much. You made a mistake, but it doesn't matter anymore. Peter and Frank are together; they're talking, although not too amicably, but they're working it out. Don't blame yourself for what you did then."

He laid his head back and closed his eyes. "At some time in your life, you have to accept the blame for the bad things you've done."

"And the credit for the good," she reminded him. "I know that the good you've done far outweighs the bad. And in this case, Bryce, there's plenty of blame to go around. You don't need to take it all. Good heavens, you were only a boy when all this started."

"But I was a man when I did my part to prolong it."

Smiling fondly, she got up from the sofa and tugged at his hand. "Come on."

Opening his eyes, he resisted her. "Where?"

"To bed."

"Where?"

"In my room."

He studied her critically. There was no change—no dismay or disgust, no contempt. He had just told her the single worst thing he had ever done in his life, and she didn't care. She loved him anyway. He stood up and hugged her close for just a minute. "Have I told you that you are the most remarkable woman I've ever known?" he murmured before kissing her.

She teased him with her tongue. "No," she replied, also in a murmur. "But why don't you come to my room and show me there?"

Chapter 9

They called Christmas the season of miracles. Leah was beginning to believe it. As if the gift of Bryce's love wasn't enough to give her faith, the day after their return from Philadelphia, Peter and Frank announced that they had resolved their feud, once and for all. Although Leah couldn't find much difference in their behavior toward each other—they still liked to fuss and grumble—she was grateful to have their mysterious past settled.

"I could use a few more miracles, God," she said softly, raising her eyes heavenward. Christmas was only ten days away, and she had a million things left to do to get ready. Planning a wedding on top of that was simply beyond her capacity, but Bryce had generously agreed to wait on that— but only until January, he warned her. If she wasn't ready by the middle of the month, he was taking her to the nearest judge.

Briefly she thought that might be best. She was only nine days from her thirty-sixth birthday, and this was the second marriage for both of them. Maybe they should simply go to the courthouse and get it over with.

But every romantic, feminine part of her rejected that idea. That was the kind of wedding she and Terence had had, with Martha and Peter the only ones present. It had been solemn, brief and the most unromantic occasion she had ever experienced. Now she dreamed wistfully of a real wedding, with a white lace gown for herself and a tuxedo for Bryce, with candles, flowers, attendants, champagne and dancing. She knew it was unrealistic—she wasn't a young, innocent, virginal bride getting married for the first time. But she was certain she could find some middle ground, something not too formal, but romantic enough to give her a lifetime of memories. If only she had time!

That was the miracle she needed—time. Twenty-six hours in a day would do nicely, for a start. But barring that, less daydreaming and more working would have to suffice. Firmly she put the wedding out of her mind and turned to the papers in front of her.

Following tradition, she was hosting a reception at the inn on Christmas Eve. Engraved invitations had gone out weeks earlier, and the acceptances had begun to come in almost immediately. She had worked out every last detail with Martha, Colleen and Vicky, but she was going over the plans again. If anything could possibly go wrong, she wanted to find it and fix it first.

She fingered one of the extra invitations. Something similar would be nice for the wedding, she mused, but less formal. Just their names, the date and time...

Groaning aloud, she covered her face with her hands. How could she get any work done when all she could think about was Bryce and the wedding?

The knock at the door provided a welcome distraction. She called an invitation, and Peter stepped inside. "Martha said you have a box ready to go to Asheville. I'm going down this afternoon, so I can take it to the shop, if you'd like."

She smiled wearily at her father-in-law. "I would appreciate that."

"Why don't you walk out to the workshop with me to get it? You look like you could use some fresh air, and I— there's something I'd like to say to you."

She agreed, even though she was certain he wanted to discuss Bryce. Maybe he would surprise her by not being critical of her fiancé.

He did surprise her when he finally began talking. "I owe you an apology, Leah," he said awkwardly. "When I first heard that Bryce had returned to Angel's Peak, I said some pretty nasty things to you for letting him stay here. I'm sorry about that."

"It's all right, Peter. You were angry. I don't even remember what you said." It was a lie, but her intentions were good. This time, that made it all right.

"I can't say that I would have chosen him as a husband for you, but I do hope you'll be happy together." He smiled faintly. "You know, you light up whenever he's around. It's like seeing the sun on a cold, snowy day."

"Like Martha," she said softly, "when she sees you."

The old man turned red. After more than forty years of marriage, she marveled, he could still blush.

"I'm glad you and Frank have worked things out."

"Well, if his son is going to marry my daughter-in-law, we've got to get along—for your sake, as well as the kids'. If that old goat is going to play step-grandfather to *my* grandchildren, I'm going to have to teach him how."

"So everything from the past is settled."

He looked down at her. "Not everything, but . . . we've done the best we could. I can't make it right, Leah—that's not in my power. All I can do is tell him how sorry I am that it ever happened, and he's accepted that. He understands about you and the kids. . . ." His voice trailed off, as if he had said too much, and he quickly looked away.

She looked puzzled. They were near the guest house when she stopped walking and turned to study her father-in-law's face. "What about me and the kids? What do we have to do with the feud? We weren't around then."

"No, of course not." He looked at everything but her, scratched his head, frowned, shifted his weight from foot to foot, then uttered a frustrated curse. "I know I ought to tell you everything, to clear my conscience, but Lord, I hate to. I don't want you to hold this against me. I don't want to lose your respect, Leah. I've loved you like a daughter for eighteen years. You've been more like my own child to me than Terence ever was."

She laid a hand on his arm. "Peter, there is absolutely nothing you could do to make me stop loving and respecting you. You and Martha will always be two of the most important people in my life." More gently she added, "I *would* like to know how the children and I figure in the past problems between you and Frank, but you don't have to tell me unless you want to."

He looked around them once more, then gestured to the rockers on the porch of the guest house. "Let's sit down," he said wearily. "This might take a while."

Leah didn't suggest that they go inside out of the cold, but chose a rocker and seated herself.

"My father died when I was about Matthew's age," he began, staring off into the distant past. "Mama raised Frank and me alone, and I liked to think that she'd done a pretty good job of it. But I was wrong."

He fell silent. Leah rocked back and forth, waiting patiently, letting him proceed at his own rate.

"Frank had a job with a company down the mountain in Asheville—a sales position. When Katherine was still alive, they lived there, but after she died, he moved back here with Bryce, so Mama could help take care of him. They lived in this house here. Martha and I were living in the same house we're in now."

He paused again, then continued in that halting fashion. He told of his love for the house and the land, of his pride in his family, in their history. He also talked of the frequent trips Frank's job required. His older brother was gone from Angel's Peak for days at a time, leaving Bryce in Anna's care, leaving all the work around the estate to Peter.

"After one of Frank's longer trips, he and Mama argued. She was old, her health was failing, and she wanted him to settle down, to quit traveling. Caring for Bryce was more than she could handle—not that he was a bad kid, just that she was a sick old lady. She wanted Frank to stay home, to take care of his son, to learn to take care of the estate, since it would be his one day. Well, Frank told her that he liked traveling, and he didn't need to learn to manage the estate because I was here, and I could do it for him. Whether he learned or not, he said, it would still be his when she died. It was family tradition, you see, for the eldest son to inherit.

"That made Mama mad. When he went out of town again against her wishes, she called the family lawyer and had a new will drawn up, leaving the estate to me." He looked away, but not before Leah saw the deep shame in his eyes. "It was my idea. I was trying to turn her against Frank. Leah, I loved this place more than I loved my life. It was my home, and I had put everything I had into it. I just couldn't bear the thought of Frank inheriting it, when to him it was just a piece of land, just a house. He would have let it decay and fall down around our heads, or sold it out from under us."

So he and the attorney, a good friend, had persuaded Anna to disinherit Frank. On his brother's return, Peter had spitefully informed him of the new will. Frank, predictably, had been furious. He and Anna had argued, then had refused to speak to each other for months.

After a while, Anna had had a change of heart. It wasn't right, she'd told Peter, to break a hundred and seventy-five years of family tradition because Frank wouldn't do what she wanted. After all, he was a grown man; he had to do what he thought was best for Bryce and himself. Peter had argued, pleaded and begged, but Anna had been adamant.

With two servants as witnesses, she had drawn up a new will, once again leaving the property to Frank, with the stipulation that it had to remain in the family. If for any reason he no longer wanted it, ownership would pass to Peter.

She had told Frank about the second will, and he had naturally boasted of it to his younger brother. Then, during Frank's next business trip, Anna had died.

Leah sat unmoving in her chair. "But . . . how did you get the estate? Why didn't Frank inherit it?"

"As I said, he was out of town when she died. I found her. I had been trying every day to convince her to destroy the second will, to let the other one stand. I had gone to her room for yet another argument, and I found her. She had died in bed the night before. And I found the will." His voice was so low and heavy with humiliation that Leah could barely understand him.

"You found the new will. The one giving the house to Frank." Understanding came slowly, along with shock, but she tried to hide it.

Covering his face with his hands, he nodded. "And I burned it in the fireplace."

"Didn't the lawyer have a copy?"

"No. Because he was my friend, Mama decided she couldn't trust him with it. That was the only one, and I destroyed it."

"So that made the first will, naming you as heir, valid." She was having trouble keeping the dismay and disappointment from her voice. It wasn't her place to judge him, she reminded herself sternly. She wasn't going to betray him that way.

Leaving her chair, she knelt in front of his and put her arms around his shoulders. "Oh, Peter," she said, sighing. "And you've lived with this ever since. I'm so sorry."

"So you see what I meant when I said I can't make things right for Frank. All I can do is apologize."

She did see. She saw too clearly. The only way to make things right would be to return ownership of the estate to his brother, and he couldn't do that, because he no longer owned it. She did.

She drew back and got to her feet, cold, numb, stiff. Her land, her house, her business—they weren't hers at all. They belonged rightfully to Frank, and eventually they would have passed on to Bryce. They were his birthright, but because of Peter's deception, they were hers. An unpleasant shiver passed through her.

Peter stood up and laid his hands on her shoulders. "Can you forgive me, Leah? Can you understand why I did it and forgive an old man for a stupid mistake?"

She hugged him. "I told you, Peter: there is *nothing* you could do to make me stop loving you. I understand." And she did. What he had done was shocking and wrong, but loving the land and the house the way she did, she could almost understand his motives. Almost.

After a moment he released her and took a step back, embarrassed by the show of emotion. "If you'll get that box for me..."

Inside the workshop she added the last few items to the box and sealed it, then handed it over to her father-in-law. "Be careful," she said absently.

"I will. Are you going back to the house now?"

"Not yet. I'll be up in a little while."

He hesitated, shifting the box in his grasp. "Want me to build a fire for you?"

"No, I won't be here that long. You go on now." She closed the door behind him, then walked to the fireplace, taking a seat on the stone hearth. It was no warmer inside than out, but she didn't notice. Cold had never bothered her much, especially when all her senses were frozen with shock.

The estate rightfully belonged to Frank. All her work, all her dedication, all her love, and the house and land belonged to Frank. She didn't think she could have been more stunned if someone had told her that one of her children belonged to someone else.

How could Peter have done it? He had practically destroyed his own family, all for a piece of land. Then he had
kept his secret, had passed on the property to Terence and
seen Leah take ownership of it, had watched her build her
dreams, her hopes and her future on it, and had never told
her that it belonged to someone else.

How it must have galled Frank, and Bryce, too, to have
to ask permission to stay in the house that should have been
theirs. At least the property had remained in the Cameron
family. Once she and Bryce were married, Frank's ties to the
estate would be strengthened even more.

Once she and Bryce were married . . . It was an ugly
thought, as cold as the hearth where she sat, and it slith-
ered its way into her mind. Once they were married, they
would share everything jointly—the children, the love, the
responsibilities . . . the estate?

No. She wouldn't think that. She *couldn't*. Bryce was a
good man, an honest one, and she loved him. She trusted
and believed in him. He wouldn't do that to her.

Sighing heavily, she stood up. Like Peter, she couldn't
"make it right," but she had done the best she could in giving them both rooms at the inn for as long as they wanted
them. That would have to be enough.

Feeling older, wearier and sadder, she left the cottage and
returned to her office, turning her mind once more to work.

"What do you want for your birthday?"

Leah pretended to carefully consider Megan's question
before answering, "To be young and beautiful."

Her daughter made a face at her. "You're already beautiful, Mom."

Leah laughed softly, contentedly. "But not young?"

"Well, you're not *old*. Seriously, what do you want?"

"Anybody who has a birthday on Christmas Eve doesn't
deserve birthday presents," Douglas teased, leaning back
against Leah's chair.

"Anyone who has a birthday three days after Christmas doesn't deserve presents, either," Megan shot back.

Leah snipped a thread from the jacket she was mending for Peter, an oversize red velvet coat that was part of his Santa suit. "I'll be happy with whatever you want to give me."

"Mom . . ." Megan turned with a sigh to Bryce, who was lying on the sofa with Matthew stretched out in front of him. "What about you? What do you want for Christmas?"

Bryce was absorbing the warmth of the homey scene around him: Leah, his love and his lover, soon to be his wife, and her children. His children. His family. It took him a moment to realize that Megan was speaking to him.

He could have said that he had everything he wanted right here in this room, but that answer would have displeased Megan as much as Leah's had. So he told her honestly the only thing he wished for. "I want January to get here." He was impatient for the holidays to pass and their wedding date to arrive. For all practical purposes they were already as good as married—he spent his days working with Leah in the office, his evenings with her and the children, and his nights in her bed—but it wasn't official yet. Until his ring was on her finger and she had traded Terence's name for his own, he wouldn't let himself fully relax.

"You guys are no fun," Megan said, a pout darkening her face. Buying or making gifts for her brothers and Laurel was easier, because they had each made up a detailed wish list.

"You know what *I* want for Christmas?" Matthew raised his head from the pillow of Bryce's arm and looked at his older sister. "I want a new baby brother."

"Hey, that would be neat," Laurel said, turning from the television set for the first time all evening. "Are you guys going to have a baby?"

Before Leah could answer, Douglas spoke up. "Don't you think you're a little old to be getting pregnant again, Mom?"

She smiled gently at her son. "Don't you mean that *you're* a little old to be getting a baby brother?"

A flush colored his cheeks. "Well, it would be kind of odd, you know? I'd be old enough to be his father."

"So *are* you, Mom?" Laurel demanded. "Are you going to have another baby?"

Bryce was waiting for her answer, too, she realized, as curious as the children. She looked at each one of them, Douglas, Laurel, Megan, Matthew. For most people four kids would be enough, but there was always plenty of room for another one, especially for one whose father would love him as much as Bryce would. "I don't know," she said, meeting his eyes, her own soft with love. "We might."

He questioned her about it later, when they took their evening walk. "Would you really be willing to have another baby?"

She linked her arm through his, then directed a mock-haughty look his way. "Do you share Douglas's opinion that I'm too old?"

"No, not at all. But... are you serious?"

Because she knew how much it meant to him, she didn't tease. "Yes, I'm very serious. I realize that I'm almost thirty-six, but I'm in good health, and all four of my pregnancies were normal and easy. I don't see any reason why I couldn't manage one more, if the doctor says it's okay." She leaned against him, squeezing him hard around the waist. "I love you, Bryce. Why wouldn't I want to have your baby?"

"Kay always said my desire for children was nothing more than male ego."

"She was wrong. You have a lot of love to give. It's natural to want to give some of it to your own children." She slid her hand into his coat pocket, linking her fingers with his. "Bryce? Peter told me today about what happened between him and your father. I'm sorry."

"What did he tell you?" After twenty-six years of hostility, he couldn't help wondering what version Peter had given her—his own, or the truth.

"That he had convinced your grandmother to leave the estate to him instead of Frank. That when she changed her will to reinstate Frank as heir, he destroyed it, so that he would inherit."

Shaking his head, he chuckled softly. "I'll be damned. The old bastard actually admitted it to you?"

She nodded. "Why didn't Frank take him to court? The servants who witnessed the last will could have testified in his behalf."

"He *did* take it to court. It was the scandal of the century. The whole town took sides. You were only a little girl then. I don't guess you would have heard anything about it."

They stopped at the fallen tree trunk, where Bryce sat down and pulled Leah snugly between his legs. "The two servants were the only ones who had actually seen the new will. The day Gran died, Peter sent them away. I always suspected that he paid them off—he inherited a large sum of money along with the property. And they might have known there would be a bitter fight over the will and simply not wanted to be caught in the middle. Whatever, Dad's lawyers never found them, so it was his word against the will Gran's former lawyer had drawn up."

"If Peter hadn't destroyed the will, your father would have inherited the property. Eventually it would have belonged to you, but instead *I* own it. Does that bother you?"

He smiled faintly. "It doesn't matter anymore."

"Why not?"

He shrugged carelessly. "As soon as you and I are married, what difference will it make whether you own it or I do? It's all in the family."

She felt a chill creep through her bones. It was a simple, logical conclusion—one that she had reached herself only a few hours earlier. Why, then, did it bother her so much coming from him?

Leah lay awake most of the night, listening to Bryce's slow, even breathing and to the soft, settling sounds of the old house. His response to her question had left her too troubled to sleep. Why hadn't he left it at "It doesn't matter"? Why had she pressed him for reasons? And why was she letting it bother her? She believed that he loved her, didn't she? She trusted him, trusted his love, so she had to accept his response at face value. She had to believe that it didn't matter to him that she owned his father's land.

But if it did matter, it would explain a few other questions that had plagued her. Such as what a handsome, successful, sophisticated man like Bryce saw in an average, ordinary woman like her. Such as why he was willing to give up his life in Philadelphia to move to tiny Angel's Peak. Why, after six years alone, six years with very little involvement with women, he had suddenly fallen in love with her. Why, after the pain and heartache of his first marriage, he was willing to marry again. Why he was willing, even eager, to take on the burden of raising another man's children. And why he had never said the three simplest and most important words a man could say: "I love you."

He had assured her that he cared. He had shown her a tenderness that she had only dreamed about. He had treated her as if she were the most important person in his life. But he had never told her that he loved her.

She stared dry-eyed at the ceiling in the moonlit room. Did he love her but simply have trouble putting it into words, as she had convinced herself, or did she want his love so badly that she had fooled herself into believing that she had it?

She couldn't find the answer in the night stillness. Only the man sleeping beside her could give her that answer, but she could never ask the question. Asking him for the words would negate the meaning behind them. Anyone could say the words. She needed to know if he felt them.

And she needed to know soon.

Saturday morning Leah remained in the dining room long after the others had left. Colleen had brought her a fresh pot of coffee, and she was on her third cup when Bryce returned to sit across from her.

"What's wrong?" he asked after a moment.

Slowly she raised her eyes to his face. She didn't know when he had joined her, whether he'd been there ten seconds or ten minutes. She didn't even know how long *she* had been sitting there until she looked at her watch. Breakfast had ended nearly an hour earlier, she realized, and she hadn't stirred from her seat. "Wrong?" she echoed dully.

"You didn't sleep much last night, did you? There are dark circles under your eyes." He reached across the table to touch her cheek, then pretended that he wasn't hurt when she moved back to avoid his hand. "You hardly spoke to the kids this morning, and you didn't even notice that the rest of us were here. What's bothering you, honey?"

When he reached for her hand this time, she accepted the contact, but couldn't stop herself from questioning it—his touch, his concern, even his endearment. Was this what it would be like from now on? she wondered unhappily. Always questioning his motives when he touched her, spoke to her, or made love to her?

He rubbed his thumb over her engagement ring. Her silence concerned him. Something was obviously troubling her, but he couldn't think of anything that could have upset her so much. She had been completely normal last night. They hadn't made love when they had gone to bed, but she had done nothing to indicate that that had bothered her. "Leah, I can't read your mind," he said softly. "The only way I can help you is if you talk to me. Tell me what's wrong. Please."

She pulled back her hand and picked up her coffee cup. "Nothing," she said, but her smile, meant to be reassuring, was pathetic. She made no effort to sustain it. "You're right. I didn't sleep well last night. I'm just tired."

He didn't believe her, but he didn't have the heart to call her a liar. Instead he rose from his chair and bent to kiss the top of her head. "I'm taking Matthew shopping this morning. I thought we'd have lunch in town. Is that all right?"

She nodded silently.

He walked toward the door, then turned back and hugged her tightly. "Whatever's wrong, we'll work it out, okay? We'll make it right, Leah, I promise."

When she was certain that he had left the house, she got her coat and went to her workshop. Half a dozen projects were scattered across the table—dated ornaments that she made for each of the children every year and small keepsakes for the guests who spent Christmas at the inn—but she ignored them, lighted a fire and sat on the hearth instead.

Bryce had often accused her of complicating matters, so maybe she could look at this simply, unemotionally—only the facts. He had returned to Angel's Peak to make arrangements for his father's return. He loved his father very much; there was nothing that he wouldn't do for Frank. He had a good job, a beautiful home and wonderful friends in Philadelphia. He had never said that he loved her.

There was more, but fear and self-doubt got in the way, preventing her from continuing. When he had asked her to marry him, she had believed that he *must* love her; after all, there was no other reason to marry her. But now there was— the land. The land that Peter had betrayed his brother and his mother for. The land that Terence had married Leah for. Now it seemed that Bryce was willing to marry her for it, too.

Could she bear that? Could she stand knowing, for the rest of her life, that marriage to her was the price he had paid to regain the estate that was rightfully Frank's? She had married Terence under similar circumstances and had nearly withered away from the lack of love. Could she endure it with Bryce?

He came to the cottage when he returned from town with Matthew, and the moment he walked in the door, she knew the answer was no. She had accepted the circumstances of her marriage to Terence because she hadn't really loved him. She had called it love, but she had been a lonely, affection-starved teenager who had known nothing about love except that she wanted it—wanted to give and to receive it. Now she knew the difference, and she couldn't live with less.

He didn't offer a greeting as he removed his coat and gloves. In spite of the fire, it was chilly in the room, so he put another log onto the grate before sitting down at the opposite end of the hearth.

Whatever had been bothering her earlier was tearing her apart now. He could see it in the bleakness in her eyes, in the taut line of her mouth, the tense clenching of her hands. He was torn between the desire to yell at her for refusing to confide in him and the need to hold her and offer his silent, unfailing support. In the end he did nothing.

"Why did you ask me to marry you?"

His smile was somber, with none of its usual joy. "Because I want to spend the rest of my life with you."

She gave him a long, unblinking look. Dissatisfied with his answer, she restated the question. "Why do you want to marry me?"

"Why do you find it so hard to believe that I want you?" he asked with an uneasy smile, trying to tease, to ease the tension between them, to ignore the sharp twist of dread forming in his stomach.

"No one else has ever wanted me." She said it plainly, unemotionally. A simple statement of fact that revealed none of the heartache and anguish behind it. "Terence didn't. My own mother and father didn't. Why should you?"

He knew what she wanted to hear—three tiny little words that would mean the world to her. The three most difficult

words in the language for him. Saying them would give her
the power to destroy him, as Kay had very nearly done...but
she already had that power, didn't she? Whether he said the
words or not, she already had his love. "Leah..."

He had waited too long to speak. She interrupted him
with another cold, blunt question. "Is it because of this
place? Because I own the house and the land that should
have gone to your father?"

Bryce stared at her, his mouth open. Surprise wiped the
words of love from his mind and dissolved the painful knot
in his stomach. "Is that what this is about? The estate?" He
gave her a hug, then kissed her soundly, so relieved that he
didn't realize that she was stiff and ungiving in his arms.
"Lord, you scared me. I thought something was *really*
wrong. Do you think I care one way or the other about this
property? As long as it stays in the Cameron family, what
does it matter whose name is on the deed?"

She pushed him away, her face cold and pale, then stood
up to pace. To keep him at a distance. "It matters to me,
and I think it matters to you, too—a lot. I've been trying to
figure out why you were interested in me. You could have
any woman you wanted. Why me?" She didn't pause long
enough for him to answer, but rushed on, needing to say it,
to get it all out. "I knew part of it was the kids. You've
made no secret of how you feel about them, especially
Matthew. He's been the son you never had. But you don't
marry someone for her kids. There had to be something else
that you wanted."

Bryce folded his arms over his chest, feeling the pounding of his heart, and leaned back against the fireplace
stones. "There was," he said quietly. "You. Yourself. Your
love."

Sadly she shook her head. "I don't think love had much
to do with it. *I* was the only one who ever mentioned love
between us. You told me that you loved your father, your
home, even that you loved my children. But you never said
anything about loving me." She sat down once again on the

stones, drawing her knees to her chest and locking her hands together. The position effectively shut him out. "Maybe you *did* want my love," she murmured, almost to herself. "Maybe you were selfish enough to want it all. Or maybe it was just the price you would pay to get the rest of it—the house, the land, a son."

"You don't believe that, Leah." His voice was hoarse, his throat dry from the fear. "I wanted to tell you," he said quietly, "but I needed time to be sure—sure that you loved me, that it was going to last, that you wouldn't change your mind and leave me and take away everything I needed to be happy." He looked at her then, his eyes dark and sad. "You know, saying the words doesn't change how I feel about you. It doesn't guarantee that you'll love me in return. It doesn't mean that you'll stay with me. I used to tell Kay that I loved her practically every day, and look what it got me." He saw her stiffen at the mention of his ex-wife and swore under his breath. "I've tried to show you, Leah, in every way I know. You have to believe that I love you."

"That's what I kept telling myself all those times when you talked about wanting and needing and forever. All those times when I told you that I loved you, and you said nothing in return." Her voice grew softer until it was a whisper, faint and quavery with emotion. "I thought, because of the way you treated me, that you *must* love me. But you haven't given me special treatment. You've been nice and gentle, but that's the way you are with everyone else. I just wanted so badly to believe that I was special to you."

"You *are* special, Leah, and I *do* love you."

She smiled sadly. "How easily the words come now, when it's too late."

The fear expanded, filling every part of him. "It's not too late!" he said fiercely. "Damn it, Leah, listen to me. I don't care about this place! Marrying you isn't going to give it to me, anyway. If I only wanted the land, I would take you to court, not marry you!"

"Why drag the Cameron name through another trial when it would be so much easier to. . ." She couldn't say it aloud. She believed it, but she couldn't say it.

Bryce was staring at her, his eyes dark with derision. "To seduce you?" He had no trouble saying it. "You think I seduced you, asked you to *marry* me for this property?"

She dropped her head to her arms, hiding her face. If she was wrong, if somehow, for some reason, he *did* love her, she was insulting him outrageously. But those were very unlikely ifs.

He surged to his feet, unable to sit still another minute. He tugged his hand through his hair as he walked restlessly to the end of the room and back, then shoved his hands into his pockets. "Of course, you're right," he said sarcastically.

Leah's head flew up, her eyes seeking his. The shock and hurt in her eyes did nothing to soothe his own pain.

"After living in Philadelphia for twenty-six years," he went on, "I decided that I absolutely had to have my rightful inheritance, so I came here to disgrace my family by proving that my uncle was a thief. But when I got here, I discovered that my uncle no longer owned the house. My cousin's beautiful, innocent, insecure widow did. You're right—it was so much easier and so much more pleasant to seduce you for the land rather than fight for it. Of course, it meant that I would have to marry you, but, hell, I can make a few sacrifices, can't I? I can put up with you and your kids in exchange for the estate." He swore viciously. "For God's sake, Leah, be reasonable!"

There was a painful silence. He stared at her, and she gazed sightlessly at the floor. He wasn't reaching her. He could see it in the slump of her shoulders, in the emptiness of her expression. Nothing he said was getting through that solid wall of fear and doubt and insecurity. Because he hadn't told her that he loved her before she'd found out about the feud, he was going to lose her.

Slowly he knelt in front of her, hesitantly reaching for her hands, afraid that she would shrink back from his touch. "What kind of man do you think I am?" he whispered. "Do you really believe that I'm capable of doing what you said?"

She heard the pain in his voice and ached to know that she had caused it, that she was going to increase it with her answer. "It's easier to believe that you would do that than to believe that you love me."

Pulling away from her, he stood up. "If you can believe that, Leah, then you don't love me. You *can't* love me, because you know nothing about me." He didn't mean that. If there was one person in life who loved him, it was Leah. But he couldn't stop himself from saying it, because he was hurt. Disappointed. Frightened. He looked at her for a long time, waiting for her to say something, to tell him that he was wrong, that she did love him. Then he got his coat and left the cottage.

Only last night he had thought that his life was perfect. Except for the mere technicality of the wedding, he had everything he had ever wanted. How had he lost it all so quickly, so completely?

He walked through the woods, circling the perimeter of the estate time after time, unmindful of the cold or the snow that had begun falling.

Every problem had a solution. If he thought long enough and hard enough, he would find the solution for this. He would find a way to convince Leah that he loved her—her and not this damned land. It didn't help knowing that it was his own fault for not telling her sooner. He had known from the start that she was unsure, that her confidence was nonexistent. He should have realized that she, of all people, would need to hear the words, but he had been too concerned with protecting himself, too afraid of losing again. Refusing to admit his love hadn't protected him from anything; instead, it had hurt both of them. How could he make her believe him now?

He could offer her a prenuptial agreement, relinquishing all claim to the estate. But what would that accomplish? Married or not, he *had* no claims, and no desire for any. He could ask her to live someplace else with him, to sell the inn and remove it completely from their lives.... No, he couldn't, he acknowledged with a fresh ache. She loved this place—more than she loved him.

He looked up at the night-dark sky as heavy, wet flakes of snow fell onto his face. He had been walking for hours, and he was numb all the way through from the cold, yet he was no closer to a solution. He had made only one decision: he wasn't going to let her go this easily. He wasn't going to live without her.

When he returned to the house, it was dinnertime. Every seat at the family table was filled, except his and Leah's. "Do you know where she is?" Martha asked him worriedly.

"The last time I saw her, she was in the workshop." He had come to tell them that he wasn't hungry and to get a look at Leah, to see if she might listen to him. He had nothing new to say—just "I love you"—but if he said it often enough, maybe it would make a difference. He was afraid that he didn't have anything else to offer.

"The lights aren't on out there," Frank said. "I checked."

Douglas started to rise from his seat, but Bryce laid his hand on the boy's shoulder. "I'll see if she's still there."

He got his coat, still cold from the solitary walk, and crossed the backyard to the cottage. Just inside the door, he stopped to let his eyes adjust to the darkness. There was the glow of embers in the fireplace, but the room was as cold as it was outside. "Leah?"

She was sitting on the hearth, in the same place he'd left her hours ago. She made no response, and for a long time he couldn't think of anything else to say. He just stood there and looked at her, feeling her pain as sharply as his own, wishing he could soothe it, wanting only to heal her with a love that she didn't believe he could feel.

After a moment, he closed the door and went to her, crouching down in front of her and taking her hands in his. Even through his gloves he could feel how cold her fingers were. "My God, Leah, you're half-frozen," he murmured. He released her, put a log onto the fire and added chunks of kindling. As soon as it was burning, he added another log, then sat down beside her.

When the heat from the flames reached her, she shuddered violently, suddenly aware of how cold she was, and moved closer to the fire. Closer to Bryce.

His eyes were closed, but he could feel her, could hear the chattering of her teeth, could smell her fragrance. He longed to hold her, but didn't try. "They're worried about you up at the house."

"Tell them I'm all right," she whispered.

He gave a short, bitter laugh. "You've destroyed *my* life, but *you're* all right. God, Leah, I trusted you. How could you do this to us?"

How could he make her the villain? she wondered numbly. *She* wasn't the one who had been willing to trade marriage and love for a piece of land.

"Maybe that's part of the problem," he continued. "I trusted you . . . and you don't even know what that means."

Slowly she turned her head to look at him. In the light of the fire she was a warm mix of gold and copper. For a long moment their eyes met, reflecting the same emotions. Pain, sadness, sorrow. Then she spoke quietly. "Go away."

She hadn't given it any thought, but as soon as she heard her own words, she knew that was what she wanted. He had to leave. She couldn't go on living in the same house with him, eating at the same table, sleeping down the hall. One of them had to go, and even though her claim to the inn was dubious, her name was still on the deed. That meant Bryce had to move out.

"I'm not going to leave you like this, Leah. Listen to me. Trust me—"

She shook her head. Trust had gotten her into this predicament, but it couldn't get her out. It couldn't heal her heart. "I want you to leave the inn."

He was stunned. In the short time he had been there, the inn had become home to him. Leaving it now would be harder than it had been twenty-six years ago, because this time he would be leaving behind everyone he loved. "Are you kicking me out?"

Still looking into his eyes, she nodded. "I want you to go."

Maybe the damage between them was worse than he had realized. If she was forcing him to leave the house against his will, maybe he had been right earlier. Maybe she didn't love him. What irony. He had never told her that he loved her, yet he did, and she had said it often, but apparently she didn't. "Are you forbidding me to visit here?"

She couldn't go that far. It was still his home—more his than hers—and his father was here. Reluctantly she shook her head. "You can still see Frank."

"And Matthew? And the other kids?"

"I think—I think it would be best if you stayed away from them." All she knew for sure was that he had to stay away from *her*. She couldn't bear seeing him and knowing that she had lost him—worse, that he had never loved her.

"I see. So we're all to be punished because of your fragile little ego." He gave the words an ugly twist, flavored with anger grown out of pain. "Damn you, Leah."

He was halfway across the room when she spoke his name. In spite of his anger and frustration, hope leaped inside him, hope that she would relent, that she would let him stay and give him a chance to convince her of his love. But when he turned back, that last bit of hope died, leaving him cold and empty inside. She was holding out her hand, and firelight glinted off the diamond that was cradled there.

Although he didn't want the ring, he accepted it. Maybe someday she would take it back. If she never did, he thought, it would serve as a bitter reminder never to trust a woman again.

Chapter 10

Three days had passed since the scene in the cottage—the worst three days of Leah's life. She pretended that everything was all right, that Bryce's leaving made no difference to her, that her heart wasn't broken solidly in two. The family pretended to believe her act, but she knew she wasn't fooling anyone. Bryce was gone, she had made him leave, and she was dying without him.

If anyone knew where he had gone, they weren't talking. She knew he hadn't returned to the inn to see his father, and Frank hadn't made any trips into town, although he had received several phone calls. She assumed that Bryce was at a motel in Angel's Peak, or possibly Asheville—either place too far away, yet far too close.

She had put off discussing his absence with the kids until she was certain she could handle it without falling apart. Tonight she had asked them to meet privately with her following dinner.

The living room was brightly lit, every lamp on, the small tree lighted, candles burning on the tables and the mantel.

Like the rest of the house, the room was decorated for Christmas, with greenery, pine cones, mistletoe, a miniature Christmas village, a Santa music box and stockings. Crowded together on the mantel were nine angels holding nine stockings, including one next to Leah's, painstakingly embroidered with Bryce's name. After Christmas, she thought sadly, she would take it down and give it to Frank to give to Bryce.

Laurel and Megan were the first to arrive, followed by Douglas. Matthew came late, avoiding his mother to sit next to his brother.

Leah sighed. She loved her children very much, and there was no doubt that Bryce had loved them, too. Was she being selfish in depriving them of a father, simply because he hadn't loved *her*? He had respected her, had treated her well. Why hadn't that been enough for her?

Because she needed love. She had lived a lifetime without a man's love, and she needed it—needed it from Bryce. If he couldn't give that, none of the rest mattered.

She took a deep breath, then let her gaze rest for a moment on each child. Douglas, only a week and a half from his eighteenth birthday, looked more like his father—and more like Bryce—every day. In the last few days he had voluntarily taken on the task of spending more time with Matthew, trying to make up to his younger brother for Bryce's absence.

Laurel was sitting in the armchair opposite Leah's. She was growing up, too, losing her girlish roundness and slowly growing into a body that had become awkward in the last few years. Sprawled on her stomach on the floor was Megan, a younger, less formed version of Laurel. Neither girl had commented on Bryce's leaving, but Leah knew they both missed him. The bond they had formed with him was less demonstrative, less adoring than Matthew's, but strong all the same.

And Matthew. He sat on the sofa next to Douglas, clutching a bright green Tyrannosaurus. He had asked Leah a half dozen times a day when Bryce was coming back, where he had gone, why he had left without saying good-bye. He was the one who would be the most disappointed, who would hurt the most. It was his reaction that she dreaded the most.

She looked down at her left hand, where she had worn the beautiful diamond for less than a week. The older kids had noticed that it was gone and knew what that meant. Matthew didn't.

"I wanted to talk to you guys about Bryce." She twisted her hands together in her lap, wishing for the easiest and least painful way of saying this.

"When's he coming home?" Matthew asked, rubbing his nose with one small hand.

"We aren't going to get married."

She was only confirming what the older three had already guessed. They, along with Leah, turned their attention to Matthew. "But when is he coming home?" the little boy repeated.

"He's not." Leah felt tears stinging her eyes for the first time. "He's not going to live here anymore, honey."

His first reaction was confusion, then anger. "But why not?" he demanded. "He liked it here—he liked living with us! Why isn't he coming back?"

"Honey—"

"What did you do to him? It's all your fault! You made him leave, didn't you?" he accused, tears pooling in his dark eyes.

"Yes," she whispered, unable to see through her own tears. "But, Matthew—"

"I hate you!" he cried, jumping to his feet. "I hate you, and I don't want to live with you anymore!" He raced from the room, leaving his family in silence.

Finally Laurel got to her feet. "I'll check on him," she said awkwardly.

"I'll go with you." Douglas hesitated, then looked at his mother. "He didn't mean it, you know. It's just... he really liked Bryce a lot."

"We all did," Megan added as she, too, stood up. She received an elbow in the ribs from her sister. She glared at Laurel, but finished what she wanted to say. "We wanted him to be our father. I sure wish you hadn't sent him away, Mom."

They left her alone then in the brightly decorated room, and the tears came at last, scalding, heartbreaking tears of sorrow. Of loss. Of love.

Five days after leaving Angel's Peak, Bryce was back in Philadelphia and no closer to a solution than he'd been when he had left North Carolina. He just couldn't see any way to convince Leah that he loved her—especially from six hundred miles away.

Maybe he should return to Angel's Peak. He couldn't force his way back into residence at the inn, but at least he would be nearby, in town. At least he could see her. But he couldn't touch her. He couldn't hold her, or make love to her, or be a part of her life. That would be intolerable.

The worst part, he decided, was that he wasn't the one she was fighting. Deep down inside, she had to know that he loved her. What she doubted was herself, her own judgment. She doubted that she had anything to offer a man, that any man could want her, but she didn't doubt *him*. If only he could make her see that!

He called Frank every afternoon, keeping tabs not only on his father, but on Matthew and the others. On Leah. Frank had told him yesterday that the children knew the marriage was off, and that Matthew hadn't taken the news well. The old man had suggested that Bryce talk to the boy the next time he called, but Bryce had refused. Leah had made it clear that she didn't want him in contact with her son.

He propped his feet on the coffee table and sipped his coffee. He had to make plans. If he was going to stay in Philadelphia, he needed to take the house off the market, unpack the boxes that had never been shipped, find a job. But most of all he needed to accept that he was no longer going to be a part of Leah's life, that he wasn't going to be her husband, her lover or her children's father, that he wasn't going to have any children of his own.

And if he couldn't accept those things, he had to go back to Angel's Peak. He had to make her accept him. There were no other options.

"What are you doing here? I thought you were in South Carolina."

The honey-rich, cultured voice cut into his thoughts like an unwelcome, icy wind. He slowly lifted his gaze to see his ex-wife. "North Carolina," he corrected.

Kay removed the mink jacket that had been his thirteenth anniversary gift to her and let it drop onto the sofa. "Whatever," she said with an indifferent shrug. "Why are you here?"

"It *is* my house," he reminded her. "Why are *you* here?"

"I came over to decide which pieces of furniture I want."

"The agent gave you a key?" he asked sourly.

"I've always had one. You never asked for it when I moved out. Where is Leah?"

"Not here."

She sat down and crossed her silk-stockinged legs. "I can see that. Is there trouble in paradise?"

He sent her a warning glare. "I'm not in the mood for this, Kay. Leave me alone."

"There *is* trouble." She was sincere when she added, "I'm sorry. She seemed ideal for you."

His expression mocking, he tried to determine if that was an insult or a compliment. With another shrug she explained. "She's the kind of woman you should have married instead of me."

He acknowledged her accuracy with a nod.

"What happened?"

He couldn't believe that he was having this conversation with his ex-wife, of all people, but answered anyway. "You should enjoy this, Kay. She decided that she didn't want me, didn't trust me, didn't need me. She didn't do it with your finesse, but she got her own hits in."

For the first time he could ever remember, Kay looked embarrassed. "I've always regretted the way things ended between us," she admitted. "You were being so damned nice about the whole mess, and I just wanted out. I said a lot of things in anger—things that weren't true. I've never mentioned it since then, because I knew you were too intelligent to believe any of them, but ... I am sorry, Bryce."

"I *did* believe them," he confessed quietly. "For a long time, Kay. You almost destroyed me with your anger."

"Does that have anything to do with why you're not fighting for Leah?"

His admission came haltingly, painfully. "I don't have any ammunition. How can I make her believe that I love her when she's convinced that I only want her land?"

Kay clamped her hand over her mouth to hold back a startled laugh, but didn't quite succeed. "I'm sorry, Bryce," she apologized quickly, seeing that he was offended, "but that's so ridiculous. You're the least materialistic man I've ever known. You never cared about property or houses or cars or clothes. All you ever wanted was a family." Understanding lighted her eyes. "She has one, doesn't she?"

"Two sons, two daughters."

"And you love her."

He nodded.

"And the kids."

He nodded again.

"Then what are you doing here? Go back to North Carolina. *Make* her believe you. Do such a good job of loving her that she can't help but believe you."

"It's not that easy," he protested.

"No," she agreed with a smile. "But it will be worth it."

* * *

He was still considering the conversation with Kay when the phone rang several hours later. Only Frank knew that he was here at the house; for an instant he worried whether something had gone wrong at the inn, but his father sounded the same as usual.

"Matthew is sitting here beside me," the old man said without wasting time on greetings. "I think you should talk to him."

Bryce rubbed his eyes in dismay. "Dad, I told you, Leah doesn't want me to have anything to do with the kids."

"Please."

After a moment, his answer came with a sigh. "All right."

Frank shifted the phone; then Bryce heard a tiny little "Hey." The boy sounded a million miles away, as lonely and depressed as Bryce felt.

"Hey, Matthew, what's up?"

There was a long silence; then Matthew answered, "I want to come live with you."

He should have refused the call. He wasn't prepared for this. Nothing could have prepared him for this. "Matthew, I miss you," he said cautiously. "I miss you a lot, but you can't come here. You have to stay there in Angel's Peak with your mom."

"I don't want to stay with her. She's mean, and I don't love her anymore. Please, I want to come and live with you. I'll be good. I won't cause you any trouble, I promise."

"Don't ever say that about your mom again," Bryce warned, coming instantly to Leah's defense. "You have the best mother any boy could want, and I don't ever want to hear you say anything like that again."

"But she made you go away. I wanted you to be my dad, and she made you leave."

Matthew was crying, and Bryce felt close to it. "It's not your mother's fault, Matthew. I had to leave. Listen, little guy, I need you to stay there, to take care of your mom for me. I want you to make sure that she's all right."

"She cried," the boy admitted. "I never seen her cry before, but she did the other night. She never cried when you were here. We sure wish you would come back."

Did Leah also wish he would come back? Not likely, he admonished himself. If she wanted him, all she had to do was tell Frank. She knew he would come running.

"Will you be here for Christmas?"

"No," Bryce answered regretfully. He would be spending the holiday alone this year. "But my presents for you and the others are under the tree."

"We don't get the baby, do we?" That had been Matthew's Christmas wish. A new baby brother. It had been Bryce's, too.

"No," Bryce whispered. "I don't guess we do."

When the phone rang again Friday morning, Bryce was reluctant to answer it. He knew it wasn't going to be Leah, and she was the only person he wanted to talk to right now.

It rang again, echoing in the stillness. Tomorrow was Christmas Eve. Leah's birthday. She would be hosting a reception in the early evening, and after dinner the family was having a private party for her. He had been looking forward to sharing both events with her. Instead he would be alone in his empty house. What a way to spend Christmas.

The third ring seemed louder. He wondered how long the caller would wait before giving up. If it was his father, he would let it ring forever.

He picked it up in the middle of the fourth ring. It *was* his father.

"You've got to come home," Frank said, interrupting his son's hello. "You're not going to believe what that woman has gone and done. When can you get here?"

"Come home for what? What's happened? What has Leah done?"

"Isn't there a flight that leaves around noon? If you can be on it—"

"Dad, tomorrow is Christmas Eve. The only way I'm going to fly out of here on such short notice at Christmas is to sprout wings. Now calm down and tell me what's wrong." His fingers ached from clenching the phone so tightly, but he couldn't force them to relax. Would he always worry this way whenever he heard Leah's name? Would there ever come a time when what she did didn't matter anymore? The answers were depressingly simple. He would always worry, and she would always matter. Always.

"I *am* calm!" Frank insisted, not caring that he didn't sound it. "I don't want to discuss this over the phone. I'll just tell you that Leah no longer owns the estate." He knew that would catch his son's attention. "Now, when can you get here?"

Bryce leaned back against the cushions numbly. She had sold the estate? She had let it pass from the Cameron family without even giving them a chance to take it off her hands? "Why did she do it?" he asked in dismay. "Where is she going? What is she going to do?"

"She hasn't decided yet," Frank answered in an imitation of her prim tone. "You make your reservations. When you get here, come to Peter's house. We'll talk there."

Bryce was able to get a flight to Asheville. Because of the holidays, he had to take a circuitous route that included hour-long stopovers in four different cities, but by ten o'clock that night he was once again back in Angel's Peak.

He parked his rental car next to the little cottage where Peter and Martha lived, then stood for a moment in the snow, looking up at the inn. The Christmas lights he had hung with the boys were on, round and bright in the clear night air. Lights burned in the sitting room, where through the open draperies he could see guests gathered in small groups. He couldn't tell if Leah was entertaining them tonight, or if that task had fallen to someone else.

The porch light came on behind him, and he heard his father's voice. "Bryce? Come on in here, son."

With one last wistful look at the inn, he turned toward the cottage.

Martha was at the house with the guests, his father informed him as he ushered him into the kitchen. Peter sat at the table, a pot of coffee and three cups in front of him. He filled the cups and set one in front of each man.

"All right," Bryce said with a grim sigh. "What's going on? What has Leah done to make you send for me?"

"Take off your coat and sit down," Frank urged. While Bryce obeyed, he pulled a folded document from the envelope in front of him. "I got these papers today. The lawyer was going to call you, too, but I told him that I would take care of it."

Papers? Lawyer? Bryce sat down in the closest chair and held out his hand. Frank laid the papers in it.

He skimmed over the document, but it made no sense. Reading it again, he forced himself to concentrate, to put the words together into sentences, and at last he understood what they were saying. His hand trembling, he put the papers down, then looked from his father to Peter. "She can't do this." His voice was a stunned whisper, weak and unsubstantial in the quiet room.

"She most certainly can," Peter disagreed. "The property belongs to her. She can do whatever she wants with it." He hesitantly reached out to his nephew but didn't touch him. "Leah is a good woman—honest and loyal and just. She's trying to make amends for what *I* did so long ago in the only way she knows."

"Make amends?" Bryce echoed. He picked up the transfer deed, then threw it onto the table again. "She took everything I love away from me, and *this* is supposed to make up for it?" He shook his head in disgust. "What is she going to do now? Where is she going to go? What about the kids? How is she going to support them? For God's sake, what's wrong with her?"

When neither man offered an answer, Bryce once again picked up the legal document and looked at it. One half of the estate had been transferred to Frank, one half to Bryce. She was giving up any claim to the property and the business, and she and the children would vacate the house before January 1.

And go where? he wondered. Angel's Peak was the only place she'd ever known, the estate the only real home she'd ever had.

He never should have gone back to Philadelphia. If he had stayed here, he might not have convinced her that he loved her, but maybe he could have stopped her from signing those papers. Through some misguided sense of justice, she had given up everything. Now she had nothing for herself, for her children . . . or for him.

Dropping the papers once again, Bryce walked to the window and stared at the inn. For the past week he had been searching for a solution to this problem with Leah, and she had handed it to him, neatly gift-wrapped in the deed transfer. It was so simple, so beautifully simple, that he knew she, with her knack for complication, hadn't even realized what she had done.

"Well?" Frank asked testily. "What are you going to do about this?" He was tapping one long, bony finger on the papers, waiting impatiently for his son's answer.

Bryce was smiling as he turned to face the two older men. "First I'm going to thank Leah for the gift. Then I'm going to ask her to marry me."

"She's sent you packing once already," Peter pointed out. "What makes you think this time will be any different?"

"That." He nodded toward the papers. "Is her birthday party still scheduled for tomorrow night?"

Frank nodded.

Bryce addressed his next question to his uncle. "Can I stay here until then?"

After exchanging curious glances with Frank, Peter also nodded.

"Thanks. I'll get my bags." Outside at his car, he turned once more toward the inn. Leah had given him two precious gifts: his home, and her love. Tomorrow night he was going to give her a gift in return. Her doubts and fears would be put to rest forever, because tomorrow night she would know how much he loved her.

Leah stared into the open closet, her gaze skimming over the clothes hanging there, looking without touching for something suitable for tonight's party. She had never felt less like going to a party in her life, but she had made it through this evening's open house, and she would make it through the birthday party, too, for the children's sake.

It seemed as if, all her life, she had done everything for the children's sake. Yet yesterday, for the first time ever, she had made a decision that wasn't in the children's best interest. They didn't even know about it yet, but she would find the courage to tell them. Not until after Christmas—they deserved one more Christmas in the house that had been home to them all their lives—but soon she would tell them that they were moving. She didn't know where, she didn't know if she could even explain why, but she could tell them when.

She stared at the clothes, her eyes dark with fear. What was she going to do? She had always prided herself on her strength. After all, when you had no one else to rely on, you had to rely on yourself. But she was tired of being strong. She was tired of depending on herself, and of everyone else depending on her, too. Most of all, she was tired of being alone.

If she called Bryce, would he come back? she asked herself in a weak moment. Not if he had any brains. Only a fool kept coming back for more pain, and Bryce Cameron was definitely no fool. He had probably returned to Philadelphia, where he had a lovely home and wonderful friends and a boss who wouldn't hesitate to rehire the best executive he'd ever had. Why should he even consider returning to her?

At last she chose a light green dress. It was simple—plain, like herself, she thought disparagingly. She tugged it over her head and let the skirt fall softly around her calves. Fastening a darker green belt around her waist, she stepped into shoes of the same color, then went to the mirror above the dresser to brush her hair once more.

Staring at her reflection, she tried a smile. It wasn't very convincing, but considering the state of her life, it was acceptable. The kids wouldn't question it, and the adults would understand.

Everyone was waiting in the private living room when she entered. They sang "Happy Birthday," and she received hugs and kisses all around. Before she was allowed to cut the cake Colleen had baked, the children dragged her to the sofa to open her gifts.

Douglas handed her the final present. It was a small box, wrapped in elegant gold paper with a tiny silver bow. She held it flat in her palm, looking at it curiously. She had already opened gifts from each of the children, Peter and Martha, and Frank. Who was this one from?

She removed the bow and the thin strip of ribbon that encircled the box and pulled the paper loose. It was a green velvet jeweler's box. The same kind her engagement ring had come in. Her hands shook when she opened it to find the familiar, beautiful, precious ring inside, and tears filled her eyes. She looked up hopefully and saw Bryce leaning against the wall, just inside the door. His pose was casual, but the intensity of his gaze as he watched her made her shiver.

The rest of the family moved back, leaving a clear path between them. They had known that he was here, she realized, every one of them. Not even Matthew was surprised by his appearance.

She finally brought her gaze back from him to the ring. Removing it from the box, she held it in her palm. She had worn the ring for only a few days, but her hand felt bare without it. Just as her life felt bare without Bryce. "I . . ." She stopped to clear her throat. "I can't accept this."

He struggled to remain composed, hiding the fear that her refusal aroused. His throat was constricted, and his palms were sweating. Last night his theory had seemed so reasonable and logical, but tonight, face-to-face with her, nothing seemed reasonable or logical. His future depended on tonight. If he was wrong...

Slowly he straightened, pushed his hands into his pockets and walked toward her. He looked at the ring in her hand, wishing it were on her finger instead. He picked it up, the gold warm from her flesh, then closed his fingers around it.

The brief contact of his fingertips made her hand burn, the heat spreading through her. Was that it? Was he going to take his ring and leave, without saying one word to her?

Even as she thought it, he spoke. "You have nothing to give me."

She flinched at hearing it stated so bluntly, but it was true. She didn't own anything but her clothes. The furniture, the dishes, all the household goods had come with the house. The house that now legally belonged to Bryce and Frank.

"No car, no land, no house, no dishes to eat off, no bed to sleep in. You have nothing, Leah, but your children and yourself."

There were nine people in the small room, and except for Bryce, all of them were absolutely silent. But it wouldn't have mattered if they'd all been shouting. He wasn't even aware of them. All he could see, all he could think of was Leah.

Avoiding his gaze, she bit her lip to stave off the tears that were burning her eyes. Not on her birthday, she vowed. Not on Christmas Eve.

"But that's all I've ever wanted," he continued in a quiet, firm, unemotional voice. "I never cared about the property, or the house, or anything else you had, Leah. I loved *you*. You accused me of wanting you only for the land, but now the land is mine—mine and my father's. And I still want you. I still love you." Kneeling in front of her, he gently took her hands in his. "I still want to marry you."

Leah sat very still, the urge to cry gone. What he said made a crazy sort of sense. If he wanted to marry her now, when she could give him nothing but herself, then he had to love her, didn't he? Only love could make a man take on an insecure, vulnerable and sometimes foolish woman like herself. Only love could make him want to marry her.

He watched her for a moment, his fears slowly easing. She was considering his statement, looking at each word for flaws, for truth. In her own complicated way she would analyze everything he had said; then she would reach a conclusion. This time he knew it would be the right one.

She looked down at their hands. The ring was still in his palm, the stone pressing into the soft flesh of her fingers. Christmas was the season of miracles, and she had just been given one—a second chance with the only man she had ever loved. He was everything she wanted and everything she needed. He was strong and dependable, gentle and tender, and he would never leave her alone. On top of that, he loved her and loved her children. All she had to do was accept him, and the miracle would be complete.

When she raised her eyes to him, she was smiling that sunlight smile that transformed her into the loveliest woman he had ever seen. Her eyes were blue and soft with happiness and joy. With love. She held his hands tighter and asked in a husky, drawling whisper, "Forever?"

Bryce smiled, too, gently, peacefully. He turned her hand over and slipped the diamond ring onto her finger, sliding it into place, then raising her hand to his mouth for a kiss. "Forever," he agreed. "I'll love you forever."

There were excited murmurs of approval from the family; then the party resumed, but neither Leah nor Bryce noticed. He kissed her, a short touch of his mouth that only hinted at the hunger inside him, then drew back to look at her. "Happy birthday," he whispered, tenderly brushing a hand across her cheek.

She admired her ring for a minute, then hugged him close and whispered in return, "Merry Christmas."

And it was, he thought with satisfaction. The merriest Christmas of his life.

* * * * *

WOMAN HATER

DIANA PALMER

Chapter One

When Gerald Christopher first suggested going to his family ranch in Montana to rest his recently diagnosed ulcer for a few weeks, Nicole had instant reservations. He was the boss, of course, and if he wanted to go to Montana, there was no reason he shouldn't. But Nicole liked the pleasant routine of life in Chicago, where she'd spent the last two years working for the Christopher Corporation. At twenty-two, Nicole White had found a nice, pleasant rut for herself and she didn't particularly like change.

The problem was that if Mr. Christopher went to Montana for a month, as he was threatening, and closed down his personal office while he was gone, Nicole would be out of a job until his return. Despite her adequate wages, trying to live for a month without any salary was a frightening thought. That was almost laughable considering her background, because Nicole's family had been one of the old moneyed ones of Kentucky. Her father, in fact, was still one of the jet set, a noted sportsman as well as a horse-racing magnate, and lived the part. Nicole had long since renounced her share of the family fortune and gone to work for a living.

Her mother's death had been the last straw. Her father had been with his latest mistress at the time, not that he'd ever been home a lot. That hadn't mattered at the time, because Nicole had been sure that her new fiancé, Chase James, would set up their marriage and that his job as a real estate agent would make it possible for him to support the two of them. She'd figured wrong. Once Chase found out that Nicole had been foolish enough to give up her family fortune—and when he realized that she couldn't possibly be talked out of it—he asked for his ring back. His immediate defection to one of Nicole's moneyed and eligible girlfriends had shattered her young life.

At the age of twenty, she'd left the elegant brick mansion of her childhood in Lexington, Kentucky, and a racehorse farm worth millions, to live the frugal life as a secretary in Chicago, where she had a friend with whom she could room. She smiled, remembering her lack of skills at the time, and how patient Mr. Christopher had been until she'd crammed in some courses at the local secretarial school. Lucky for her that he'd liked her personality and had decided to take a chance on her secretarial skills improving. They had. She'd graduated from the course at the top of her class.

It all seemed a long time ago now, a part of her life that was like some slowly fading photograph of a reality she no longer belonged to....

"You'll like it there, Nicky," Gerald Christopher said dreamily, staring out the window. "The ranch is in the southern part of the state, nestled in the Rocky Mountains. It's rich with forests, lakes, rivers, peace and quiet. Just the thing to help me get over this ulcer they've diagnosed. We can work in peace and you can have plenty of free time to yourself."

"But your brother and his family—won't they mind having your secretary to house and feed?" she asked, her pale green eyes hesitant in a plain but interesting oval face, surrounded by naturally curling short dark hair. Despite the fact that she'd worked for him for two years, she knew very little about his private life. He'd never made a habit of talking casually about anything personal, as some employers did. She knew he had a brother, and he'd mentioned a woman named Mary, whom she'd assumed was his sister-in-law. But that was really all she knew about him in any personal way.

"Winthrop doesn't have a family," he said, smiling as he turned toward her. He was tall with brown hair and dark brown eyes. Not a bad-looking man and he seemed pleasant enough, but he wasn't a woman chaser or a ladies' man. He was very businesslike and a terrific boss, and Nicky adored him. In a purely businesslike way, of course. Her heart was pretty impregnable these days, hardened by Chase's cruel defection. That had ended her dreams of marriage. The hated wealth that had blinded her to men's greed was gone now, too. And without her designer clothing and her diamonds, men didn't seem to notice her at all. Of course, her manner was stiff and off-putting with most men, but she didn't even realize it.

"Your brother came to the office once, didn't he?" she ventured, recalling vaguely a tall, very cold sort of man she'd barely glimpsed on an unusually hectic day and had learned later that it was Mr. Christopher's mysterious older brother.

"Yes, he did," he said. "Winthrop owns a small share in the corporation, you see, but he's the silent partner. He doesn't care for desks and boardrooms. Dad left him the ranch, which is worth a mint, and I have an equally small share in that. He's primarily a cattleman, and I'm a businessman, so we each have what we like most. He's something of a loner. But as long as we keep out of his way, we won't have any trouble."

That sounded ominous. She looked at the green-lined white steno pad in her lap. "A month is a long time," she said slowly.

"Come on, Nicky, what have you got going that you can't walk away from?" he chided gently. "No boyfriends, no evening classes. A month in the country would do you good. If that wealth of potted plants you surround your desk with is any indication, you must be a country girl at heart. Or at the very least, a frustrated gardener."

She laughed. "I do love plants. And, yes, I'm a country girl. I was born and bred in Kentucky," she confessed, "and I guess I do miss it sometimes. My people were farmers," she added, tossing off the white lie as easily as she twirled the pen in her slender hand. That was the story she told people, anyway, and it prevented a lot of embarrassing questions about why she'd given up all that money.

"And farming isn't the best profession to be in these days," he agreed with a fond smile. "I can see why you came to the big city. But since you do like the country, I presume, where's the problem?"

She sighed. "It's not quite orthodox."

"No, little puritan, it isn't," he agreed. "But for the next month, you're my private secretary and I'll even increase your salary to make it more acceptable."

"Oh, but that's not nec—" she began.

"Certainly it is," he countered, waving a lean hand at her. "I'm tired of the rat race, Nicky. I need rest or this ulcer is going to put me in the hospital. We'll both benefit from some mountain air."

"It's October," she reminded him. "Late October. Doesn't it snow in Montana in late October?"

"Oh, frequently," he agreed. "And the ranch is way up in the Rockies, near the Todd place—" he paused, glancing at her with an odd expression "—you remember Sadie, don't you?"

"Yes. She was very nice." A nurse, in fact, and Nicole's taciturn young boss had dated her and had been devastated when she left several months ago to take care of her invalid mother. Hmm, Nicole thought; that was about the time his health problems reared their ugly head.

"Anyway, the ranch is near the Todd place," he continued, "and we used to get snowed in a good bit. But we always get a chinook when we need one, and we can dig our way out. Stop worrying."

"What's a chinook?"

"A warm wind that comes unexpectedly to melt the snow," he said, smiling. "You'll love it there, Nicky. I promise."

I hope so, she thought. All at once she wondered if he had more than just health reasons for wanting to work at home. Sadie had managed to drag him out of his shell, and there had been a tangible something between them before her abrupt departure. It might turn out to be an interesting trip. "All right, I'll go," she agreed. "But you're sure your brother won't mind?"

He looked vaguely disturbed for a second. Then he smiled. "Of course I'm sure."

Nicky wondered later about that hesitation. Mr. Christopher had hardly ever mentioned his brother in all the time she'd worked for him. But through the office grapevine there had been some small bit of gossip about the Montana rancher, something someone had whispered just after his brief visit. If only she could remember it.

Becky, a blond and vivacious woman who worked for one of the vice presidents, breezed into the office after Mr. Christopher had left for the day.

"What's this I hear about some exotic vacation you're taking with the big boss?" she teased.

Nicky laughed. "If you call the backwoods of Montana exotic, then I guess it's true." She sighed as she covered the computer. "I do hope you'll come to my funeral. I have visions of being eaten by a puma or carried off by a moose."

"You might be carried off by Winthrop." Becky grinned. "Or haven't you heard the grizzly tales about him?"

Nicole turned, her eyes wide and curious. "Is he terrible?"

"A wild man, from what we hear. They said some society girl threw him over a few years back, and he actually went to her engagement party with a Hollywood movie star—a girl who turned out to have been a school friend of his and owed him a favor. He called up the friend and paid her expenses all the way from Hollywood, just for the occasion. Ruined the event, of course, since the movie star got all the attention. He used to be a ladies' man and he's always been well-to-do, and he traveled in those very ritzy circles. But since then, he's pretty much given up his playboy status and turned to the great outdoors. They say his experience with the blond heiress has soured him against rich women in a big way. Can't blame him too much, can you?"

"He sounds... interesting." Nicky chose her words carefully; it wouldn't do to show her fear.

"Looks that way, too, except for the scars and the limp. Although the scars had faded nicely the day he was in here." She grinned at Nicky. "He sure gave you a look, but you were so busy you didn't even notice him."

"I remember him, but I didn't look long enough to see the limp." She frowned. "How did he get it?"

"From the wreck. Deanne Sharp—of the Aspen Sharps, you know, ski-resort wear and accessories, and Winthrop's fiancée at the time—was driving. They crashed. He almost lost his leg, and during his recovery, she walked out on him. I guess she only liked him for his athletic ability. He was an Olympic-quality skier and they met on the ski slopes. He missed the Olympic team by a few points when he was younger."

"That was what I was trying to remember. Someone said he'd been in a wreck, but I forgot what happened."

"The lovely Deanne happened. I hear she's on husband number three now, and has millions. But all that happened three years ago, the year before you came to work," Becky said. "We all heard about it. What he did at that woman's engagement party might have sounded cruel, if you didn't know it all. We were in Winthrop's corner, all of us. He got a bad break. As it is, he gets around pretty good, but he isn't the pinup he used to be. An experience like that could make a man bitter, you know."

Nicky drew in a slow breath. "A real woman hater."

"Now that's the truth," Becky laughed. "No, he doesn't like women. So if you go to the ranch with the big boss, make sure you take lots of warm clothing. That way you won't get frozen—by the weather or Winthrop."

"We may get snowed in," Nicky moaned.

"The snows come big in Montana," she was told. "Six feet deep and more, sometimes. My best friend worked at the hospital here until she had to go back to Montana to take care of her invalid mother a few months ago. You might remember her—Sadie Todd? The boss used to take her out."

"Yes, I remember," Nicky said with a smile, and kept her mouth shut about what Mr. Christopher had told her.

"They grew up together," Becky added. "I visited her once. Montana is lovely country, but brutal. It's frozen a lot of people, but if you want to get away from the world, there's no better place."

"I don't think I want to go."

"Don't be silly," Becky chided. "The big boss is a doll. Winthrop can't be too horrible."

But Nicky still wasn't sure. She went home and got her small apartment in order, still with misgivings. It didn't take long to pack, because there wasn't a lot to pack. She had jeans and sweaters, some blouses and a single jersey dress, because she had the feeling that she would be roughing it.

She took a thick winter coat as well, and some leather boots left over from the past. Her lips twisted in a thin smile when she surveyed the contents of her suitcase and she thought about the clothes and life-style she'd once taken for granted. She missed that easy luxury once in a great while, and when she had to pinch pennies to meet the rent, her principles didn't help much. But she was a different girl from the arrogant little miss her parents' financial indulgence and emotional indifference had created. And that meant a lot. She'd learned about reality in the past two years, and about real people, who didn't put a dollar sign on their friendship. Even though her friend Dana, with whom she'd roomed, had married a year ago, Nicole still had friends like Becky, and they often went to movies or the theater together.

She pulled on a pair of cotton pajamas, washed her face and went to bed. It wouldn't do any good to worry about the past or the future. It was enough to cope with the present.

A week later, Nicole and Mr. Christopher flew out to Montana in the corporation jet. She wore the gray jersey dress for the flight, along with a minimum of makeup. She looked sweet and young and totally unlike a glamorous socialite. She didn't want to start off on the wrong foot by deliberately antagonizing the elder Mr. Christopher, who had plenty of reason to dislike that type of woman.

"You don't mind if I work?" Gerald Christopher asked with a smile, looking up from the papers in front of him.

"Not at all," she assured him. "I'm not nervous of flying."

The flight seemed to take a long time, but perhaps that was because Nicole wasn't reading. She stared out at passing clouds, a little anxious about the welcome she was going to get when they got off the plane.

"Mr. Christopher, your brother does know I'm coming?" she asked him when they were over Butte and about to land.

His dark eyebrows arched. "Of course. Don't worry, Nicky, everything's going to be fine."

Sure it was. She knew that the instant they got off the plane and she got a good look at the expression on Winthrop Christopher's face.

She recognized him at once. He was a big man. Taller than his brother, broad shouldered and lean hipped. He was wearing work clothing—jeans and dusty boots, with a checked shirt under a massive sheepskin jacket. On his head was a battered black Stetson twisted into an arrogant slant over one dark eye. He looked like a desperado. He hadn't shaved, and the white line of a scar curved from one cheek into the stubble on his square chin with its faint dimple. His face was rather square, too, and his features severe. He had a straight, rather imposing nose, and his black eyes gleamed with a cold light. In one lean, dark-skinned hand he held a burning cigarette. And the look he was giving Nicky would have curdled fresh milk.

"Hello, Winthrop," Gerald said, shaking his brother's hand. He glanced at Nicky with a smile. "In our childhood days, I used to call him Winnie, but I gave it up when he blacked one of my eyes. Despite all that, I know he'd die for me," he added with a grin, which the older brother didn't return. He was too busy glaring at Nicole, his dark eyes cutting into her oval face, looking for imperfections, making an unpleasant inventory of what he saw. "Winthrop," Gerald continued quickly, "this is my private secretary, Nicole White."

"How do you do, Mr. Christopher," Nicky said politely and she actually managed to smile, but her knees felt unsteady. This was no welcome at all. Dislike was too mild a word for what she read in those eyes. Wounded man, she thought, even while she wished she could run. She understood the meaning of betrayal, because she knew it intimately. For the first few months of her exile, Chase's handsome face had imposed itself over every letter she typed, every book she read, every television program she watched.

Winthrop's dark eyes narrowed. His thin, chiseled lips pursed thoughtfully, but there was no smile to ease the hardness of that rugged, unshaven face. "Yes, I remember you," he said curtly. His voice was deep and curt. "You're young."

"I'm twenty-two," she said.

"Young." He turned abruptly, with a care that no physically fit man would have had to take. "I've got the pickup. Does your pilot want to come out to the ranch and have something to eat?"

"No, he's due back to fly one of the other executives over to New York," Gerald replied, clapping an affectionate hand on Winthrop's shoulder. Brave man, to touch that walking inferno, Nicky thought as she fell into step behind them.

"I'll get the luggage." Winthrop started toward the plane, favoring one leg, and Nicky hesitated, her eyes speaking her thoughts. He gave her a look that stopped her from moving or speaking. He could have stopped a brawl with that glance. Her half-formed offer to help was frozen solid on her lips. With a violent flush, she turned away and followed Gerald.

"Don't ever offer to help him," her boss cautioned in a soft, quiet tone. "He's a little less sensitive about it these days, but soon after it happened, he threw a punch at one of the cowboys just for offering."

"I'll remember." She felt stung. The older brother was going to be hard going, and her first impulse was to ask if she could go back to Chicago.

Gerald Christopher seemed to sense her feelings, because he put an affectionately careless arm around her shoulder. "Don't panic," he teased. "He doesn't bite."

"Thank God I've had all my inoculations," she sighed, but she smiled back.

Behind them, the older man was watching that exchange of smiles and the arm around Nicky and putting his own connotation on what was going on between his younger brother and his secretary. The look in his eyes was both threatening and disapproving as he picked up the cases and followed them to the cream-colored pickup truck.

It was a long ride to the ranch, down a highway dwarfed by the towering, autumn-hued peaks of the Rockies. Soon Winthrop turned off onto some mountainous dirt roads that didn't actually seem like roads at all. To Nicky, squashed between the two men, it was a cold and unnerving experience. She could feel Winthrop Christopher's long, powerful leg come in contact with hers every time he pressed on the accelerator, and her body was reacting to the feel of his shoulder against hers in ways she hadn't expected. He made her tremble with awakening sensation, made her feel alive as she hadn't felt since her late teens. She didn't like that, or him, and her face took on the hardness of stone as the road wound on and on, through fir trees so tall and thick that Nicky stared in fascination at their girth. The forested areas were becoming thick now that they were off the rolling plain that had led to them, down country roads where houses were miles apart and traffic was practically nonexistent. Nicky, who'd read about Montana, hadn't been prepared for its vastness, or for the glory of orange-tipped aspens with their thin silvery trunks, and cottonwoods fluffy and yellow-hued, and those incredibly big pines. Or for the sheer splendor of the mountains and the crisp, clean coldness of mountain air. She watched, rapt, as the mountains shot up in front of them. Winthrop turned onto a tiny dirt road and they started to go up.

"Not what you expected, Miss White?" Winthrop chided as she stiffened on a sudden hair-raising curve as he gunned the truck up what seemed like a mountainside. "Montana isn't all pretty little photographs in coffee-table books."

"It's very mountainous," she began.

"That it is." He wheeled around another curve, and she got a sickening view of the valley below. It was just like the Great Smoky Mountains, only worse. The Smokies were high and rounded with age, but the Rockies were sharp and young and much higher. Nicky, who had no head at all for heights, began to feel sick.

"Are you all right, Nicky?" Gerald asked with concern. "You've gone white."

"I'm fine." She swallowed. Not for the world would she let Winthrop see what his careless wheeling was accomplishing. She held onto her purse for dear life and stared straight ahead, her jaw set, her green eyes unblinking.

Winthrop, who saw her stubborn resolve, smiled faintly to himself. Nicky might have been surprised to know how much it took to make him smile these days.

Another few miles, and they began to descend. The valley that opened before them took Nicky's breath away. She forgot her nausea in the sheer joy of appreciation. She leaned forward, with her slender hand on the dash, her eyes wide, her breath whispering out softly.

"Heaven," she breathed, smiling at maples gone scarlet and gold, at huge fir trees, delicate aspens and fluffy cottonwoods and the wide swath of a river cutting through it all, leading far into the distance like a silver ribbon. "Oh, it's heaven!"

Winthrop's eyebrows levered up another fraction as he slowed the truck to give her a better view. At the end of the road was a house, a huge sprawling two-story house that seemed part of its environs. It was made of redwood, with decks on all sides and an enormous porch that seemed to go all the way around it. It had to have fireplaces, because smoke was coming from two chimneys. Maples were all around it, too ordered not to have been planted deliberately years before, and with the mountains all around, it had a majesty that a castle would have envied.

"Lovely, isn't it?" Gerald sighed. "Every time I leave it, I get homesick. Winthrop hasn't changed a single thing about it, either. It's been this way for forty years or more, since our mother planted those maples around the house when our father built it."

"I thought they looked as if someone had planted them." Nicky laughed. "They're in a perfect semicircle around the back of the house."

"Some city people might think that trees grow in perfect order," Winthrop mused, glancing coldly at Nicky. "Amazing, that you were able to pick it out so easily."

"Oh, Nicky grew up on a farm, didn't you, country girl?" Gerald grinned, tweaking her hair. "Way over in Kentucky."

"Good thing they plant trees in perfect order in Kentucky, and teach native sons and daughters to recognize the difference between a planted tree and a naturally seeded tree," Winthrop said without looking at her. "I guess there are people who assume God planted them in rows."

That was a dig, and Nicky wondered what the big man would do if she leaned over and bit him. That amused her and she had to fight to keep from grinning. He was watching her again, his eyes darkly piercing. He disturbed her so much that she dragged her gaze away and felt her cheeks go hot. It was incredible how easily this man got through her defenses. She was going to have to be careful to keep out of his way.

"Did I write you about the Eastern sportsmen I'm expecting week after next?" Winthrop asked Gerald unexpectedly. "I've organized a moose hunt for them, but I'll warn you in plenty of time to keep out of the section I'm planning to hunt."

"I remember," Gerald nodded. "I hope they have some savvy about weapons. Remember the solitary hunter who came one winter and shot your prize bull?"

Winthrop glared at him. "That wasn't funny," he said and glared at his two passengers, who were fighting smiles. "Damned fool couldn't tell a stud bull from a deer...." Winthrop wheeled the truck up the dirt drive. "These are my Herefords," he added, nodding toward the red- and white-coated herds grazing across the flat plain toward the river. "They're in winter pasture now. I rent some government land for grazing, but I own most of it. It's been a bumper crop of hay this year. There's enough to spare for a change."

Nicole, who knew about farming and winter feed, nodded. "The southern states aren't having such luck," she remarked. "Drought has very nearly ruined a lot of cattlemen and farmers." She didn't question the way he spoke with possession about the family ranch, since Gerald had already told her that Winthrop had complete control of it.

Winthrop frowned as he glanced at her, but he didn't say anything. Her name, her last name, rang a bell, but he couldn't remember why. No matter, he thought; he'd remember eventually where he'd heard it before.

He parked the truck at the door of the huge house and got out, leaving Gerald to help Nicky to the ground.

A big, elderly woman came ambling out onto the front porch to meet them. She had high cheekbones and a straight nose, and she was very dark.

"That's Mary," Winthrop said, introducing her. "She's been here since I was a boy. She keeps house and cooks. Her husband, Mack, is my horse wrangler."

"Nice girl," Mary muttered, watching Nicole closely as the three newcomers came up onto the porch. "Long legs, good lines. Plain face but honest. Which one of you is going to marry her?" she demanded, looking from Gerald to Winthrop with a mischievous smile.

"I wouldn't have a woman, fried, with catsup," Winthrop replied without blinking, "but Gerald may have hopes."

Before Gerald could say anything, Nicky got herself together enough to reply. She did it without looking at Winthrop, because her cheeks were flushed with temper and embarrassment.

"I'm Mr. Christopher's secretary, Nicole White," Nicky said quickly, and forced a smile as she extended her hand. "Sorry to disappoint you, but I'm only here to work."

"And that is a disappointment," the woman sighed. "Two bachelors, all the time. It weighs heavy on my heart. Come. I will settle you."

"Mary is Sioux," Winthrop told Nicole. "And plainspoken. Too plainspoken, at times," he added, glaring at Mary's broad back.

Mary whirled with amazing speed for such a big woman and made some strange gestures with her hand. Winthrop's eyes gleamed. He made some back. Mary huffed and went up the long, smooth staircase.

"What did you do?" Nicole asked, amazed.

Winthrop looked down at her from his great height, his eyes faintly hostile but temporarily indulgent. "The Plains Indians spoke different languages. They had to have some way to communicate, in the old days, so they did it with signs. This," he added, drawing his hand, palm down, across his forehead, "for instance, means white man or paleface. The sign refers to this part of a man's forehead that was usually covered by a hat and so didn't get tanned like the rest of him. It was pale. This," he continued, rubbing two fingers in a long oval on the back of his left hand, "means Indian."

"Winthrop and Mary used to talk about the rest of us at the table—" Gerald chuckled, tugging affectionately at a short curl beside Nicky's ear "—using sign language. None of us could understand a word."

"It's fascinating," Nicky said, and meant it.

"If you ask Mary, she might teach you a little," Winthrop told Nicky, smiling with cool arrogance. In other words, that look said, don't expect any such favors from me.

She wondered how she was going to survive a month around him, but she did come from a long line of Irishmen, so maybe her spirit was tough enough to cope. She turned back to Gerald. "Do you want to work today?"

"No," Gerald said with certainty. "Today we both rest. Get on some jeans and I'll show you around."

"Great!" She ran upstairs, careful not to look at Winthrop Christopher. It was going to be imperative that she keep out of his way while she was here. He wasn't going to pull his punches, apparently, or accord her any more courtesy than he would have given to any other woman. Remembering what Becky had told her, it was even understandable. But it was going to make her stay here more uncomfortable than she'd expected. The fact that he disturbed her only added to her discomfort. Becky had said that Winthrop had been watching her the day he came to the office. And it was vaguely unnerving to think of those black eyes watching her in an unguarded moment. And why had he? Did she remind him of the woman who'd crippled him? She wasn't blond, of course, but perhaps her facial features were similar. She'd have to ask Gerald.

She was only sorry that she couldn't dislike Winthrop as forcefully as he seemed to dislike her. Quite the contrary; he disturbed her as no man ever had, scarred face, limp and all.

Chapter Two

The room Mary led Nicole into was delightful. It had pink accents against a background of creamy white, complete with a canopied bed and ornate mirror and even a small sitting area with pink, satin-covered chairs.

"This was their mother's room," Mary said. "Pretty, yes?"

"Are you sure I was meant to go in here?" Nicole asked hesitantly.

"Oh, yes, very sure. Mr. Winthrop said so." She winked at Nicole without smiling. "With his hands, you see."

Nicole shook her head. "He seems very..." She turned, shrugging as she tried to find words.

"His path has not been an easy one," Mary told her. Those dark eyes were sizing her up while she spoke. "Gerald was the favorite. He was a gentle, easy child. Winthrop was forever in trouble, always fighting, always in turmoil. He was the eldest, but not the most loved. And then came her. She with the blond hair and city ways, who was like a clear morning to me, and I saw through her. But Winthrop could not see through to the greed that motivated her. She crippled him and left him.''

Nicole searched the smooth old face quietly. "He hides," she said perceptively.

Mary smiled. "You see deep."

"I know a survival instinct for what it is," came the quiet reply. "We all hide inside ourselves when we've been hurt." She met the dark eyes levelly. "I won't hurt him."

"I see deep, too," Mary mused. "He won't let you close enough to do harm. But watch yourself. He has no love for women. He might take out old wounds on you."

"I'm a survivor," Nicole said, laughing. "I'll manage. But thank you for the warning."

Mary only nodded. "Come down when you are ready. Are you hungry?"

"I could eat a moose," the younger woman sighed.

"Lovely idea. I have moose in the freezer. How would you like it? Baked, fried or in a stew?"

Nicole burst out laughing. "I love stew."

"Me too." Mary grinned and left her.

Nicole put on a pair of faded jeans with a long-sleeved, gray knit shirt, because the air was chilly, and her pink sneakers and went downstairs without bothering to fix her makeup or comb her hair. She wasn't trying to catch any eyes, after all, so why irritate Winthrop by making it look as if she were making a play for him?

There was no one around, so she went outside and found a comfortable seat on the porch swing. It was peaceful. Birds twittered and somewhere a dog barked. Farther away, cattle were lowing. Nicole closed her eyes as the breeze washed around her. Heaven.

"I see you've found the swing."

She jerked upright as Winthrop came out onto the porch. He was bareheaded, still in the jeans and blue-checked shirt he'd worn to the airport. He'd taken time to shave, because his face was dark and smooth now, with the hairline white scar more visible without the stubble of a beard to hide it.

"I like swings," she said. Her pale green eyes wandered over him. He was terribly attractive without his jacket. Muscles rippled in his long legs when he walked, in his arms when he lifted them to light a cigarette. Despite his size, there wasn't a spare ounce of fat on him. He looked lean and fit and a little dangerous, despite the faint limp when he moved toward her.

"Deer come up into the yard sometimes," he observed. He dropped into a big rocking chair and crossed his long legs. "Moose, elk ... it's still pretty wild here in the valley. That's why we attract so many bored Eastern sportsmen. They come here to hunt and pretend to 'rough it' but they've lost something that mountain people have all their lives. They've lost hope." He glanced down at her. "I hate rich people."

She felt as if he knew something, but she was afraid to bring the subject out into the open. "I'm not rich," she said, and it was the truth. "But I thought you were."

It was the wrong thing to say. His dark eyes kindled and his face took on the sheen of stone. "Did you?" he asked deliberately, and the mockery in his face was daunting. "Was that why you came with Gerald, or is it his money you're after?"

"You don't understand—" she began.

"I understand women all too well," he returned coldly. He moved away from her without another word, almost colliding with Gerald, who was coming out of the house as he was entering it.

"Sorry, Winthrop," Gerald murmured, curious about the expression on his brother's face. "I was looking for Nicky."

"I'm out here, Mr. Christopher!" she called.

"Oh, for God's sake, I'm Gerald here," he said shortly, joining her with a resigned glance over his shoulder as the door slammed behind Winthrop. He looked even younger in jeans and a pullover shirt. Nicky moved over to make room for him on the swing, and struggled to regain her lost poise. Winthrop was going to make her life miserable, she just knew it, and her stupid careless remark had provoked him. "Mr. Christopher was my father," Gerald continued, "and he was *Mister* Christopher, too," he added with a faint smile. "Our mother was on a camping trip up here. She wandered off and he found her. He nursed her back to health and she left, thinking that was the end of it."

"Was it?" Nicole asked.

Gerald laughed. "No. As a matter of fact, Dad followed her all the way to New York, found her at some social gathering, picked her up and carried her to the train station and brought her here. Eventually, to save her reputation, she agreed to marry him."

"I guess he was used to getting his own way," Nicky mused, and in her mind's eye she could see Winthrop doing exactly the same thing. Her fine skin flushed just a little at the unexpected thought.

"They were happy together," Gerald said. "She died one spring of pneumonia. He died six months later. They said it was a heart attack, but I've often wondered if it wasn't loneliness that did it." He paused for a moment, then said suddenly, "I'm sorry Winthrop's so inhospitable." He glanced at Nicole's quiet face. "You aren't afraid of him, are you? If you are, don't ever let him see it. He's a good man, but he's pretty hard on women."

"I'm not afraid of him," she said. And she meant it. She wondered if there was any chance that he found her as disturbing as she found him. That didn't bear thinking about.

"You must miss all this in Chicago," Nicole said, looking up at her boss.

"I miss this, and other things," he replied. He stared at a house far on a hill in the distance, his eyes narrowed and unexpectedly sad. "Sadie Todd lives over there," he said absently, "with her invalid mother. We'll have to go and visit her while we're here."

"She was nursing at the general hospital, wasn't she?"

"Yes. She had to give up her job and come home when her mother had a stroke. Mrs. Todd is completely paralyzed on one side and doesn't seem to want to get any better. Sadie said she couldn't leave her at the mercy of strangers. Her father is dead."

She knew almost to the day when Sadie had left, because Gerald Christopher had withdrawn into a tight little shell afterward and seemed to walk around in a fog. He'd put enough pressure on himself thereafter to give him that ulcer. But it had surprised her that he wanted to come home, because he worked like a Trojan all the time lately. She was almost sure that Sadie was the reason he felt the need of a month's vacation in Montana. She smiled to herself.

"I'd like very much to go and see her," she said.

He smiled down at her. "You're a nice person, Nicole." He got up. "I'm going to make a few phone calls. Just sit and enjoy the view, if you like."

"Yes, sir," she promised.

He went inside, and she lounged in the swing until Mary called her to have a sandwich. She sat in the spacious kitchen, enjoying a huge ham sandwich and a glass of iced tea while Mary prepared what promised to be the world's largest moose stew. They talked about the ranch and the country and the weather, and then Nicole went out the back door and wandered down to the river, just to look around.

She could imagine this country in the years of the Lewis and Clark expedition. She'd read a copy of their actual journal, enjoying its rather anecdotal style, seeing the country through their eyes in the days before supersonic jets and superhighways. Trappers would have come through here, she mused, kneeling beside the river with her eyes on the distant peaks. They'd have trapped beaver and fox and they'd have hunted.

Kentucky had its own mountain country, and Nicole had been in it a few times in her life. It had been a different setting then. Elegance. Parties. Sophisticated people. Wealth. She sat down on a huge rock beside the river and tore at a twig, listening to the watery bubble of the river working its way downstream. She much preferred this kind of wealth. Trees and cattle and land. Yes.

"Daydreaming?"

She turned to find Winthrop Christopher sitting astride a big black stallion, watching her.

"I like the river," she explained. "We have one in Chicago, of course, but it's not the same. We have concrete and steel instead of trees."

"I know. I've been to Chicago. Even to the office, in fact." His eyes narrowed. "You don't remember me, do you?"

She did. Even that brief glance had stamped him onto her memory, but it wouldn't do to let him know that. She avoided a direct answer. "It's always hectic. I don't pay a lot of attention to visitors, I'm afraid."

"The morning I came, you were sitting at that computer with a stack of steno pads at your elbow and a telephone in your hand. You barely looked up when I went into Gerald's office." He smiled mockingly. "I was wearing a suit. Maybe I looked different."

"I can't quite imagine you in a suit, Mr. Christopher," she said, thinking, top that, cattle king.

"Winthrop," he corrected. "I'm not that much older than you. Eleven years or so. I'm thirty-four."

"How old is your brother?" she asked, curious.

He lifted his chin. "Thirty."

"Sometimes he seems older," she mused. "When they call the stockholders' meetings, for instance."

He glanced into the distance. "No doubt. I'm glad I don't have to deal with those damned things. That's Gerald's sole province now. I just run my ranch, and the only stockholder I have to please is myself. Gerald doesn't own enough shares to squabble over the decisions I make.''

"You inherited the ranch, didn't you?"

He stared at her for a minute, and she swallowed hard, sure that he was going to give her some sarcastic financial rundown and chide her for asking. But, surprisingly, he didn't. He just nodded. "That was the way my father wanted it. He knew I'd hold it as long as I lived, no matter what. You'll find that Gerald isn't terribly sentimental. He'd just as soon have a photograph as the object itself.''

She pursed her full lips and studied him. "I'll bet you saved bobby pins and bits of ribbon when you were a teenager," she said daringly, just to see what he'd say.

He blinked, then laughed, but it wasn't a pleasant sound. "I had my weak moments when I was younger," he agreed. His eyes darkened. "Not anymore, though, Kentucky girl. I'm steel right through.''

She wouldn't have touched that line. She turned, glancing at the distant ribbon the river made running into those towering, majestic peaks. "I was thinking about Lewis and Clark," she murmured, glancing toward the horizon, so that she didn't catch the look on his face. "A man died during the expedition. What they described sounded just like food poisoning. They wouldn't have known, of course. How much we've learned in over a hundred years. How far we've come. And yet," she said softly, "how much we've lost in the process.''

"The expedition went down the Missouri and Jefferson rivers," he said slowly. "We're on a tributary of the Jefferson, so they may have camped in this valley." He looked away. "They used to call it Buffalo Flats. The buffalo are gone, though. Like the way of life that existed here long ago." He shifted restlessly. "Where's Gerald?"

"Back at the house, I suppose," she said, bothered by the curtness of his tone. "He said he had some important phone calls to make. I would have stayed, but he said we wouldn't work today."

"Want a ride back?" he offered, and then seemed to withdraw, as if he regretted the words even as he was speaking them.

Some devilish imp made her smile at him. "Suppose I say yes?" she asked, driven to taunt him. "You look as if you'd rather sacrifice the horse than let me on him." And she grinned, daring him to mock her.

He felt a burst of light, but he wouldn't give in to it. "Damn you."

She grinned even more. "I won't accept, if you'd rather not let me aboard. Anyway—" she shuddered with deliberate mockery and more sarcasm than he could know, because she'd practically grown up on horses "—I'd probably fall off. It looks very high."

"It is. But I won't let you fall off. Come on." He kicked his foot out of the stirrup and held down a long arm, giving in to an impulse he didn't even understand. He wanted her closer. He wanted to hold her. That should have warned him, but it didn't.

He had enormous feet, she noticed, as she put a foot in the stirrup and let him pull her up in front of him. He was amazingly strong, too.

She hadn't realized how intimate it was going to be. His hard arm went around her middle and pulled her back against a body that was warm and strong and smelled of leather and spice. She felt her heart run away, and that arm under her breast would feel it, she knew.

"Nervous?" he asked at her ear, and laughed softly, without any real humor. "I'm not dangerous. I don't like women, or haven't they filled you in yet?" She's a woman, he was reminding himself. Watch it, watch yourself—she'll sucker you in and kick you down, just like the other one did.

"Yes, I'm nervous," she said. "Yes, you're dangerous, and you may not like women, but I'll bet they chase you like a walking mink."

His eyebrows arched. "You're plainspoken, aren't you?" he asked, gathering her even closer as he urged the restless stallion into motion, controlling him carefully with lean, powerful hands and legs.

"I try to be," she said, still uneasy about the double life she'd led since leaving Kentucky. To a man who'd been betrayed once, it might seem as if she were misleading him deliberately. But the past was still painful, and she'd forsaken it. She wanted it to stay in the past, like the bad memories of her own betrayal. Besides, there was no danger of Winthrop becoming involved with her. He was too invulnerable.

She held onto the pommel, her eyes on his long fingers. "You have beautiful hands, for a man," she remarked.

"I don't like flattery."

"Suit yourself, you ugly old artifact," she shot right back.

It had been a long time since anything had made him laugh. But this plain-faced, mysterious woman struck a chord in him that had never sounded. She brought color and light into his own private darkness. He felt the sound bubbling up in his chest, like thunder, and then overflowing. He couldn't hold it back this time, and the rush of it was incomprehensible to him.

She felt his chest shaking, heard the deep rumble of sound from inside it. She would have bet that he didn't laugh genuinely very often at anything. But she seemed to have a knack for dragging it out of him, and that pleased her beyond rational thought.

The lean arm contracted, and for an instant she felt him in an embrace that made her go hot all over. What would it be like, she wondered wildly, if he turned her and wrapped her up in his embrace and put that hard, cruel mouth over hers. . . .

She tingled from head to toe, her breath catching in her throat. It shouldn't have been like this, she shouldn't still be vulnerable. She had to stop this, or it was going to be an unendurable month.

"Watch out, Miss White," he said at her ear, his voice deep and soft and dangerous. "Save the heavy flirting for Gerald. You'll be safer that way."

He let her down at the porch, holding her so that she slid down to the ground. For an instant his dark face was very close, so close that she saw his dark eyes at point-blank range and something shot through her like lightning. She pulled back slowly, her eyes still linked to his. What had he said? Something about flirting with Gerald. But why should she want to flirt with her boss?

"See you." He wheeled his stallion and rode off, and she watched him with mingled emotions.

Supper was an unexpectedly quiet affair. Winthrop was out when she and Gerald sat down to eat, along with the ranch foreman, Michael Slade, a burly man of thirty who seemed perfectly capable of handling anything.

"Boss said he wouldn't get back in time for chow," Michael told Gerald with a grin. "Had to go into Butte for some supplies he needed. I offered, but he said he had some other things to do as well."

"Odd that he didn't do it before he met us at the airport." Gerald sighed as he took his medicine and glared at his plate. The doctor had told him that they didn't treat ulcers with bland diets anymore, but Mary hadn't believed him. Amazing, how disgusting green pea soup looked in a bowl, and he did hate applesauce. He glanced at Mary, sighed and then gave in to her, as he had done even as a child. He picked up his spoon and began to sip the soup. "Oh, well, that's Winthrop. Unpredictable. How's it going, Mike?"

The foreman launched into grand detail about seeing to the winter pasture, fixing fences, storing hay, culling cows, doing embryo transplants for the spring calving and organizing other facets of ranch life that he'd expected would go right over Nicole's head.

"One of my family was into embryo transplants when it was barely theory," Nicole interrupted. "They had some great successes. Now there's a new system underway, implanting computer chips just under the skin to keep track of herds...."

"Say, I've read about that," Mike agreed, and Gerald sat and stared while the two of them discussed cattle.

"Mr. Christopher must be feeling pretty proud of himself to have someone like you on the payroll," Nicole told the foreman when they reached a stopping point. "You know your business."

"Forgive me, ma'am, but so do you," Mike grinned, his ruddy face almost handsome with his blue eyes flashing. "I never knew a woman who could talk cattle before."

"I never knew a man who talked it as well," she grinned back.

"I thought you were from Chicago," Gerald sighed, shaking his head, when Mike had gone and they were sipping coffee in the living room. "Until you admitted that you were a Kentuckian, at least," he added. His gaze was warm and faintly questioning. "Amazing, that we worked together for two years and knew nothing about each other."

She smiled at him. "I guess most bosses and secretaries are like that, really," she agreed. "You're very nice to work for, though. You don't yell, like some of your vice presidents do."

He laughed. "I try not to. Winthrop, now," he said, watching her face as he spoke, "never yells. But it's worse that way, somehow. He has a voice like an icy wind when he loses his temper, which isn't often. I've seen him look at men who were about to start fights and back them down. One of our ancestors was a French fur trader up in Canada. Our grandmother used to say Winthrop takes after him."

"He has expressive eyes," she agreed, glancing at Gerald warily. "He doesn't want me here, you know."

His shoulders rose and fell. "He's buried himself up here for three solid years," he said irritably, staring into his coffee. "No company, except these hunting parties that he tolerates because it gives some variety to his life. No women. No dating. He's avoided women like the plague since Deanne left him. He uses that limp like a stick, have you noticed?" he asked, lifting troubled eyes to hers. "It isn't all that bad, and he could walk well enough if he cared to try, but it's as if he needs it to remind him that women are treacherous."

"I'd heard that he was something of a playboy in his younger days," she probed, curious about Winthrop in new and exciting ways.

"He was," Gerald agreed with a faint, musing smile. "He broke hearts right and left. But Deanne liked him because he was a new experience. I don't think she really meant to hurt him. She was young and he spoiled her, and she liked it. But when he got hurt, she had visions of being tied to a cripple for life, and she ran. Winthrop was shattered by the experience. His black pride couldn't deal with the humiliation of being lamed and deserted, all at once."

"Poor man," she said gently, and meant it.

"Don't make that mistake, either," he cautioned quietly. "Don't ever pity him. He's steel clean through, and if you give him half an opening, he'll make a scapegoat of you. Don't let him hurt you, Nicky."

She colored delicately. "You think he might?"

"I think you attract him," he said bluntly. "And I have a feeling that you aren't immune to him, either. He doesn't like being vulnerable, so look out."

Hours later, when she went up to bed, she was still turning that threat over in her mind. She could picture Winthrop behind her closed eyes, and the image made her sigh with mingled emotions. She'd never felt so empty before, so alone. She wanted him in ways that she'd never dreamed she could want a man. She wanted to be with him, to share with him, to ease his hurt and make him whole again. She didn't quite know how to cope with the new and frightening sensations. Nicky had her own scars and she didn't want involvement any more than Winthrop did. But there was something between them. Something that was new and a little frightening, and like an avalanche, she couldn't stop it.

She was almost asleep when she heard slow steps coming past her door. She knew from the sound that it was Winthrop, and her heart beat faster as he passed her room. Odd, how deeply she could be touched just by his step. She wondered if he was as curious about her as she was about him, despite his understandably deep distrust of women. He was like her, in so many ways, hiding from a world that had been cruel to him. They had more in common than he seemed to realize. Or perhaps he did realize it, and was drawing back because he didn't trust her. She closed her eyes as she heard a door close down the hall. In no time at all, she was asleep, secure because the master of the house was back, and she was safe.

Chapter Three

Winthrop's horses attracted Nicole immediately, even though he'd given her a terse warning at breakfast about going too close to them. One of the happiest memories of her childhood was watching old Ernie at her home in Kentucky as he worked the thoroughbreds when they were ready to be trained.

Besides his saddle horses, mostly quarter horses, Winthrop had at least two thoroughbreds with unmistakably Arabian ancestry, judging by their small heads. All American thoroughbreds, she remembered, were able to trace their ancestry to one of three Arabian horses imported into England in the late 1600s and early 1700s: Byerley Turk, Godolphin Barb and Queen Anne.

Winthrop's horses had the exquisite conformation and sleek lines that denoted thoroughbreds, too. She'd watched them during her brief stroll around the stables and corral. One was a mare about to foal, the other a full stallion, both with sleek chestnut coats and exquisite conformation. She'd wanted to ask Winthrop about them over scrambled eggs and steak that morning, but he'd been unapproachable. Frozen over, in fact, and she knew why without even being told. He didn't want her too close, so he was freezing her out.

She'd finished her two hours in the study, taking dictation from Gerald, and now cozy and warm in tailored gray slacks and a white pullover sweater, she was lazing around the corral looking for the horses. The stallion was there, but she didn't see the mare anywhere.

A noise from inside the big barn caught her attention. She couldn't see inside, but it sounded like a horse's whinny of pain. It was followed by a particularly virulent curse from a voice she recognized immediately.

She darted into the dim warmth of the big barn, down the neat corridor between the stalls that was covered with pine shavings.

"Winthrop?" she called quickly.

"In here."

She followed his voice to the end stall. The mare was down on her side, making snuffling sounds, and Winthrop was bending over her, his sleeves rolled up, bareheaded, scowling.

"Something's wrong," she said, glancing at him.

"Brilliant observation," he muttered, probing at the mare's distended belly with tender, sure hands. "This is her first foal and it's a breech, damn the luck! Go get Johnny Blake and tell him I said to come here, I can't do this alone. He'll be—"

"The mare will be dead by the time I find him," she said matter-of-factly. She eased into the stall, ignoring Winthrop as she gently approached the mare, talking softly to her with every step. While Winthrop watched, scowling, she slid down to her knees beside the beautiful, intelligent creature, watching the silky brown eyes all the while. She sat down then, reaching out to stroke the mare. And slowly, she eased under the proud head and slowly coaxed it onto her knees.

She drew her fingers gently over the velvety muzzle, talking softly to the mare, gentling her.

"She'll let you help her now," she told Winthrop softly, never taking her eyes from the mare's.

"Yes," he said, watching her curiously for a few seconds before he bent to his task. "I believe she might. You'll ruin that fancy sweater," he murmured as he went to work.

"Better it than lose the foal," she said, and smiled at the mare, talking gently to her all along, smoothing the long mane, cuddling the shuddering head, as Winthrop slowly worked to help the colt in its dark cradle. She knew instinctively that the mare would realize that she was trying to help, and not hurt her.

Minutes later, guided by patient, expert lean hands, hind fetlocks appeared suddenly, followed rapidly by the rest of the newborn animal. Winthrop laughed softly, triumphantly, as the tiny new life slid into the hay and he cleared its nostrils.

"A colt," he announced.

Nicole smiled at him over the mare, amazed to find genuine warmth in his dark eyes. "And a very healthy one, too," she agreed. Her eyes searched his softly, and then she felt herself beginning to tremble at the intensity of his level gaze. She drew her gaze away and stroked the mare again before she got slowly to her feet so that the new mother could lick her colt and nuzzle it.

"A thoroughbred, isn't he?" she replied absently, her eyes on the slick colt being lovingly washed by his mother. "The stallion has a superior conformation. So does the mare. He might be a champion."

"The stallion is by Calhammond, out of Dame Savoy," he said, frowning as he moved away to wash his hands and arms in a bucket of water with a bar of soap, drying them on a towel that hung over it. "How did you know?"

"Kentucky is racehorse country," she laughed, sidestepping the question. She didn't want to tell him how much she knew about thoroughbreds, although she'd certainly given herself away just now, and she'd have to soft-pedal over it. "I cut my teeth on thoroughbreds. I used to beg for work around them, and one of the trainers took pity on me. He taught me a lot about them. You see, one of the biggest racing farms in Lexington was near where I lived—Rockhampton Farms." Actually Rockhampton was her grandfather's name; her mother's people had owned the stables there for three generations. But it wouldn't do to admit that to Winthrop, because he'd connect it with Dominic White, who was her father and the current owner. He might even know Dominic, because he entertained sportsmen, and her father was one of the best.

"I've heard of it," Winthrop told her after a minute. He turned, staring hard at her with dark, curious eyes as he rolled down the sleeves of his brown Western shirt and buttoned the cuffs with lazy elegance. White. Her name was White. Wasn't that the name of that jet-setting sportsman from Kentucky who was coming with the Eastern hunting party? Yes, by God it was, and Dominic White owned Rockhampton Farms. He lifted his head. "The owner of Rockhampton is a White," he said in a direct attack, watching closely for reaction. "Any kin of yours?"

She held onto her wits with a steely hand. She even smiled. "White is a pretty common name, I'm afraid," she said. "Do I look like an heiress?"

"You don't dress like one," he commented, with narrowed eyes. "And I guess you wouldn't be working for Gerald if you had that kind of money," he said finally, relaxing a little. He didn't want her, but it was a relief all the same to know that she wasn't some bored little rich girl looking for a good time. He couldn't have borne going through that again. "I've been to Kentucky, but I've never been on the White place. My stallion and mare came from the O'Hara place."

"Yes, Meadowbrook Farms," she murmured. She could have fainted with relief. She didn't want him to know about her background. Of course, there was always the danger that he might someday find out that she was one of those Whites, but with any luck she'd be back in Chicago before he did, and it wouldn't matter anymore. Right now, the important thing was to get her boss well and not upset him with any confrontations between herself and Winthrop.

Winthrop had every reason to hate rich society girls, and he might be tempted to make her life hell if he knew the truth. And probably it would be worse because she hadn't told him about it in the beginning. Her character would be even blacker in his eyes for the subterfuge. For one wild instant, she considered telling him. But she knew she couldn't. He disliked her enough already. And it was suddenly important, somehow, to keep him from finding new reasons to dislike her. It did occur to her that someday he might hate her for not being truthful with him. But she'd discovered a tender streak in his turbulent nature while he was working with the mare, and she wanted to learn more about that shadowy side of him. That might not be possible if he knew the truth about her.

"I couldn't have managed that alone," he said quietly, watching her. "I'm obliged for the help."

"I like horses," she said simply. "And he's a grand colt."

"His father has been a consistent winner, but he was hurt in a race last year. I bought him to stand at stud rather than see him put down. I had a lot of money that was lying spare, so I developed an interest in racehorses. I've spent a good deal of time at racetracks in the past year."

Another chink in the armor, she thought, thinking about his compassion for the stallion as she looked up at him.

He saw that speculative gleam and it irritated him. She wasn't working out the way he'd expected. She had too many interesting qualities, and he didn't like the feelings she aroused in him. He'd buried his emotions, and she was digging down to them with irritating ease.

"You don't like me, do you?" she asked bluntly. "Why? Is it because I'm plain, or because I'm only a secretary..."

"You aren't plain," he said unexpectedly, his dark eyes tracing the soft oval of her face. Big green eyes. Pretty mouth. High cheekbones. Skin like satin, creamy and young. She was young. He sighed wistfully. "And I'm no snob. I just don't want women around."

"That's straightforward," she said softly. "And I hope it won't offend you if I speak as bluntly. I know a little about what happened to you and why. I'm very sorry. But hating me and making my life miserable for the next few weeks isn't going to erase your scars. It will only create new ones for both of us. So can't we be sporting enemies?" she asked, her green eyes twinkling. "And I'll promise not to seduce you in the hay."

His eyebrows shot straight up. Unexpected wasn't the word for this little firecracker. He'd have to think up a new one.

"What do you know about seduction, Red Riding Hood?" he asked with blithe humor, and she got a tiny glimpse of the man he'd been before the accident.

"Not much, actually," she said pleasantly, "but that's probably in your favor, because it will save you a lot of embarrassing moments. Just imagine if I were experienced and sophisticated and out to sink my claws into you!"

Her earnestly teasing expression made him feel as if he were sipping potent wine. He had a hard time drawing his eyes away from her soft mouth and back up to her laughing eyes. Incredibly long lashes, on those eyes. Sexy. Like the rest of her. She was tall, but she wasn't overly thin. He liked the way she looked in tailored slacks and that white sweater. Both were thick with horsehair about now, and she'd smell of horse....

"She'll want some water now," she reminded him, unnerved by that slow, bold scrutiny and hoping that it didn't show.

It did. His chin lifted just a little, in a purely male way, and his chiseled mouth twitched. "Nervous of me?"

"If all the gossip I've heard about you is true, I have good reason to be, and that isn't conceit on my part," she added proudly. "Playboys don't usually mind who they charm, because it's all a game to them."

The light in his eyes went out, like a cavern succumbing to darkness. "I don't play games with virgins, honey," he said unexpectedly, catching her chin with a lean, steely hand. "And you'd better remember it. I've forgotten more about lovemaking in my time that you've ever learned, but I'm not low enough to take out my hurt on you."

He was so close that she could feel the strong warmth of him. Her heart ran wild. She'd never had such a powerful, immediate reaction to a man before. Not even to Chase. This was new and wildly exciting, and she wanted more.

"How do you know that . . . about me?" she whispered, shocked that he could so easily discuss the most intimate subjects.

"I don't know," he replied quietly, searching her soft eyes. His blood warmed in his veins, and he felt his heartbeat slowly increase. Her scent was overpowering, drowning him, seducing his senses. He knew a lot about her, knowledge that only instinct could have supplied.

Her lips parted on a rush of breath. The dimness of the barn was warm and cozy, shutting them away from the world. Winthrop was closer than ever, towering over her, drowning her in a narcotic kind of hunger.

She took an involuntary step toward him. "I . . . don't understand," she whispered, her voice shaking. One slender hand went hesitantly to his chest and pressed against it, feeling the shock of warm muscle and a spongy wiriness that might have been hair underneath. She felt him tense, even before his hand came up to remove hers with abrupt impatience.

"Don't do that," he ground out, glaring at her. "I don't want your hands on me."

Her own forwardness shocked her more than his irritable statement. She turned away, feeling a rush of tears that she couldn't let him see.

"I'd better get back to the house," she said quickly. "Your brother was going to make a phone call and then finish his dictation. I'm glad the mare's okay." She said it all in a mad rush and threw a vague smile in his direction before she went out of the barn as if her shoes were on fire.

He watched her go with mingled emotions. Anger. Irritation. Hunger. Frustration. He couldn't sort them out, so he didn't bother. He went back to feed and water the mare and see about the colt. Damn women everywhere, he thought, and limped more than usual as he went about his business.

Nicole made a point of avoiding her boss's unpredictable brother for the rest of the day. But there was no getting away from him at the supper table, and she had to fight not to look at him.

Cleaned up and freshly shaved, wearing a white shirt that suited his darkness, he would have drawn any woman's eyes. It was easy to see how he'd appealed to women when he was younger. He was still a striking man, and it wasn't just his looks. There was an indefinable something about him, a vibrant masculinity that was almost tangible and certainly overpowering at close range. Her hands trembled just sitting next to him at the long table.

Gerald was quoting figures on some real estate he'd acquired, and Winthrop was listening with barely half his mind. He was watching Nicky while he pared his steak and chewed it deliberately, trying not to let her know that he was watching her. She was wearing that gray jersey dress that clung so lovingly to her curves, and the memory of the effect she'd had on him in the barn wasn't doing his appetite any good.

He finally grew impatient with her downbent head and stopped eating and just stared at her intently while Gerald went on talking without realizing that he was talking to himself.

Nicole felt that intent stare and looked up into Winthrop's dark eyes. And her heart stopped beating.

Electricity danced between them. She couldn't drag her eyes from his, any more than his were willing to be tugged away. The look they exchanged was long and piercing and shattering in its intensity. It was as personal as a kiss, so steady and unblinking that she felt her body tremble in intimate response to his blatant interest.

His gaze held hers for a shuddering moment, and then it dropped to her mouth, and she felt her lips part helplessly for him.

"Winthrop, are you listening?" Gerald asked suddenly, breaking the silence when he discovered that his brother was apparently staring into space.

"What?" Winthrop turned back to him. "Something about real estate values?" he asked absently. He didn't like the way his body responded to that look in Nicole's eyes. He was going to have to do something. But what?

Nicole was having as difficult a time with her own body. She shifted restlessly and drank coffee that was, by now, hopelessly oversugared. While Winthrop's dark eyes had been openly making love to hers, she'd put six spoons of sugar in the black liquid. She took a sip and shuddered and left it in favor of the glass of water Mary had provided for each of them. So much for common sense. It was time to retreat.

For the next few days, she and Winthrop avoided each other—ignored each other—to the extent that everybody noticed, and Mary began asking gentle questions that Nicole smiled at and avoided answering. And that might have gone on for another week if she hadn't tripped on the steps coming in from a walk late one afternoon, to be caught by Winthrop in the gathering darkness.

He'd apparently just come in from the corral himself. He smelled of cattle and he needed a shave, but his arms in the sheepskin jacket felt strong and warm, and instead of pulling away like a sensible girl, Nicole had sighed and relaxed against his tall, strong body.

Winthrop muttered something, but he didn't push her away. His hard arms contracted, drawing her against him under the unbuttoned jacket, and he stood holding her in the dusky light, savoring her softness, his cheek against her dark hair.

It seemed so natural, somehow. So right. His eyes closed and all the reasons why he shouldn't allow her this close vanished. He didn't make a sound, and neither did she. The wind sang through the tall lodgepole pines, whispered through the aspen and maples, whipped her hair against her flushed cheek. She pressed closer with a tiny, inarticulate sound, too hungry for the contact to listen to the warning bells going off in her head. He was warm and strong, and it was sheer delight to be held by him. She felt her body tremble with exquisite pleasure.

"We could hurt each other badly," he whispered in her ear, his voice deep and soft and slow. "You don't have the experience to understand the risk, and I can't be sure that I wouldn't take out old hurts on you, even though I wouldn't do it consciously. This is crazy."

"Yes."

He nuzzled his cheek against her hair. "I mean it, Nicky."

She sighed, reluctantly drawing away from him. She looked up, curious, excited. "Afraid of me, cattle baron?" she asked softly.

"In a way," he agreed unexpectedly, but he wasn't smiling. He touched her cheek with the back of his fingers in a soft caress. "I don't like to start things I can't finish."

"Meaning?" she persisted. If it was digging her own emotional grave, she couldn't help it. She had to know.

He stared into her eyes for just a second, and then drew back, physically and emotionally. "You'll figure it out. Don't wander out of the yard when you go walking. One of the men thinks he spotted a wolf today. I don't want anything to happen to you, little Eastern girl. I may never be your lover, but I'll take care of you, all the same, while you're here."

And with that surprising statement, he turned and walked off. Nicole stared after him with eyes that brimmed with unshed tears. He was very protective of her, and she wondered if he realized it. He wasn't saying what he felt, but she knew instinctively that he shared some of the warm feeling that was growing inside her. But whether he'd ever give in to it was anyone's guess. As for Nicole, it had shocked her to realize that she had none of her usual defenses when he was near her. And that realization kept her quiet all through supper and beyond bedtime. What an unexpectedly complicated thing this vacation of her boss's had become. She hoped that she was going to be able to cope with the new and disturbing feelings that Winthrop had unearthed in her.

Life sailed into a pleasant routine after that. She and Gerald settled down to work, and Nicole spent her free time exploring outdoors or watching Mary in the kitchen. Winthrop was pleasant enough, but he kept things cool, although from time to time she found those dark, quiet eyes watching her in a way that excited her beyond bearing.

Two days later, she heard cattle bawling and excited male voices, and she succumbed to the need to see Winthrop. The cattle were massed at a makeshift corral just away from the barn and the stables, and Winthrop was on his horse, helping to drive cattle into a holding pen where they were apparently being vetted and vaccinated and examined and treated for diseases or infestation by grubs.

That weak leg didn't seem to bother the big man one bit on horseback. He could cut and rope with the best of them, and the wilder the horse, the better he seemed to enjoy himself. He laughed deeply and with obvious pleasure the whole time. She imagined that when he was in the saddle he could forget how ungraceful he was on the ground.

Not that a limp made him any less a man. He bristled with masculine sensuality. She could see quite easily how he'd gained a reputation in his youth as a playboy. He was devastating physically, and he had a voice that even in memory could make her flush with pleasure. Her heart hadn't been the same since that unexpected embrace on the porch. She could close her eyes and hear his voice all over again, as it had been that evening, and she could almost imagine it in a dark room, coaxing, deliberately seductive....

Warmth coursed through her and she forced herself to watch the men and the cattle. Winthrop had climbed off the horse to help catch a calf, apparently one that needed doctoring. He looped his rope and undid it, lazily coiling it while one of the other cowboys threw the calf and began to do something to it. Winthrop was rubbing his leg, and the limp was even more pronounced when he turned, leading his horse by the reins.

He saw Nicole at the fence, and he stood very still for an instant. She could feel his anger even at the distance, and made a discreet and quick withdrawal. He was headed in her direction, so she changed it and walked quickly into the forest that encircled the house.

Why she should have been embarrassed, she didn't know. But she knew he was angry, even before he caught up with her minutes later.

She stopped, catching her breath. He was right behind her, still leading the horse. As he walked, he favored that right leg.

"Running away?" he taunted. "Why?"

She stared at him. It was silly to be so ill at ease with him, but his expression wasn't at all welcoming. "I don't know," she said quietly. She was wearing jeans and a long-sleeved yellow sweater. He had on a shirt the same shade of yellow and brown as his jeans, and she thought illogically how well they matched.

He lifted his dark head. "Don't you? What are you doing—spying? Did you want to see if the cripple could still throw a calf?"

She went forward without thinking and put her soft hand over his mouth. "Don't," she said softly. "Don't do that to yourself. You're not a cripple. You're a man with a limp."

The feel of her fingers shocked him. The gesture was unexpected and it threw him off balance. He caught her smooth hand, holding it near his cheek as if he couldn't quite decide what to do with it.

He stood over her, breathing roughly, his eyes dark with pain and anger as they searched hers. His fingers contracted absently around hers, bruising a little, but she didn't protest.

"I don't want you here," he said quietly, his eyes narrow, piercing.

"Yes, I know." She moved her fingers experimentally, and he let them go. She touched his cheek, tracing the long scar down his jaw, into the dimple in his chin. It was incredible how secure she felt with him, and not the least bit afraid. She sensed something in him, something vulnerable and tender, and she wanted to reach it. She needed to reach it, although she didn't understand why. "You don't talk about it, do you? Not ever."

His broad chest rose and fell. He was very close. Too close. She could feel the muscles ripple when he moved, feel him breathing, feel the warmth of him in the chill air.

His fingers slid into her hair, hesitantly, feeling the curls as he moved his hands to her nape and turned her head up with firm gentleness.

"It's been one hell of a long time since I kissed a woman," he said half under his breath, looking down at her coldly. "Don't you realize that you've been inviting that for days? I'm not a boy, and I've gone hungry in recent years. I can't play games, I even told you so. You could start something that would ruin both our lives."

She let him pull her head back. She looked up at him unafraid, her eyes soft with understanding and compassion. "I'm not afraid of you," she said softly.

"I could make you afraid, Nicole."

His voice was velvety soft and deep. Her lips parted, because it was as sensuous as she'd imagined it would be. She liked being close to him. She wanted his mouth and her lips parted in subtle invitation. She might have imagined herself in love with Chase James, but never in her life had she felt anything as sweet as this.

He looked down at her soft mouth, seeing it open, and something in him snapped. He bent quickly, covering it with his hard lips. He wanted to hurt her. She was a child, playing at sensuality, and he wanted to make it so rough that she'd stop tormenting him with emotions he never wanted to feel again....

She yielded completely, no thought of fighting him. His mouth was hard, warm and tasted of tobacco and it was only then that she realized how expert he really was. He made no allowances for her youth, and despite her small experience with Chase, this was her first real taste of passion. It was devastating, this helpless feeling he caused in her. She sighed hungrily, letting him draw her completely against the powerful hard length of his body, letting him crush her against it. Her mouth yielded eagerly to his insistent lips, tasting the tobacco tartness of his tongue as it pushed into her mouth, penetrating her in a silence that blazed with kindling sensations.

Her hands grasped his shirtsleeves, holding on, because her knees were getting weak. His arm at her back arched her, the hand at her nape tangled in her curly hair. He made a sound deep in his throat and lifted his head, his eyes black and blazing as they probed her dazed ones.

"Aren't you going to fight me?" he taunted with a faint, mocking smile as his mouth poised over hers.

"No." She reached up, sliding her arms around his neck. Her mouth was soft, parted and waiting, tempting his. "Oh, no, I want it, too!"

"Nicky..."

It was a groan, her name on his lips. He bent, half lifting her up to him. But this time, he didn't try to hurt her. This time, he was achingly gentle. His hard mouth slowed and softened on hers, and he kissed her with a subdued passion that aroused all her protective instincts. Poor, tormented man, she thought. So much love in him, all wasted on the wrong woman. And now he was driven to hurt back, out of fear that it was going to happen again. But it wasn't, she thought, her heart blazing with compassion. It wasn't, because she'd never hurt him.

She closed her arms tight around his neck and opened her mouth for him, drawing it over his as she was learning he liked it. Her tongue teased at his full lower lip and he made a sound that corresponded with the tautening of his body.

"I'm sorry," she whispered against his lips. "I don't...know much about this. I'm sorry if I did it wrong."

He lifted his head again. He was breathing roughly, and his eyes had a haunted look. The hand in her hair caressed gently. "You really are a virgin, aren't you?" he murmured with a tenderness he wasn't aware of.

"I guess it shows," she whispered dryly. She looked down at his shirt, missing the sudden shocked delight in his eyes. "I haven't had a lot to do with men in the past few years."

He brushed the curly hair away from her face, touching her with pure wonder. Yes, this was what he'd been uneasy about, this vulnerable side of her that attracted him. He'd tried so hard to avoid this confrontation. Ridiculous, really, when it was inevitable that he was going to feel her warmth in his arms, savor the soft nectar of her mouth. He'd known she was nearby, back at the corral. He'd sensed her somehow. "Why were you watching me?" he asked.

"I don't know. I needed to." She shifted, burying her face against his broad shoulder. "You disturb me," she whispered shakily. "It frightens me."

"It shouldn't." He held her, rocked her. His mouth touched her forehead in a kiss as gentle as the arms that held her. "I won't hurt you again."

She nuzzled her face against him. "It's very exciting, being kissed like that," she whispered shyly.

He smiled. "Is it?" He tilted her chin up and searched her eyes. "Then let's do it again," he whispered into her open mouth.

It was wilder this time, hotter, more unbearably sweet. She gave him her mouth and melted into the hard contours of his body with a soft moan. It wasn't until she felt the tautening, felt the sudden urgency in the mouth devouring hers, that she realized things were getting out of control.

She put her hands against his wildly thudding chest and pulled her lips away from his. "No," she said shakily.

He bit at her lower lip, his head spinning. "No?"

"You're a man...and experienced," she whispered. "I've never...and I can't. I'm sorry."

He was breathing roughly, but he didn't seem to be angry. He brushed his mouth over her eyes, closing her eyelids. "Do you want to?" he whispered, smiling.

"What a ridiculous question. I expect you know the answer," she said dazedly.

"I suppose I do, at that." He sighed, wrapping her up against him. "Hold tight. They say it passes, eventually. I can't vouch for it, of course. I'm not in the habit of drawing back at this point."

"Oh, I'm sorry," she moaned.

"I won't die." He nuzzled his cheek against hers, rocking her. His arms had a faint tremor, but his breathing was calmer now and his heartbeat had stopped shaking them both. "What a potent little package you are. I didn't plan this. I meant to...hell, I don't know what I meant to do. Scare you, maybe."

"You did."

He laughed. "Like hell I did, you were with me every step of the way. I could have laid you down in the grass and—"

"Hush!"

He drew back then and looked down at her, frowning, his eyes wary and searching. She was flushed, and her eyes had an unnatural brightness, as if she were holding back tears.

"What are you so afraid of?" he asked quietly, touching her eyelid gently to release a long, silver tear. "It was passionate, but still just a kiss. I didn't even try to touch you in any way that would have offended you."

"It isn't fear," she whispered. She lowered her eyes. How could she explain to him the intensity of her feelings, the aching tenderness she was beginning to feel for him?

"Are you afraid of intimacy?" he asked very quietly.

She lowered her eyes to his chest and closed them. "I'm afraid of getting involved. Just as afraid as you are," she added. And it was true. She'd given her heart to Chase—she'd almost given her body to him. And he'd betrayed her trust. How could she risk it again?

"Why?"

She looked up at him. "Why are you?" she countered, searching his quiet eyes.

He bent and touched her forehead with lips that were breathlessly gentle. "I loved her," he whispered, "in my way. It was the first time I'd ever felt more than a physical hunger for a woman. When she walked away from me, I wanted to die. I swore I'd get over it, but I don't know that I really have. The scars go deep."

She touched his face gently, running her fingers slowly along his hard cheek. Amazing, how exquisite it was to be near him.

"I got thrown over by my fiancé," she confessed. "He decided he wanted a rich girl, and I wasn't..." She almost added "anymore" but she caught the word in time.

He searched her soft green eyes. "You didn't sleep with him," he said, gazing at her intently.

"That's hard to explain." She stared at his top shirt button. It was undone, and thick dark hair peeked out against his tanned skin. "I wanted the first time to mean something. What hurts the most is that I never felt that way about him. I thought I loved him, but I never thought about sleeping with him."

That was the truth. Seeing how fast living had ruled her parents' lives had soured her on that part of life. Intimacy had become to them as careless as handshakes, and Nicole had determined that it would be treated more reverently in her own life. Perhaps, in retrospect, that was one of the reasons Chase had left her. He'd pushed her toward intimacy more and more after their engagement, but she'd resisted stubbornly. And now, standing close in Winthrop's arms, she was savagely glad she'd resisted.

There was more to it than that, he knew, but she wasn't volunteering any more information. He studied her quietly, thinking how much like him she was. He ran his finger down her cheek. Secretive, too, but he'd get more of an explanation eventually. It was insane to be so pleased that she was still innocent. It excited him, as sophisticated women never had.

"I could eat a moose," he said conversationally. "Why don't we rush back to the house and raid the freezer? Can you cook, in case Mary decides to try out for the Rockettes one day?"

She laughed at him. His humor had surprised her. Was this the real man? Had that cold veneer finally melted away?

"Yes, of course I can cook. Why would Mary want to try out for the Rockettes?"

He shrugged. "She threatens it once or twice a winter. She saw them on television once and was sure she was just the right height, even though her legs were a bit large. I haven't taken her seriously in past years, but as I get older, my stomach worries."

"Don't you worry, Mr. Christopher, I'll take care of you," she murmured and turned toward the house. "Are you walking or riding?"

He sighed and grimaced. "I guess I'm riding," he muttered. "Damned leg hurts like hell."

She had a feeling he wouldn't have admitted that to anyone but her. It was the best kind of compliment. She smiled and shook her head when he offered to let her ride with him after he'd painstakingly mounted the horse and was sitting regally on its back.

"It wouldn't do your leg much good," she reminded him. "I'll just walk alongside and look up at you adoringly, if you don't mind."

"That'll be the day," he mused.

She looked up. "What happened to your leg?" she asked softly.

"Bone damage and torn ligaments. I was pinned in the car when she wrecked it," he said simply. "The surgeons repaired it as best they could, but there were complications. I'll always limp. And when I overdo, I'll always hurt." He glanced at her. "I had a choice between limping or giving up the leg. I came in with a matched set and I intend to go out the same way."

She pursed her lips, feeling mischievous, and almost asked an outrageous question. Then she blushed wildly and turned away.

He guessed the question and burst out laughing. "No," he murmured. "It doesn't cramp my style in bed."

She gasped, glaring at him. "I never—"

"You might as well have written it in twelve-inch letters on canvas," he retorted.

Her mouth opened and then closed while she thought up searing retorts, none of which came to mind. Later, she'd think up hundreds, she was sure. But the thought of him in bed with another woman made her feel jealous and angry. And it showed.

He stopped, fingering the reins in one lean hand and waited for her to look up at him. His dark eyes, shadowy under the wide brim of his hat, watched her. "I'll qualify that," he said after a long exchange of eyes. "I don't think it will cramp my style. I haven't been with a woman since it happened."

Her breath caught, but she didn't look away. It was such an intimate thing to know about him, and she struggled to think of a suitable reply.

"That wasn't fair, was it?" he asked with a slow smile. "And I can't tell you for the life of me why I wanted you to know that. But I did. We'd better get home. It's getting dark."

She lowered her eyes to the trail that led back to the house. His revelation shouldn't have mattered to her, but it did. She smiled softly to herself, unaware that he saw the smile, and understood it.

He lit a cigarette and rode along beside her with a carefully hidden smug expression while he smoked it. "How about dinner tomorrow night? I'll drive you into Butte."

She felt chills to the tips of her toes and a wild excitement that was new, like the sudden tenderness between herself and Winthrop. "If Gerald doesn't need me, I'd love to," she said.

He hesitated. He looked down at her curiously, but he didn't speak. "Okay."

She wondered about the reason for his withdrawn expression and the odd silence the rest of the way to the house. That was good, because it kept her from thinking about the way he'd kissed her. She'd never felt more threatened in her life, and the worst of it was that she wasn't even afraid of what might happen between them.

He glanced at her just once, shocked by the surge of jealousy he felt at her remark about Gerald. It was that, too. Jealousy. He was afraid that there was something between this woman and his brother, and his own sense of honor and family wouldn't allow him to trespass on Gerald's territory. He wanted her to be heart-whole. He wanted that desperately. Could she have kissed him that way and still belong to Gerald? Surely not!

He pulled his emotions up short. It wouldn't do to give in to this unexpected yen for her. He was playing with fire, and God forbid he should get burned a second time.

Nicole, unaware of his thoughts, was having some difficulties of her own trying to figure out his taciturn somberness after the new and delicate camaraderie between them. She guessed, rightly, that he was holding back out of apprehension, and she even understood. But she didn't want him to leave her alone. She was beginning to love him, and it was only when she admitted it that she realized how desperately she wanted him.

Chapter Four

Winthrop wasn't at the supper table. Nicole didn't really expect him to be, because it was early November now, and according to Gerald, the boss was getting his management program in gear for winter. That included culling cattle; weaning, preconditioning and delivering calves; making the initial selection of replacement cattle and starting them on feed; and all the veterinarian-related chores that that entailed. With the sheer immensity of the cow-calf operation, it was a full-time job for the boss to keep up with what was going on. Mike, the foreman, relieved Winthrop of a lot of headaches, but even with a firm of accountants to do the paperwork, Winthrop still had to make the big decisions. No wonder he was putting in so many late hours, Nicole thought after Gerald had explained his absence.

Later that evening, Gerald had some correspondence for her. They went into the study to work. The room had Winthrop's personality stamped all over it. There was a bear's head on the wall, and burgundy leather furniture. The rugs were Indian, and the huge stone fireplace was made of native rock in comparable colors. The desk was oak, the chairs man-size and comfortable. There was a copper kettle on the hearth, and it reminded Nicole of the huge copper mining operation she'd seen as they came through Butte on the day they'd arrived. On the wall was a portrait of a man in buckskin, and she wondered if that was the French trader who was an ancestor of the Christophers.

"By the way, Sadie's invited us for dinner Friday night," Gerald said as he sorted out his mail, which had been forwarded from Chicago that afternoon. "Is that convenient for you?"

"That's fine," she said. "I look forward to meeting her again." She sat poised with her steno pad on her lap. "Uh, Winthrop asked if I'd go into Butte with him tomorrow night. To a restaurant."

Gerald pursed his lips and smiled mischievously. "I see," he mused. "So Winthrop's out to take my girl away from me, is he? I'm not sure if I like that."

It was an old joke between them, dating from her first six months as his secretary when two of the vice presidents had tried to steal her out from under his nose. She laughed and he was smiling. But the man out in the hall, overhearing him, didn't see that. Winthrop was within reach of the doorknob, but his lean hand faltered.

"He's not likely to try to take me away from you, so you can stop worrying," she said, tongue in cheek. "Anyway, he couldn't do it, you're quite unmatchable. Are you reassured?"

"I am." Gerald sighed theatrically, his brown eyes playful. He wasn't at all bad-looking. He just seemed very young beside his brother. "What a frightening thought!" he added with a mock shudder. "That I could lose you to my own brother. But Winthrop is too much a gentleman to steal from people, so I can relax. Now, suppose we get down to work?"

Winthrop turned and walked out the front door. His footsteps were so soft, and the closing of the door so quiet, that the occupants of the study didn't hear him.

He hadn't expected Nicole to be like that. He'd been sure that her ardor was real, that she'd felt the same tenderness he had. And here she was telling Gerald that there was no chance Winthrop could turn her head. He felt sick to his stomach and furiously angry. He couldn't bear the thought of being near her anymore, not after hearing her conversation with Gerald. What a close call, but at least he'd been spared. His face hardened as he began to work out what he was going to do. Thank God, she'd never know just how close she'd come to getting under his skin.

There was no sign of Winthrop for the rest of the evening, and the next morning, Gerald found a note waiting for him when they sat down to breakfast. He read over it, obviously puzzled.

"Winthrop," he said, waving the slip of paper. "He's gone to Omaha, God knows why. Something about a cattle deal. He said he's sorry about this evening, but he'll have to take a rain check on your dinner date."

"That's all right," she said, hiding her disappointment. "I'm sure he couldn't help it."

Gerald, who knew his older brother a little better than Nicole did, was uneasy. Winthrop hadn't offered to take a woman out to dinner since that blond barracuda did him in. Nicky had touched something in him, something cold and dormant, and now Winthrop seemed determined to fight it to the last breath. Gerald studied Nicky, wondering if she had any idea how disturbing Winthrop must find her. Probably not. She was a sweet person, a little reserved most of the time. Gerald was fond of her, in a brotherly way, and he felt responsible for Winthrop's unexpected coolness toward her. Knowing how his brother felt, Gerald should have been more wary of bringing a woman to the ranch. But it had been Winthrop who'd mentioned bringing Nicky. Come

to think of it, Winthrop had asked a lot of questions about
her after he'd seen her that day at the Chicago office. He
pursed his lips. Well, well. Big brother had an Achilles' heel,
it seemed. He smiled as the thought warmed his mind. And
now that Winthrop had the quarry near the hook, he was
going to play her for a while, was that it? Or had he gotten
cold feet and was now running?

"You're very quiet," Nicole said hesitantly.

"I'm just thinking. By the way, with Winthrop gone,
would you rather spend tonight at Sadie's?" he asked with
old-world politeness.

She smiled. "You're a nice man. Would you mind?"

"Heavens, no," he murmured. Besides, it would give him
an excuse to see Sadie again the next day, when he went to
fetch Nicky. And it would kill any potential gossip stone
dead. Winthrop might appreciate that one day.

They went that night to have dinner with Sadie. She was
a tall woman with blond hair and soft brown eyes. Nicky
had always liked her, and the two of them found plenty to
talk about when Sadie had come by the office to wait for
Gerald.

"I'll be delighted to have you stay the night," Sadie told
her enthusiastically. "It gets lonely with just me for company. Mother likes people."

"How is she?" Gerald asked gently.

Sadie sighed and shook her head. "No better. No worse.
She just lies and looks at the wall and begs to die." She bit
back tears. "Here, Nicky, help me get the food on the table, will you? Gerald, would you like to go in and ask
Mother if she needs anything?"

"Certainly," he agreed, and paused to exchange a look
with Sadie that was long and bittersweet.

Sadie watched him leave the room, her eyes wandering
over his tall figure in the becoming tan suit.

"I'm hopeless," Sadie sighed, smiling shyly. "I love him to death, but there's not a thing I can do about it. I love Mother, too. I can't leave her."

Nicky studied the wan face. "He hasn't been well, either," she said.

Sadie glanced up. "Oh, dear."

"An ulcer," Nicole said. "Just an ulcer. But he pushes so hard."

"He always has. Competing, you know," she added with a loving smile. "He feels he has to come up to par with Winthrop."

"That would be a tall order," Nicky said without thinking as she laid the table.

Sadie glanced at her as she filled cups with steaming black coffee. "He's a cold man."

"Not really," Nicole replied softly. "He's just hurt, that's all."

The older woman pursed her lips. "How did you wind up on the ranch?"

"Mr. Christopher wanted to come home for a month to rest and work. I have car payments, furniture payments, payment payments..." She grinned. "I couldn't afford to lose a month's pay, so I came, too."

"And now Winthrop's done a vanishing act. Why?"

"I don't know," Nicky said honestly. "He asked me out to dinner tonight, and then this morning he left." She shrugged. "He's very difficult to understand."

"He always was. I've known the two brothers for years. I went to school with Gerald." She filled the coffee cups and then placed them in their lovely china saucers on the linen tablecloth. "Winthrop was always a loner, although he was something of a rounder in his younger days. He broke hearts..."

"I'll bet he did," Nicky murmured. She looked up. "Did you know about the blonde?"

"Everybody around here knew about the blonde," Sadie replied. "It was a nine-day wonder. The gossip went on forever, as it does in small communities. Winthrop got back on his feet and lived it down, but I imagine he hasn't really gotten over it. She was a first-class barracuda. She'd have cut him up like fish bait if they hadn't been in that wreck. She'd have taken him for everything he had, and left him bleeding without a backward glance. She married an oil millionaire, you know. They say she's got a closet full of mink coats."

"How sad," Nicky said genuinely, her green eyes full of bitterness. "So many people marry for money. Or try to."

"I'll bet you never would," Sadie said unexpectedly. "Gerald always did like you. I'm a bit jealous of you."

"Me?" Nicky grinned. "Thanks, but he's too nice a man to make a play for his secretary. I'd do anything for him, but only in the line of duty. I'm shy that way. Most men don't appeal to me physically."

"Does Winthrop?"

Nicole flushed and flapped around while Sadie burst out laughing.

"I'm sorry, but your guilty secret is safe with me," Sadie said with a laugh. "Oh, Nicky, what a man to get hot and bothered by. The iceman!"

"It could be worse. I could develop a case for some married man with twenty kids."

"True, true." She put the finishing touches on the table arrangement. "Come and meet Mother, and then I'll show you where to put your overnight case."

"You're nice to let me stay," Nicky said. "You and I know that nothing would go on, but people talk. I don't want any gossip about my nice boss."

"Neither do I, and I'm glad you're old-fashioned." The nurse narrowed her eyes. "You really are old-fashioned, aren't you?" she asked with startling perception.

Nicky cleared her throat. "I always thought...well, marriage is nice. They say white only means it's your first marriage, but it means a lot more than that to me. I had old-fashioned grandparents."

She didn't add that she had wildly liberated parents and a succession of stepparents, or that her grandparents had gone to court to save her from the glitter.

"Good for them," Sadie said. "Her room's through here."

Sadie's mother was small and withered and very quiet. She looked like a little doll lying there, white hair and pale blue eyes and a beaten look about her. She could only move one side of her body—even one eye and part of her mouth were affected. It must have been a massive stroke.

"Mama, this is Nicky," Sadie introduced her.

Gerald moved. He'd been sitting on the bed beside the little old woman, holding her hand. He got up so that Nicky could sit and take the wrinkled little fingers in hers.

"Hello, Mama," Nicky grinned. "Or should I call you Mrs. Todd?" She raised her eyebrows.

"You may call me Mama if you like," Sadie's mother said, with the first hint of a twinkle in her eyes.

"That would be nice," Nicky said, smiling. "Mine died a long time ago. I don't have one. So if Sadie doesn't mind, I can share you. It's a pretty big deal," she added with mock solemnity. "I live on a tight budget, so working another person into my Christmas shopping list is a great honor. I give Godiva chocolates as presents," she whispered.

The old lady actually laughed. Her thin fingers tightened on Nicky's. "Do you?" she whispered.

"Do you like chocolates?"

Mama managed to smile. "I love them!"

"Lucky you, to have just adopted me," Nicky said. She searched the tired old eyes. "I'll bet you were as beautiful as Sadie, at her age," she mused.

"Yes, I was," the old woman said emphatically. "Sadie...show her."

"This was Mother at my age." Sadie held up a small portrait study. The woman in the photograph was standing beside a tall, dark man, and she was the image of Sadie.

"Weren't you a dish?" Nicole sighed, studying it. "You're still a dish," she added, glancing down at the smiling woman. "What can we bring you to eat? I saw roast beef and mashed potatoes and a salad...."

"Mashed potatoes and gravy," the woman replied eagerly. "And is there pudding?"

"Yes," Sadie said quickly, although there wasn't and she'd have to rush back and make one.

"I'll have pudding, too," came the pleased reply. "Now go and eat," her mother said. "Then Nicole can visit with me while you and Gerald put everything away."

"Nicky's staying the night. Winthrop's away," Sadie explained.

"If it's all right," Nicky asked.

"It's all right," the old woman said fiercely. "Go and eat, child. If I adopt you, you must be fattened up. I don't want any thin children."

Nicky laughed, her green eyes sparkling in her elfin face as she got to her feet. "I'll double up on portions. And I'll bring your pudding myself."

Sadie just shook her head when they were back in the dining room. "Never," she whispered, smiling. "I've never seen her so animated. She just lies there and hates it. Tonight, for the first time, she came alive. Nicky, what did you do?"

"I stirred her up," Nicky said with twinkling eyes. "That's all. People need stirring up now and again, especially when they're bitter."

"You should see what Nicole did to Winthrop," Gerald mused. "He left home."

"That wasn't my fault."

"Tell me about it," Gerald invited, a mischievous twinkle in his dark eyes.

"It wasn't. All I did was..." She hesitated, her face turning red as she thought about what she'd done and the way she and Winthrop had kissed so hungrily in the woods.

Gerald raised an eyebrow and exchanged a glance with Sadie.

"Is everything on the table?" Nicky asked quickly, sitting down.

With the subject safely changed, they took their places and began to eat. Watching Gerald and Sadie, she could easily see that they felt something for each other. Nicole's gentle heart went out to them, because it was obvious that they couldn't have any kind of future together in this situation. Putting Mrs. Todd in a nursing home would be condemning her to death. And Nicole had a feeling that she was very possessive about her daughter, perhaps without realizing it. Sadie was shy and so was Gerald, to a large extent. It was a difficult situation.

Sadie made a vanilla pudding and when it was dished up, Nicole took a tray to Mrs. Todd's room.

"I haven't enjoyed anything so much for a long time," Mrs. Todd sighed when she finished. "It's so hard to bear, being like this. I was always active, able to do as I pleased. And now..."

"Won't you get better?" Nicole asked quietly.

"I don't know. The doctors said I might. But that was a year ago; I think they've given up now."

Nicole put the tray to one side. "That's a nice bird feeder outside the window," she remarked, glancing at the elaborate chrome and glass affair.

"I love birds," the old lady explained. "I can watch them."

Nicole pursed her lips. "Do you have any binoculars?"

Her eyes gleamed. "No."

"I'll get you some. How about a book on birds, so you can identify them?"

The old eyes got brighter. "I'd love it!"

"Done. Just give me a few days. Now, how about a good murder mystery? There's one on television, one of those Agatha Christie ones, and I won't even tell you who done it."

Mrs. Todd actually laughed. "You should be with the young people, Nicole."

"The young people are—what did you flappers call it—spooning," she whispered conspiratorially. "At least, I hope they are. Gerald's very shy, and I think your daughter is, too."

"Yes, she is, poor child. She's such a good girl, and she's been so sweet to come and look after me. A lot of children would have turned their backs, or put me in a nursing home," Mrs. Todd said worriedly. "She hasn't said anything about it, but I know she's lonely here."

Nicole patted the old hand. "She loves you."

Mrs. Todd looked up. "And that young man . . . is he yours?"

She shook her head. "But I think he might be Sadie's. Would you mind?"

Mrs. Todd thought about it for a minute. "Well, no. He's a good boy. Not a patch on Winthrop, mind you, but the Christophers are fine people. I knew their mother. She was a dream girl."

"I hear their father was a nightmare man," Nicole said, fishing for information.

"Oh, no. He was a dynamo. We were all so jealous when he went to New York after Margaret. She didn't want to come, they'd had some terrible falling out. But he made her, kept her down at that house a virtual prisoner, until she agreed to marry him. Just between you and me, I think he took unfair advantage, too, but she loved him like a tigress. They were very happy."

"Did he look like Winthrop?" Nicole asked softly.

The old eyes seemed suddenly young. "Yes."

"A big man?"

"Body and heart. How is Winthrop? Is he getting over that woman?"

"I don't know him that well."

"Of course you don't, but you light up when I mention him, all the same. Turn on the television, child, and save your blushes. And then why don't you say good-night to the young lovers for us both and we'll hope something nice develops."

Nicole laughed delightedly as she followed the smug instructions. She tiptoed down the hall. It was unusually quiet, and when she reached the hall door, she saw why. Gerald, who seemed such a quiet and shy man, had Sadie in an embrace that spoke volumes and the way they were kissing said everything. Nicole tiptoed back and shut Mrs. Todd's door.

"Did you say good-night?" she asked Nicky.

Nicky said no with a straight face. "They're having a lively discussion. I expect it will be some time before we hear from them."

Mrs. Todd settled back against her pillows. "Lovely. I think it would do Sadie good to have company more often."

Nicole just smiled and settled down to watch the movie.

It was late the next morning before Nicole heard the sound of a vehicle coming up the driveway. That would be Gerald, she thought and she smiled at Sadie.

"I've had a lovely time," she told the other woman. "Thanks for letting me stay."

"I'm glad you did," Sadie mused. "Mother hasn't enjoyed herself that much since the stroke. You were just what she needed to shake her out of her lethargy. And now that I know you aren't making eyes at my Gerald, I'll be your best friend."

Nicole's eyebrows arched in surprise. "You didn't think that?"

"Of course I did," Sadie replied, amused. "So did everybody else. Gerald isn't the kind of man who brings women home, even secretaries, unless they mean something to him. Or at least, that's what we all figured."

Nicole wondered then about Winthrop's strange behavior, and if he could have thought the same thing. She went back over her easy friendship with her boss and began to see what an outsider might have seen.

"He's a very nice man," Nicole began quietly, "but..."

"That 'but' saved your life," Sadie whispered conspiratorially. She looked up as a knock sounded on the door and she went to open it with wide, bright eyes. But it wasn't Gerald standing outside. It was Winthrop.

Chapter Five

Sadie's face fell, although she tried not to let her disappointment show. "Oh, hello," she faltered. Winthrop's expression didn't encourage any pleasurable outbursts. He looked out of humor and unapproachable. Nicole, watching him, thought that he'd had time to build walls again, and he'd done it with enthusiasm. So much for her optimistic outlook on the future; the iceman had frozen over.

"Where's Gerald?" Nicole asked hesitantly. Her question made the situation even worse.

He positively glared at her. "He's at home on the phone, coping with some office disaster that one of his vice presidents is in the middle of. He's drinking buttermilk by the gallon, eating antacid tablets by the handful and generally getting sicker by the minute."

"Winthrop, you should have disconnected the phone," Sadie sighed.

He smiled at Sadie. "How's your mother?"

"Doing better, thanks, and all because of Nicky. She built a fire under Mama," Sadie grinned.

Winthrop stared at Nicole speculatively. "She's good at starting fires, all right," he said, but it wasn't a compliment. He was spoiling for a fight.

Nicole glared back. He was wearing jeans with a chambray shirt and the familiar sheepskin jacket, and a wide-brimmed hat shadowed his cold face. He looked very Western and deliciously sexy. Nicole wondered why he always seemed to button his shirts up almost to the throat, and found herself unexpectedly curious about what was underneath. Hair peeked out at his throat, and she remembered the springy feel of his chest under her hands that evening he'd caught her on the steps....

Winthrop was telling Sadie something about a party.

Nicole snapped back to the present. "A party?"

"Gerald thinks you're getting bored without some fun, buried out here in the sticks," Winthrop told her. "He wants to give a party. There'll be a band and all the neighbors will come. You too, Sadie. I'll drive Mary up to sit with your mother."

"I haven't been to a party in a long time," Sadie confessed wistfully.

"Neither have I, but I guess we'll have to make the best of it," Winthrop said with unflattering resignation. "It'll be Friday night, around six. I'll drive Mary up and fetch you."

"Couldn't Gerald?" Nicole suggested.

Winthrop openly gaped at her. "What?"

"He'll have to welcome his guests and so will you," Sadie reminded Nicole.

Nicky sighed. "I guess so." She picked up her case, which Winthrop promptly took away from her, and followed him out to the truck with a rueful wave at Sadie.

He got in under the wheel, threw up a hand at Sadie and reversed the pickup with deft, controlled movements. He didn't speak until he had it headed down the long, winding road toward the ranch.

"I didn't expect to find you here," he said curtly, lighting a cigarette as he drove. The wind was fierce and the truck lurched. It was getting dark against the horizon, heavy blue clouds building over the peaks.

"It wouldn't have looked right, to have Gerald and me under the same roof alone," she faltered.

He glanced at her. "Then, my God, how does it look to have the three of us under one roof?" he shot back.

She hadn't thought about that. She flushed scarlet and moved her gaze out the window. "How was your trip?"

"Fine."

"When did you get back?"

"About an hour ago."

She stared at her hands in her lap. She'd felt her heart soar when he walked into Sadie's living room, but now all she felt was miserable. He'd left town because he didn't want to take her out, and now he was as remote as the clouds. She felt abandoned.

"Don't look like that," he said abruptly.

"Like what?" she muttered.

"Lost. Wounded."

She studied her hands in her lap, twisting the small emerald ring she wore on her right ring finger. "You've been spoiling for a fight ever since you came in the door."

"And you don't know why?" he taunted, and his eyes cut at her. "Or hasn't it occurred to you yet that I want you?"

It had, but only in a vague way. She felt her face flush at hearing it put into words, and so bluntly. She couldn't even look at him. She was feeling a tenderness she'd never experienced, and he'd reduced it to something casual and physical and faintly irritating.

"That's plain enough," she said in a soft tone, forcing herself not to react violently when what she wanted most to do was push him out the door and down a sharp ravine.

He wouldn't back down, he told himself, no matter how miserable she looked. His jaw tautened as he wheeled the truck around a sharp curve, scattering dirt and gravel on the unsurfaced road.

"You get under my skin," he said abruptly. "I don't like it."

Her heart shifted uncomfortably. She stared out at the tall trees in the graying horizon. "You have the same effect on me," she said curtly, "and I don't like it, either."

"Then suppose we keep out of each other's way," he suggested. "You won't be here that much longer."

"That might be wise."

He drew on his cigarette, and then he turned and looked at her just as she lifted her eyes to his. The truck almost went off the road. He braked easily enough to stop the truck, but his gaze didn't waver. Her eyes were greener than new leaves on spring trees, he thought absently, his own narrowing with kindling hunger. She was young and soft and sweet and she made him ache as he had in his youth, made him feel invulnerable and all male.

Her lips parted, but she couldn't look away. It was like holding a live wire in bare hands. Her breath shuddered out of her throat and she felt throbbing fire in her blood.

"If I touched you now, there wouldn't be any stopping for either of us," he said in a deep, slow tone. His broad chest rose and fell heavily, and his eyes were narrow, dark. "You knock me off balance."

"You said yourself," she whispered, trying to be rational, "that you'd been away from women for a long time."

"And you think it's proximity that's causing my reaction to you?" he asked with a mocking smile. He reached out a lean hand and idly linked her fingers into his with a caressing pressure that was as arousing as a kiss. Her heart began to race, and her breath came in smothered whispers that she tried not to let him see.

"That," he whispered, "is chemistry. It doesn't have anything to do with proximity, or age, or sanity. I touch you, and my body aches. And if the way you're breathing is any indication, Kentucky girl, you're on fire for me.''

She bit her lip, hard. But the tremors wouldn't stop. She tugged her hand away from his and he released it with careless indifference and went back to smoking his cigarette.

"Don't worry," he said with cool mockery, "I won't tell your boss. I love my brother. His happiness comes first.''

She frowned slightly. "I don't understand."

"Don't you?" He turned back to the steering wheel and put the truck into gear without another word.

She rode beside him in an uncomfortable silence. She wanted to tell him that he'd gotten it all wrong, that she and Gerald were only boss and secretary. But he looked too unapproachable and she wasn't sure of him. Her feelings for Winthrop were new and a little frightening. She didn't want to have to face them.

When they got back to the house, he got out to carry her bag up to the front porch, all bristling masculine humor. He limped more than he usually did, too, and she wondered if it was due to his bad temper or if he was in pain from the walking he must have had to do on his trip.

"I don't understand why you're so angry at me," she murmured as she joined him on the porch. "I haven't done anything...."

"This is why," he said quietly. He looked down at her from his formidable height and, aware of Mary standing just inside the door, he did something with his hands, in sign language—first a movement like someone drinking out of a cup, and then an odd movement with his elbows and closed fists. "See if you can get Mary to translate that," he chided, turning. "And you'll know it all."

She stared after him wistfully, loving the lines of his elegant body, the muscular fitness that emanated from him despite that limp. He was the most attractive man she'd ever known. And if he'd looked back, and seen her standing there watching him, it might have erased some of the ill humor from his dark face. But he went away without a backward glance and Mary seemed to vanish into thin air as Nicole went inside with her overnight case.

"There you are," Gerald moaned, rubbing his stomach as he appeared in the doorway of Winthrop's study. "My ulcer is killing me. Have Mary pour me some buttermilk, will you? Then we've got to get some paperwork done and see if we can sort out this mix up in taxes. Hurry, Nicky!"

"Yes, sir!"

She got the milk from the kitchen, curious about Mary's oddly smug look.

"There's something I want to ask you." Nicole hesitated. "Those signs Winthrop made on the front porch—you saw them. What did they mean?"

Mary grinned, showing even white teeth. "Interesting things."

"What did he say?"

Mary folded her arms over her ample bosom. "Much."

"Well?"

"Hard to translate into English," Mary continued. "Many Indian signs have no equivalent in English."

"Yes, but you must have some idea what he said," Nicole persisted.

"Good idea, all right, but I must give thought to the proper manner of expressing it to you." Mary turned back to making a thick-crusted apple pie. "Some time soon, I will translate it for you." Then she grinned again over her shoulder and giggled.

Nicole, no wiser than before, sighed and carried the milk to Gerald.

The tangle took time to straighten out, especially over the phone, and by the time it was done, Nicole was too tired to do anything except eat a light supper and go to bed. Winthrop, as usual, was out working, so she didn't have to worry about keeping peace with him.

During the next few days, as she helped Gerald plan the party in her honor, Nicole puzzled over Winthrop's cool behavior and Gerald's continued stomach pain. Gerald and Sadie had gotten off to such a great start, and now he seemed morose and moody and worried.

Nicole had planned a menu of hors d'oeuvres and finger foods for a buffet, and arranged for a local band to play. Gerald had called the neighbors to invite them.

"This will be fun," he said as he finished. "There hasn't been any music in this house since Winthrop announced his engagement." He seemed far away for a minute and wistful. "There was music that night, and the neighbors came over, and we danced until after midnight. Mrs. Todd was fit as a fiddle back then, and she danced, too." He glanced at Nicole from his comfortable armchair. "Winthrop hasn't allowed music in the house since, although I can't blame him. He won't go near a party, either. He says he can't dance because of his leg, but I think the memories are stopping him more than any physical pain."

"I guess he really loved her," she said, remembering what little Winthrop had told her about his feelings at the time.

"It's been three years. He should be healing, mentally at least."

She didn't like to think about Winthrop's broken heart, or the cause of it. Her feelings were too turbulent, and jealousy was still topmost.

"Will he even come to the party?" she asked.

"He'll have to," he chuckled. "Or the neighbors will talk about him. He hates gossip more than he hates music. At least, he does since the accident. It never used to matter in the old days."

"We haven't heard from Sadie lately," she said with deliberate casualness.

He looked uncomfortable. "Her mother hasn't been well."

She studied his wan face. "Hasn't she?"

He shifted restlessly, crossing his legs. "She doesn't want to lose Sadie," he said curtly. "She's afraid of being alone, or at the mercy of strangers in some nursing home. I can't blame her, Nicole. It's just that Sadie's so young to be buried alive like that."

"Couldn't Mrs. Todd get better if she had more interest in life, in living?"

"Perhaps," he agreed. "But it's very hard to keep that interest going. You made a good start with her. Unfortunately, she's only enthusiastic when people are around. The minute they leave, she goes back to brooding."

"Doesn't she have relatives besides Sadie?"

"She has a sister in Florida," he murmured. "Ten years her junior and a live wire. She wants Mrs. Todd to come and visit, but Mrs. Todd is terrified to leave here. She has some idea that she'll die if she does. Meanwhile," he sighed, "Sadie is trapped. She loves her mother, you know."

"And you love Sadie," she said quietly.

He started to deny it, and then he saw the gentle compassion in Nicole's green eyes. "Yes."

"Give it time," she said. "And we needn't rush back to Chicago," she added with a faint grin.

"Even if that means watching Winthrop do a job on your nerves?" he probed. "Because he's wearing them down, isn't he?"

"I bother him," she said, then looked up at Gerald. "He bothers me, too."

"Good. You both need a little shaking up," he said with a smile. He got to his feet, grimacing. "I need some more buttermilk."

"And your tablets," she added.

"And my tablets. But you're good medicine, Nicky."

She smiled. "Thank you. And thanks for the party, too. It was a nice thought."

"I hope you enjoy it."

"Oh, I think I will," she said. She was already thinking about breezing down the staircase in a billowy white gown, dragging a black mink coat behind her, dripping diamonds so that Winthrop would fall at her feet. Of course, she didn't have a white gown or a black mink or any diamonds. It would be the gray jersey dress and he'd be too out of humor about the whole thing to notice if she waltzed down the staircase stark naked. She sighed and went back to the typewriter.

The night of the party, Nicole dressed carefully in the hated gray jersey and did her face with a minimum of makeup. The band, a very good country and western one, was already in full swing when she went to answer the door with Gerald.

Winthrop came in behind Sadie, glaring at Nicole and Gerald with coal dark eyes. He was wearing a white shirt with dark slacks and a leather jacket, a creamy dress Stetson atop his neatly combed straight hair. He and Nicky had barely spoken in recent days. He'd commented that a party was just what he needed the night before his group of Eastern hunters arrived—which they were scheduled to do that Saturday. But Gerald had made soothing noises to the big man and he'd calmed down.

But only temporarily. His eyes were already promising retribution on Nicky's poor head.

"Good evening, Winthrop," she drawled softly as Gerald led Sadie off to the punch bowl, since she was the last to arrive and there were no more guests to receive.

"Good evening, Miss White," he replied. His dark eyes ran down her body like exploring hands, slow and very thorough. "I gather that you only brought one dress with you?"

"I didn't think I'd need more than one," she explained quietly. Her pale green eyes swept over his dark face and she felt tingles of pleasure from just looking at him. "It isn't too drab, is it?"

"You know you look lovely in anything you wear," he said suavely. He took off his Stetson, settled it on the hat rack, then hung up his jacket.

Watching the muscles ripple under the white shirt he wore with a blue patterned tie, Nicole wanted to stand in his arms and feel him holding her. It was a hunger that bordered on obsession. She moved closer to him as the band swung into a slow dance tune.

"I want to dance," she said quietly, aware of the guests watching them. Nobody was dancing yet; everybody seemed to be waiting for someone else to get things started.

He stared her down. "I don't dance anymore," he said coolly. "I can't. My leg won't hold me up under sudden turns and dips."

"It would if you danced slowly," she said. She moved even closer, her perfume floating up into his nostrils, her warmth teasing, seductive. "Hold me, Winthrop," she whispered, laying both palms slowly, hesitantly, flat down over the hard muscles of his chest.

He shuddered a little, and his chiseled lips parted. "I won't, damn it," he bit off.

She laid her head against his shoulder. "You want to," she whispered, "and I want to. Everybody's watching." Her own forwardness was beginning to embarrass her, but the need to be held by him was so strong that she fought down the urge to give in.

"No!" he bit off.

He started to turn, but she blocked his path. Everyone stopped talking, and she held her breath while he decided.

With a glance behind them and a muffled curse, he pulled her into his hard embrace and began to move very carefully to the slow rhythm of the music.

Gerald and Sadie watched the tall man's slow, hesitant movements with quiet smiles, amazed that Nicole had been able to manage such a small miracle. Winthrop was giving in, at least for the moment. His dark face was threatening, but he was holding her with such tenderness that it was almost tangible despite his temper.

Nicky savored her small victory, closing her eyes in wonder. Dancing with him was as sweet as she'd imagined it would be. He might hate her for it, but right now it seemed worth every expected bit of pain. He was tall and strong and warm, and he smelled of spice and soap. The lean, sure hand that held her made her feel safe and protected. She sighed with pure delight.

He felt that soft yielding and was furious at her for making a spectacle of him, for drawing everyone's eyes to his disability. Damn her, what was she trying to do to him?

He gave in with ill-concealed irritation and drew her slowly against him, one lean hand possessing hers. He began to move to the rhythm, a little clumsily at first, but quickly with more and more confidence. She melted into him, then, careful not to knock him off balance, she smiled against his shoulder.

"There," she mumbled happily, "I knew you could."

"I could wring your neck," he said, forcing himself to smile at her while all around them other people were finally joining them on the dance floor.

"It's your house," she reminded him. "The host is supposed to open the dancing. There are rules about that kind of thing."

"I can't dance with this leg," he said through his teeth.

"You're doing it, aren't you?" She drew back a little and looked up into his darkly glittering eyes. "But if you're sure you can't do it, then why don't you fall on the floor or something?"

"Lady," he breathed through his teeth, "you're brave in company."

"If we were alone, what would you do to me?" she asked with open curiosity, her green eyes wide and twinkling.

The look in them softened him, just a little. She was a handful, but her heart was in the right place. She wouldn't let him feel sorry for himself, or slide into thinking he had to give up living because he had a bum leg. And until now, he hadn't even realized how much he'd used that leg to keep him away from people. It had become his excuse for being a recluse, his excuse for avoiding involvement.

His fingers edged between hers and caressed them as he turned her with amazing flexibility. He smiled then, the cold anger in his eyes melting into reluctant pleasure.

"You danced before the accident, didn't you?" she asked, smiling. "You loved it, too. You're very good, despite that leg. You move with such grace for a big man."

"And what would you have done, Pollyanna, if I'd gone down on the floor with the first turn?" he asked.

"Oh, I'd have made sure I went down with you," she said matter-of-factly, "so that everyone would have thought I tripped you."

He felt his heart start pounding. Something stirred in him that he hadn't felt since his youth, something young and daring and utterly reckless. He pulled her against him and stood there for one long minute, fighting the urge to kiss her in front of everyone. He liked the way her body melted into his when he drew her close, he liked the faint trembling of her legs against his. She was his the minute he touched her, and he especially liked that. His eyes narrowed as he remembered the feel of her soft mouth, the exquisite pleasure it gave him to kiss her. She'd been engaged once, she'd told him. He felt a sudden heat of unreasonable jealousy. What had the man been like? Why had he jilted her? Was there some secret in her past that she was afraid to share with him?

"Are we doing statue imitations?" she asked breathlessly.

His lips pursed. "I'm trying to decide whether to kiss you."

"Not in front of all these people, for heaven's sake," she burst out.

"These people—or Gerald?" he asked softly.

Her eyebrows went straight up with surprise. "Well, come to think of it, I'm not sure how he'd react to it," she had to admit. Gerald hadn't said anything about her interest in Winthrop, and she didn't think he'd fire her over it. But, then again, she wasn't sure....

Winthrop sighed, and drew her back against him. "Never mind, daffodil. Just dance."

"Why did you call me that?"

He smiled against her temple. "There's nothing more full of hope than a daffodil. It comes before the last snow is gone, fluffing up yellow and pretty and optimistic in the middle of all that freezing white. It takes a lot to kill a daffodil. They're glorious."

Tears stung her eyes. He could call her daffodil forever, if he liked. She snuggled closer. "What a nice compliment," she said.

"I meant it."

"I know. You're not the kind of man who spouts insincere flattery."

"Perceptive of you, Miss White."

"You bet, Mr. Christopher."

He was quiet then, circling the floor lazily with her soft weight against him, feeling his head whirl with delicious sensations. His leg was beginning to throb from the unfamiliar strain, but he'd have fallen on the floor before he'd have given in to it now. He didn't want to let go of her. He wanted to pull her closer, and bend his head and take her soft mouth fully under his....

All too soon the music stopped, and Gerald was there, waiting.

"My turn," he grinned. "Sorry, big brother."

Winthrop stared at his brother for a long minute, searching the younger man's eyes curiously. And for just a minute, he thought about refusing. Then he came to his senses. She was just a woman, for God's sake, and women were treacherous. He wasn't going to fight with his brother. If Gerald wanted her, he could have her, Winthrop thought angrily. He smiled, but there was no humor in it. He nodded with a mocking smile at Nicole and then walked slowly away to the punch bowl, pausing to talk to some of the other men on the way.

"You angel," Gerald said, hugging her. "At first I thought he was going to breathe fire at you."

"So did I, but I bluffed him out. Doesn't he dance beautifully?" she murmured dreamily, staring past Gerald at Winthrop.

"Indeed he does, with the right partner." He whirled her around. "You've brought him back to life. I'd given up hope that he was ever going to put things into perspective. You're very good for him."

"Where's Sadie?" she asked.

"Phoning Mary to make sure Mrs. Todd is all right." He slowed down a little. "I wish I could decide what to do about it."

"Why don't you do what you want to and solve all your problems when the time comes? You can't cross a bridge until it's in front of you."

"Where did you learn so much?" he asked curiously. "You're not at all what you seem."

"I've had plenty of practice," was all she'd admit. And then that dance, too, was over, and she went from partner to partner for the rest of the evening.

Winthrop didn't dance with her again, but she felt his gaze on her wherever she went. Her eyes were on him just as much, when she thought he wasn't looking. He was so good to look at. Dressing up suited him. Even in a simple white cotton shirt and dressy tie, he looked elegant. It made him seem darker than ever, more sensuous. She wasn't even surprised to discover that she loved him. That seemed as natural as breathing.

All too soon, the guests were leaving. Nicole had the crazy idea of being alone with Winthrop while Gerald took Sadie home. But he looked in her direction with an expression on his face that chilled her to the bone. It was as if he hated her, and perhaps he did for what she'd done to him. Dragging him onto the dance floor in front of all the neighbors might not have been the way to his heart, she realized. And because she was confused and a little hurt by his coldness, she asked if she could ride with Gerald and Sadie. They took one look at her face and agreed without protest.

When they got to Sadie's house, Mrs. Todd was asleep, and Mary was watching a gory horror film on television. It was just ending and Mary sat with a big bowl of popcorn on her ample lap, refusing to budge until the last drop of blood was spilled.

"Good movie," she enthused, walking out with Nicole while Sadie and Gerald said a lingering good-night indoors. "You like horror films?" she asked.

"I like vampire movies," Nicole said. "But I like science fiction better."

"You and Winthrop," she shook her head. "Those films are noisy. Too noisy. I like quiet movies."

"With screaming and lots of victims," Nicole chided.

Mary stared at her, stone-faced. "Beats all those noisy machines."

Nicole laughed delightfully. "I guess so. How did Mrs. Todd do tonight?"

"Done fine. We had pudding. I like pudding."

"So do I," Nicole said, smiling. "It was a good party. Winthrop and I started the dancing."

Mary's eyes widened. "Winthrop was dancing?"

"Yes. He does it very well."

"He used to," Mary agreed. "But I have not seen him dance since the accident. How did you manage it?"

Nicole chewed her lip a little and peeked at Mary. "I stood in front of him on the dance floor and wouldn't move."

Mary laughed. She did it seldom, but when she did, it was wholeheartedly. "Good medicine," she told the younger woman. "We should bottle you."

"I'd most likely ferment and become illegal. There's Gerald."

He joined them, looking a bit hot under the collar and flustered. He grinned. "Ready to go?"

"Been ready quite some time," Mary said. "Long past my bedtime."

"There, there, too much sleep can kill a good woman," Gerald said soothingly. "Think of how I'm saving you from certain death."

"Saving me from much needed rest," Mary countered, climbing into the pickup between him and Nicole. "Winthrop danced, she tell you?"

"She didn't have to. I saw it with my own eyes," he volunteered, grinning past her at Nicole. "I wish I could have taken a picture. Nobody will believe it."

"Isn't it cloudy tonight?" Nicole was trying to change the subject, but it really did look cloudy, and it was getting colder.

"Snow clouds," Mary said. "We get buried in snow pretty soon."

"Not in November," Nicole said.

"This is Montana. Snow comes early and late—you can't predict mountain weather. And snow in November is pretty routine," her boss informed her. "Lord, I hope we don't get shut up with that horsey set from back East. They'll be here tomorrow." He glanced at Nicole. "By the way, one of Winthrop's guests is from Kentucky, an expert on thoroughbreds. Winthrop wants him to take a look at the colt and give him an opinion. He wouldn't be able to race it for a couple of years, of course, but he's thinking along those lines."

Nicole knew a number of people in the horsey set. She was afraid of meeting someone from her old life, someone who knew her father, who might tell him where she was and what she was doing now. She didn't want him to know anything about her new life. There were deep scars from those young years. She wanted nothing to do with the man who'd driven her mother into a succession of lovers, followed by a fatal accident. Nothing at all.

"Did he tell you the man's name?" Nicole asked quietly.

Gerald glanced at her. "As a matter of fact he did," he replied. He grinned ruefully. "But I was on the phone at the time and I didn't catch it. There's a Murdock woman, and a couple of brothers named Harris. But I don't think the Harrises know much about horses."

Nicole consoled herself with the thought that there must be hundreds of horsey sportsmen in the world besides her father. She only nodded, closing her eyes as they went back to the Christopher ranch.

The house was quiet when they got there. If Nicole had hoped to see Winthrop again, she was disappointed. He was nowhere in sight. She said good-night to Mary and Gerald and went reluctantly to her room.

She didn't sleep. She lay awake staring at the ceiling for what seemed hours. Finally she got up and decided to make herself a cup of hot chocolate. Perhaps that would do the trick; she really couldn't stay awake all night.

Since the household was asleep, she didn't stop to fumble through the closet for a robe. Besides, her long flannel pajamas were more than decent, with their pale-pink rose pattern. She looked very young without her makeup and barefoot, as she went down the long, dark staircase. She hoped the house didn't have ghosts, she didn't fancy meeting one.

The kitchen light was on. She opened the door and paused, stopping dead at the sight of Winthrop bending over the stove. He was wearing pajama bottoms, nice brown striped ones, but no top. His chest was…incredible. Broad and bronzed and thick with a wedge of hair that covered his rippling muscles.

He turned, his dark hair tousled, and stared at her. "Looking for someone?" he asked.

"For some hot chocolate," she confessed. "I can't sleep."

"I'm making some," he said. "Come in and find some mugs."

She stared at herself. "I should get a robe…"

"Why?" he asked, glancing at her. "You're covered up in all the right places, and I'm hurting like hell. I'm not in any condition to lay you down on the kitchen table with evil intent."

She smothered a giggle, went in and closed the door behind her. "How savage sounding," she mused as she searched the cupboard for cups. "Think of the splinters!"

"A nice girl like you. Shame on you." He took the hot chocolate off the stove and poured it into the mugs before he put the pan in the sink to soak. He was limping rather badly, and she grimaced as he sat down with a hard wince.

"That's my fault, isn't it?" she asked gently. "I made you dance when you didn't want to, and you hurt it because of me. I'm sorry."

"Nobody makes me do a damned thing," he said curtly. He had two pills. He took them, swallowing them down with a sip of the hot chocolate. "I could have walked away from you if I'd wanted to."

"But you didn't."

He turned, his dark eyes holding hers. "I didn't want to. I like holding you. The excuse isn't particularly relevant."

Her face colored, and he smiled slowly.

She lowered her eyes to her cup and lifted it quickly to her mouth. She sipped at it for a long time, her mind hungry with sweet longings, her eyes darting to his broad, bare chest and back to her cup. He was through with his chocolate, but he sat back, quiet and faintly threatening and just looked at her until her body began to tremble.

"Did you wonder what I looked like under my shirt, Nicky?" he asked with blatant seduction in his voice.

Her lips parted on a husky sigh. She couldn't quite meet that searching gaze. She clung to her empty mug as if it were a life jacket. The silence was suddenly too sweeping, the loneliness of the deserted room staggering in its implications. They were alone. And he wanted her.

She felt him move before she saw him. He took the mug out of her hands and drew her up in front of him, holding her gently by her upper arms.

"There's nothing to be afraid of," he whispered. "Nothing at all."

He bent his head and she saw the shadow of his face, felt his chocolaty breath as his mouth brushed against hers. She relaxed then, because he was very slow and sure of himself. He wasn't in any hurry, and the leisure of his movements stopped the panic inside her. She began to unwind, feeling the softness of his mouth along with its hardness, liking the delicate probing of his tongue just under her upper lip. Amazing, she thought, how sensitive her mouth was to that light touch.

She lifted toward him a little, and heard his breath catch. She couldn't know that he was on fire with need, that he was in agony trying to hold back enough to keep from frightening her.

"Sweet," he whispered against her lips. "You're so sweet."

He had a lover's voice, she thought, very deep and seductive. She loved to hear him talk anytime, but particularly like this, in hushed whispers. She put her hands against him and felt them tingle where they touched the thick hair that covered him. It was wiry against her palms, deliciously abrasive when she began to draw them over his broad chest, disturbing the muscles so that they rippled under her fingers.

His breath caught. He stopped and suddenly moved back. His eyes held hers, searching them. "I want more than this," he said tautly.

She couldn't look away. "How... how much more?"

His eyes went to her pajama jacket. "Nothing terribly indiscreet," he said quietly. His hands followed his gaze. He hooked his index finger into the V neckline of her pajamas and tugged her toward him. "Don't panic, okay? I promise I won't let it go too far."

She wanted to protest. But her eyes went down to his lean fingers working the buttons with such deftness, and she couldn't look away. He undid them slowly, and then drew the fabric back from her high, pink breasts with a leisurely expertise that hypnotized her.

Then his gaze was on her, looking at her with blatant possession. Winthrop was a man with an eye for beauty, and the expression in his dark eyes told her that he found her beautiful. Her nipples went hard under his scrutiny, and she was embarrassed and tried to cover them. But he stopped her, shaking his head gently.

"It isn't sordid or shameful to let me see you," he said quietly, his voice very slow and deep. "God never made anything more beautiful than a woman's breasts."

Her breath stopped in her throat at his words. She looked up at him, her gaze sharing secrets with him. Then he smiled, and it was like the sun coming out.

He touched her cheek, gently tracing it. "Come here and let me hold you, Nicole," he breathed, drawing her. "Feel my body and let me feel yours. Let me teach you how beautiful it can be to touch skin against skin."

She let him draw her close, feeling the sting of tears as she went into his arms. Her eyes closed at the first contact with his warm, hard body, and she cried out as her nipples stabbed into his skin, burying themselves in the damp, abrasive mat of hair that covered the hard muscles. "Winthrop," she murmured.

"Yes." His hands spread against her silken back, under the pajama top. He drew her very close, closing his own eyes as her soft body melted into him. He was aroused, and she knew it. He felt her stiffen as her legs came into contact with his.

"Don't flinch away from me," he murmured at her temple, coaxing her back against him. "This is natural, too, and good and sweet and right between a man and a woman. Don't be afraid of it."

"It's so intimate," she whispered shakily against his warm, broad chest. His skin tasted of cologne and soap. Masculine smells. Good smells.

"Intimate," he agreed at her ear. "Yes, it's that. It's exquisitely sweet, having you close to me this way." His arms tightened and trembled a little. So did his tall, fit body. "Nicky," he breathed on a groan, bending his head over her. He began to rock her, fostering a new kind of intimacy between them, one that should have shocked her but was strangely familiar now. She clung to him, letting him hold her, yielding to his strength.

"Your leg..." she said a long minute later.

"What leg?" he murmured.

She drew in a long breath, and he shuddered as he felt her breasts swell against his skin.

"It's scary, isn't it?" she whispered. "Holding each other like this."

"Scary enough," he agreed on a bitter laugh. "You can't possibly imagine the thoughts going through my mind."

"I'll bet I can, too," she said. She nuzzled her cheek against him, loving the rough feeling of the hair over his chest. "Do you like that?"

"Can't you feel how much I like it?" he asked with blatant mockery. "Give me your mouth."

She lifted her lips to meet his, her hands sliding around him to his back, loving the feel of him, the vibrant masculinity of him. He kissed her slowly, warmly, and even that was intimate, his tongue probing softly in her mouth.

He shifted her a little so that his hand could find the soft curve of her breast and tease it into arching toward those tormenting fingers.

"Do you want me to keep going?" he whispered at her lips.

"Yes," she whispered back, her voice breaking. She wasn't old enough or sophisticated enough to hide her hunger.

"Like this?" he murmured, with a teasing touch around the nipple, his fingers faintly callused and deliciously abrasive on her soft skin. "Or like this?"

His thumb rubbed suddenly at the tiny hardness and she cried out, a whimper of sound that worked on him like a narcotic. His hand covered her breast and he lifted his head to look into her misty eyes while he caressed her.

"I'm on fire," he whispered. "Burning."

"So am I," she moaned. "Winthrop..."

His head bent to her body, and as she watched, fascinated, he arched her and opened his mouth and put it completely over her breast.

She thought that as long as she lived, she'd never get over the sensation. It went on and on, tearing at her, shaking her, making her too weak to move, to breathe, to think. She was an instrument, and he was playing her with an expert touch, teaching her things about her own body that she'd never known.

She arched farther, her hands in his dark, cool hair, inciting him, begging him. His mouth slid from one breast to the other, and she moaned like a wounded thing, feeding on the sweet ardor of his mouth, living only through him.

Dazed, shuddering with sensation, she barely felt him move. And then she was on his lap in the chair, and he was holding her, cradling her while she cried. She hadn't even been aware of the intensity of her emotions until she felt the tears like rain on her face.

"Shh," he whispered gently, his mouth soothing her now, touching her hot cheeks, her wet eyelids and eyelashes, her nose and mouth and chin. "It's all right. Hush, darling, it's all right now."

"Winthrop," she whispered tearfully.

"Nicole," he breathed, wrapping her up in his arms. He rocked her against him hungrily, laughing a little at her headlong response even now. "Wildcat! Never in my life, not ever... You damned near pushed me over the edge with those little cries you made."

"I couldn't help it," she said, hot-faced. "It was what you were doing to me..."

"I couldn't help that, either," he murmured dryly. He kissed her gently. "You have exquisite breasts, Miss White," he breathed huskily. "As soft as satin, as warm as velvet. I'd rather cut off my arm than cover them, but if I don't, you and I are very likely to become lovers within the next few seconds, right here on the floor."

And while she was getting over the shock from that statement, he sat her up on his lap like a big doll and proceeded to do up the buttons on her pajamas. When she was covered again, he drew her back down, holding her lazily while he pressed tender, undemanding kisses on her damp face.

"You're very quiet," he remarked finally. "Why? Are you shocked? Outraged? Embarrassed?"

"I don't know," she confessed, snuggling closer. "Not outraged or ashamed, although I suppose I should be embarrassed. I'm not in the habit of... behaving this way with men."

"I know that." He brushed the damp hair away from her cheeks. His dark eyes held hers. "Is this all new to you?"

It wouldn't do to lie to him, she supposed. She searched his dark eyes. "Yes," she said quietly. "My fiancé..." she said quietly. "He wanted me, but I could never give in to him. I...didn't like it when he tried to touch me." She lowered her eyes to his broad chest. "And when I found out what he really wanted, I felt used and cheap and ashamed. I don't feel any of those things with you." She lifted her eyes again, because it was important to make him understand. "It isn't like a physical thing with you, however silly that sounds. It's..." She searched for the right words. "It's..."

"Beautiful," he said for her. "Poignant. Profound."

"Yes." Her pale eyes lit up, making her beautiful.

He kissed her very tenderly. "Any other woman I'd have in bed by now," he murmured. "But you aren't the kind of woman who can play around with sex. Not even in the throes of an urgent need."

"Nevertheless," she said slowly, choosing her words, "I wouldn't refuse you."

"I know. That makes it worse. I can't take the responsibility alone." He touched her mouth with a gentle finger.

"Responsibility?" she whispered.

"I could make you pregnant," he said gently.

Her body felt wildly hungry. Her lips parted and the look in her eyes made him want to throw back his head and scream.

His fingers trembled as they touched her face. "Nicky," he whispered.

"Do you want a son?" she asked in a husky, loving tone.

"Yes," he bit off. "I want one with you...."

Her body shuddered. She looked into his eyes and knew that she was lost, that she couldn't stop, that he couldn't. In his eyes, she saw the coolness of white sheets and the outline of two bodies in the darkness....

And all at once, she was standing and he was five feet away from her with a burning cigarette in his hand.

She was so numb she could hardly feel. Her eyes traced him, saw the faint shudder of his long legs.

"Go to bed, sweetheart," he said without looking at her.

"You aren't angry?"

"No," he said, his voice deep and slightly choked. "I'm not angry."

She turned toward the door, only half understanding. She paused with her hand on the knob and glanced back. "Winthrop, are you all right?" she asked, her tone exquisitely gentle.

"Team sports and cold showers will save me," he said on a husky laugh. "Go to bed."

She flushed because that explained it all. "I'm sorry," she said. "Really sorry."

"For what?" He glanced at her finally, and she was shocked at how pale and drawn his face was. "Nicky, you were in as deep as I was. I'm a little shell-shocked, that's all. But we can't stay here. Things are getting out of hand. I don't want anything to happen that we might regret."

She smiled at him. "I wouldn't regret anything."

"I can't be sure of that. It's easy to lose sight of things in the darkness. I want you very badly. I know you want me just as much. But let's stop and think before we commit ourselves that completely. I can't take you to bed one night and walk away from you the next morning. At my age, sex is a commitment, not a toy."

Her face colored. "I guess it is, when you start talking about making people pregnant," she murmured dryly.

"That, Miss White, I would enjoy," he said lazily, and his dark eyes glittered playfully. "And so would you; I'd make sure of it. So suppose you go up to bed and give it some thought. And tomorrow we'll discuss terms."

"What kind of terms?"

He smiled slowly. "That would be telling."

She turned back to the door. "If it means I get to live with you, I'll agree to most anything," she said and ran for it. Behind her, she heard rich, thunderous laughter, and by the time she got to the top of the staircase, she was laughing, too. Life was sweet and Winthrop had to feel the same way she did, because he was hinting at a lot more than a brief affair.

If he trusted her that much, it must mean that he loved her. And God knew, she loved him with all her heart. She was so preoccupied dreaming about Winthrop's arms holding her in the darkness, and little boys and never leaving this exquisite valley as long as she lived that it was hard to fall asleep.

For an instant, she had a twinge of guilt about not sharing her past with him. But there was still time, she told herself as she snuggled under the covers. Plenty of time, to explain why she'd kept it a secret, to show him that she loved him, that she'd never betray him. Yes, there was time.

Chapter Six

When Nicole woke up the next morning, it was to an odd kind of silence. Although she was used to that particular stillness in winter, it was unfamiliar in autumn. But usually it meant snow.

She threw off the covers and ran to the window. Sure enough, the lacy white flakes were coming down like cotton out of the clouds, gently blanketing the trees and the grass. She sighed, vividly remembering last night and the newness of what she'd shared with Winthrop. Like a daydreaming child, she propped her elbows on the windowsill, put her face in her hands and mused about how it would be if she and Winthrop had been snowed in together, just the two of them.

Her daydreams were rudely shattered by the loud noise of an approaching vehicle—a four-wheel-drive vehicle, at that.

A huge Cherokee wagon came into view with Winthrop at the wheel, and several passengers. They must be the hunting party, she guessed. The group didn't look too bad. There was a willowy redhead dressed from head to toe in white fur, followed by two older men, one in a wool plaid coat, the other in leather. And there was one more passenger, a big, white-headed man with an imposing nose, wearing tweeds. . . .

Nicky came away from the window feeling sick. She'd go back to Chicago alone, right now. She'd pack her things and get out while she could. The memories came back hauntingly. The loud arguments, the fights that never seemed to end. Her father apologizing halfheartedly for his latest infidelity, her mother's mocking laughter. She put her hands against her eyes, feeling all over again like the little girl who used to run into the kitchen and hide her face against Lalla's ample bosom and cry her eyes out until the argument ended.

"Nicky!" came Gerald's voice outside the door. "Nicky, come down! Guess who one of our visitors is? It's your father!"

Along with that horror came a new one. She hadn't told Winthrop who her father was, or that she'd renounced her inheritance. What was he going to think?

"I'll be right down," Nicky called back.

She got dressed in a daze, pulling on her gray slacks and white sweater, the ones Mary had miraculously cleaned. She'd been wearing them the day she'd helped Winthrop deliver the colt. Perhaps that memory, if her clothing triggered it, would make the next hours easier.

She ran a brush through her hair and smoothed on some lipstick. She looked pale and haunted, but that couldn't be helped. Why did it have to be her father, she wondered miserably. Of all the sportsmen in the world, why him? She'd suspected it, of course, when Winthrop had mentioned that he'd been to Kentucky and knew Rockhampton Farms. Since her father was a well-known sportsman, it wasn't far-fetched to imagine that he might enjoy hunting in Montana.

There were voices in the living room when she went downstairs, but the only face she saw immediately was Winthrop's. The tender lover of last night might have been a dream. His expression was hard, ice-cold. He barely looked at her before he turned back to his guests, a cup of coffee in one lean hand.

"Here she is," Gerald said with a grin, coming to meet her. His hand on her arm gave her the strength to walk into the room. "Look who's here," he added, pulling her toward the big white-haired man in tweed.

"Hello, Nicky," her father said coldly. "Long time, no . see."

"Not long enough," she replied, and the bitterness of the past was in her eyes.

Winthrop frowned. It wasn't the reunion he'd expected to see at all.

Dominic White stood up, but he didn't approach her. His careless green eyes swept over her wan face and dismissed it. "This is Carol Murdock," he said, introducing the willowy, very young redhead in ski pants and a mohair sweater under all the fur. "She's visiting with me for a while."

"Hi," Carol said breathily. She beamed up at Dominic, who was at least fifteen years her senior, probably more like twenty. "Your dad sure is a lot of fun. He's going to show me how to shoot a moose."

"Oh, you'll enjoy that, I'm sure," Nicky told her. "It's easy. You just load the gun and point it and pull the trigger."

"I taught Nicky to shoot when she was twelve," Dominic told the group. "She could match any man on the place with a rifle. Even won trophies at it."

Winthrop, quietly smoking a cigarette, studied her curiously. "A girl of unusual talents."

"An unusual girl altogether," her father replied. He laughed shortly. "We haven't spoken in two years, have we, Nicky? I'm in disgrace, you see. I made the unforgivable error of falling out of love with her mother. Nicky holds me responsible for Brianna's death. And for cutting her off without a dime after the funeral," he added with killing precision. "She's been living by her wits ever since, haven't you, darling? Which one of these rich Christophers have you set your cap for?"

Just like old times, Nicky thought, feeling panicky. Her father was turning everything around, taking the blame off himself and throwing it at others. Winthrop's expression told her that he believed her father, and it grew even harder.

"I'm Gerald's secretary," she said with what little pride she had left. "And I'm not chasing anyone."

"You mean you've learned to love being without those Dior gowns you fancied and having to make do with the same fur several years running?" her father persisted. He looked like some middle-aged playboy even in his hunting clothes, and Nicky wanted to scream at him. All her life he'd made her feel inferior, and now he was destroying her one chance at happiness. He was convincing a once-betrayed man that he was being betrayed all over again. How would she ever make Winthrop listen to her?

Nicky's fists clenched by her sides. Her father had always enjoyed creating scenes. He should have been an actor, she thought bitterly.

"Let me introduce you to the other guests," Winthrop interrupted, wondering even as he did it why in hell he should bother to save her any discomfort after the way she'd deceived him. She'd pay for that, he promised himself. "Ben Harris—" he nodded toward the man in leather "—and Jack, his brother." He indicated the other, thinner man, in the plaid. "They come up every year looking for a good rack to go on their walls back in Kentucky. This year Dominic decided to come with them."

"I don't suppose you knew I was here, of course," Nicky asked her father with some of his own flair of stealing the advantage.

"I haven't known where you were in two years," he re-plied shortly. His eyes, so like her own, searched her face. "I haven't cared," he added with a mocking smile. "There's been a noticeable financial difference since you moved out, honey. I can balance the checkbook these days."

"Stop it," she whispered, near tears of enraged helpless-ness. "You know that's not true."

He simply turned away from her, refusing to take any notice of her embarrassment.

It wasn't the way he'd insinuated. She hadn't wanted his money—not even the trust her mother had left her. She'd refused all of it, but he was making sure both Christophers thought he'd done it himself, and that she was out for what she could get in the way of financial security. And it wasn't true.

"I hope you find someone to support you, honey, but it won't ever be me again," Dominic laughed, bending to brush a kiss across Carol's hair. "Your mother was enough."

"Don't you talk about my mother," Nicky said huskily. Her green eyes spit fire at him. "Don't you dare!"

Dominic laughed. "You always were dramatic."

As if he'd have noticed, with his eternal philandering. She almost said so, but Gerald was looking worried, and Winthrop's eyes were promising a confrontation.

"Do you have TV?" Carol asked, searching around. "It's so boring, just sitting around."

The woman was bored already? Nicky thought with sur-prise. Boy, was Carol in for a shock. Neither Gerald nor Winthrop watched much television. But Nicky was taken aback herself when Winthrop abruptly got up, and led Carol off to show her the TV and VCR in the living room.

"Fast worker, isn't he?" Dominic asked Gerald with a smile that wasn't quite friendly. "He'd better remember that she's my property."

"Your good manners are exceeded only by your arrogance," Nicky remarked coolly. "And if you try it on Winthrop, you'd better be wearing body armor. He doesn't like jet-setters."

Dominic glared at her. He stuck a diamond-ringed hand in his pocket and pulled out a cigarette case. "Something you've already discovered?" he asked with a pointed smile.

"Why did you do that to me?" she asked, searching the face that was so like her own. "Why did you make me out to be a cheap gold digger?"

"Tit for tat, darling," he drawled, and his own eyes kindled angrily. "You didn't think about the effect your defection would have on things at home, did you? I was blamed for everything. I don't like being humiliated. I don't think you will, either. And just for the record," he added coldly, "I didn't kill your mother, although I felt like it a time or two. She was no saint, Nicky, for all that you're trying to canonize her posthumously."

"So you've always said," she returned. "And who are you to judge anyone, you with your bought-and-paid-for playmates?"

"I'm not a plaster saint," he shot at her. "Your mother turned me out on the town as soon as she knew you were on the way, in revenge for what I'd done to her. Making her pregnant was a cardinal sin, in case you didn't know. She paid me back twenty times over. Are you shocked, Nicky? Didn't you realize that people are human?"

Nicky listened, only half hearing him. Why should her mother have hated him for that? She was suddenly aware of Gerald, an unwilling eavesdropper to the argument. The Harris brothers were sitting in the corner, talking hunting, and hadn't heard much. She shifted away from her father, and tried to smile.

"Do you have anything for me to do?" Nicky asked Gerald, her tone conciliatory and faintly hopeful. He caught on quickly.

"As a matter of fact, we've got about ten letters to get out this morning," Gerald replied. He smiled vaguely at the three men. "If you'll excuse us..."

"Is he your partner?" Dominic asked Nicky, frowning.

"He's my boss," she replied coolly. "I'm his secretary."

Her father stiffened. "You're joking, of course," he said curtly. "No White has worked for a living for three generations—"

"Until now," Nicky interrupted with a mocking smile. "Some of us like the real world better than the artificial life of upper-crust luxury. You ought to try it. It has a humbling effect on a haughty spirit."

"You should know," Dominic countered coldly. "You were a haughty enough child."

"Living in a combat zone does have that effect on children." She turned and left the room.

"So he's your father," Gerald murmured when they were in the study with the door closed. "He wasn't originally supposed to be included in this group. He invited himself along with the Harris brothers at the last minute. Odd that Winthrop didn't connect you with Dominic White, since you were from Kentucky, too."

"He did," she said reluctantly, averting her eyes. "But I lied to him. I told him that White is a common name. I imagine I'm about the most unpopular person in Winthrop's acquaintance right now, especially after what my father just said about me. And it's not true."

"You don't have to defend yourself to me," he replied gently. "Your father strikes me as a vindictive man."

"You don't know the half of it," she replied. "He's used to cutting people's throats. That's how he got so rich."

"Well, he can't be all bad," he said after a minute.

"He's not," she said pleasantly. "He likes his horses, and once I saw him feed a hungry dog. He just doesn't like me. He never wanted children." That was true enough, but she'd always thought that her mother wanted her. She was still puzzling over what her father had said.

Gerald didn't press further. Instead he chose a different tack. He pursed his lips, stared at her and asked, "Why didn't you tell Winthrop the truth?"

"Because I was sure he'd get the wrong idea," she sighed. "He'd think I was a bored heiress out for a good time. Ironically, that's probably exactly what he thinks now, thanks to my father and his big mouth. I must sound like the world's most experienced spendthrift and a gold digger as well."

"You don't like him, do you?"

"My father, you mean?" Her green eyes gleamed. "I do not. I'm sure he has some good points somewhere, but I've never found them."

He searched her face quietly. But he didn't say another word. He pulled up a chair and sat down behind the desk. After a minute, he began to dictate.

Nicky spent the rest of the day trying to avoid the other guests, and the snow continued to fall. Mary never said a word about the extra people to look after. She just kept cooking, imperturbable even when Carol dashed into the kitchen and asked in all innocence if there was a boutique anywhere close by because she wanted to shop for a new fur.

Nicky had to bite her tongue to keep from asking if the girl knew that in these parts, a mink set consisted of a trap and a skinning knife.

But to Nicky's irritation and her father's frank anger, Winthrop seemed to enjoy Carol's company.

"Maybe she forgot who she came with," Nicky muttered to Mary late that day as she helped the older woman set the long dining table.

"Not likely," Mary said. She glanced at Nicky. "Winthrop looks through you today. Why?"

Nicky hesitated before she put down the last plate. "He thinks I lied to him because I didn't tell him about my background. I let him think I came from a poor family. But it's true in a way," she added, her face open and sad. "I was poor in love, at least."

"And your father?"

Nicole pursed her lips. "You tell me. What kind of man is he?" she asked, because she'd learned how perceptive the Sioux woman really was.

"He is a sad man," Mary said surprisingly. "He draws attention to himself out of loneliness and pain. He has not learned to admit fault, only to find it in others. I pity him. As you should. In your youth, you have twice his wisdom."

Mary left and went into the kitchen, leaving the younger woman thoughtful and quiet.

If Nicole thought the day had been bad, she soon found that the evening meal was an even worse ordeal. Winthrop sat at the head of the table with the hateful Carol on one side and Gerald on the other and completely ignored Nicky and her glum father. The Harris brothers ate and sipped their coffee merrily, exchanging pleasantries and hunting experiences with Nicky, but she hardly heard them. She was watching Winthrop's dark eyes light up as he spoke to the nubile redhead, and hating the other woman for arousing the tender side of the man she could no longer reach.

"You wear your heart on your sleeve," Dominic said coolly. He stared over his coffee cup at his daughter. "Never let it show."

"Never cry. Never show emotion." She laughed shortly. "A page right out of your book. You're frozen clean through. I suppose I'll be just like you when I'm your age. What a lovely future to look forward to."

"It beats having your emotions lacerated twice a day," he said nonchalantly. He stared hard at the redhead. "She's barely your age," he mused. "And your host is a hell of a man, limp and bad temper and all. I won't like losing her to him. I'm not a good loser."

"Winthrop doesn't want a society girl," she replied. "He's had enough misfortune because of one."

"I remember reading about the wreck," her father said surprisingly. "Deanne something-or-other, that ski heiress. I had a fling with her myself. She was a real honey. The kind who'd stroke your fevered brow while stealing your wallet."

It hurt, knowing that her own father was that kind of man. An aging playboy with no real emotion underneath his elegant facade. "You ought to compare notes with Winthrop. I'm sure he'd be interested," she said sweetly.

"Stop sniping at me, Nicky," he said coolly, and his green eyes met hers. "All your regrets and all mine won't change the past. Neither will giving up your rightful legacy. Brianna wouldn't have wanted that. She had high hopes for you."

"Did she? I don't remember her being sober enough to discuss them in the past."

"I thought you'd become wiser with time, but you still see the past with blinders on," he remarked. "Grow up, honey. Life isn't all black and white. Your mother was neurotic. She couldn't handle responsibility. In fact, neither could I. We were two kids playing at life, and when you came along, the dream fell apart. Neither of us could cope and you got caught in the middle. I'm sorry, but I can't remake the past."

"If neither of you wanted me, why did you bother to have me?" she asked, wounded by the confession. "Or was I just an accident?"

She read the answer in his face before he could even try to disguise it. And suddenly, her whole childhood made more sense. The endless fights, the indifference of her parents to each other's life-styles, the drinking and womanizing...

"So," she let out the word as a sigh. "So that's why." She smiled ruefully. "Thank you. At least now I know why you both hated me so much."

"Oh, Nicky," he said, "that's not so. We never hated you."

"You never had time for me, either of you."

"That's true," he admitted. His green eyes searched hers and he smiled wearily. "We were just kids when you came along, Nicky. Both of us. Kids playing house. And then there we were with a real live baby, but we couldn't put you back on the shelf. We had to be responsible for you. That wasn't an easy task for two people who'd never known what it was to be responsible."

She stared at him as if she'd been slammed in the head with a pole. She'd never thought of her parents as people, only as parents. This new perspective was enlightening, but disturbing.

"You don't understand, do you?" her father asked quietly. "You thought because we were your parents, we had to be perfect. But it doesn't work that way. Parents make mistakes. They aren't perfect."

She shifted restlessly. "Mother drank herself to death because of your womanizing," she said accusingly.

"Your mother drank herself to death because she was unhappy," he replied, without heat. He leaned back, and despite the trendy shirt and the gold chains he wore, he looked old and tired. "So was I. I ran after women looking for my rainbow, and she climbed into a bottle looking for hers. Neither of us ever found it." He pursed his lips and studied her. "Have you found yours, Nicky? Does anybody ever really get the brass ring in life?"

"There are better ways to try for it," she began.

"Sure there are," he agreed. "But when you've got all the money in the world, why look past your wallet?"

"I can think of some very good answers to that question," she told him. "I've watched you buy people all your life. I hate the ugliness that money can bring out in people."

"You can't bribe an honest man, honey," he said sagely. "Can you?"

"But everyone has a price. Some prices are less materialistic than others—a promotion, a holiday for a hardworking parent, a hospital bill for a sick child. Those are less obvious prices, but they still mean people can be bought."

He nodded. "So you begin to see."

"What you and mother had wasn't a marriage," she accused him, all the hurt of the past coming back.

"We didn't love each other enough," he said simply. "In the beginning, maybe we did. But we had families that lived in each other's pockets and constant interference. We were never let alone, not even when you came along. You were the last straw, Nicky. You were the knot that we couldn't untie. Divorce, in our day, was scandalous. Our families had never had a divorce."

"Better a divorce than unending war," Nicky shot back.

"My sentiments, exactly. And your mother's. If we'd divorced, she'd have married one of her old beaux and I'd have married—probably several more times," he acknowledged with a wicked grin. "And we'd both have been very happy. As it was, we sought our separate remedies and your mother's was fatal. Nobody's fault," he tacked on, watching her. "Nobody's fault at all. But you can't accept that, can you?"

"Somebody has to be at fault," she said doggedly, glaring at him.

"Why?"

The question threw her off balance. She stared at him. "What?"

"Why does somebody have to be at fault?" He fingered his chains. "Your mother and I were nice people, separately. We just weren't compatible. Who do you blame for that?"

She felt herself losing ground. He always had been like a trial lawyer, able to twist things around to suit himself. If only he didn't make so much sense. She'd blamed him for two years for her mother's untimely death, just as she'd blamed herself. But what if neither of them were responsible?

She shifted a little and finally got to her feet, looking down at him. He always seemed laid back, very relaxed. Nothing seemed to bother him.

"I'm a black sheep, Nicky," he said. "I always have been. I like women and I'm rich enough to indulge that habit, and I try to come out ahead in business. But I never hated you, honey. I never could."

She tried to smile. "No? It seemed like it when you got here."

"That was dirty pool, all right." He glanced down and then up again. "I missed you," he said curtly, as if he hated even saying the words. "I missed Brianna. Everybody left me at one time. Damn it, how do you think I felt?"

He got up and stormed out of the room without even a backward glance. Nicky stared after him with confused emotions. He'd sounded, and looked, hurt. Perhaps he had cared about her mother in his fashion. Maybe even about Nicky, too. But the wounds were still raw and she couldn't cope with this new facet of her father just yet.

She turned, oblivious to the others in the room, and went upstairs. Her father was only forty-one, she realized with a start; he wasn't even old. And there was no reason he shouldn't have women friends. It was just . . . she'd wanted him to love her mother. She'd wanted her mother to love him. She'd wanted a warm family life . . . and she'd never had it.

She changed back into her jeans and the yellow sweater, hating the gray dress. She wished she had something as slinky and svelte as Miss Kansas City downstairs, so that she could tempt the antagonism out of Winthrop's dark face. But she'd probably lost her chance with him. He hadn't come near her since her father's arrival, he hadn't spoken to her or acknowledged her. He'd even avoided looking at her.

It was amazing how deeply his turning on her had hurt. She sat down at her vanity and ran a comb through her hair, dreading the return trip downstairs. She'd never felt quite so lost and alone, not even as a child. She missed her mother suddenly and wished that they could have talked. There had been a few precious times when her mother had been sober, when she'd actually listened to her daughter's rambling.

The door opened, cutting into her thoughts, and the comb paused in midair over her short, dark hair as Winthrop walked into the room and slammed the door behind him.

He'd unbuttoned his long-sleeved chambray shirt at the throat. His dark hair caught the light and gleamed, like his unblinking dark eyes under that jutting brow. He stared down his straight nose at her and bad temper mingled with pure male arrogance in the way he watched her.

"Go ahead," she sighed, putting down the comb to sit with her hands folded in her lap. "Get it out of your system. Shall I start it for you? I betrayed you, lied to you—"

"You could have told me," he replied. His eyes narrowed on her face. "I even asked you point-blank if you were related to Dominic White and you sidestepped the question."

"Guilty as charged," she confessed. "I should have told you the truth. And if I had," she continued, turning to face him, "you'd have shot me off the ranch like a bullet."

"Trust comes hard to me," he said unexpectedly. "I won't be able to forget that you didn't level with me."

Even though she had expected it, the words hurt. She tilted her chin up and looked at him, drinking in the sight of his face, adoring it with her soft green eyes. "I'm not a bored heiress. I've lived in Chicago for two years—"

"Patiently," he agreed with a smile that would have been pleasant any other time. "Waiting for your chance. Gerald was first choice, I realize that, but I was the second-string, wasn't I?"

She blinked. "I don't follow you."

"You set your sights on Gerald, honey," he replied. "He was going to be your meal ticket. You played him for two years—"

"I what?" She got to her feet.

"I'm no fool," he ground out. "You've been hanging on him ever since you got here! I overheard what you said to him, about no other man ever being able to take you away from him. I heard it all. And you even held back last night, because you were afraid of what he might say if he saw us together."

"I did? Amazing, how much restraint I showed in the kitchen, wasn't it?" she taunted.

His jaw tautened angrily. "I'm no innocent boy. I've had my share of adventures with women. And this morning, I got a good look at the real Nicole White. No, honey, you won't pull the wool over my eyes again. I'm on to you now. And there's no way I'm going to be your meal ticket. Neither is Gerald. I'll see to that."

She couldn't believe what she was hearing. All the growing tenderness between them, everything he'd said last night... After all of that, he could believe her father's lies, could he? How could he believe that she was just a gold digger?

"Gerald's in love with Sadie," she said, almost in a daze.

"Is he? Too bad. I guess you're brokenhearted. So that's why you turned to me, was it?" he laughed coldly. "And if your father hadn't arrived, I might still be deluding myself. What a lucky break. One cheap adventuress in a lifetime is damned enough."

"Oh, Winthrop," she sighed achingly. "Are you so afraid to believe what you feel, instead of what you hear? Can't you take my word for it?"

"I did," he reminded her, his tone icy. "And look where it landed me."

"My father was getting even," she said, moving closer. "He was paying me back for walking out on him after Mama's funeral. It was just revenge. He's over it now, he'll tell you the truth if you ask him!"

"I know the truth." He lifted his chin as she came closer, and the expression on his hard face was not welcoming. "You've been stalking me. I knew it was no accident that you wound up at the corral that day and you deliberately came on to me at the dance last night."

"That's right," she said sarcastically as she looked up at him. Her heart was breaking and he didn't even care. "That's right, all I wanted was to get my hands on your wallet. I never cared a fig for you!"

She pressed against him and his steely hands caught her, holding her away.

"Do I make you nervous, big, bad rancher?" she teased, moving as close as his hands would allow. Her eyelashes fluttered at him, her fingers went to his chest and her nails drew lazily across the cotton fabric, making sensuous little scratchy sounds there. His heartbeat increased sharply.

"No," he denied. But he was looking down at where her hands were touching him, and something flickered in his dark eyes.

"Well, you make me nervous," she whispered. "You make me shake all over when you touch me, and that doesn't have a thing to do with how much money you've got in the bank. And I didn't lie to you about being innocent, I am."

"You and Madame Bovary..." he chided, but his touch had become caressing on her arms.

"And when we made love in the kitchen, I would have died for you," she breathed ardently, her lips parted, welcoming, pleading as she looked up into his eyes.

His hands tightened while he tried to fight what she made him feel. His body suddenly went taut but he couldn't help it, he wanted that soft mouth under his until it was madness.

"Damn you, Nicky."

"Winthrop." It was a moan, and he covered it with his lips.

He muttered something under his breath, but Nicky didn't hear it. She was lost in the strength of his arms, the ardent hunger of his hard mouth as it moved breathlessly on hers.

It seemed to take a long time for him to realize what was happening. Her warm body in his arms drugged him. The soft warmth of her mouth, trembling gently as he explored it, made him vulnerable. But minute by aching minute, the past came back. Deanne had once melted like this against his hard body. She'd murmured words of love, promised heaven. And then...

He eased his mouth away from Nicky's, steeling himself not to care about the soft accusation in her drowsy eyes as she watched him pull away.

"Please..." she whispered, and made a move to go to him.

"No, thanks," he said quietly. And the very tone of his voice halted her in her tracks. He was as politely indifferent as if he were refusing a drink of water when he wasn't thirsty.

She looked up at him with slow comprehension. He didn't even seem to be affected by that sweet interlude. He was just indifferent. She felt a sudden, sharp emptiness. Was this how it was going to be from now on? Was he so uninvolved that it didn't require any effort for him to draw away from her? She'd banked everything on his desire for her; she'd seen it as her one way to reach him. But it hadn't. She'd lost. He didn't trust her. And now he was showing her that he didn't even want her anymore.

"I'm not a gold digger," she said with what pride she had left. She was trembling, and he had to know it. She wrapped her arms around herself and watched him, like a hurt child. "Money doesn't matter to me. Surely you can see that?"

"I don't know you," he answered. His dark eyes narrowed as he studied her face. "And maybe it's better this way. I remember telling you once that we could hurt each other badly. I let you get to me last night, honey, but I won't make that mistake again. The last thing I want is involvement."

"But you said...I mean, I thought..." she faltered, trying to put into words what she'd felt the night before, what she'd thought he meant.

"I've been alone a long time, daffodil," he said with a mocking smile. "And I'm no saint. A man gets lonely from time to time."

In other words, she'd been a nice little interlude with no strings attached, but now it was broad daylight and he'd come to his senses. He'd just proved his indifference by showing her that he could pull away from her anytime he wanted to without regret.

"That's plain enough," she said quietly, studying his dark, impassive face. It was a long way up, despite her own height, and she felt at a disadvantage. "I guess I misread the whole situation."

"Just as long as you realize you'll never get to first base around here, except in business. Get my drift?"

She should have pasted him one, but she was disillusioned and sick at heart. Her dreams were shattered. "I can't really blame you for the way you feel," she said dully. "I should have told you the truth in the beginning. I guess it was a hard knock."

"Nothing I couldn't handle," he replied coolly. "Don't flatter yourself too much. A few kisses doesn't make a relationship."

"Oh, I know that," she laughed coldly. "And just for the record, I was lonely, too. You see, men haven't noticed me for a long time; not since I had money, in fact," she said with a cynicism that suddenly matched his. She felt old and world-weary and battered. "Too bad I can't go home to Daddy and accept that trust my mother left me. That would up my bank balance by about three million."

She went to the door and opened it, watching him scowl as her remark registered.

"Dream on, honey," he said, but without a lot of conviction.

"You don't believe that, either, of course," she nodded. "Why don't you ask my father why my fiancé threw me over? The answer might open your eyes."

He stared at her for a long moment. "If you've got that kind of money, why work for my brother?"

"Because I got sick of a warped life-style where promiscuity and alcohol and pills seemed to replace love in my parents' relationship! Because I got lost somewhere and went hungry for just a little love!" Tears welled up in her eyes and she set her lips together to try to stop the trembling. "The man I thought I loved walked out on me the day he found out I'd given up all that nice money. And here I am, two years later, being accused of the very thing he was guilty of. You think I'm mercenary," she said in a husky whisper. She laughed tearfully. "How's that for irony?"

He stopped in the doorway to look down at her. His conscience and his pride were at war. "You lied to me once, damn it!"

"So you can't ever trust me again," she returned. "Okay, you've judged me and found me guilty. I don't want your pity. I don't want you at all. My father was right all along—everybody's got a price. I should go home with him and let him teach me how to buy people!"

"You're talking nonsense," he said curtly.

"I'm talking sense," she said on a laugh, although her chin was trembling. "I've been chasing rainbows. Thanks for putting me back on the right track."

"You're crying," he said half under his breath and lifted a hand to catch a stray tear.

But she jerked away from his hand like a wounded thing, raw from his rejection, sick at heart. "Go away," she whispered furiously. "I hate you! I hate you, Winthrop! I wish I could leave here tomorrow and never have to see you again as long as I live!"

He tried to speak, but he couldn't seem to find words. In the end he turned and stormed off down the hall, smoldering. He was the wronged party, so why in hell did he feel guilty? He didn't even want to think about how he might have messed up things if she was telling the truth. Surely she wasn't. She'd lied to him once, hadn't she? He closed his mind tight. He just wouldn't think about it. She was another Deanne. He was well rid of her.

She watched him go with a sore heart. Well, if he wouldn't believe the truth when it was staring him in the face, who cared? She closed the door and gave up any idea of going downstairs again. She took off her clothes and cried herself to sleep.

Chapter Seven

Somehow, Nicky got through the night. Winthrop had excused himself and gone out to help his men keep a check on the cattle. The snow had made the mountain roads impassable except with a four-wheel drive. The hunters didn't seem to mind. In fact, they were apparently used to mountain weather and since they were planning a week-long outing on the ranch, they settled in with easy acceptance.

Carol, however, became a pill. Nothing pleased her. Her room was too cold, the bed was lumpy, there were no shopping centers and she couldn't even get a manicure. Furthermore, she missed her parents, whom she visited every few days. She wanted to go home.

Nicky's father spent the better part of the second day, in between cleaning his hunting rifle and getting himself kitted out with the proper attire, calming down his playmate. It seemed he had a knack for communicating with Carol, because he finally got through to her that it would be impossible to get out until a chinook blew in. That could be any day, he'd added with careful insight.

Mary had already told Nicky that the snow could go on for days or even weeks, but Nicky wasn't sharing that tidbit with the excitable redhead. After Dominic's comforting statement, anyway, Carol went off into the living room and watched a popular science-fiction thriller until even Winthrop started to grow tired of the film.

At dawn on the third day, the hunters piled into Winthrop's Jeep and headed down the valley. Gerald and Nicky worked alone in the study, leaving Carol to her science-fiction habit.

"I can't tell you how sick I am of light sabers," Nicky remarked after the sound became louder in the next room.

"Sure you can," Gerald invited, leaning back in his chair. "Go ahead. Then I'll tell you how sick I am of laser cannons. And then we'll make silly faces in the mirror and see about renting straight jackets in a matched set."

She giggled. "Let's pray for a chinook."

"I'm for that. The Sioux used to have a prayer for it, come to think of it. We'll ask Mary."

She looked at her steno pad. "Winthrop said something to her at breakfast with sign language. Mary's been teaching me a little bit of signing, so I tried to watch carefully."

"I watched for years and never learned a thing," he confessed. "What did he say, do you know?"

She smiled ruefully. "Either he wanted bicarbonate of soda or he was melancholy."

He frowned. "What?"

"When you want to express melancholy or gloom, you make the sign for *heart* and then the sign for *sick*. It's really a fascinating insight into another language," she added. "For instance, if you want to say that you're disgusted, you sign *heart* and then *tired*. The sign for enemy is *friend* and *not*. Drunk," she grinned, "is expressed by making the signs for *whiskey*, *to drink*, *much* and *mad*. See?"

He shook his head. "Fascinating. Smart girl."

"Intelligence is this," she said, touching her right index and middle fingers to her forehead.

"How about smart aleck?" he taunted.

"I'm not that good, yet," she sighed. But she was learning. Already, Mary had taught her enough that she could translate what Winthrop had "said" to her on the porch the morning he'd brought her home from the Todds'. He'd said that he was jealous of Gerald, and that he wanted her very much. How different things might have been if she'd known that at the time. But Winthrop had become a coolly considerate host and nothing more. All the lovely soft feeling that had been growing so gently between them was gone forever.

"I'm worried about Sadie and Mrs. Todd," Gerald said abruptly, tapping a pencil on the blotter. "I tried to phone them an hour or so ago, and the lines are down. Sadie had to put their Jeep in the shop a couple of days ago, so I know they don't have any transportation. I drove by there before the snow started, just to say hello."

"Could you get Winthrop to run up and check on them?" she asked.

"Winthrop is in a snit lately, haven't you noticed?" he asked miserably, his gaze apologetic as he added, "Your father did a job on your character. Although, to give the man credit, he tried to tell Winthrop it was mostly just bad temper and vengeance. But Winthrop didn't listen. He walks off every time your name is mentioned."

"We had an argument and didn't exactly part friends," she told him, without going into details. She didn't add that Winthrop's attitude had broken her heart. "You wouldn't want to go back to Chicago anytime soon?" she added hopefully.

"Poor Nicky," he said, smiling at her knowingly. "I'm sorry it turned out like this. In the beginning, Winthrop was so different when you were around. He smiled and laughed and seemed to enjoy life for the first time since the accident. I'm sorry it fell apart."

"So am I," she confessed, feeling her eyes sting with unshed tears. "I guess he's soured on me because I didn't tell him who my father was. He thinks I lied to him. And perhaps, in a sense, I did. But I didn't mean to be devious. I was only trying to forget the past. My childhood was pretty rough, and my mother's death shook me up. There are so many scars. I guess that's why I understand Winthrop so well. I have scars, too, and time isn't all that healing when your emotions have been ravaged."

"I guess so." He got up and went to the window. "I wondered why Winthrop was flirting with Carol. I supposed he was trying to make you jealous."

"On the contrary," she laughed, "he was showing me that I don't matter. And believe me, he's succeeded. I wouldn't go near him now with a whip and a chair."

"I can understand how you feel," he said, turning. "But you have to understand how it's been for my brother, Nicky. It was several months after the accident before he was even able to walk without a cane, and they'd threatened at first to take off the leg entirely. Winthrop said they'd take it off after he was dead, and he meant it, but he doesn't realize even now how close it came to that. It took one of the best orthopedic surgeons in the country to save it—and he performed an operation that used techniques he invented as he went along. One of the bones in his lower leg was shattered; the surgeon completely rebuilt it, like putting a jigsaw puzzle together."

"He said there were complications," she probed.

"His impatience," he said, confirming her suspicions. "They told him exactly what he could and couldn't do, and he ignored them and tried to ride a horse the day after he came out of the hospital. He tore the cartilage and had to go back into surgery to have it resewn. Consequently it hasn't healed as well as it could have. But the doctors said he could get rid of that limp if he'd work half as hard at his exercises as he's worked at fighting them tooth and nail over the manner of his recovery. Winthrop," he added dryly, "is impatient."

As if she hadn't already noticed that, she mused sadly. "I suppose at the time he didn't much care what happened to him."

"It was the closest I've ever seen him come to the edge," Gerald agreed. "He took chances and pushed himself even harder than he used to in his wild days. Finally I asked him if the stupid woman was worth his life. And that seemed to snap him out of it. But he's not the same man he was."

"What was he like then?" she asked, because she wanted to know everything there was to know about him.

"Full of fun," he said. "Reckless, with a devil-may-care attitude, but in a suave kind of way. He liked music and parties and skiing—in the water or in the snow. He was forever on the go. The ranch was important to him, but not in the way that it is now. He left Mike in charge and went out to beat the world. Now," he said softly, "he just sits up here in the mountains and broods. Less since you've been here, I have to admit, but he still has that streak of melancholy."

"Maybe he found out that money and glitter don't wear well," she said. "I learned it young."

"Perhaps he did." He studied her quietly for a long moment. "It hurts you that he believes your father, doesn't it?"

"More than I can tell you."

"Give him time, Nicky. Trust comes hard to a man who's been betrayed. But if the feeling is there, inevitably it's going to break through the ice."

"Think so?" She smiled. "I wonder."

They went back to work, but she brooded about what Gerald had said. Would Winthrop eventually come to his senses? Or had it been just a mild physical attraction and he wanted nothing more to do with her? She didn't know.

Later that afternoon, Gerald began to pace, and rubbed his stomach as if it were troubling him.

"Need an antacid?" Nicky asked.

"What?" He glanced at his stomach. "Oh. It's just acting up. I forgot my medicine. I guess I'd better take it. No, it isn't that," he said suddenly, turning. "I'm worried about Sadie."

"Then let's go see her. Isn't there a four-wheel drive around here somewhere that we can use?"

He grinned. "Sure. Are you game? It could be dangerous."

"I'd like some fresh air myself." She glanced toward the living room door, where the sound of laser blasts was echoing loudly. "And I need a reprieve from that movie that I loved until we got snowed in with her."

"My sentiments, exactly. I'll tell Mary where we're going. Dress warmly."

Warmly meant putting on her jeans, two pair of socks, boots, a long-sleeved shirt, a sweater, and her heavy coat, gloves and a stocking cap. Even that was hardly enough against the thick snow and biting wind. The mountains were cold in November, she learned quickly. And the snow was flying at them in an unending sheet of white, provoked by a wild wind. Nicky had misgivings about this trip, but she had more about being cooped up inside with Carol.

Gerald had the old Jeep idling when Nicky climbed in beside him. She glanced around her with a curious smile. "Will it get us there?" she asked hesitantly.

"I hope so," he confided. "It hasn't been used for a while, but Mike has one and Winthrop has the other new one, so we're stuck with this. I think it will be all right."

The vehicle sputtered and lurched as he put it in gear, and the chains on the heavy tires made a nice clanking sound as he shot down the mountain road. Thank God it was a wide one, but by the time they turned off onto the dirt road that led up to the Todd place, Nicky was regretting her decision to go with him. Gerald wasn't the driver Winthrop was, and as the heavy snow continued to fly at them, Gerald swung too wide around a curve and the Jeep suddenly left the road.

Gerald moaned something. The Jeep lurched crazily sideways and slid down onto a lodgepole pine and hung there, shuddering. Nicky pitched against his shoulder, and got a sudden and terrifying view of a sheer drop out his window.

"Oh, for heaven's sake!" she squeaked.

He caught his breath, staring beside him. "Damn," he breathed. "I couldn't see the roadbed and I ran right off. Nicky, we'll have to get out of here. This is a dead pine, and if it gives way..." He glanced at her with pure terror in his dark eyes.

"Then we'll get out," she said, more calmly than she felt. "How?" she added.

"Well..." He studied the Jeep's position for a minute. "I think it might be easier if we tried to get out on your side. The tree will balance us. You go first. I'll help."

Climbing out of the Jeep looked impossible, but there was no choice; plunging down that deep ravine would be as sure as death. She thought of Winthrop and wondered if he'd miss her if she pitched down there. Morbid thoughts, and she shook them off. No, sir, she wasn't about to give him the satisfaction of dying.

With Gerald's help, she managed to lever herself up to the passenger door and gingerly open it. The Jeep pitched a little, and she caught her breath and shuddered, certain that the end was near, but the vehicle remained fairly secure against the pine. She prayed as she caught hold of the opening and began to drag herself up and over. She got grease from the dirty undercarriage all over herself, but in the end, she managed to tumble out. Then she reached up to help Gerald, who managed the task with more deftness than she had.

They cleared the Jeep and collapsed onto the thick, soft snow, almost buried in it while they caught their breath. Behind them, the Jeep lay on its side against the tall pine, unmoving, despite the fierce wind.

"At least it hasn't gone over," Gerald sighed. He held his stomach and groaned. "Damn. I wish I'd stopped long enough to take that medicine."

She stared at him, snow sticking to her face. She felt bitterly cold. "Can you make it?" she asked, frightened.

"I think so," he sighed. "My ulcer isn't sure, but I am," he said with a wan smile.

"So am I." She smiled back. "Well, shall we start out?"

"We're closer to the ranch than the Todd's place," he said when they were standing in the road. But the snow was coming harder and thicker, and it was blinding, stinging their eyes. "We can follow the road back..."

We hope, she added silently, because the blizzard wasn't letting up. If anything, it was getting worse. The brilliance of the snow was as blinding as the flakes whipped up by the biting cold wind.

She leaned into that wind, pulled the cap and her collar down to cover as much of her face as possible, and started walking. Beside her, Gerald kept up the pace. But when they'd gone a few hundred yards, the going got harder and harder. Incredibly, she started to feel hot in all the freezing cold and snow. She wanted to throw off her coat and walk in her sweater, but Gerald shook his head sharply when she started to do it. He mouthed something that looked like "frostbite," but she wasn't sure.

She concentrated on putting one foot in front of the other, watching her boot sink into the deep snow. It came over the boot top and down into her warm socks, wetting them, chilling them. She'd left her gloves in the Jeep, like an idiot, so she had to keep her hands in her pockets, but they were freezing cold, too.

They rounded a bend, and found the road suddenly buried under a huge drift of snow. Nicole stopped, her eyes on the blanket of white around them, but there was no alternative route. They had to get through that drift or die.

Gerald moved close to her, panting. "Oh, God," he muttered, clenching his hand over his stomach. "It's hurting, Nicky. How in hell are we going to dig through that?"

She looked at it dubiously. She didn't have gloves and Gerald was in no condition to do it alone. There were no tools. A ranch hat like Winthrop's Stetson would have helped or even a shoe, but if she took off her boot, her foot would freeze. She stared at the huge mound of snow with helpless frustration.

"Oh, damn," she wailed, hating the hot sting of tears in her eyes. She wasn't beaten. Oh, God, she couldn't be beaten! She had to do something, but what?

"I'm so tired," Gerald sighed. He sank down with his back to the snowdrift. "So tired ... stomach hurts ..."

"You can't go to sleep," she burst out. "It's fatal! Gerald, we have to go on."

"How? The snow's too deep. We can't get through, Nicky." He closed his eyes, leaning back against the bank that angled against the snowdrift. "Nice ..."

Nicky shook him, but he was too weary to try anymore. She looked around at the white forest, its tall trees rising over them like shrouds while the wind blew and the snow fell and the world was as hushed as a cathedral.

She sank down beside Gerald and sat there, looking around at the deadly white beauty of it. A hundred years before, men must have seen such sights and been killed by them, she thought. The Lewis and Clark expedition probably had its share of snowstorms, and they'd survived. But they were strong, well-equipped woodsmen. Nicky was a city woman with no woodcraft skills. She didn't even know how to build a fire, if she could have made her hands do the work.

Her green eyes went up to the sky. Well, it wasn't such a very bad place to die, she mused as drowsiness swept over her. She was near Winthrop, even though he didn't care anymore. Maybe he'd bury her here, and she'd be near him forever...

She closed her eyes. Somewhere she heard an organ. It was making beautiful music in the distance, and there was singing. It was an old hymn of some kind, exquisite in the stillness...

"Amazing Grace."

Her grandfather used to sing it when he worked with the horses. "Amazing Grace, how sweet the sound..." she began to hum.

Voices...coming close. The organ stopped, but a cat was purring. Something touched her. Shook her. That voice—it was deep and urgent and somehow familiar—but she didn't understand what it was asking. She was warm and safe and she protested when someone tried to move her. She fought, but she was subdued. Then she was rising, floating. White clouds. Snow. Cold. The organ drifted in and out. She tried to open her eyes, but it was just too much work. She slept.

Her head ached. She sneezed and the sound echoed around her. Was she dead?

She opened her eyes slowly. A ceiling. Very white. A canopy, pink, overhead. She turned her head and there was Winthrop. He was unshaven, his hair needed combing. He was sprawled beside the bed in a chair half his size, his booted feet splayed, his mouth open. He was snoring.

She stared at him for a long moment, memorizing him. He looked good, even without a shave. His shirt was open, and his hair-roughened chest looked like leather. She wanted to touch it, smooth her hands over its masculine contours, feel his heart beating under that rough skin. His hands were clasped over his lean waist, darkly beautiful masculine hands, their strength evident even in rest. She remembered their delicate touch on her soft flesh, and trembled a little with pleasure.

"Winthrop." His name sounded rusty. She frowned, because it had hurt her throat to call him. Her hand went to it. Her fingers were cold, but they didn't hurt. Had she escaped frostbite? She held out her hands, palms down, and looked at them.

"You were damned lucky," Winthrop said, opening his eyelids without moving a muscle. He glared at her out of eyes as black as night. "You didn't even get frostbite, although you'll have a hell of a cold."

"Gerald?" she rasped.

"He's fine, thank God. What possessed you two greenhorns to scale the Rockies in a blizzard?"

"He was worried about Sadie," she defended.

"Sadie had the good sense to stay inside," he said coldly. "I sent Mike up to take supplies to her and her mother. They're fine. More than I can say for you and Sir Galahad."

"We can't all be brilliant mountain men," she said sweetly.

"Do you want something to drink?" he asked.

"Not until I can have it analyzed for poison," she threw back at him.

"I'll send Mary with it," he replied. "I might not be able to resist the temptation, at that."

She watched him get up and tears gathered behind her eyes. Such an ordeal, only to find him still unforgiving and hateful at the end of it. He might have said he was glad she was alive or smile at her, or something.

"Sorry to put you to the bother," she muttered.

He bent over her, his eyes dangerous. "Don't bait me," he threatened softly. "I've had a hell of a night watching you fade in and out. You little fool, people have died in snowdrifts out here!"

"Sorry, but I do seem to be alive. I hope you aren't too disappointed . . . oh!"

The exclamation was in response to the sudden, unexpected descent of his mouth, square over hers.

"Disappointed—" he bit off, and kissed harder. His hand at her throat tilted her face at a more inviting angle and he caught his breath as his lips became gentle and began to play with hers. His breath was as ragged as her own now, but he didn't even care. She could have died. Knowing it made him wild.

Her hands went to his hard cheeks, trembling and cold as they pressed there, holding him to her mouth. Her brows knitted in exquisite anguish. Dreams came true like this, she thought achingly. Dreams. She'd lived on them for so long.

"Oh," she whispered softly, a tiny whimper of sound that echoed in his mind.

His mouth opened against hers, lifting, teasing, his breath mingling wildly with hers while his hands caught hers and pulled them down to the bed beside her head, his fingers interlocking with hers.

"I could ravish you," he ground out huskily, and the eyes that glanced at her were blazing.

"I thought . . . you hated me," she breathed unsteadily.

"I did. I do. I hate what I feel when I touch you." He bent again, tormenting her mouth with his lips, brushing, lifting, teasing until she began to writhe on the sheets. "Yes, that's exciting, isn't it?" he whispered roughly, watching her face. "I'm going to make you wild, Nicky, and then I'm going to walk off and leave you with it. . . ."

She arched softly, her eyes wide and quiet, her body trembling. "No, you won't," she whispered. "Because you'll be just as wild as I will."

His jaw tautened as he looked down at her, his pride aching, his body aching. She was killing him. His eyes went to her bodice, where her breasts were outlined under the gossamer-thin white cotton of her gown. The arousal she couldn't help was blatant.

His fingers, linked with hers, contrasted roughly. His eyes adored her breasts, caressed them. "That," he whispered slowly, "is beautiful."

"Everything is beautiful with you," she said, her heart in her eyes as she looked up at him, too much in love with him to even be embarrassed at his bold stare.

"Nicky!" He groaned her name as he bent, his mouth so tender, so exquisitely gentle with hers that tears ran hotly down her cheeks. He was the world, and everything in it. She loved him so.

Even as she thought the words, she whispered them under his warm mouth, breathed the truth against him, echoed her feelings like a prayer.

"No." He drew back suddenly, sharply. His fingers pressed hard against her lips while he sat over her, trying to breathe, with eyes as black as the night outside the window. "No. Don't say it."

"But I do love you," she said, her face like a child's, full of pleading and hope.

His thumb rubbed against her lips roughly in a reluctant caress. "I don't want that," he said quietly. "I'm sorry. But I... can't, Nicky."

"I can't help it," she whispered softly. "I'm sorry, too, but I do. I do, I do!"

His thumb pressed harder and he caught his breath. "Listen, I've been alone a long time. I've gotten used to my own company. I don't want anyone with me. I don't want ties, commitment. For God's sake, Nicky, I'm not a marrying man!"

Her face flamed when she realized where the conversation was leading. She stared at him, horror-struck. She hadn't meant that, but he'd assumed she was begging him to marry her.

"I... I didn't mean ..." she faltered.

"I can't saddle myself with a wife," he said flatly. "And you're too frail for this country, even if I went crazy and invited you to live with me. You're too used to the city. This is a man's country, Nicky, not a woman's. You'd never survive it."

She bit her lower lip. "Are you sure?"

"Yes." He took her hand in his and smoothed over its softness, wondering at the delicious sensation that washed over him as he savored it. "Just as I'm sure that I don't want a woman here," he added deliberately, holding her gaze.

She searched his dark eyes quietly. "All right. I'm sorry if I've embarrassed you."

"I think you're more embarrassed than I am," he mused, smiling gently at her red cheeks. He frowned a little as he studied her. "Are you sure this isn't reaction? You've had a rough time of it lately."

She took the out he was offering her, grateful for a little salvaged pride. "Probably it is. Being rescued, and all," she explained. "You don't hate me anymore, do you?" she added weakly, the expression in her eyes so eloquent that he felt himself choking to death on pride.

"No, I don't hate you," he said shortly. "I never did. I hated being lied to, that's all." And she had lied, he recalled. Numbly, he laid her hand down on the covers, wondering why he felt so empty. It had warmed him when she'd whispered that she loved him, God knew why. Love wasn't something he coveted these days. His eyes drifted up to hers, but she was concealing them under her lids. Could she love him?

He bent toward her, watching her face lift for him, her mouth part. Yes, she wanted his mouth, that was sweetly evident. He looked into her eyes while he kissed her, seeing the pupils dilate, the lids close drowsily. That excited him more, and he drew back before he got in over his head. He scowled down at her curiously. She disturbed him all too much. He didn't need this. She'd already betrayed him once, he wasn't giving her a second shot at him. It might be an act, even this talk of loving. Just an act. He couldn't trust her.

"I'll see about some orange juice," he said with a faint smile. "Want some soup?"

"I guess I could eat something, if it won't put Mary to too much trouble," she added quietly.

"I can't remember the last time any woman guest considered Mary," he mused, his gaze quietly possessive. "Get some rest. I'll be back after a while."

She watched him get up, trying to hide her feelings. But he limped suddenly and she sat up, her breath catching. "Winthrop, you're hurt!" she burst out.

The caring note in her voice cut him to the quick. He didn't want it, or what he was feeling for her. He glared at her. "I don't need a nurse," he bit off. "Get yourself well. I can take care of myself. I've had years of practice."

He went out and slammed the door, leaving her stunned and hurt. She wished she knew what she'd done to make him so angry. She felt like she'd made an utter fool of herself by telling him she loved him. Tears stung her eyes as she lay back. Well, maybe he'd believe she'd lied, or, as he'd said, that it was reaction. He'd made it all too obvious that her love was the last thing on earth he wanted. So she'd just have to learn to hide it from him.

Chapter Eight

Soon after Winthrop left the room, Nicky had an unexpected visitor. Her father, neatly dressed in a gray suit, came in and took the chair Winthrop had vacated.

"Feeling any better?" he asked, and seemed to be genuinely concerned. Nicky could remember being sick as a child and having neither of her parents come near her.

"I'll be all right," she said. "I just feel a little tired."

"I guess so," he said with a smile. "Your nose is red."

"It feels red, too." She returned the smile. "Did anybody shoot anything?"

"I got a deer," he said. "Six-point buck. Nobody else had any luck." He pursed his lips. "I offered Carol a jacket made from the skin and she stormed off in a snit. I shot Bambi, you see."

Nicole laughed in spite of herself. "You cold-blooded killer, you."

"I love venison," he sighed. "Mary's fixing us a big stew out of the hindquarter, but you won't get any until lunch tomorrow. She says it has to simmer a long time to get done right.''

"She's a good cook."

He leaned back in the chair to study her. "What possessed you and your dim-witted boss to go driving in a snowstorm?" he asked pleasantly.

"He was worried about Sadie Todd," she explained. "And I just wanted to get some fresh air."

"In a snowstorm?" he asked.

"Well, we were kind of getting tired of watching science-fiction movies . . ."

"That's no reason to commit suicide. Snow is deadly, as you damned near found out. If Winthrop hadn't decided to call it quits early, the two of you would have frozen to death."

"I guess Winthrop was pretty angry."

"Angry." He pursed his lips. "That's an interesting choice of words. Mild, considering his reaction when he found you. I thought I had a good command of four-letter words, but he taught me some new ones. He carried you over that drift all by himself, weak leg and all. I guess he's hurting like hell, from the way he limps, but he was determined."

She felt her heart leap with the pleasure that knowledge gave her. She toyed with the sheet. "He's quite a man."

"I think so," he agreed. "I told him the truth, by the way. I think you've paid enough for the past."

"Thanks. But it won't do much good. Winthrop isn't a marrying man," she added when he didn't seem to understand. "And I'm not a liberated woman."

Dominic sighed heavily. "Well, different people, different attitudes." His green eyes twinkled. "I'm very liberated, myself. But I'm kind of glad you aren't. And do you think I'm ever going to get any grandkids?" he added thoughtfully.

She flushed, averting her eyes. "Not anytime soon. I'm barely twenty-two."

"Kids are nice. I wish I'd enjoyed you more, while I had the chance." He frowned. "Say, would you like to go to a carnival or something? I could buy you cotton candy and ride the rides with you. Or we could go fishing...."

"This sounds serious," she said with mock fear. "Are you suffering from an attack of fatheritis?"

"Feels like it." He grinned. "We could at least speak. Maybe we could exchange Christmas cards. Then, as time goes by, you might come to Kentucky to see me."

"Or you might come to Chicago to see me." She sighed. "You and Carol," she amended.

"Carol won't last," he shrugged. "She's temporary. They all are. You see . . . in some crazy way, I loved your mother, even if we couldn't quite get our act together. She's pretty irreplaceable." His eyes fell. "God, it hurt when she died. I couldn't even tell you how it hurt."

"I don't think I would have listened if you'd told me then." She sat up straighter. "I think I understand a little better now. And maybe we could exchange Christmas cards."

He grinned at that dry remark. "Maybe we could." He got up. "Well, I'd better go rescue Mary. Carol is trying to teach her how to walk like a model."

"Carol models?"

"Doesn't it show? She's got style, all right. And Mary was just eating it up." He scowled. "She mentioned something about the Rockettes...."

"That's kind of a family joke," Nicole said, enlightening him. "Thanks for coming up to see me."

"You look a little peaked to me," he said. "Mary was fixing chicken soup in between parading around with a book on her head. I guess she's going to bring you some."

"No, she isn't," Winthrop said from the doorway, limping heavily toward them with a tray on which were perched a soup bowl and a teacup and saucer. "She's too busy try-ing to do a pivot without falling into the venison stew."

"Sorry about that," Dominic murmured sheepishly. "I did tell Carol to stay out of the kitchen."

"No harm done. Mary seems to be having the time of her life." With a hard glare, Winthrop bypassed Dominic and put the tray down on the bedside table. "Well, don't just lie there, prop yourself up. You can't eat flat on your back."

"I was just trying to do that," she shot back, "and you don't have to snap at me!"

"I'll check on you again, Nicky," Dominic said as he started toward the door.

"Okay."

He closed the door and Nicky tried to take the soup from Winthrop's steely hands without letting him see how much hers were trembling. But the bowl seemed pretty unsteady even before she touched it.

He looked down into her eyes and they exchanged a glance that set her heart running away.

"Here, this won't do," he said under his breath.

He sat down beside her on the bed and began to ladle the soup gently into her mouth. She watched him, fascinated at his unexpected tenderness. The way he pampered her, the way he looked at her—even the gentle smile that touched his hard mouth as she accepted the soup like a child—tugged at her heart.

"Feeling better?" he asked.

"Much, thank you." She swallowed some soup. "Winthrop, my throat hurts," she whispered.

"Yes, I imagine so. I've got something for that, and for your cold. Nonprescription, but they're what our doctor always prescribes for head colds. I'll take care of you, daf-fodil."

"Somebody needs to take care of you," she said softly, studying his hard face. "Your leg must hurt terribly."

"It usually does after a day as hard as this one," he said carelessly. "I've got something to take for it."

"Well, thank you for rescuing us, anyway."

"Gerald sounds worse that you do," he told her. "You're both greenhorns."

"You were out in it, too," she reminded him.

"That's so," he said agreeably. "But I'm a woodsman, honey. I know how to survive a snowstorm. You and my citified brother are lucky to be alive."

"Yes, I realize that." She took the last bit of soup and sat quietly while he mopped her up with a napkin. She knew she must look terrible. Her hair hadn't been combed, her face was pale and her throat felt scratchy. But Winthrop was looking down at her with pure pleasure . . . almost possession.

"You need sleep," he said.

"I've been asleep on and off since you brought me home," she said. "I don't want to sleep."

"It will help you heal." He got up, put down the bowl and offered her a cup of steaming tea to swallow down the capsules he'd put in her hand. She hesitated but he looked determined, so she swallowed them, finished the tea and lay back against the pillows.

"I hope you don't catch my cold," she said.

"I don't usually get them," he replied. He smiled slowly. "Even from kissing sick little girls."

Her face colored and she lowered her eyes to his chest. That was even worse. He had a sexy chest, and she wanted very much to draw her hands over it.

"You have expressive eyes, Nicole," he murmured, watching her intently. "You want me, don't you?"

The color in her cheeks deepened. She glared at him. "Well, I do realize that it isn't mutual. You don't have to throw it in my face. It isn't something I can help."

His eyebrow arched. "Was I doing that? I didn't mean to. I'm pretty used to speaking my mind."

"Well so am I." She stared at the coverlet. "What I said...earlier," she faltered, glancing at him and then away. "I was overwrought and tired, and I guess I kind of got carried away."

"You mistook a chill for true love?"

She glared at him. Damn that mocking smile. "I got carried away."

"You're one of a kind, Nicky," he mused. "As for getting carried away, if you weren't so frail, I'd throw you back against those pillows and lie down against you. And in a very few minutes, we'd both know what you feel for me."

He was doing it again. She felt completely out of her element when his voice dropped into that sensuous drawl and his eyes began to make love to her body. She felt her breasts tautening and drew the sheet slowly over her bodice so that he wouldn't see what he was doing to her.

But he did see her response. His eyes seemed to darken at the proof of how easily he could arouse her. She couldn't know that it made him feel ten feet tall.

"Don't worry," he said as he picked up the tray, still watching her. "I've got sound survival instincts. I meant what I said about commitment."

"You'll grow old all alone," she said quietly, her eyes steady on his hard, dark face. "You won't have anyone to look after you or care about you. Eventually, you'll grow a thicker shell than you have now, and no one will be able to touch you. Is that really what you want?"

For just an instant, his expression was open. "No," he replied. "But I don't want my heart torn out of my body a second time, either. I like my life as it is."

"Unhampered," she said.

"Exactly." He left her with that parting shot. He was still limping badly, and he was scowling when he left the room.

Nicky must have slept then. She wasn't aware of the quiet, watchful man sitting beside the bed. He looked at her as if he couldn't help himself, staring at the steady rise and fall

of her firm young breasts under the sheet. She looked innocent in sleep. Everybody did, he reminded himself.

But there was something different about this woman. She
was special. Much too special. He was going to have to get
a grip on himself before he pitched headfirst into that
sweetly baited trap. He'd fought it too long to give in now.

He closed his eyes finally, with a long sigh, and tried to get
comfortable in the chair. His knee was giving him hell.
Probably he'd torn a muscle. But he hadn't wanted anyone
else to touch Nicky. She belonged to him. She was his responsibility.

The sound of the windup alarm clock was unnaturally
loud. It woke Nicky in the early hours just before dawn. She
opened her eyes and glanced at the tall man sprawled again
in the chair, grimacing as he breathed. His leg was probably hurting, and here he sat, when he could have been comfortable in bed.

Nicky got up, just staring at him. Even unshaven and un-
kempt, he was a sexy man. His shirttail had been pulled
from his jeans, and his shirt was half unbuttoned down a
chest thick with hair and dark from exposure to the sun. He
might not love her, but he was oddly protective of her these
days. That was some small comfort.

She touched his hard, warm cheek with her fingertips,
tracing its high cheekbones.

"Winthrop?" she whispered.

He made a sound and his head turned, but his eyes didn't
open.

"Winthrop, come to bed," she whispered.

He never did wake up completely. He let her tug him out
of the chair and he sprawled onto the bed with a mumbled
protest. Nicky was glad that he'd already taken his boots off,
as she wouldn't have relished trying to remove them. She
eased his legs onto the bed, careful not to jar the bad one.
Then, with a mischievous grin, she crawled back under the
covers and snuggled close.

His arm came around her instinctively, drawing her cheek to the soft cotton of his shirt. His fingers caressed her hair gently, and she thought that she'd never been quite so close to heaven. She lay quietly beside him in the dim light of the lamp and tried to imagine how it would be if they were married, if she had the right to lie in his arms every night like this, while the wind howled angrily outside the darkened window and snow fell.

It was so sweet that she lost all fear of the future and simply went to sleep, Winthrop's chest rising and falling steadily against her.

A drum was beating somewhere. She heard it in the back of her mind, its steady rhythm comforting. It was nearby. Growing louder. Louder. It stopped suddenly and then increased. Something moved against her. Her head fell back onto a pillow and she mumbled when she felt the mattress lower then return to its normal position.

The sound of footsteps grew dim. A door opened and closed. What a crazy dream, she thought, and drifted back to sleep again.

The light streaming in the window woke her. This time she opened her eyes, and found Mary standing at the curtains.

"How you feel?" the Sioux woman asked.

"Fi..." Her voice sounded hoarse. She tried again. "Fine. I think."

"You look pale. I bring oatmeal. Best thing for scratchy throat and cold. Also buttered toast and coffee with lots of cream. Sound good?"

"Oh, yes," Nicky sighed. "I'm so hungry!"

Mary paused beside the bed and bent down to touch Nicky's forehead. "No fever. Good. You live yet." She pursed her lips at the clear indentation of a head in the pillow beside Nicky's. "You have pajama party last night?"

Nicky grinned. "He was sprawled in the chair and groaning in his sleep. I figured his leg was giving him the devil. So I got up and led him over here and tucked him in. He never knew."

Mary's normally placid face came alive. "He never knew?"

"That's right," Nicky told her, smiling broadly. "He was gone when I woke up, but I'll bet he doesn't remember how he got in the bed."

"Well, well. New weapon, hmm." Mary grinned, too, showing even white teeth. "Poor man. Shame on you. You should not take advantage of the helpless."

"He wasn't very helpless yesterday, was he?" Nicky asked with pride. "He carried me through a snowbank."

"That leg is not as bad as he thinks it is," Mary returned. "If he exercised it more and favored it less, it would heal properly. It is his hiding place, Nicky. He cannot accept being a whole man again because that would make him vulnerable to his emotions."

"Not so anyone would notice," Nicky sighed ruefully. "He can be pretty formidable."

"He is still only a man." Mary tucked Nicole back into bed. "Need medicine for your throat?"

"A lozenge would be wonderful. It's scratchy." She paused to sneeze and grab for a tissue. "And I think I have a cold."

"It would seem so. I will bring your breakfast. And I will bring you venison stew for lunch. That should help clear your head."

"It may take more than venison stew to do that," Nicky replied.

"I make it with Tabasco sauce." Mary leaned over her. "Trust me." And she grinned again before she went out.

To Nicky's dismay, Winthrop didn't come back all day. She expected him every time the door opened. Mary brought breakfast and then Gerald came, red-nosed and sniffling, followed by her father and even Carol, who gave her a pretty scarf to cheer her up. But no Winthrop, not even when the venison stew was served.

When Mary came back after lunch to pick up the dishes, she cocked her head at Nicky's forlorn expression.

"Something troubles you?" she asked.

"Of course not." Nicky finished her cup of hot black coffee and set the cup on the tray Mary was holding. "I don't care if he ignores me. I'll just lie here and die."

"He cannot get up just yet," Mary said after a minute.

Nicky was immediately contrite and worried. "It's his leg, isn't it?"

Mary nodded. "The strain, you see. I think he may have pulled a tendon. I have made a poultice for it, which will take away the pain and make it heal. But in the meantime, he is an invalid. Mr. Mike has taken the hunting party out for him, and Miss Carol is watching...would you care to guess?"

"I thought I heard laser cannons," Nicole replied grimly. "Does he have something for pain?" she persisted, her green eyes troubled.

"He will not take it," Mary grumbled. "Even now, he is trying to work with a board across his lap on which to write."

"It sounds as though he might need a little nursing," Nicky suggested.

"You need it more. Lie down."

"I could talk to him. It's only a cold and a reaction," she said and then added when the other woman looked doubtful, "Oh, please, Mary. How can I lie here knowing that he's in pain?"

Mary shrugged. "Good point. All right. But put on your robe and leave door open." Her dark eyes held Nicky's with subtle warning. "He is still a man."

"I love him," Nicky said simply.

"Yes, I know. That will make it harder for you. He is a man who does not trust love." The expression on her face was serious. "He will fight being vulnerable. Now more than ever."

"I wouldn't hurt him," she said.

"You will have to prove that to him. And it will not be easy. But I would think less of you if you did not try," Mary added. And she smiled as she went out.

Nicky put on her long white chenille robe and went along to Winthrop's room, a little nervous about how she'd be received.

Her nervousness was justified as it turned out, because he was moody and restless and more irritable than she'd ever seen him.

He glared at her from his bed, where he lay taut-faced with only a sheet drawn haphazardly over his lean hips for cover. His dark hair was disheveled, his face unshaven. His long, powerfully muscled legs were bare, like his tanned chest, and all of him was covered with a very masculine feathering of black hair. He looked like an outlaw in his sprawled dishabille, and Nicky wondered if any woman could see him like that and not be affected. Her heart began to run away from her the minute she knocked on the door and was invited to open it.

"What do you want?" he asked curtly, and she noticed the scattered paperwork that had apparently been cast to one side with irritation.

"I thought you might need something," she said, hesitating.

"If I did, Mary could get it."

"Mary's got her hands full with your hunting party."

"They've gone out again. Carol's watching movies. Gerald's on the phone. So all Mary has to do is look after me. In any event," he said with a mocking smile, "that's what she gets paid to do."

"And here I am about to cause a labor dispute by offering to do it for free," she sighed. Her throat still felt a little raw, but at least her nose had stopped running. She moved closer to the bed, eyeing him warily. "How about some fruit juice?"

His dark eyes narrowed. "How about telling me how in hell I wound up in bed with you last night?"

Her eyebrows arched. "You were in bed with me?" she asked with pretended horror. "How scandalous!"

His lips made a thin line. "Don't be cute," he ground out. "And it wasn't scandalous. Nothing happened!"

She lifted her chin. "A likely story," she said.

He sat up, disrupting the sheet, but her eyes stayed on his face so that she didn't see what it revealed. "Nothing happened," he enunciated. "I don't ravish women in their sleep."

"Ah, but you don't know what I might have done to you," she said, lifting her eyebrows mockingly.

The glare got worse. "Cute. Real cute."

"Anyway, you rejected me," she reminded him. "You cut and ran before I woke up. But not," she added with a slow smile, "in time to fool Mary, who saw the imprint of your head on the other pillow and asked how it got there."

His eyes widened. "What did you tell her?"

"Oh, nothing at all," she assured him. "I told her I didn't have the slightest idea how you'd gotten in my bed."

"Oh, my God." He put his face in his hands.

"It's all right, she understands perfectly that these things happen. She didn't say a word; she just grinned."

"Oh, my God," he repeated.

"And she promised she wouldn't tell anyone except family and close friends and any acquaintances that happen past the mailbox."

"Oh, my God!"

"Now, now, you don't have to get upset, this is the twentieth century, after all—"

"This is rural Montana," he said, half shouting. His eyes blazed at her. "You little fool! Your reputation will be in shreds!"

"People in Chicago don't notice things like that," she reminded him. "And Gerald and I are going back next week, you know. Your reputation will have hardly a blemish. In fact, it might even make you more desirable to some of the local belles if it gets around that you're the same devil-may-care rake you used to be."

He narrowed one eye. "How do you know what I used to be like?"

"I asked Gerald, of course. He said you used to score with every woman you dated—"

"Nicky!"

"Well, not in exactly those words, of course," she amended at his shocked expression.

"Have you lost your sweet mind?" he demanded. "What were you trying to do?"

"Get you comfortable and warm," she said with a smile. "You were groaning and I knew your leg was hurting you. Since you seemed determined to sit up with me, I thought you should be comfortable. So I led you into bed, and you went with me just like a lamb."

"Which wasn't what I felt like when I woke up," he replied curtly. "Your gown was up around your hips and half off your shoulder, and men have it rough early in the morning anyway. Oh, honey, you had a close call you didn't even know about!"

"I did?" Her eyes were wide, trusting and innocent. He sighed impatiently.

"Never mind. What did you really tell Mary?"

"The truth. She grinned and mumbled something about a new weapon."

"It will backfire." He bit his lip suddenly and grimaced. His hand went to his knee, where she noticed a poultice tied with white gauze.

"Will that help?" she asked.

"Mary says so. She usually knows. Even the local doctors have a measure of respect for her way with herbs. In the old days, the Indians had to have a healthy knowledge of it, since they didn't have a neighborhood clinic.''

"Mary's told me a lot about Montana and the way it used to be," she said. "It's a fascinating country. Big and sprawling and special.''

"That's why I stay here," he said. He leaned back against the pillows, studying her face. "I have no desire to go back to the life I used to lead.''

"Well, that's one thing we can both agree on," she said quietly. "Neither do I.''

His chiseled lips pursed thoughtfully. "Are you really worth three million?''

She nodded. "If I sign the necessary papers. But I don't want three million dollars. If I refuse that trust, do you know what the money will be used for?''

"No.''

He seemed honestly curious, so she told him. "It will fund a research program to find new ways of treating cancer in children.''

"Three million would go a long way," he said.

"Yes, wouldn't it?" She smiled. "And since I've gotten used to working for the Christopher Corporation, and nobody's fired me yet, I expect I can support myself without that trust.''

He stretched lazily, watching her eyes drop to his chest with the movement and follow the sensuous tautening of muscle under thick hair. He liked the way it felt to let her look at him like this.

"You're a surprising girl, Nicole," he said, his voice dropping an octave, deep and sexy.

"Am I? I thought I was a gold digging adventuress.''

"That sounds bitter," he mused.

She shifted from one foot to the other and stared down at the thick beige carpet. "It felt bitter, too. You never believed a word my father said, really, but it gave you the excuse you needed to draw back before things got complicated.'' She looked up, catching the surprise in his dark eyes even as it registered that she'd hit on the truth.

"I told you at the beginning that I didn't want commitment,'' he reminded her sulkily.

"I don't remember asking for any,'' she replied.

"You said you loved me.'' His dark eyes slid down her body. "Several times.''

"You'd just saved my life.'' She steeled herself not to let him see how vulnerable she was. She'd thrown herself at him for the last time. He didn't want to make a life with her, and there was only one other thing he might offer. She couldn't accept that kind of relationship, so what was left?

His face didn't reveal a single emotion. "And it was only gratitude?''

"Gratitude, and a natural response to a very experienced man. Which you are,'' she said, watching his eyes narrow. "I must have been a real pushover.''

"You're twisting it.'' His voice was deep, but a little more curt now. "What I saw in your eyes wasn't completely physical.''

"I'm young, as you keep reminding me,'' she shot back.

"Yes.'' His gaze swept over her face, memorizing lines and curves and expressions. "Eleven years my junior. Almost another generation, especially in sensual ways.''

"You don't have to remind me about how experienced you are.''

"In my day, I was,'' he agreed. He propped himself against the pillows, righting the sheet with a careless hand. "But in recent years, I've given up jet-setting around the world. I've changed my values, Nicole.''

"Through choice?'' she asked gently. "Or just because you were unsure of being accepted with your battle scars?''

"Honey, you believe in cutting to the bone, don't you?'' he asked with a half-angry laugh.

"You aren't the kind of man to be spoon-fed things, are you?'' she returned gently.

"No." He drew up his left leg and studied her quietly. "Why did you think I'd order you off the place if I knew your real name?"

"You'd already said you hated rich people, and Gerald said you had no use whatsoever for jet-setters. I guessed that if you knew I was in that class, it would make you hate me," she said simply.

"You might have given me the benefit of the doubt."

She managed a smile. "I didn't have enough self-confidence for that. As it was, you were only tolerating me."

"I thought you and Gerald had something going," he said. He studied the coverlet. "I love Gerald. I couldn't take away something he wanted as badly as he seemed to want you."

"And all along, he was in love with Sadie. I've never had ulterior motives," she added, wanting to make him understand. "I don't want a rich man, Winthrop. I have a job I enjoy, I can make my own way in life. I was never looking for a . . . a meal ticket."

"I didn't know that. All I had left were my instincts, and they'd already let me down once. I haven't trusted a woman since this happened." He touched his knee.

"Were you ever in love before her?" she asked hesitantly, because it was suddenly important that she know that.

He met her searching gaze. "Love is an illusion. I don't believe in it. I never did. I wanted Deanne until she was an obsession with me. I got drunk on her. When she walked out, I thought I was going to bleed to death, and for two years I felt like a zombie. Is that love? I don't know. It's the most intense thing I'd ever felt, so maybe it was. But I'm over her now and I have no inclination whatsoever to go through it again."

He'd probably never spoken so candidly about his feelings before, and she was flattered that he'd trusted her even

that far. She sat down slowly on the bed beside him, her soft
weight moving the mattress.

"Love shouldn't be all physical," she told him, her voice
as gentle as the fingertips that went hesitantly to his firm
mouth and touched it. "It should be a sharing between two
people. A bonding of thoughts and hopes and dreams. A
linking of intangible things. Companionship. Friendship.
Openness and honesty."

"You lied to me," he said curtly. His fingers caught her
wrist.

"What do you care?" she asked. "You don't believe in
love, and you don't really want it anyway. You're safe from
ever being hurt again. Nobody can reach you. If you stay up
here another ten years, you'll be a walking dead man!"

"At your age, what do you know about love?" he demanded. "You said you loved me, but we both know all you
feel is pity. I've been hurt and I'm scarred, so you see me as
a charity case!"

Her eyebrows went up. "You?"

The one word was more expressive than any argument she
could have made. He glared at her and let go of her wrist.
"You feel sorry for me," he continued doggedly.

"I feel sorry for anybody who gets close to you all right,"
she mumbled. "You aren't my idea of the perfect lover."

"How would you know, when you've never had one?"

"You said my innocence was all an act—"

"Oh, for God's sake, I was mad as hell, I'd have said anything! I didn't mean it. I know lack of experience when it
stares me in the face. You blushed that night in the kitchen
when I looked at you."

"I wish you'd stop bringing that up. I was...over-
wrought," she concluded helplessly.

"You got too damned close," he said suddenly, every last
bit of caution gone. His eyes glittered dangerously. "You
got under my skin. What did you expect me to do—lie back

and enjoy it? I won't be owned by some little city girl with a rich daddy!''

''Now just hold on one minute,'' she said slowly. ''What do you mean 'with a rich daddy'?''

''Your father mentioned that if I wanted to marry you, he'd give us a racehorse for a wedding present, and an interest in the farm to boot.''

She was horrified. Absolutely horrified. In his usual bulldozing way, her father was trying to help. This scheme sounded like his idea of building a fire under the man he thought Nicky wanted.

Somehow she got to her feet, her heart slamming in her throat. ''How nice of him,'' she said huskily.

''He needs looking after,'' he replied. ''He shouldn't be let out alone. And you're not much better. Neither of you do things the right way.''

''Which is?'' she taunted.

''Straightforward. Don't you know how to get what you want in life?''

''Your way would probably be to reach out and grab it,'' she muttered.

''You're catching on, sugarplum.''

Before she could react, he had her by the wrist again. He levered her down onto the bed, on her back, and loomed over her with a purely arrogant look in his dark eyes.

''I don't want to be another one of your conquests,'' she told him, struggling.

''Sure you do. If you keep thrashing around like that, you're going to dislodge my sheet and the mystery of life will be over!''

She stopped immediately, glaring at him with wide green eyes as she tried to catch her breath. Smiling down at her, all unshaven and with his hair down over his forehead, he looked sensuous and a little dangerous.

''You don't want commitment, remember?'' she reminded him bitterly.

"I don't have to propose marriage to kiss you," he returned, bending.

"I have a cold—I'm contagious!" she squeaked.

"I have a sore leg, and that's not catching. But desire is," he whispered against her lips. "Shall I show you how easy it is to catch?"

"It isn't fair," she wailed.

"Probably not. But it's sweet, all the same." He nuzzled her face with his, in soft, gentle caresses that wore her down all too easily. "You smell of gardenias, Nicky. You smell sweet all over. Here," he breathed, taking her hand in his to press it against his hard, warm chest. "Touch me."

Her hand faltered shyly, but he guided it over the hard muscles, letting her feel the silky hair that covered him, the ripple of muscle under rough skin. "You feel furry," she whispered.

"And you feel like satin." He traced her cheek with his fingers as he kissed her very lightly, and his hand slowly lowered to the buttons of her bodice under the robe.

"No," she protested.

"Go ahead, fight for your honor," he chided. "And I'll wear you down anyway. It's only going to be a token resistance. You want to be touched as much as I want to touch you. So just give in, Nicky, and enjoy it."

"You conceited ape!"

"Enjoy it," he whispered. His fingers moved to the edge of her breast, tracing around it with maddening expertise, making her moan and stiffen suddenly in an explosion of unexpected pleasure.

"Winthrop!" she gasped.

"It isn't new," he whispered, drawing his mouth slowly over hers. "We did this in the kitchen that night...you let me touch you then, too. You let me kiss you."

"You shouldn't," she whispered shakily.

"You belong to me," he said simply as he began to unfasten buttons. "I have every right in the world."

"You don't," she tried to protest, but his hand was inside the gown now, his lean, cool fingers against virgin flesh, teasing, tracing, until she arched up and trembled.

"Mine," he breathed against her mouth. Her movements were exciting him, her little cries caught in his lips, making him hungry. "All of you. Here and here...sweet young body, ripe for my hands. I could make a meal of you, Nicky."

He had her gown around her waist, and she couldn't even protest. Her eyes closed, tears falling down her cheeks while he looked, touched, delicately tasted her pretty, firm breasts. She let him, and his whirling mind registered her complete abandonment to his ardor. She wasn't resisting him anymore—verbally or physically. He could do anything now and she'd let him.

And that realization was what slowed him down. He lifted his head quietly, looking at the helpless reaction of her body to his lovemaking. She was beautiful, he thought, and he stared at her with something akin to reverence in his dark, tender gaze.

His fingers traced around an erect nipple, gently loving. "I've never seen anything so perfect, Nicky," he whispered. "It's like touching satin."

Her eyes opened. She was embarrassed, and her face felt hot as she met his gaze. "I'm afraid," she whispered.

"There's no reason to be frightened. I'm not going to ravish you." He drew the backs of his fingers against her, loving the way she tensed with pleasure. "But I could, couldn't I? You want me pretty badly right now."

"Obsessively," she confessed. Her voice shook a little. "Do you enjoy humiliating me?"

"Is that what you think I'm doing? Think again." He lifted his hand, and she saw its faint tremble. "That isn't faked, Nicky," he added solemnly. "I go just as high as you do when we make love. It's mutual, this chemistry. It has been from the very beginning."

"I won't have an affair with you," she said quietly.

"I wouldn't let you," he returned. He nuzzled her nose with his. "On the other hand, I don't want marriage."

"I'll have to leave," she whispered, feeling her heart break.

"Inevitably," he agreed. He looked down at her as his fingers drew tenderly over her bare breasts and she trembled. "It knocks the very breath out of me to touch you this way," he breathed.

"You aren't the only one," she said shakily.

He bent and put his mouth gently on the soft curve, and then he drew back, while it was still just a whisper of sensation. "You'd better sit up and pull up your gown, honey. Someone's coming up the steps very loudly."

His words registered, but she felt as if she was caught in a dream. In the end, he helped her up, buttoned her gown and belted her robe with exaggerated indulgence. He'd only just finished when Mary ambled into the room with two mugs of steaming black coffee.

"Still here?" She clicked her tongue at Nicky. "You should be in bed. You will never mend this way."

"We were talking," Winthrop said. "Don't run her off just yet. I'm not through."

"Yes, you are," Mary said with unexpected stubbornness. "Must get her well, first, and you back on that leg. Then you can talk. Up!"

Nicky managed a rueful smile at Winthrop, feeling disappointed and a little shy. His expression, on the other hand, gave nothing away. He didn't protest, so she went with Mary, too subdued to even notice the twinkle in the older woman's eyes.

But Nicky didn't go back to Winthrop's room again, and he didn't ask for her. It was a kind of world-weary truce, but without any fraternizing. She didn't even see him, but Mary said that he was almost on his feet again. That was good news.

Meanwhile, Mike brought Sadie and Mrs. Todd down the mountain for the duration, so at least Nicky had someone to talk to. That is, she had Mrs. Todd to visit with, not Sadie, who was taking a delicious pleasure in nursing her Gerald back to health.

The little group got along very well. That was unexpected and enlightening, because Nicky had thought they wouldn't fare that well. Even Carol found things to talk to Mrs. Todd about. And Dominic White discovered that his lady love had a compassionate side to counterbalance her mercenary tendencies. He didn't seem to want to cut at Nicky anymore, although he did keep mentioning fairs and cotton candy....

Nicky was back taking dictation when Gerald felt up to it, in between wondering why Winthrop hadn't come near her and how she was going to bear to leave him when she and Gerald had to go home to Chicago. Even living in the same house separated from Winthrop was agony. How was it going to feel when she was hundreds of miles away, separated for life?

Chapter Nine

It was Saturday, and the hunters were packing to go home. A chinook had blown in Friday to take away the snow, unlocking the grip the storm had on the ranch, leaving the roads passable if slushy.

"Well, it's just been great," Carol sighed as she left. "I can't think when I've enjoyed anything as much. Especially your movies," she added, smiling demurely at Winthrop in the hall.

"You'll have to get Dominic to bring you again," he returned with a smile.

"I might be persuaded," Dominic said. He put an arm around Carol. "This one might be worth keeping."

"Well, she's certainly pretty enough," Nicky volunteered. "And I like her, if that carries any weight."

Carol's eyes brightened. Impulsively, she hugged Nicky. "We won't tell anyone that I'm only five years older than you are. We'll just let people gape when you call me Mom, okay?" she laughed.

"Okay," Nicky said gently. She winked at the redhead.

"By the way," Dominic hesitated, luggage in hand, "I, uh, put my foot in it again, Nicky."

She knew what he was going to say, about trying to buy Winthrop. He was a rascal, but he was still her father. She liked him sometimes, warts and all.

She hugged him briefly. "I've fouled things up all by myself, thanks. You just added your two cents' worth. I like you anyway."

Dominic looked uncomfortably emotional for a minute before he pulled himself together. "Come see an old man once in a while," he managed finally.

"I don't know any old men, but I guess I could come see you. If I get to help Eddie with the horses," she added. "It's been a while since I've ridden."

"We can remedy that. Don't wait too long. See you, Nicky."

"See you, Dad."

They went out, followed by the Harris brothers who were mumbling their own thanks and goodbyes. Nicky found herself alone with Winthrop, who towered over her in jeans and that huge sheepskin jacket he liked to wear with his creamy Stetson.

"You seem to have arrived at a truce with your father," he mused.

"I misunderstood a lot of things. Grief plays havoc with the brain," she said quietly. "I loved my mother very much."

"So did he, unless I miss my guess." He touched her short hair, the simple gesture sending thrills down her spine. "Was she like you, to look at?"

"Oh, no. She was beautiful," she recalled gently. "Long black hair and pale blue eyes—Irish. She even had the lilting speech. She was a lady, in every sense of the word. I adored her."

"And what does that make you—the ugly duckling?" he chided. He tilted her chin up, searching her suddenly flushed face. "Nice eyes. Big and soft. Pretty little mouth. High cheekbones. Soft skin. You'll do, sugarplum, even without long hair. But let it grow anyway. I like long hair."

He turned her loose then and started out the door, still limping a little.

"Your knee . . . is it better?" she asked hesitantly.

He half turned toward her, his dark eyes alive and quiet. "It's no worse, at least. Why? Were you thinking of offering me a massage?"

"I don't go around playing with men's legs."

"Oh, you're one of those kind of women, are you?" he taunted. "Marriage or nothing?"

"I don't want to marry you. I'm sorry if that breaks your heart."

He smiled slowly, the sight of it almost knocking the breath out of her. Heavens, he was handsome! Bigger than the whole outdoors, sexy, sensuous . . .

"Tease," he accused.

"You're the one making references to playing with men's legs. Which I don't do."

He grinned at her high color. "I know a lot of things you didn't do until I came along," he mused, and his eyes went straight to her yellow sweater.

"Aren't your guests going to miss the plane?" she asked in a high-pitched parody of her normal voice.

"That's their problem, not mine."

"You're driving them, aren't you?"

The roar of the Jeep interrupted her.

"No," he answered as it sped away. "Mike's driving them. Gerald wants you in the office, by the way. He's got a hundred letters to get out yesterday."

"Thanks a lot," she muttered darkly.

"Better toe the line, honey, or you could get fired. Since you're throwing away money hand over fist lately, you do need the work now, don't you?" he asked, playfully looking down his arrogant nose at her.

It had only just occurred to her that he was teasing. It was new, like that look on his dark face, that twinkle in his eyes. Her heart skipped a few beats and she turned her head, a little unsure of this new Winthrop.

"Yes, I guess I do," she admitted. But the words didn't match what her soft, searching eyes were telling him. Not at all.

He tilted her chin up with a lean, strong hand and looked down at her. "I'm going out to check on my purebred herd," he murmured. "I'd take you with me, but you're a distraction, Kentucky girl."

Her pulse jumped again. "I thought...you said...you didn't want me around," she managed breathlessly.

"Did I say that?" he asked, lifting his eyebrows. "My goodness, it must have been the painkillers."

"Listen here, Winthrop—"

"Say it like that again," he whispered at her lips, taunting them from a fraction of an inch away, so close that she could almost taste him.

"What?"

"Whisper my name like that again," he repeated, and his nose brushed lazily against the tip of hers.

"Win...Winthrop," she obliged.

"Mmm," he murmured. His lips nuzzled hers, tempting them, urging her closer to him in the dim light of the hall. "Come up here...."

He actually lifted her off the floor with two steely hands at her waist. "That's better," he whispered. "Now open that pretty mouth and kiss me properly."

He had the most incredible way of getting to her. She was lost and witless, drugged on his nearness. She gave him her mouth, parted her lips, and moaned when he deepened the kiss hungrily and his arms swallowed her up against him.

Time got lost somewhere in the middle of that long, sweet kiss. A dog barked, and pans banged in the kitchen. A door opened and closed. Winthrop finally lifted his head, his breath coming hard and quick on her faintly bruised lips.

"Do you like it that way?" he whispered roughly. "Or do you want me to be gentle with you?"

She buried her face under his chin, trembling with reaction. "I like it . . . any way at all, with you," she whispered, clinging to him.

"Same here." He let her slide down his powerful body to the floor, savoring the feel of her against him. Her eyes were wide and soft and drowsy, and he couldn't help bending to brush her mouth once more with his. "Don't overdo it. You're not quite fit yet."

"Look who's talking."

"And no sass." He tapped her on the cheek. "See you."

He was gone, then, and she watched him until he was out of sight.

In between long talks with Sadie, Gerald managed to give a little dictation. Mrs. Todd had decided at long last to go and visit her sister in Florida, and it didn't really come as a surprise when Gerald announced a little hesitantly that he'd asked Sadie to marry him.

"It's about time," Nicky said, beaming. "Congratulations!"

"I can hardly believe it after all this time," Sadie sighed, leaning her head against Gerald's shoulder. "But I've never been happier."

"Neither have I. And I'm sure your mother's going to love Florida. The climate will be good for her. We can visit her every other week if you like."

"Well, maybe once a month anyway," Sadie compromised, her eyes bright with love and happiness.

Nicky had to look away. There wouldn't be any such happiness for her. She'd go back to Chicago and take up her job, and try to forget Winthrop. That wasn't much of a future. She wondered how she was going to manage without him. He might enjoy teasing her and kissing her, but he'd said too often that marriage wasn't for him.

"You look glum, Nicky. What's wrong?" Gerald asked.

She forced herself to smile. "Nothing at all. I'll get my pad and take down some of that correspondence you're so anxious to get rid of."

"Good girl." He smiled down at Sadie. "I think life is going to be a lot easier to cope with from now on."

For him, at least, Nicky agreed. Not for her.

She couldn't quite handle sitting at the supper table without the buffer of guests to protect her from Winthrop's dark, searching gaze. So she offered to have hers upstairs with Mrs. Todd. Mary gave her a hard look, but she fixed two trays and helped Nicky carry them upstairs.

"It is not like you to run away," Mary said stoically at the door to the guest room Sadie and Mrs. Todd were sharing.

"I'm very good at it, actually," Nicky replied. "Especially when I'm outgunned."

"The biggest fish are the hardest to land."

Nicky shrugged. "Sometimes they're the boniest, too."

Mary grinned. "Good bones, though." She opened the door. "Nicky is having supper with you," she told Mrs. Todd. "Thought you might enjoy some company."

"Why, Nicky, how thoughtful," Mrs. Todd said with a smile. "I'll enjoy that."

"Mary even fixed you a pudding," Nicky said, nodding toward the creamy vanilla treat.

"My favorite. How kind, Mary."

"No trouble," the older woman said. "I like them, too. Hearty appetite."

Mary left them, and Nicky arranged Mrs. Todd's tray and silverware before she sat down to eat her own food. It tasted like cardboard, but she forced herself not to pick at it. She'd have to get used to not seeing Winthrop across the table from her. Now was a good time to start.

"My sister is looking forward to having me stay with her," Mrs. Todd said. "She's been alone for five years now, since her husband died. She lives in one of those retirement communities, and she says there are lots of things to see and do. Best of all," she sighed, "the weather is warm and sunny. This chill goes right through me. I haven't been comfortable with the cold weather, but I didn't have the heart to tell Sadie. She was so happy, especially when Gerald came here on his holiday."

"He really came to see Sadie, I think," Nicky laughed. "And I'm glad it all worked out so nicely."

"So am I. Sadie will take care of him, and he of her." Mrs. Todd's gaze searched Nicky's face curiously. "Why are you hiding up here?"

Nicky jumped. "Hiding?"

"Hiding. You can't tell me it's my company you want. Are you and Winthrop trading blows again?"

Nicky shifted restlessly, crossing her jean-clad legs. "We just agree to disagree, that's all."

"He's a stubborn man. You'll have to be patient if you want him."

"I don't want him!"

"Don't be silly, of course you do," Mrs. Todd said nonchalantly. She finished the last of her pudding. "When it comes time, he won't let you leave. Mark my words, he knows a good thing when he sees it."

"Think so?" Nicky wanted to believe the old woman's words, but she knew Winthrop too well. He didn't want a long-term relationship. In fact, he'd probably be happy to wave her goodbye. The thought depressed her even more.

The last thing she expected was to find Winthrop at the door when it opened suddenly. She'd thought it was Mary and hadn't looked up until she heard his voice.

"There you are," he said pleasantly. "I wondered where you'd gotten to. How're you doing, Mrs. Todd?"

"Very well, Winthrop, thanks to you," the older woman beamed. "It's been like old times visiting here."

"I'm glad you're enjoying it. I thought I'd walk Nicky down to the barn and let her look at my colt. She helped deliver him, you know."

"I didn't! Nicky, that's quite a feat for a city girl."

"But she isn't," Winthrop said proudly, watching her. "She's a country girl. Kentucky-born and reared. Her people were horse fanciers."

"How interesting."

"How is the colt?" Nicky asked, keeping her voice steady when her heart was racing wildly in her chest.

"Growing like a weed. Come on and I'll show you. Good night, Mrs. Todd. Mary will be up soon to check on you."

"Thank you, Winthrop. Good night, Nicky, and thanks for keeping me company."

"It was my pleasure," Nicky assured her, bending to kiss the wrinkled cheek. "Night."

She followed Winthrop out the door with faint hesitation. He seemed friendly enough, but she sensed something beneath the outward calm. Something disturbing. Exciting.

"Isn't it late to be looking at horses?" she asked as they walked down the staircase.

He glanced down at her. "Why? Are you afraid to be alone with me after dark?" he asked.

She hated that arrogant look. "Of course not!"

"Then why ask the question?"

"I thought you might have better things to do."

"I could do some bookwork, I guess." He glanced at her. "Or watch the VCR—"

"I'd just *love* to see the colt!" she interrupted.

He chuckled softly. "I thought you would."

He led her down the side hall and helped her into her coat and stocking cap. "It's still cold, although the snow has stopped."

She couldn't imagine why he wanted her company, but she was touched beyond reason that he did. It felt so good to be with him, alone with him under the wide sky, crunching through the snow toward the barn.

"Did Dad look at the colt while he was here?" she asked.

"He sure did. He thinks I've got a young champion on my hands. He said that if I wanted him to, he'd train him for me."

"That's not a rash offer," she said. "He's good with horses, and he's never backed a loser yet."

"So I hear." He took her arm and turned her at the barn door. "Turning down three million dollars is crazy. You could accept the trust and still give a million to research."

"I don't want to be rich," she said simply. "I tried it, and I didn't like it. My values got fouled up. I like them the way they are."

He sighed. "I can understand that. It just seems a waste. You could do a lot with that kind of money."

"You can only wear so many diamonds at a time, and fur makes me sneeze," she said with a straight face.

"You'll be working for the rest of your life, damn it. What if Gerald ever fires you? What will happen to you?"

The prospect really seemed to bother him. She searched his dark eyes, shadowed by the wide brim of his hat. "I might get married someday," she said. "I like children. I'd like to have a family."

He touched her arm lightly, smoothing her coat sleeve. "Yes. I'd like that, too, one day. Kids are nice."

"How many do you plan to adopt?" she asked.

His eyebrows arched. "Adopt?"

"You said marriage wasn't in your vocabulary," she reminded him. "So if you want children, you'll have to adopt them."

He moved restlessly. "A wife would be an encumbrance."

"So would children."

"It's not the same thing."

"It is."

He glared at her. "I won't marry you, honey, if that's what you're hinting at."

She glared back. "Who asked you? I don't want a walking icicle."

"I'm anything but an icicle in bed," he told her.

"Talk is cheap!"

"Not half as cheap as that statement," he returned. He scowled down at her. "How in God's name did we get on this subject?"

"You said you wanted children—"

"Well, I don't. Not anymore." He started walking again. He glared at the barn door as he opened it. "Women! They twist everything around to suit themselves."

"So do men."

He stood aside to let her enter the barn. "Marriage was invented by women to legalize sex."

"Don't look at me," she said airily. "I don't want to marry anyone. I'm just twenty-two. I have years and years of living to do before I tie myself to a man's housework."

"Time passes quick. Before you know it you'll be my age."

"God forbid," she glared up at him. "I'm not ready for the Home."

"Stop that," he grumbled. "I'm not old."

"Neither is the Statue of Liberty," she said with a sweet smile. "Where's the colt?"

"Over there."

She followed his irritated gesture and leaned over the gate, watching the little chestnut colt nuzzle at his mother's belly.

"Aw," she cooed. "Isn't he cute?"

"I'm not old," he repeated, still nettled by her offhand remark.

She looked up at him carelessly. "All right. You're not old. Isn't he cute?"

"Thirty-four is a man's prime."

"If you say so."

"It is, damn it!"

"Was I arguing?" she asked innocently.

He pushed back his hat with an irritable sigh. "Gerald says you and he are going back Monday to get the office shipshape so he and Sadie can get married Friday and have an extended honeymoon."

"That's nice," she said absently. She hadn't known, but it was good to have it out in the open. Two more days to be with Winthrop. It would be heaven and hell.

"You won't lose your pay. He's going to let you handle his office while he's gone."

"That's nice, too."

"Don't you know any other words?" He glowered down at her. "Look here, Nicole, we won't see each other again."

"Yes, I know." She looked up at him quietly. "That should please you. It must be hell, having a lovesick woman making calves' eyes at you all the time."

He shifted restlessly. "I've gotten used to having you around," he said reluctantly, but he wouldn't look at her.

Like an old shoe, she thought miserably. She watched the colt in silence for a few moments, then said, "I imagine you'll get used to not having me around just as easily."

"I guess so."

She peeked up at him. His face was hard and cold, but his eyes were glittering faintly as he looked down at her.

"I'll always limp," he said unexpectedly. "Gerald says I can work the kinks out, but the doctors don't agree. There's always going to be a degree of impairment."

"That's too bad," she said.

"Is that all you can say?" he growled.

Her eyebrows arched. "What would you like? Shall I sit down on the ground and start crying?"

"I'm a cripple!"

"Sure." She stared back at the colt. "You and the Marine Corps."

"Nicky..."

"If you want to limp, go ahead. I don't care."

"You aren't listening."

"Of course I'm listening. You're telling me what a bad risk you are, and I'm agreeing with you. You've been right all along, Winthrop. I need a younger man who doesn't limp, who wants marriage and children. You're absolutely right, so now I'm going to go back to Chicago to find one." She looked at the growing anger in his hard face. "That should satisfy you."

"Would you like to know what would satisfy me right now?" he asked under his breath.

"Not really. I'm tired and I'd like to go to bed."

"At last, we agree on something." He moved toward her.

"Oh, no, you don't. I'm saving myself for my future husband."

"Thank you."

"It won't be you," she told him doggedly. "I'm not crazy enough to think that. You aren't a marrying man, remember? You don't want commitment."

"I don't know what I want anymore," he muttered.

"Well, I do," she said. "I want to go home."

"To a lonely apartment in Chicago?"

"It won't be lonely long," she assured him. "I'm going to start my very own lonely hearts chapter."

"Over my dead body."

"Nobody would want to meet over your old dead body."

"Nicky..."

She got as far as the barn door and opened it to freedom. "You only want my body," she burst out. "And that's not enough!"

"Will you listen to me?!"

"*No!*"

She turned and ran for the house, easily outdistancing him. She passed Gerald and Sadie on the steps, shot up the staircase into her room and locked the door. So much for trying to reason with Winthrop. All he wanted to do was back her into a corner and seduce her. Well, he wasn't getting another chance to do that! She'd just avoid him until she could leave. Better to walk away with a broken heart than a broken spirit as well. She loved him, but she couldn't settle for a one-night stand. Not even with the only man she'd ever wanted.

She tossed and turned all night, thinking about the ironies of her life. Even if nothing else had come out of this trip, at least she'd made peace with her father. But she wished that Winthrop could have returned just a little of the feeling she had for him. Her heart was going to break in two when she walked out that door Monday morning. And Winthrop wouldn't even miss her. On that thought, she cried herself to sleep.

Chapter Ten

It was as if Nicky's impulsive action had brought a wall down between herself and Winthrop. He wasn't around the next morning when Gerald and Sadie and Nicky got into the Lincoln to go to church in Butte. He wasn't around when they got back, either, and Gerald remarked on it, because Winthrop almost always went to church.

The day wore on, and Nicky got her things packed since they were leaving early the next morning. The corporation jet was scheduled to pick them up about eight.

Gerald spent all his free time with Sadie, finalizing their wedding plans. A special plane was taking Mrs. Todd to Florida that afternoon, so that she could make the flight in luxurious comfort. Gerald had arranged everything, and Mrs. Todd was enthusing about her future son-in-law to anyone who had time to listen.

Since there was a chance that Winthrop might show up, Nicky stayed behind when Gerald and Sadie drove Mrs. Todd to the airport. But Winthrop was still missing.

"Gone hunting, he said," Mary told her with a curious glance. "Funny thing, to see him hunt on Sunday when he curses if others do same."

"He's avoiding me," Nicky murmured.

"Thought as much. What did you do?"

"He was telling me all the reasons I ought not to get involved with him and I agreed, that's all," Nicky sighed.

Mary grinned from ear to ear. "Just like man, to state truth and then get mad when others agree."

"I suppose he'll never speak to me again." Nicky was remembering their talk. Perhaps he'd been trying to say something and she hadn't given him the chance. Either way, she'd never know now. She was going home and he wouldn't follow. Most likely, he'd be glad to be rid of her.

"Winthrop is deep," Mary said unexpectedly. "Hard man to predict." She glanced at Nicky. "But be sure that he thinks before he acts. Weighs the odds. He is surefooted."

"I used to think I was, too," Nicky said. "But I'm not anymore."

"Give it time."

"Now that," she replied, "I have plenty of. What's for supper?"

"Something different," Mary told her secretively. "Old family recipe. You'll like it."

"But what is it?"

Mary leaned forward. "Moussaka."

"You're putting me on," Nicky laughed.

"Had Greek uncle. Taught me to make it, eggplant and all. Nice change of pace."

"I'll bet!"

"Here." She handed over the utensils. "Set the table. No doubt Gerald and Sadie will be late. They have much to discuss."

"They'll make a happy couple."

"Yes."

Since there was no more reply than that, Nicky went about her business and began to set the table in the dining room. And all the while she wondered where Winthrop had gone and why he hadn't come home. She had so little time left here. It was going to be agonizing to go off and leave him, and here he was wasting precious minutes they might have spent together. But why should he care, she reminded herself. He didn't trust her. He might want her, but he didn't love her. He'd said himself that love was an illusion. Besides that, he didn't ever want to marry. So why bother about him?

She finished the place settings and put napkins all around. At least her nice boss was going to come out ahead, she thought. Gerald would marry Sadie and have a perfectly wonderful life while Nicky grew old taking dictation. It didn't bear thinking about.

Maybe she could do what she'd threatened Winthrop with—get married and have children. Sure. Nothing easier. First, she had to find a man. And who could measure up to old stone face?

Even as she was asking herself the question, the kitchen door opened suddenly and Winthrop came in with something furry by the tail.

Mary stared, but Nicky went forward. "Oh," she exclaimed. "A wounded squirrel! Wait, I'll rush and get a bandage!"

"Oh, for God's sake," Winthrop ground out. He slid the squirrel onto the sink for Mary to deal with and glared at Nicky as he eased out of his sheepskin jacket and hat, dumping them untidily on the floor.

"There ought to be a law against shooting unarmed squirrels," Nicky muttered for something to say.

Winthrop went to the sink to wash his hands, ignoring her.

"Nice squirrel," Mary defended him. "Plump. Make good stew."

"I'll bet he was somebody's daddy," Nicky murmured.

"You're breaking my heart," Winthrop said nonchalantly. He dried his hands on a towel and looked straight at her. "Where's Gerald?"

Her heart was beating double time, but she wasn't about to let him know it. "He and Sadie drove Mrs. Todd to the airport. She left for Florida today."

"I know. I said goodbye before I went out. What's for dinner?" he asked Mary.

"Moussaka."

"That stuff with eggplant?" He made a face. "Whatever happened to beef and potatoes?"

"Need change of pace."

"No, I don't," he argued. "I like having the same thing every day. It gives me a sense of security."

"Then why go out and kill an innocent squirrel when you really wanted a steak?" Nicky asked.

"He wasn't innocent," he replied. "I have it on good authority that he was a rounder with unspeakable taste in women squirrels."

"Well, in that case, let's all eat him," Nicky agreed.

Winthrop actually grinned at her. She had to spoil it all by blushing.

"Sit down. I will bring the dishes," Mary told them.

Winthrop motioned for Nicky to go ahead, and even pulled out her chair for her.

"I'm impressing you with my manners," he informed her.

"Are you really?" She smiled vacantly. "When do you begin?"

"Watch it, Kentucky girl." He sat back in his chair and studied her intently while Mary brought in the main course, followed by rolls, vegetables and fruit.

"We leave tomorrow," she said when they all three were seated and enjoying Mary's exotic dish.

"Yes." He didn't seem disturbed. But when he finished his meal, he lit a cigarette. That was the first time Nicky remembered seeing him with one since her early days at the ranch.

"Bad smell," Mary scowled at him. "Why you do that? Thought you quit."

"I quit several times a month," he reminded her. "I'll start quitting again tomorrow."

Mary shrugged as she got up to fetch the coffee pot for refills. "Your lungs, not mine."

"Thank you so much," he said with a mocking smile.

Mary hit him on her way to the kitchen.

"You sure are cheerful tonight," Nicky remarked. "It wouldn't be because I'm getting out of your hair tomorrow?"

"The thought did cross my mind."

"I'll bet it did."

She sipped her coffee and he stared at her for so long that her heart began to run wild and her breathing became quick and labored. She gripped the cup tighter so that he wouldn't see how badly her hands were trembling.

"You aren't limping," she said suddenly, shocking herself with the flat statement. But he hadn't been. He'd been walking straight and steady.

"I've been practicing," he replied easily. He tapped the ashes into an ashtray. "Nice of you to notice."

"Are you going to cut Mary off by auditioning for the Rockettes yourself?" she asked demurely.

"I'd never pass muster," he replied. "My legs are too hairy."

"Ah, well, another career shot to hell by lack of a straight razor."

"Cute." He chuckled softly.

"Thank you, my mother always said I was."

"How did she die?" he asked unexpectedly, and stared at her until she was forced to answer.

"She fell into the swimming pool and drowned during a party," Nicky told him, and the dark memory was reflected in her eyes. "Nobody even noticed, can you imagine? She fell in front of two dozen people and drowned right there. And nobody noticed."

Something in her expression caught his eye. "And where were you when it happened?"

Her face drew in. "Haven't you guessed?" she asked in a faint whisper and forced a smile. "I was one of the two dozen people who didn't notice...."

He got up without haste, crushing out the cigarette in the ashtray and pulled her up into his arms. "Stupid," he accused, drawing her close to him. "Holding it in like that, never telling anyone."

"I didn't see her," she wept. "Winthrop, I didn't see her. I was dancing with Chase and I never even looked. Not until someone screamed...."

"Your father?"

"He wasn't around. I guess we both had our share of guilt over it, wondering if we could have saved her if we hadn't been so caught up in the glitter." Her hand came up to wipe away a tear. "She was so unhappy. And so alone."

"We're all alone," he replied quietly. "Some more than others."

She looked up at him, searching his dark eyes. "Do you remember your mother?"

He smiled. "Very well. She and my father were deeply in love. It never faded, all the long years." He touched her face lightly. "I was looking for something similar. I found Deanne instead."

"All women are not like Deanne," she said doggedly.

His thumb rubbed lazily across her lips. "Maybe. Maybe not."

"Cynic," she burst out, exasperated. "You're scared to death to find out."

His eyebrows arched. "I like not having my heart used for target practice. Which reminds me—your father said you were something of a markswoman."

"I used to be," she corrected. His thumb caressing her mouth was disturbing. "I used to ride, too. But I'm out of practice."

"You might come back with Gerald for the wedding," he said abruptly. "I could give you a refresher course."

Her heartbeat increased. But even as she heard him say the words, she knew that the minute she left the ranch, he'd forget her. She'd be out of his thoughts. His offer was just a sugar pill—something to keep her happy until she left. He didn't mean it.

"That would be nice," she said, without any real conviction.

"Nicky..."

Whatever he was about to say was lost, because Mary came back in with the coffee pot and didn't lift an eyebrow at the two of them practically standing in each other's arms.

"More coffee?" she offered, and the spell was broken.

Winthrop watched Nicole for the rest of the meal, and then Gerald and Sadie came back, and the conversation centered on the wedding. Bedtime came and there wasn't a single opportunity for any more discussion. Nicky went to bed halfheartedly, more disappointed than she could ever remember being. She loved Winthrop, but he was making it patently obvious that he didn't return that feeling. But, then, what had she expected?

The next morning, before she had time to plan what she was going to say, she and Gerald were in the Jeep with Mike and being driven to the airport. Winthrop was long gone, apparently out hunting again. Nicky didn't even get to say goodbye to him before she flew back toward Chicago.

Chapter Eleven

Back at work, Nicky found herself haunted by a particularly vivid ghost. Winthrop drifted around in her thoughts constantly so that she couldn't eat or sleep or rest. She didn't understand why he couldn't have managed the time to say goodbye to her. Of course, there was always the possibility that he was simply indifferent.

She was a nervous wreck by the time Thursday rolled around. Gerald was equally anxious, all thumbs as he waited for the driver to take him to the airport. And tomorrow was the wedding at the ranch.

"Why aren't you packed and ready?" Gerald asked suddenly, as if it had only occurred to him that Nicky wasn't coming.

"I'm not going," she said quietly.

"But why not?" he asked, and smiled. "Winthrop invited you, didn't he?"

"I suppose he felt obliged to," Nicky confessed. She sighed heavily. "You see, I . . . well, I kind of . . . I told him I loved him," she concluded, and went scarlet. She buried her face in her hands while Gerald gaped at her. "Of all the stupid things I ever did, that was by far the stupidest. He told me right up front that he didn't want commitment. I should have listened."

"Oh, Nicky," he murmured. He patted her shoulder awkwardly. "Nicky, I'm so sorry. With all due respect, you could have found a more approachable man. Winthrop has too many scars and he's lived completely alone for so long.... I'm just really sorry. If I'd thought anything like this would happen, I'd never have forced you into going to Montana with me."

"It's not your fault," she reminded him. "I didn't have to go." She forced a smile. "But I can't quite manage the wedding. I hope you understand. Having to be around him, and having him know how I feel ... I just couldn't bear the embarrassment."

"I'll make some kind of excuse for you. Don't worry." He studied her worriedly. "You'll be all right?"

"Sure I will. I thought I might go and spend the weekend with my father. Christmas is coming up in three weeks."

"So it is." He patted her shoulder again. "Can you cope while I'm on honeymoon?"

"You bet, boss," she said brightly.

"Okay. Well..." The driver appeared in the door and announced that he was ready when Gerald was.

"Kiss Sadie for me," Nicky said.

"I'll do that with pleasure. You'll have to come over for supper one night when we get back in town."

"That would be nice."

"I'll see you soon, Nicky."

"Yes, sir." She smiled, and waved goodbye to him.

She wanted to go to the wedding. It would have been heaven to stand and look at Winthrop just once more. But she'd do better to get him out of her mind, and going back to the ranch would only open old wounds. She'd had enough torment. And he'd never led her on. He'd told her exactly how he felt, so if her heart was broken she could only blame herself.

She settled back into the office routine the next day, fielding questions and phone calls and correspondence with a flair that would have pleased her absent boss.

She wasn't prepared for the phone to ring and an angry, irritated Winthrop to be on the other end of the line.

"Where in hell are you?" he demanded coldly.

She stared at the phone as if it had grown teeth. "I'm ... here. Working," she faltered.

"You were invited to the wedding," he reminded her.

"Yes, I know."

"Then why aren't you here?"

She stared at her feet. "I didn't want to come," she said in a ghostly tone.

"I don't bite," he grumbled. "And I hadn't intended to drag you off into the underbrush."

"I know that," she moaned. She bit her lower lip. "I made a fool of myself," she said after a minute, almost choking on the words. "I ... couldn't face you."

There was a pregnant pause. "Made a fool of yourself? How?"

She twisted the cord around her fingers. "I threw myself at you like a lovesick teenager."

"Was I complaining?" he asked unexpectedly.

"I know how you feel about women."

"Do you?" he asked in bemusement. "I'd planned to take you hunting with me."

Her heart leaped. "Had you?"

"Your father tells me you can handle a .30-.30 with the best of them," he added. "I thought we'd hunt deer."

"I would have liked that."

"It's not too late," he reminded her. "Gerald could send the plane for you."

She closed her eyes and prayed for strength. "I don't think it's a good idea, Winthrop."

"Why not, for God's sake?"

"Because I can't live on dreams," she burst out. "And the sooner I face it, the better off I'll be. I know you mean well, but it . . . it tears the heart out of me, that's all. I won't come."

She hung up quickly, before he could talk her into going to Montana. He was offering her comfort, but he didn't realize the torment it would cause her. Loving him, being near him, and knowing he didn't care for her would have been the last straw.

All the rest of the day she expected him to call back. But he didn't. And she went to Kentucky and spent the weekend with a surprised and very different father. They talked, she and Carol went shopping, and when the time came to go back to Chicago, she was frankly reluctant to go.

"This has been fun," her father remarked, grinning. "We'll have to have a big Christmas this year. I'll get a tree and everything."

"And we'll have a party," Carol added, clinging to his arm with real affection. "Nicky needs to meet some men her own age. I know at least one with a good character I could invite." She glanced at Nicky ruefully. "Notice I didn't say with money—just with character."

"Yes, and I appreciate that," Nicky grinned back. She liked Carol. The more she saw of the redhead, the more depth she found in the other woman.

"Come home for Christmas," her father coaxed. "We'll have a big time."

It would at least keep her mind off Winthrop. "All right," she agreed, smiling. "I'll plan on it. See you in a couple of weeks, then."

"I'll send a plane up to get you," he grinned.

She went back to her apartment feeling vaguely happy. But the bubble burst at work the next morning. Becky was waiting in her office with a cold message from Winthrop.

"The iceman calleth," Becky said, whistling through her teeth. "And was he in a snit! He said to tell you that you can—" She cleared her throat. "Well, that you can sit up here in the city and freeze for all he cares, and that if he never sees you again, it will be too soon." She cocked her head at Nicky. "Does he drink? Because he sounded as if he had a snoot *full*!"

That didn't sound like Winthrop. "Are you sure it was Winthrop?" she asked.

"Boy, am I sure." Becky shook her head. "He even spelled it for me." She smiled with mischief in her eyes. "He got it right on the third try, anyway."

"Oh, my."

"Oh, my, isn't what the switchboard operator had to say. She's thinking of filing charges against him for his use of language." She turned to go back to her own office, still shaking her head. "Poor old guy. What did you do to him, Nicky?"

Nicky wasn't sure. But if he was that angry, she must have gotten under his skin a little. She sat back and waited for new developments.

But when a week went by with no more word from him, she fell into a black depression. Gerald came back to work a new man. The honeymoon in the Bahamas had been ecstatic, and he could hardly keep his feet on the floor while Nicky brought him up to date on what was happening in the office.

"Yes, I can handle all that," he sighed. He watched her closely. "I hear Winthrop called you."

She flushed. "Sort of."

"I hear he was drunk at the time," he added.

"How did you hear that?"

"Mary," he said. "She was snickering so hard that I could barely understand her. She said he went off into the mountains and dared anybody to bother him."

"Will he be all right?" she asked with concern she couldn't help.

"Winthrop?" he asked as if she'd taken leave of her senses.

"Well, he isn't Superman."

"Don't tell him that. He's just taken out another lease on the cape," he murmured.

"If he wants to go off in the mountains in a snit just because I wouldn't come to the wedding, that's his problem," she said shortly. "Anyway, he didn't really want me there."

"That isn't what Mary said."

"What do you want to do about this letter?" she asked, attempting to change the subject.

He started to speak, then changed his mind and settled for work. They fell back into a pleasant routine, and Winthrop wasn't mentioned again. Nicky was sure that he was only angry because she hadn't fallen all over herself getting back to Montana. She didn't dare hope it was because he'd started to care for her.

He didn't call. He didn't write. Christmas Eve came and Nicky gave up hoping that she'd hear from him. She wished her boss a merry Christmas, sent her love to Sadie and went to Lexington for the holidays.

Her father met her at the airport in his Lincoln, with Carol beside him, and took time to have the driver run them through town so that she could see the beautiful Christmas decorations.

"It's just like old times," Nicky sighed. "I always did love the way they decorate the city."

"Me, too. You ought to see the decorations we have at the house," her father said with a twinkle in his eyes.

"And your present," Carol added, also twinkling. "It was really hard to wrap, so I gave up trying and just stuck a bow on it."

Nicole had presents for both of them in her luggage: a pipe for her father and for Carol a bottle of her favorite perfume. But she frowned, wondering what they could have gotten her that made them both look so smug.

She didn't have long to wait. They piled out at the steps and she walked toward the enormous brick house with feverish curiosity. It was decorated with boughs of holly and red velvet ribbon, and she took a minute to tell Carol how pretty it looked.

"Thanks," Carol laughed. "I did it all myself. With a little help from your dad," she acknowledged with a wink in his direction.

"Your present's in the living room," her father added as he helped Carol out of her mink coat. "We'll go see about some hot cider while you open it."

"Aren't you coming?" she asked.

Her father helped her out of her tweed coat, nodding at the pretty green silk dress that matched her eyes. "You look very nice. No, we're not coming. Not just yet. Go on, now. And Merry Christmas, sweetheart."

He kissed her cheek and then went away, whispering to Carol, who glanced over her shoulder at Nicky and giggled.

Boy, it sure was some strange Christmas, she told herself as she opened the living room door. And then she stopped dead. Because her present wasn't under the huge lighted Christmas tree. It was sitting on the sofa, looking toward her furiously, with a glass of whiskey in one lean hand.

"Merry Christmas," Winthrop said curtly.

Her mouth flew open. He had a bow stuck on the pocket of his gray vested suit, and he looked hung over and pale and a little disheveled. But he was so handsome that her heart skipped wildly, and she looked into his dark eyes with soft dreams in her own.

"You've got a bow on your pocket," she said in a voice that sounded too high-pitched to be her own.

"Of course I've got a bow on my pocket. I'm your damned Christmas present. Didn't you listen to your father?" He got up, setting the glass down with enough force to shake the table, and started toward her, limping just a little. He didn't look like a present, he looked murderous. "I can't eat," he said accusingly. "I can't sleep, I can't work. I spent a week up in the mountains trying to get you out of my head, and all I got was drunk. I'm hung over, bleary-eyed and half mad with wanting you."

"Oh, I'm so glad, Winthrop," she whispered. Her heart went wild. "Because I'm half mad with wanting you, too...Oh!"

The tiny cry was lost under his devouring mouth. He had her up in his arms, barely pausing to kick the door shut before he carried her back to the sofa and stretched her out on its velvety length under the formidable weight of his body.

She protested the intimacy of his hold, but he shook his head and took her mouth under his again, glorying in its breathless response.

"No more fighting," he breathed into her parting lips. "There's no need. You're mine, now. That gives me the right to take any liberties I please with you, and this is only the beginning. You're going to marry me, lady. I've got all the necessary papers. All we need is a blood test, and that's scheduled an hour from now. We're going to have a Christmas wedding."

Tears stung her eyes. She looked up at him through a drowsy haze, her body intimately pressed to his, her eyes wide and soft and loving. "You don't want to get married," she whispered.

"Yes, I do," he corrected her. He looked stern and solemn and very adult. But the look in his eyes was so tender that it knocked the breath out of her. "I just didn't know it until I let you walk out the door. And then I couldn't get you to come back. I thought I didn't care." He bent, brushing her mouth with exquisite gentleness. "But I can't quite make it without you, Nicky," he added huskily. "I've never been so alone. Come home where you belong. I'm too old, and too cynical, and not quite the man I used to be, but I..." He took a slow breath. "I love you, little one."

Tears ran down her face. She didn't imagine he'd ever said that in his life, and she felt the faint shudder that ran through his body when she arched hers to search blindly for his mouth.

"I love you, too," she breathed. "Deathlessly. Hopelessly. With all my heart!"

"Yes, I know, you say it quite often," he murmured, nuzzling her nose with his. "After a while, I began to enjoy hearing it. You got under my skin from the very first time I saw you, so busy at your desk. I convinced Gerald that he needed to bring you out with him," he confessed lazily, shocking her. "I didn't realize why, of course, until I had you in my arms. Then it all fell into place, and I did my best to run. But I was caught, even then. God, I've been miserable without you!"

He kissed her hungrily and she felt his hands at her hips, lifting her up into an embrace that made her shudder and gasp and go scarlet.

"This is part of loving," he whispered into her mouth. "Part of marriage. It's beautiful. Don't be afraid of it."

"I'm... not." She looked straight into his dark eyes and imagined how beautiful it would be joining with him in loving union, softness to hardness, tender rhythm on cool sheets in the darkness. And she gasped again. "Oh, my," she whispered shakily.

"Oh, my, indeed," he whispered. "Yes, sweet, just that way. Intimate and ardent...your body and mine. For all the long, achingly sweet nights of our lives. I'll be your fulfillment, and you'll be mine. And there'll never be another secret between us."

She cradled his head in her hands and pulled it gently toward her. "I'll give you children."

He smiled softly. "Yes." His head bent. "Merry Christmas, sugarplum."

She smiled back as she gave him her mouth. "You delicious Christmas present, you..."

Outside the door, two people with a bottle of champagne and four glasses were congratulating themselves on their little surprise.

"Should we knock?" Carol asked.

Dominic White pursed his lips. "Sounds a little premature." He grinned at the muffled laughter behind the door. He lifted an eyebrow. "Suppose we sample the champagne? Just to make sure it's not corked?"

"A brilliant idea," Carol agreed, linking her hand through his arm.

"I have another. How do you feel about a double wedding?"

Carol reached up and kissed his cheek. "Ecstatic," she sighed. "Can we get a blood test and a license in time?"

"Honey, I ain't a millionaire for nothin'," he drawled.

"As long as you know I'm only marrying you for your money," she reminded him with a mischievous smile.

"Mercenary hussy," he accused. And he grinned. They went into the office and closed the door. And after a minute, laughter was coming from that room, as well. Outside, the first flakes of snow began to fall. A white Christmas was well under way.

* * * * *

TWO FABULOUS AUTHORS
ARE BRINGING YOU...

Two magnificent stories...each filled with love, laughter and, of course, romance!

MARILYN PAPPANO

REGARDING REMY (Southern Knights)
Silhouette Intimate Moments #609
Available this month!

Wounded Special Agent Remy Sinclair needed some down-home TLC, and nurse Susannah Duncan would do just fine. But it seemed that Remy's sexy angel of mercy had secrets...deadly secrets.

DIANA PALMER

THAT BURKE MAN (Long, Tall Texans)
Silhouette Desire #913
Man of the Month March 1995

He's rugged, lean and determined. His name is Burke, and he's March's *Man of the Month—* Silhouette Desire's 75th!

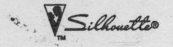